Texas Conquest

Texas Conquest

A Texas Legacy Romance

Holly Castillo

TULE
PUBLISHING

Dedication

This book is dedicated to all of my friends and family who always stood beside me and encouraged me to follow my dreams.

A special dedication goes to my husband, who is my hero in real life, and the inspiration for the hero in this book.

Also a special dedication to my Editor, Meghan Farrell, who believed in me and my writing so much that she made my dream come true. Much love to all of you!

Chapter One

San Antonio, Coahuila y Tejas
November 1835

S UPPLIES HAD ARRIVED. Anjelica Torres gnawed on her lip as she watched the weary mules trudging up the dusty road, three wagons in tow. She had no doubt they held precious provisions; blankets, boots—even guns. All things that the army camped across the river desperately needed.

"What if we took one?"

"Don't be foolish. You know they won't let us leave town with a whole wagon."

Angie let the curtain fall back over the window, her mind racing as she looked at her sister. "What if they have guns? Do you know how much that could—"

"No, Angie. It's way too dangerous. Besides, how will you carry them? We have a hard enough time as it is with the food. I just wish I knew where it came from. Santa Anna hasn't sent supplies in months."

Angie folded her arms across her chest and kept gnawing on her lower lip, staring through her sister, Olivia. "There has to be—"

"Get the idea out of your head." Olivia shook her head,

1

her lips pulled into a tight, thin line. "We can't do anything about it. You don't even know it's supplies." She kept shaking her head, the severe bun not allowing a single hair loose. "No. Now come and help me clean the kitchen. It's already getting late. It will be dark soon and we have much to do."

Angie nodded, not quite meeting her sister's stern gaze.

Olivia, appeased with the reaction, turned and walked towards the back of their home. "Today we didn't have enough *tripas*. We'll need to have Grandpa prepare more for tomorrow. Now that it's a little cooler..."

Holding her breath, Angie grasped the door handle and opened it just enough to squeeze through. She backed out onto the front porch, smiling to herself as she heard Olivia still talking. The door shut with a soft click and she faced the road with determination, watching the wagons slowly making their way towards the mission where the Mexican Army camped.

Her palms were suddenly damp and she wiped them on her skirt, drawing a deep breath as she stepped off the porch and onto the road. There had to be a way she could get some of the supplies. Anything would help the Texians. The food they smuggled to them frequently helped, but the army was in desperate need for more. And if there was something she could do, she didn't care about the risk.

The wagons were kicking up plumes of dust and dirt and she coughed, waving her hand in front of her face, squinting against the fading sunlight. This wasn't getting her any-where. Frustration chewed at her nerves. She needed a plan;

at the very least she needed to know exactly what was in the wagons. The longer she took waiting, the closer the wagons drew to the Alamo.

Grandma always warned that curiosity killed the cat, and Angie was feeling very much like a feline as she caught up with one of the wagons and tried to reach for the rail. Once on the wagon, she could examine the contents. At the very least, the information would be invaluable to the Texians. She would worry about how she would get off the wagon later.

She stretched, half skipping on her tiptoes, but she couldn't quite reach the rail. She was going to have to run and jump. Her heart was pounding loud in her ears as she kept her eyes focused on the driver. He hadn't noticed her yet, but he would probably notice if she jumped onto his wagon. She cursed under her breath. She needed a distraction, something to slow them down.

Perhaps if she could stall them... if she created confusion... they might stop long enough for her to at least peek inside. If she just...

The idea tickling the back of her mind was ridiculous, but she had to try. If it meant giving the Texians an upper hand, by God, she would do it. Freedom was worth any cost at this point.

Turning down between two homes she started running, hitching up her skirts and forcing her legs to carry her quickly around the back of the house and up the other side. If she were fast enough, she would come out the other side just as the wagon...

"*Madre de Dios!*"

A mule squealed and reared in front of her, its paws striking at the air, forcing the mule tied next to it to stumble sideways. She had been running too fast and couldn't stop quickly enough. Her skirts flew out in front of her as she tried to skid to a stop, but her feet slid on the loose dirt. *Dead cat.* The fleeting thought struck her as hooves hovered dangerously over her head.

A flash of movement to her side caught her eye, but she didn't have time to pay attention. She was trying to remember every prayer and every saint. The hooves were coming down as she brought her arms up, hoping to shield herself some from the blow. The forceful slam from the side was unexpected and she was suddenly rolling, over and over into the road. Something was wrapped around her, shielding her head from the ground. Motion stopped and she lay momentarily stunned, struggling to pull in a breath. She cracked her eyes open slowly and the setting sun cast shadows over the face looking down at her.

For a brief moment, she feared her sins had caught up with her and she was in hell. For surely it was the devil that stared down at her, watching her with dark eyes. The shadows cast over his face prevented her from seeing more, but he was shaking his head.

"What in God's name did you think you were doing? You could have been killed!"

She couldn't catch her breath and realized distantly that it was partially because he lay on top of her. The man was large, his broad shoulders keeping the sun from hitting her face, and every inch of her body was covered by his. From her toes to her breasts, she could feel his muscles and a tiny quiver settled in her stomach. Humiliation tinged her cheeks as she realized they were lying out in the center of the road.

She couldn't seem to pull a rational thought into her mind. His arms were under her, his hands cradling her head, his chest crushing hers to the ground. *No wonder I can't breathe.*

His heart beat against her breast, steady and hard, and her heart skipped a beat. She had never been this intensely aware of another person's body. She once again tried to pull in a deep breath and several scents assailed her at once. He had just eaten something sweet, maybe a late blooming berry, and the scent carried on his breath across her cheek. The warm, earthy smell of sweat and travel clung to his body, mixing with what she could only assume was his own musky aroma. The combination made her light-headed while at the same time desperate to get closer to this stranger. Perhaps a hoof *had* struck her in the head.

She narrowed her eyes, trying to see past the shadows to the man who held her, when the commotion to her right drew her attention. The wagon driver gestured angrily at her as he fumbled with the harnesses to the mules, trying to correct the damage she had caused. His colorful curses were in both English and Spanish so as not to confuse anyone about the chaos.

Her cheeks felt like they were on fire. Well, at least her plan had worked. But it had brought more attention than she had anticipated. She suddenly started shaking so badly her teeth chattered. She didn't think she would ever forget the sight of those hooves coming down at her.

"Are you alright?" The devil's deep voice was soothing, gentle, and made her want to forget everything except the enjoyment of someone holding her and comforting her.

Her arms reached up to his shoulders and she pressed at them lightly, testing his strength. The quiver in her stomach intensified at the feel of his muscular arms. He was all man, and he lay on top of her in the middle of the road as though he had nothing better to do. He shifted slightly, moving so the sun cast a small amount of light on his face. His gaze was intense, his brow wrinkled in a frown.

She was finally able to gulp in air and nodded frantically. "I'm f-fine. Really."

The supplies! The thought demanded attention and her whole plan would be worth nothing if she didn't act quickly. She started to push away from him only to be brought up short by his arms tightening around her, making her aware of how intimately their bodies were entwined. The wagon seemed to suddenly be a distant concern.

"Are you hurt? That mule nearly trampled you."

He couldn't be the devil. The devil wouldn't care if she was hurt or had been trampled, would he?

His arms tightened around her again and he was suddenly lifting her off the ground. "Let's get out of the road. You're shaking hard enough to break in half."

Angie stared up at him and licked her lips, tasting dirt and dust. It was as though his voice was hypnotizing her, making her forget what she needed to accomplish. He was carrying her to the sidewalk on the opposite side of the road from the wagons, and she should be upset. He was ruining her plan and all she wanted to do was stay with him. She needed to get away from this man who held her so gently and made her forget everything else.

The driver was climbing back up in his seat, still grumbling about the crazy woman. If she didn't hurry, the wagons would be gone. The man slipped his arm out from beneath her knees and she was suddenly standing on trembling legs. She turned her gaze to his face and drew in a deep breath. She had been right to think he was the devil. The priest had said many times that *el diablo* showed himself in the form of temptation and beauty, and the man standing before her was exactly that. His hair was thick and black and curled slightly on his forehead. His high cheekbones and strong jaw spoke of an aristocratic heritage, and his face, bronzed by wind and sun, made his dark hair and eyes prominent.

His full lips twitched in a smile at her appraisal. "Do you need to sit down, *senorita*? You're still shaking."

It was true she was still trembling. But it wasn't the remnants of fear that made her quiver. She lifted her chin and tried to push her hair out of her face and suddenly became aware that he still held her, his hands gripping her waist. Her face flamed as she grasped his forearms and tried to push him away. Her heart was hammering in her chest and she could feel where each of his fingers touched her body. Surely, she had hit her head on something.

"I really am fine, *senor*. I need to leave."

He brought his hand to her face and the clean scent of

mesquite surrounded her as his thumb brushed dirt off her cheek.

His expression had turned from concern to incredulous. "I just saved your life and you're not even going to thank me?" He shook his head and his fingers tightened slightly on her waist. "You at least owe me your name."

She swayed slightly towards him. His strength, his aroma, his voice—everything about him made her want to get closer, to trust. It was an emotion she couldn't afford. Angie bit down on her lip and glanced sideways at the wagons. They were beginning to move. She looked back at him and blinked—hard. Her hands were still holding his forearms and she looked down at them, recognizing the red sleeves. Dear God, how could she not have seen it before? She looked back into his face, shaking her head. He was a Mexican soldier!

"What possessed you to run out in front of that wagon?" he demanded, his frown deepening, his thumb still caressing her cheek even though the dirt was gone.

Angie had never been good at lying. And she didn't feel like trying her skill on this soldier. She placed her hands against his chest and pushed, hoping she wasn't blushing as furiously as she felt. "I need to go…" The wagon driver cracked his whip and the mules jerked forward. She pushed harder against his chest, unable to look at him. "I need to go…"

His grip slackened on her waist, but he didn't fully release her. "Tell me your name."

With one hard shove, she pushed free of his grip and

stumbled backwards. He watched her with raised eyebrows, folding his arms over his chest. The wagon picked up speed and rumbled past them, and she wanted to curse louder than the driver had. She took a few more steps backwards, finding it difficult to take her eyes off of him. Then she spun on her heel and picked up her skirts.

His gaze burned on her back as she started to run. She ran harder, furious with herself. He was the enemy! And she had enjoyed his arms more than any sane woman should.

A LIGHT FROST covered the ground, creating a surreal appearance in the field surrounding him. Lorenzo Delgado watched the landscape, his eyes the only part of him that moved. Unlike his partner, who shifted from one foot to the other, rubbing his hands together.

"There's nothing out here," he grumbled. "If Cos wants to give us busy work, he ought to let us go find a *senorita* in town to entertain us."

Lorenzo remained silent, unmoving, the chill in the air causing his breath to plume faintly. The soldier next to him looked over his shoulder at the town that lay behind them. "I've heard the San Antonio women can provide quite the entertainment." He snickered. "If I got a hold of one of them, I'd…"

"You'd do nothing, *pendejo*. You know the orders." A third soldier swaggered up to them, casually rolling a cigarette. "For some reason Cos doesn't want the locals

HOLLY CASTILLO

bothered." He shrugged.

"And what would he do about it? He needs every last one of us."

Lorenzo cast a glance at the irritating man and frowned. "You want to be the one that finds out what happens?"

The man eyed him, his fingers fidgeting on the carbine he held at his side. "Might. Been a long time since I had a woman."

Lorenzo looked away from the soldier, returning his gaze to the fields where they were supposed to be watching for a possible attack. He understood the frustrations of the man. He hadn't thought it could affect him until he had held a sweet-smelling woman in his arms.

He had arrived in San Antonio only a few hours earlier, tired from the long trek from Laredo when he had seen the woman. Though his feet ached and he wanted nothing more than a few hours of sleep, he didn't complain when he was ordered to patrol. He was finally where the action was with the Texian Army camped so nearby.

The wagons that had followed them from Laredo were kicking up so much dust on the road that he almost didn't see her. But a flash of color drew his eyes and he stopped on the sidewalk, watching the woman walking quickly beside the wagon, unaware of his presence. Her hair was dark, falling past her waist, sweat-dampened tendrils curling at her temples. She was chewing on her lower lip, her hands gripping her pale blue calico skirts as she tried to keep up with the wagons. *What the hell is she doing?* Suddenly she disappeared between two homes.

10

He walked forward slowly, curious about the woman with olive skin and gray eyes, wondering why she had been trying to keep up with the wagons. He was about to step off the sidewalk between two houses when she came flying past, her skirts hitched up past her knees.

"Startled" wouldn't be a good way to describe the reactions around her, his lips pulling into a smile, seeing the scene in his mind instead of the frost-covered field. He hadn't had much time to really consider his reaction. One moment he was admiring a glimpse of long, smooth calf and ankle, the next she was lying beneath flying hooves.

He raced forward, a hoof glancing off his shoulder as he threw himself at her, wrapping his body around her to keep her safe from the rugged road. When their mad tumble came to a stop, he was assaulted by the feel of soft woman and the scent of lavender. He nearly hadn't been able to get his voice to work to ask her if she was all right. *How long has it been since I've held a woman?* And when he had allowed himself the improper caress of her cheek, the feel of her silken skin had nearly undone him.

Far to the side of his vision some tall shrubs shuddered. His eyes narrowed and he forced the image of the Spanish beauty out of his mind. He supposed he should be grateful he was on patrol where the cold, numbing air forced him to keep his mind on task. The Texian Army camped just outside of the town at a bend in the San Antonio River. Though the ragtag group of farmers and drifters hadn't made any true rushes at the town, Mexican General Cos was well aware how much the rebels wanted to capture the Alamo. It would be a huge achievement in their quest to free Texas from Mexico rule, but it was virtually impossible they would succeed against the much larger Mexican Army.

"Where are you going, *hombre?*" his partner asked, reluctant to leave his reclining position against the tall pecan tree.

Lorenzo was moving forward slowly, cautiously, his hand tightening on his musket. "There's something out there."

Chapter Two

"IT IS COLD tonight. Get Papa's jacket."

"And you? You will freeze."

"I am wearing extra layers. Don't worry about me. I can take care of myself. You are the one who doesn't think ahead."

Anjelica ignored her sister's comment, not wanting to have any arguments. Papa's jacket lay neatly folded on a chair, as though just waiting for him to come and pick it up. Papa hadn't been there to wear the jacket for five years. Angie rolled up the sleeves since they fell past her fingertips, drawing a deep breath. She didn't know if the jacket really still smelled like Papa or if it was just her imagination, but she enjoyed it just the same.

Olivia draped a black shawl over her head then handed Angie a similar one. Silently they blew out the candle and the basement was enveloped in darkness. Moving just by touch and familiarity, they climbed the steps and came through the dining room floor. They hesitated for several seconds, listening, breath held, to hear any other sounds in the house. All was quiet.

"I didn't think Grandma was ever going to go to sleep,"

Angie whispered.

"Hush. She might still wake up. We need to be quick."
Olivia's tone was curt and clipped.

Angie rolled her eyes behind her sister's back as she
pushed the rug back over the floor. Her sister always acted as
though no one else knew what needed to be done. Angie was
all too aware of the urgency required. And it wasn't something she took lightly.

They stood at the back door for a few moments then in
unison drew deep breaths as they stepped outside, wincing as
the back step creaked. "Remind me to fix that tomorrow,"
Olivia whispered, pulling her shawl tighter about her face as
she scanned the surrounding houses. All was dark. No one in
San Antonio was awake at this hour except those either on
patrol or causing trouble. They wanted to avoid both.

They crept along the side of the house, stepping lightly,
two dark figures sliding along almost invisibly in the darkness of the November night. They dodged from house to
house, using the buildings and carts and any other items
along the way to provide cover. Even though they could not
see anyone awake, there were eyes out there, watching
everything.

Angie tried to breathe evenly through her nose. No matter how many times they made their nighttime journey, she
couldn't seem to calm her racing heart, couldn't still the
adrenaline that pumped through her veins, screaming for
release. She feared the soldiers on patrol several hundred feet
away could hear the thundering of her heart.

Soon it was wagons, shrubs, and lumps of hay that provided their cover, and the houses of the town were beginning to spread out. By now Angie was breathing heavily and she could hear Olivia struggling for breath as well.

"Next hay stack we stop," Angie puffed out between breaths, her words leaving plumes of frost clinging to the air.

Olivia didn't spare any words, just nodded. At the next pile they hunkered down, breathing deeply, holding on to one another for support.

"Next time you carry the blasted meat," Angie spat, beginning to regain her breath.

"We've already had this discussion."

"All that bread and vegetables don't take up that much room. I just think you're using your height as an excuse."

"Angie, we'll discuss this later."

"Fine. But I still—"

Olivia's fingers dug sharply into her wrists, making Angie stop mid-sentence and hold her breath. A twig snapped. The sisters looked at each other with fear in their eyes and leaned in closer to the hay, hoping it would conceal them. Both tried desperately to hold their breath.

"You are chasing ghosts, *hombre*."

The man's voice cut through the icy night air and both women couldn't stop their reflexive flinch. Angie's fingers were now digging just as sharply into Olivia's wrists as her own.

"I saw someone. There's someone out here." A deep, rough voice floated on the frigid air.

"There isn't anything out here. Maybe it was a cow."

"Good. We need some meat. If we find it, we will be heroes." The same smooth voice spoke again.

"You're going crazy. There is nothing out here."

A soldier suddenly came into view, crossing the field. He was turned slightly away from them as he walked, though he was looking back and forth. Angie bit her lip so hard she tasted blood. *Please, God, don't let him see us. Please, God.*

He stopped only yards away from them, propping his gun against himself while he started to roll a cigarette. "There really isn't anything out here. Let's head back to the trees. At least there the wind didn't get us."

Another soldier approached, his long strides carrying him quickly across the field. He too searched the darkness, but he hadn't seen them... yet. Angie forced herself to stop biting her lip as the man came into view. It was *him*. The soldier who had saved her, the man who had held her so gently and made her heart pound so hard. Even now her heart thudded harder. *It's just nerves.* Wanting to rub her suddenly damp palms on her skirt, she was afraid to risk the motion. She couldn't take her eyes off him and feared he could feel her staring. She licked her lip and tasted the metallic flavor of blood.

"Maybe it really is just ghosts. Everyone keeps telling me this city is haunted."

The soldier stopped in front of the man smoking his cigarette. "I thought you wanted to catch a rebel."

The other soldier took a long drag of his cigarette before answering. "The only thing I want to catch is sleep. *Hijo*, I've been on my feet all day. Just forget it. There's nothing out here."

The man's eyes scanned the field slowly, and Angie held her breath as his eyes settled on their haystack. It almost seemed as though he were looking right at her. Olivia's nails dug into Angie's wrist, making her wince.

But the soldier turned, gestured to his friend. "Let's see if they'll finally let us sleep."

Angie and Olivia didn't breathe easily until the soldiers' voices had faded away and things had been silent for several minutes. An owl hooted in the distance, making both women jump then release a tensely held breath.

"That's the closest we've ever come to getting caught," Angie whispered.

Olivia closed her eyes briefly, shaking her head slowly. "I should be doing this by myself. I never should have let you get involved."

Angie gritted her teeth, tired of hearing the same thing from Olivia over and over. Standing slowly, she brushed at her skirt, glaring at her sister. "You couldn't have stopped me. I would find some other way if you didn't let me help you. Why should you be the only one trying to make things right? I want the same things you do!"

Olivia stood as well, her eyes probing the darkness where the soldiers had disappeared. "You don't understand everything, Angie. You have your doubts. I never do. That is what makes us different." Before Angie could get in a retort, Olivia continued, "Very well. Let's keep going."

The remainder of their journey seemed to move slowly, probably because they hesitated much more, stopped to listen for longer times, and were far more anxious than usual.

If they were caught, it would quite possibly mean death to the entire family. They had come too close to finding out just what the consequences would be.

Part of it was also due to Angie's frustration with Olivia. She envied her sister's control over her emotions. But she couldn't understand why Olivia didn't recognize that she was just as passionate about their cause as Olivia. If it came to such a point, she would die for their mission. But Olivia didn't know that.

They finally crossed the familiar pile of cedar logs and started to breathe easier. They were close to friendly territory. This time, when a twig snapped, they stopped where they were in the clearing, waiting for someone to show himself. If someone was really hunting them, they wouldn't have heard anything to warn them.

A plainly dressed man stepped into their sight, holding a long rifle pointed at the ground. He nodded to them, slightly doffing the loosely shaped cloth hat he wore. "Good evenin', ladies. He's up a few more paces waitin' for you."

"Thank you," they said in unison then headed further towards the large encampment that lay just over the hill.

A tall, gangly man turned at their approach and his droopy face lifted into a smile when he saw them. "Well, sisters, it looks like you made it into our neck of the woods once again."

"It was close this time," Angie muttered, taking the shawl off her head.

He looked at them with concern. "Did someone see you?"

"Possibly. But they gave up pursuit." Olivia also lowered her shawl.

The man tensed and looked beyond them towards the fields they had just crossed. "Are you certain? Should I warn—"

"No one followed us. You have nothing to be concerned about."

He studied Olivia's face for several seconds, then nodded. "Right, then. Have you heard any news?"

Angie was fumbling with her skirts and looked at him in disbelief. "No. We haven't heard a thing. We thought we'd just risk our lives to come say *hola.*"

"Angie!" Olivia snapped.

The Texian laughed, though the sound was rough, as if he had almost forgotten how to laugh. "You're absolutely right. Such a foolish question deserves such a foolish answer."

Finally, Angie's skirt gave free and with a relieved sigh the outer layer fell to the ground with several thumps. "At least fifty pounds of meat. Most of it is dried, but some of it should be cooked quite soon. It was all I could carry, Mr. Tom."

Olivia also removed her outer skirt, but wasn't as dramatic about dropping it as Angie had been. "Bread and some vegetables. We've been speaking with one of the farmers that comes to our *cocina* and he might be willing to bring a wagon of goods out here within the next couple of days. We haven't decided if he is on our side yet or not. Just keep an eye out for an older farmer."

Tom was gathering up the skirts with something close to excitement. "Any little bit helps. You are an inspiration, honestly. I wish all of the men could know the risks you put yourself through for them. It might help boost their spirits."

"I'm sure having a bit of food will be enough to boost them for right now," Angie said softly, tugging her shawl tightly around her shoulders as she looked at all of the men sleeping around small fires, their thin blankets providing little warmth. She could only see about fifty or so. There were far more further into the night that huddled the same as these.

"Morale has been low lately. It's been getting colder and the men have been talking about going home. If we don't make a move soon we might begin to lose ground. I could really use some good news for the men."

Olivia's lips pressed into a thin line. "I wish we had some for you. Cos received more men."

"I know. We got wind of it yesterday, but the details have been sketchy. Do you know how many?"

"At least one hundred. Some came into the *cocina* today and seemed to be in high spirits, though they looked tired."

"Any idea where they came from?"

"One of the soldiers spoke of Laredo. Whether that is where they originated or where they paused, it is hard to say."

"Damned convict soldiers."

"Pardon me?" Angie asked, her interest suddenly drawn into the conversation.

Tom shook his head, still concentrating on gathering up

the food. "We had heard there was a group of convict soldiers headed this way. Up from Laredo. Santa Anna told them fight or die by execution. A pretty rough group from the reports. We were trying to find them before they got here, but obviously they slipped through."

"Convict soldiers." Angie said slowly, thinking of the man who had saved her.

He was a hard man. She had seen it in his eyes and felt it in his strength. She shivered slightly, remembering his hands on her face, how she had felt so feminine in his arms. She had sensed danger from him. Now she knew why. And yet...

She nodded. "That makes sense." She hesitated, then, "There were three wagons that arrived today. I don't know what was in them, but they were heavy. The wheels made deep cuts in the road."

Tom paused, looking up at both of them. "Guns?"

Angie shook her head. "I tried to get a peek." She caught Olivia's glare out of the corner of her eye. "But I couldn't. It could have been anything."

He shook his head, returning to the task at hand. "We sure could use some of their weapons. Hell, we could use a lot of anything right now."

Tom handed off some of the food to another man wearing worn buckskin pants and a floppy, old hat. "I have a list for you that I need you to get to a man in town."

"How do we find him?"

"You won't. Hang out your laundry tomorrow, and—"

"Tomorrow isn't Tuesday." Angie shook her head at him. Tom looked at her with confusion. "We only do laundry on Tuesday. It will look odd if we hang out anything tomorrow."

"She has a point." Olivia nodded. "But we can find a way to hang out a few things. We'll spill some *chili* on some of the linens."

"Good. Hang the list with them. You'll never know he's there."

"Is there anything else we can do?"

"You've already done more than enough. I hate asking you, but if you have more food…"

"We'll be back in a couple of nights with what we can gather."

"Please be cautious."

Olivia and Angie nodded, taking back their now empty outer skirts. Pulling their shawls back over their heads, they turned to make the dangerous trip back home.

Chapter Three

"STOP PINCHING."

"I'm not."

"*Mirar*! Look at your fingers. You are pinching!"

"I am not pinching!"

"You must use your fingers lovingly... like you would caress a bambino's little cheek. Like you would caress a lover's..."

"Grandma!"

"Bah. Don't act so—so—how do you say? Ah, well, it doesn't matter. *Empanadas* need to be treated gently. Don't you see, when you smooth the edges, run your finger along it like so..."

"You mean to roll the dough."

"Eh? *Que es* 'roll'?"

"*Mirar*, Grandma, it is exactly what you are doing. I am doing exactly what you—"

"Soldiers! Soldiers coming!"

Anjelica's head jerked upright and a puff of flour hung in the air in the early morning sunlight. The side door crashed open and an auburn haired girl raced inside, her freckles prominent on her flushed face. At the stern look from the other two women in the room she smiled mischievously. She placed her hands on her hips and tapped her foot, her chin thrust out arrogantly. "There are soldiers coming."

"We are well aware, Serena, *gracias*. As I'm sure all of the neighbors are aware as well!" Angie grabbed a handful of flour and started towards the grinning girl.

With a shriek Serena dodged around her sister and into her grandmother's arms. "*Buenas Dias, Abuela.* Good morning, Grandma. Is Angie burning the *empanadas* again?"

"Ah, *que* Serri… what am I going to do with you? Look at you. What is in your hair today? What is this… what… feathers? *Hija*, you're wearing feathers in your hair?"

Angie shook her head in disbelief and headed out towards the front of the house. Her baby sister had their grandmother wrapped around her little finger. When she had been a child, her odd behavior had been cute. Now that she was almost thirteen, her oddities were making her a source of humor for the entire town.

Olivia, looking tall and slender in her shirtwaist and narrow black skirt strode toward her from the front of the house, an apron held between her teeth while she tried to tie one around herself. Her hair was pulled back in a severe bun and her collar looked like it was nearly choking her. Angie didn't even know how she could breathe. It made her feel stuffy just looking at her older sister.

"They must be hungry to be coming this early. And there's a lot of them," Olivia said, her words muffled around the fabric in her mouth.

Angie sighed as she took the apron. "I know. Serena announced it to everyone on the road."

Olivia rolled her eyes and shook her head. "I am going to have to teach her to calm down from time to time."

"That will be like taming the wind."

"Hmph." Olivia was still trying to tie her apron. Shaking her head, Anjelica turned her sister around by the shoulders and finished tying it for her. "We haven't had a large crowd in a while. We could use the business."

Olivia squared her shoulders and touched her hair, making sure the bun was still securely in place. "We don't exactly know that they are here to eat."

Angie's face blanched and she didn't say anything more, watching through the windows as a group of soldiers strolled down the road in their direction. Some wore the bright red uniforms they had become so used to, others the more casual white uniforms. At least none of them were officers.

Olivia busied herself straightening some of the tables and opening the windows on the side of their living room that served as the front of their small *cocina*. She spoke as she worked. "They look to be new recruits. Probably more of the ones that arrived yesterday. I'm sure they're here to replace the ones Cos lost at Concepcion." Not too far from San Antonio the battle at the small mission called Concepcion had been costly for General Cos and had bolstered the Texian resolve.

Angie headed towards the counter that divided the room from the kitchen to gather some napkins and utensils, trying not to think what it meant for more soldiers to be arriving at San Antonio. Texas had barely begun its fight for independence from Mexico, and yet it already felt like war surrounded them everywhere.

For a moment, the image of the tall, dark soldier entered her mind. Would he come to the *cocina*? She didn't know how she would react to him if he did.

"I don't see why Cos doesn't just admit defeat," she said, trying to think about anything else. "They destroyed him at Concepcion. Why doesn't he just give up?"

Olivia whipped around to face Anjelica, her face tense. "There are soldiers about to step in here to eat, Angie. Remember where you are."

Angie blew a wisp of hair out of her face and put a hand on her hip, seconds away from launching into an argument, when the first soldier stepped through the door. Forcing a bright smile on her face, she hurried forward to greet while Olivia stepped back into the kitchen.

"*Buenas dias, senors.* Please make yourselves comfortable. *Café?* Coffee? Would you like a cup of coffee?"

As the men filed in they looked at her appreciatively, obviously delighted to find a woman greeting them so sweetly. The room filled to nearly three-quarters full as ten men found chairs at the small round tables. Conversation swirled in both English and Spanish, and the speech was colorful to say the least.

Olivia came sweeping out of the kitchen, holding a pot of steaming coffee in one hand and balancing several cups in the other. At her entrance, Angie took off to the back to get some *pan de juevo* and more coffee. Her eyes darted around their long kitchen for Serena, but the troublesome child was not in sight.

Quickly pulling her hair into a loose knot at the base of her neck, she went to work in the kitchen, wishing she knew what the soldiers were doing and why more replacements had been sent. Footsteps sounded on the wood floor as more men filed in for a warm breakfast, and she shook her head. The business was a blessing; she only hated those that they fed were the enemy.

She was balancing four cups on her arm and hand and a pan of pastries on the other hand when she saw it. Moving from the kitchen to the opening for the living room slithered a long, green snake. Gasping back her scream the cups wobbled for several seconds before two of them crashed to the floor. The snake slithered faster. "Serena!" she yelled, feeling the vein in her neck stand out as she began to back away from the serpent. "Serena! Get in here right now!" She watched in fascinated horror as it slithered out the doorway and towards the first table. Breathing deeply, she set down the cups and tray and raced towards the door. She nearly crashed into Olivia as she entered the room.

"What are you yelling about? Don't you realize we have customers?" Olivia hissed, her eyes popping with anger.

Most of the men continued to talk, though some of them had fallen silent while they watched the two sisters. Angie grabbed her sister's arm and tugged her around so that she could see the floor in front of them. Olivia muffled her soft cry with her apron. "*Mocosa*! Where is that little brat?" she growled.

"Later. We have to get rid of that before—"

"What the—*Nombre que!*"

"The men find it."

Two men jumped to their feet, hopping about as though their feet were touching coals. "*Culebra!* Snake! There's a snake!" Chairs scraped back on the floor as men pushed away from their tables, not wanting to be surprised by the serpent.

Slowly, one of the men stood in the corner, the long, green serpent wrapped around his arm. "Is this what you are looking for, *senorita?*" he addressed Olivia, one eyebrow lifted. It was obvious he was trying to contain his amusement from the way his lips twitched slightly.

Angie's heart stuttered to a stop then raced forward. It couldn't be! Had she wanted to see him so badly that she had willed him to their *cocina?* Her eyes drank in the sight of him from his thick hair, tapering neatly to his collar, over his bronzed face with a light shadow of whiskers, down to his hated red jacket. And there she stopped, reminding herself firmly that it was foolish to want to have anything to do with him. If he found out what she and Olivia did, the whole family could be at risk. And yet, there was something about him, something that pulled at her and made her desperate to know more...

Olivia, flustered, nodded while her fingers nervously touched the top button of her collar. She had always hated snakes. Angie stepped around her and came face to face with the soldier, and for the briefest moment lost concentration on the task at hand. His eyes, a dark hazel, watched her with intensity, though they revealed none of what he was thinking. The humor was gone, and replaced by curiosity as he watched her, waiting.

She mentally shook herself out of her trance and reached for the snake. "Yes, that is exactly what we are looking for. *Gracias, senor.*" Her voice was tight. She prayed he wouldn't say anything. She would never hear the end of it from Olivia.

The soldier withheld the snake from her, stepping around the table to get closer. "It's just a harmless grass snake." The other soldiers close to him backed away, still not certain the hissing, angry snake he held by the head was harmless.

Angie couldn't take her eyes off him. There was strength in him, a power that both frightened her and intrigued her. All she could think about was his unique scent, the feel of his hands gripping her waist. The faintest aroma of mesquite teased her nose and she found it difficult to pull a deep breath. He was danger. He was not only the enemy, but he was bold and confident. She should be afraid of him, yet instead she felt incredibly safe.

Olivia gave a pointed glance to all the men who stood as far back as they could. "*Si.* A very harmless grass snake."

Out of the corner of her eye Angie saw a flash of auburn. "Serena," she spat, whirling around to capture the girl, thankful for the distraction. As always, the nimble child slipped right between her hands.

"You found him! *Es muy loco.* Did you know this foolish *gato* was going to eat him? Eat him. Can you imagine such a travesty? Well, of course I couldn't let that happen, so I brought him inside. You know, snakes like it to be warm. Why, he was already starting to move slowly with that cool air outside. He was such easy prey for that *loco* cat. So, I thought he would like to be near the stove. He didn't seem to like that much, though he did start moving faster. So then I put him in your room, Angie, since it's always a little warmer at that corner... don't know why that is. I think the ghosts like the other side of the house, because it's always cooler over there. Oh, yes, *senor* soldier. This house is haunted. But don't ask my sisters. They say that is a foolish thought, but I know they are real. You can feel them. Real cold and slimy... or at least that's what my friend says. She says she's actually seen one. But I don't think snakes are afraid of ghosts, otherwise mine wouldn't have left Angie's room like he did—"

"Serena! If you say another word, I will—"

"*Gracias, senor*, for catching my little friend."

The soldier was trying desperately not to laugh. Serena had finally paused to take a breath, and it looked like she was about to get started again.

He spoke quickly before she could. "Your little friend shouldn't be indoors. God intended for him to be outside where he is comfortable."

Angie watched him closely. He was flashing one of those smiles at Serena now and she wondered how many women's hearts he had broken. Serena was talking again and Angie's lips pursed together with frustration.

"The *gato*, though, *senor*, will surely eat him. I can't allow that to happen. I will make him a nice home in Angie's room."

The soldier's eyes darted to Anjelica's face. "Angie, is it?"

he asked softly, his voice reminding her of their intimate embrace in the road.

She tilted her head to one side, raising an eyebrow at his arrogance, though her heart was pounding madly in her chest. Having his full attention once again was making her scatterbrained.

Olivia had had enough. Stepping between Angie and the soldier, she put a firm hand on Serena's shoulder. "Take your snake, Serri." Her voice was tight.

Olivia was angry, that was for sure, and Angie wondered who was going to get the lecture this time. Serena, obviously. But she almost felt like Olivia was upset with her as well. Serena grabbed for the snake, easily and calmly dodging it as it tried to bite her and grabbed its head. Olivia and Angie cringed. Drawing a deep breath, Olivia spoke again, keeping a hand on Serena's shoulder. From the way Serena cringed, it was not a pleasant hold. "*Gracias, senor*, for your help. I apologize for my sister's mischief. You may have whatever meal you would like for breakfast. Please accept it as my expression of gratitude."

He nodded, but his gaze didn't leave Angie. "Are you ever going to tell me your name?"

Olivia drew herself to her full height, finally drawing his attention. "We are the Torres sisters, *senor*, and we are referred to as that."

The other soldiers snickered at the reprimand in her voice, relieved now that the serpent had been caught. The soldier nodded respectfully at Olivia, glancing sideways at Angie. Ducking down, Serena escaped her sister's grasp and ran towards the front door. None of the men tried to stop her as she still held the snake.

Chuckles circulated throughout the room as the men started to sit back down, all of them excited that they would have a new story to tell when they got back to their post. Olivia nodded to the soldier then turned sharply on her heel and headed to the kitchen.

Angie couldn't seem to make her feet work. She watched the soldier for several seconds, trying to think of what to say that would reprimand him as much as Olivia had, but not really certain why. She had liked the way he had said her name.

He tilted his head to the side, his smile now entirely gone. "Do I frighten you, *senorita*?"

Angie leaned back in indignation. "You? Frighten me? I think you have been smoking some of the Indian pipes." The very idea that she would be frightened by a man was laughable. And yet, this man…

His smile returned. "*Bueno*. Could I have some breakfast then?"

Her eyes narrowed at him. "Of course." She turned and headed towards the kitchen.

"Don't you want to know what I want?" he called after her.

She didn't stop walking.

Lorenzo stepped out onto the clean, white porch, shaking

his head at himself. Breakfast had been far more entertaining than he had expected.

"You will never get anywhere with those women, *hombre*. The tall one… she *es muy frio*. Very cold."

He shrugged nonchalantly as he adjusted his hat. "They are pleasant enough. And *Senorita Fria* gave me a free breakfast." But *Senorita Fria,* the older sister, was not the reason he was intrigued by the small *cocina*. He hadn't thought he would see her again. She had haunted his dreams all night long, and he had woken with the scent of lavender and gray eyes on his mind. His fellow soldiers had told him about the *cocina* with the warm, fresh breakfast and the demanding rumble of his stomach had temporarily distracted him. Until she was suddenly standing right in front of him, the scent of lavender mingling with the heady aromas drifting from the kitchen.

It had taken a tremendous amount of restraint to not wipe the tiny beads of perspiration from her forehead. His fingers craved to feel her smooth skin once again. He had waited for her return with his breakfast, but she didn't come near his table again. The desire to see her, to hear her voice again, was almost overwhelming. There was something about her that pulled at him, something hidden and mysterious in the gentle sound of her voice, yet hard glare from her eyes.

"That is the only nice thing she will ever do for you, and it was only because you caught that snake," his comrade said, drawing his mind back to their conversation.

Lorenzo's lips twitched. "They are quite the entertaining family." He glanced back at the *cocina* and noticed the curtains move. One of the sisters must have been watching. He smiled to himself. San Antonio might prove interesting after all.

⚜

OLIVIA SCRUBBED THE giant cast-iron pot furiously, her arms buried inside as she tried to clean out the grease from the day's cooking. Angie watched her from the corner of her eyes as she fastened a chili-stained tablecloth to the clothesline, a list folded carefully alongside it. Serena had received a scathing lecture that had nearly put the young girl in tears before Olivia had decided to take the remainder of her frustrations out on the daily cleaning.

Olivia hadn't said a word to Angie for the remainder of the day, but it was obvious something was bothering her. Angie placed a clothespin in her mouth as she placed another tablecloth on the clothesline, warily watching her sister. She hated it when Olivia exploded in anger.

"Why don't you just spit it out?" Angie said, turning to face her. "What is it that has you so upset?"

Olivia raised her eyes slowly, a deep scowl on her face. "I'm not upset about anything."

Angie gave a bark of laughter, placing her hands on her hips. "What is bothering you? Yes, Serena caused a disruption, but I doubt she'll do it again, and it didn't hurt business."

Olivia threw her scrub brush down in the pot and straightened. "We don't need any extra attention on this house, Angie."

"What are you talking about?"

"Today! What was that with that soldier? It was enough that Serena created all of that commotion with the snake, but you didn't have to be rude to the man who caught it!"

Angie blinked. "Rude?" The image of the dark soldier flashed in her mind and her heart skipped a beat.

He was trouble. She knew it and Olivia wanted her to be nice to him? Every instinct in her body said to get as far away from him as possible—because all she wanted was to get closer.

"How was I rude? He was being just as rude by trying to get familiar with us!"

"Just the same, you can be polite and demand respect without getting snippy and ignoring the customer. Did you ever bring him his breakfast?"

"No, you did. I saw you."

"But you were supposed to. I watched you ignore him while you fed others. I had to take him his food."

"Well, he was being inappropriate," Angie said firmly, crossing her arms over her chest.

"Be that as it may, we cannot risk angering or causing any extra attention than usual. You must be polite to these soldiers."

"Just how polite?" She could still feel his arms. She couldn't be polite to him. She didn't know where she would stop.

"Stop it. You're being disgusting now. Just try to be friendlier. If we rile even one of them, they might start watching us far more closely than we want. You know what we are doing is important. Besides, we can't risk something happening to Serena or Grandma and Grandpa."

"Why would something happen to us?"

Angie and Olivia both jumped at the voice coming from above them. Serena watched them from her high perch in the pecan tree, her eyes narrowed in suspicion. She swung her legs back and forth, chewing furiously on her thumbnail.

"Serena, eavesdropping is a sin. Get down here and go to your room, where I sent you in the first place," Olivia snapped.

Serena didn't budge. "You say *everything* I do that you don't like is a sin. What are you doing that could put me and Grandma and Grandpa in danger?"

The slight accusation to her voice couldn't be missed and Angie stomped over to the tree, tilting her head far back to look up at her. "Get down now! You've caused enough trouble for one day."

Serena was silent for several seconds, then, "I'll come down once you tell me what secret you're keeping from me. Are you talking about all the stuff you keep in the cellar?"

Angie looked over at Olivia and met her sister's startled eyes. "How did you know about the cellar?"

"I knew you were disappearing somewhere. I didn't really know where until I lost my snake again and found him under the rug. That's when I found that little door. But I've seen you sneaking off every now and then. I tried to follow you once but couldn't keep up. Where were you going?"

Olivia stood, her hands clenched into fists at her side.

"Get down here now! I will not have this discussion with you."

For a moment it appeared Serena was going to continue to ignore Olivia's orders. Then finally she turned and began to shimmy down the tree. But when her feet hit the ground she took a step away from her sisters. "I have the right to know what is going on."

Olivia took a determined step forward. "You don't need to know anything."

"Does this have something to do with Mama and Papa?"

Olivia drew up short and once again her eyes met with Angie's. "What are you talking about?" Angie asked cautiously.

"I know Mama and Papa didn't just die. I know something happened to them. Why else would everyone get uncomfortable when I try to ask questions?"

Olivia drew a deep breath and her posture slumped. "Serena... I don't know what to tell you... We—Mama and Papa..."

"Why don't you just tell me the truth?" She crossed her arms over her chest. "What happened to them?"

"Mama and Papa were killed, Serri. They were murdered for their beliefs." Olivia's lips were pressed into a thin line, her face hard. Olivia rarely spoke of their parents, and it was obvious it was difficult for her.

Serena's lower lip was trembling. "Why? What did they do? What did they do!"

Angie took several quick steps and caught her sister's shoulders, forcing her to look at her. "They fought for freedom, Serri. Our freedom, freedom for our neighbors. They were federalists, a group our president did not like. Rumor began to spread that they were traitors. They died not much later."

"They were killed," Olivia said harshly. "For some reason, they were seen as dangerous for wanting to make our lives better."

"So it was the army that killed them? They are the ones that..." Serena's voice trailed off, thick with tears.

"It was our president that had them killed."

Angie would never forget the day she realized her parents had been murdered. She and Olivia had been playing and discovered the trap door leading down to the cellar. Stepping down into the cool, earthen storage room had been like stepping back in time. Her father's jacket hung on an old, dusty chair in the corner; her mother's favorite shawl was folded neatly on a cot against a wall. And within a small cedar chest had been letters from their cousins on the Texas coast, letters telling about revolution and change, and oppression. The last letter had been a warning that the president was coming after the federalist supporters and her parents were on the list.

Serena was chewing furiously on her fingernails. "I want to help."

Olivia shook her head. "With what? Serri..."

"I know you are helping the Texians. I know you are! And I want to help, too."

"No!" Olivia and Angie spoke at the same time, looked at each other, and smiled wryly.

"I want to help. You can't stop me."

"Serena, when the time comes for you to help, we will tell you. Right now you are still too young and wild to really help us."

"What do you mean wild?"

"Do you really think that snake helped this morning?" Angie said, glancing around wondering if Serena really had left it outside as Olivia had instructed.

"Yes. We shouldn't be serving Mexican soldiers anyway. Now that I know the truth, I will make their lives miserable. I will put bugs in their food every day."

"And ruin this *cocina*. Think, Serena. You must think before you do such foolish things! Those soldiers pay good money and that keeps you warm at night and food in your belly."

"Then why are we trying to get rid of them if they're that great?"

Angie threw her hands up in the air. "She's starting to sound like Grandma now."

"There will be customers after the soldiers are gone. More people will move to San Antonio without all of those soldiers cluttering the roads. There will be freedom, and peace, and everyone will want a taste of Angie's burned *empanadas*," Olivia said with a slight smile that barely touched her eyes.

The same slight smile touched Serena's face and she wiped at the tears that clung to her eyelashes. "So, what can I do to help?"

"For right now, you will go to sleep and be a good girl in

the morning. And be nice to the soldiers. That goes for you too, Angie."

Angie said nothing as she grabbed the basket of laundry. She just hoped the man who was haunting all of her dreams didn't return to the *cocina*. "By the way, Serena, where is your snake now?" she asked cautiously.

"In your room."

"Serena!"

Chapter Four

"GRANDMA, HOW ARE the tortillas?"

"Flat."

"Funny, Grandma. Very funny. We have a hungry bunch for lunch today; you might need to make more."

"Don't worry. You're starting to sound too much like Olivia," Grandma affectionately pinched Anjelica's cheek, leaving flour on her olive skin. "Grandpa has the *tripas* on the fire and I've got another kettle of *menudo* bubbling. Just don't burn the *empanadas*."

"I know how to make *empanadas!*" Angie shook her head in annoyance.

So she burned the *empanadas* occasionally… she still had more batches that turned out perfectly fine. She chose to ignore the fact that she had nearly burnt down the kitchen a time or two.

"So you say. We'll work on your *pan frances* tomorrow, *si?*"

Angie sighed as she peeked into their wood oven, hoping not to see flames on her *empanadas*. "*Si*, Grandma."

The soldiers had come early that morning, weary from a night on patrol. Angie had barely stirred the fires when the first boots had hit the porch. The sun was only a pale glimmer on the horizon. Fortunately, there were some *empanadas* left from the previous day—salvaged from the burned ones—and the coffee didn't take long to brew. But as more men streamed in, the appetites grew and Grandma, wisely, knew they would want something hearty, like a large pot of *menudo*.

Now the sun was at its halfway point, one pot of *menudo* had already been devoured, and more men were coming. It was the most business they had seen in weeks. Olivia was thrilled. Angie was exhausted. Serena was causing her usual mischief.

Hearing more footsteps on the porch, Angie grabbed a pot of coffee and headed towards the door. She stopped mid-step, turned, and placed a quick kiss on her grandmother's cheek. "I forgot to say good morning today."

"Bah. We are too busy for such silliness. Get out there." But there was a very happy smile on her face.

Angie moved quickly among the tables, refilling coffee cups while at the same time trying to listen to conversation for anything that might be useful to the Texians. Olivia was on the other side of the room, dark circles under her eyes, but a warm smile on her lips. Angie wondered if she looked just as exhausted.

"*Hola*, Angie."

Angie blinked hard at hearing a man use her name and focused on the face of the soldier whose coffee cup she had been refilling. The snake charmer, as she had nicknamed him, smiled at her. Her heart stopped then thudded on with a hard beat. She should be angry. She was trying to be angry.

"I thought yesterday you had been put in your proper place. Do I need to remind you again?" God, she couldn't catch her breath.

Did she give him a proper reprimand? She wanted to get away, and quickly. He affected her too much, and he was only smiling at her. Vivid memories of his body pressed along hers made her feel flush. She wished she could speak as firmly as Olivia. Was she still smiling? That wouldn't help get her point across at all.

"Perhaps. Do you prefer to be called Angie or Anjelica?"

He was too handsome for his own good, and he knew it. How many other women had fallen for the warm smile, the dimple, the lock of black hair that fell over his forehead? He was a charmer, alright, and, at the moment, she felt like the snake.

What should she say? What would Olivia say to make him feel properly chastised?

"There are three of us. You'll figure out which Torres is which soon enough." She had barely stopped filling his coffee cup before it overflowed. Swallowing hard, she lifted her chin, hoping she looked calm and unflustered, far from what she actually felt. *Dear God, help me get through this!*

LORENZO LEANED BACK in his chair, feeling more relaxed than he had in days. The young woman who stood before him was a challenge, a challenge he fully intended to accept.

And by the blush that was slowly creeping into her cheeks, he had the feeling she was feeling a bit tested as well. He wondered just how far he could go.

She was alluring, her pale olive skin and dark brunette hair emphasizing the high color in her cheeks and the gray of her eyes. She was small, but not too delicate, and her curves were just enough to make him lose his train of thought. He remembered them well from the brief time he had held her in the road. It was that memory that had drawn him back to the *cocina*, made him want to see her again.

He folded his arms over his chest and watched her as she put one hand on her hip and began to tap her foot. She was a temptation that pulled at him, but temptation had nearly cost him his life before. The thought made him hesitate, the relaxation replaced with the familiar tingle of unease that followed him everywhere. He couldn't allow himself to make the same mistakes again. There was too much at stake.

She was doing her best to appear irritated with him, but her eyes watched him with a curiosity that made his blood stir. She was naïve and innocent, he was certain. *This isn't Laredo.* But the tingling wouldn't go away. "You are Angie, or Anjelica, and you haven't bothered to answer the question yet. Your tall sister over there is Olivia, and the mischief maker that just ran behind you is Serena."

"So, you have been spying on us?" She seemed extremely disturbed by the thought. She smoothed a hand apprehensively over her apron.

"No, though I might have to resort to such tactics if you keep eluding my questions. A very talkative girl with a pet snake kept me company for a while yesterday and told me all about her very stern sisters. I thought I should get to know a little more about the woman whose life I saved."

Angie's eye twitched. "Why do you care?"

He blinked, obviously thrown off by her question. "Care? About what?"

"My name. If you know anything about propriety, you would know to call me *Senorita* Torres. So why do you care so much about my name?"

"So that I won't offend you by calling you the wrong name. Eventually, I hope, you will be comfortable with me calling you by your given name. With your permission, obviously. Of course, if you don't tell me, I'll just have to create a new name for you, one that only I will use. That way you'll know that I'm speaking to you." It was too easy for him to be comfortable with her, to exchange banter and tease. He was being drawn in by her voice, the soft scent of lavender, the nervous way she fidgeted. It was too easy for him to forget the pain caused by trusting a woman.

"For some reason, *senor*, I have no doubt that you always make sure women know when you're speaking to them."

His eyes widened with surprise then he started to laugh, a rich, joyful noise that drew Olivia's sharp glance. Blushing, Angie quickly refilled the other cups around the table then began to rearrange items, items that didn't need to be touched but gave her an excuse to not look at him. "What would you like for lunch today, senor?"

"Come walking with me tonight." He couldn't stop the words before he had spoken.

Her eyes jerked to his face. "I'm afraid that's not available for you to choose."

He watched her closely, watched the eyes that searched his face. She didn't know him. She didn't know the sins he had committed. She would never know and, for his short time in San Antonio, she could make him forget them too.

"Then I'll take some *enchiladas* and hope when you return you'll have reconsidered."

Angie's hand tightened on the coffeepot handle till her knuckles were white. "It won't happen." She started to turn when his hand shot out and caught her wrist. Startled, she turned back to face him, her eyes staring at where his dark fingers encircled her pale wrist.

He felt an instant rush, as though her rapid heartbeat was suddenly pulsing into his. There was something very different about this woman. Different enough for him to risk the exposure of meeting with her to go for a walk that night. It was a tradition—when a man was interested in a woman, he would take her for a walk in town where they could be supervised by the townsfolk and determine if they had anything in common.

It was worth it for this woman. It was worth it for Angie.

ANGIE'S HEART WAS racing as his hand held her wrist. The same tingle that had covered her skin when he had touched her face that day in the road brought the same tingles to her flesh, and an odd trembling in her knees.

It was as though her skin was suddenly extremely sensitive. She could feel the calluses on his fingers, could feel the warmth of his palm. She wondered if he could feel how fast her heart was beating. She slowly raised her eyes to his and, for once, he wasn't smiling. He released her wrist, an unspoken question on his face. For the briefest moment she felt captured, just by his eyes, and she had to get away before she did something foolish.

Frustrated and flustered, Angie turned quickly to race into the kitchen. Trying to calm her racing heart, she paced their kitchen, straightening pots, folding towels, and trying to remember what she had come into the kitchen to do. To go walking with him, the way most women did who were young and could enjoy the attention of a man—the temptation...

"A Mexican soldier. You could do far worse."

Grandma's raspy voice made her jump. "Grandma! What-what are you talking about?"

"A soldier? Interested in our little Angie?" Grandpa came walking through the side door, holding a tray heaped full of steaming *tripas*. He moved slowly, showing how much his knees were aching in the cold weather, but his deeply tanned and wrinkled face didn't reveal his discomfort.

Grandma made shooing motions at him. "This is a matter between women. Do not stick your big nose in this."

"My nose isn't anywhere near as big as yours. And if you don't want these *tripas*, *bueno*. I'll go eat them myself."

"Nah, nah, nah!" Grandma grabbed the tray from him before he could get out the door. "Now go. Cook some beef.

Be productive."

Grandpa muttered under his breath about bossy women and an empty stomach as he headed back outside.

Angie was trying desperately to ignore both of them and regain her composure, hoping Grandma had forgotten the topic. She leaned over the pot of salsa and stirred it slowly, the heady aroma of cumin and tomatoes helping soothe her nerves.

"He is handsome, *sí*?"

"He is rude."

"Eh? Why do you say such a thing?"

"He speaks the same to me as he speaks to Olivia and I'm sure any other woman in this town. He is rude and disrespectful." Angie busied herself with checking various foods around the kitchen, even though they were all well cared for by her grandmother.

"Who cares? If you don't take him, maybe Olivia will. A Mexican soldier would be a fine addition to this family."

If only her grandparents knew the truth. They had been loyal to the Mexican government their entire lives. To them, the Texian rebellion was a foolish endeavor by a bunch of scraggly Americans who wanted to take over everything. They didn't see that they were being taxed blind by Santa Anna. They didn't see anything wrong with the military patrolling their streets and harassing the people of San Antonio. In their minds, if someone got in trouble with the Mexican government, they had it coming to them.

Angie shook her head, wishing that sometimes, just sometimes, Grandma could keep her opinions to herself. She scooped rice and beans on to several plates and was scooping up enchilada sauce when Olivia came sweeping into the room.

She moved in next to Angie, helping fill the plates so Grandma could not hear her words. "What did we talk about last night, Angie? Don't you remember?"

"What are you talking about?"

"You need to be courteous out there! We don't need any unnecessary attention!"

"What—I have been going out of my way out there..."

"Then why does that soldier look so unhappy out there?"

Angie's reactions were torn. He was unhappy? Because she had told him she wouldn't go walking with him? What did Olivia expect of her? They had both turned down suitors in the past. Had she forgotten?

"Probably because I didn't beg him to flounce my skirts!"

"Angie! No more of that. No more! Do you understand? I don't care that they are the enemy... we must keep things as smooth as possible around here. Do you understand?"

"Yes. I understand just fine. I'll start tossing up my skirts in the back room to keep everything 'smooth.'"

"Angie! Don't you ever—Angie, we are not finished with this conversation. Angie, come back here!"

If Olivia expected her to be cordial, she would. She would go beyond that. She would keep the customer happy, just as Olivia obviously wanted her to. Angie strode out to the snake charmer, balancing three plates. She plopped the first down in front of him, barely missing him with a splash of *enchilada* sauce.

"I accept." She spat out as she handed out the other plates around the table.

The soldiers at the table fell silent.

The soldier was looking at her with surprise. "You accept? As in you have reconsidered walking with me, something you had assured me wasn't going to happen?"

"It is best you don't say anything further. I can reconsider my reconsideration." She blinked, wondering if what she had said had made sense.

He held up his hands. "I won't argue. This evening?"

"Let's meet at the fountain." Angie was suddenly doubting her rash decision.

His eyes darted to the doorway and she knew that Olivia had just entered the room. She could almost feel her sister's glare on her back.

"At the fountain," he said, nodding to her.

"Good," she snapped then turned on her heel and stomped back to the kitchen. *My God, what have I just done?*

Chapter Five

S HE WAS JUST going for a walk. That was all. Just a nice, harmless little walk. With a Mexican soldier she didn't even know. With the enemy.

Angie groaned and put her face in her hands. Her bed held her only two good skirts that didn't have patches or worn spots from scrubbing out chili stains. One of the good things about not being rich was having certain decisions limited to few choices.

"Just calm down," she muttered, once again concentrating on her clothes.

It didn't matter what she wore. She hadn't thought her actions through when she had accepted his offer, knowing in the back of her mind that her decision would upset Olivia.

And it certainly had done that. When Olivia heard what she had done, she was furious. By the time the last customer had left for the day, Olivia's bun was coming loose and she was looking more flustered than Angie had ever seen her. And the angry tension around her mouth gave Angie no doubt what she was so flustered by. Olivia had made it clear to her a long time ago that the men of the Mexican Army could not be trusted. And now Angie was going walking with one of them.

Finally choosing the red skirt with fine black stitching on the hem, she paired it with her fitted black blouse with long flowing sleeves and a heavy shawl that she threw over her shoulders. It had been cool all day, and the evening would probably be even colder.

She hesitated with her hand on the knob to her door. She could back out at any time. She had gone as far as she needed to irk Olivia and try to make her point. But something else pulled at her, making her mouth dry and her palms slightly damp at the thought of meeting him. She remembered the way he had held her in the street, remembered the way he had touched her cheek, the feeling of his hands on her waist, and her cheeks flushed.

Was he a convict soldier? How dangerous could he really be? She bit down on her lower lip and placed her forehead against the door. Her grandparents were thrilled she was going for a walk with the strong, Mexican soldier. Olivia hadn't spoken to Angie at all, yet. It felt like she had a thousand butterflies in her stomach whenever she pictured his face.

Whatever this feeling was, she had to fix it and get him out of her mind. She and Olivia couldn't risk the danger of having a Mexican soldier get too close to their family. He could learn too much, and then… they would all be executed, just like her parents.

Taking a deep breath, she opened the door and headed down the hall, wondering if she was going to have a confrontation with Olivia. Angie was working through every possible answer she could give her sister as Olivia came through the dining room.

"So you're really going to go."

Her sister's voice held no censorship, just disappointment. Angie stopped and turned towards her sister who stood in the doorway to the kitchen, wiping her hands on a towel. She looked exhausted. She looked—defeated. Angie's heart hit her feet.

"It was a mistake. I know that now. But I'm afraid... I'm worried..." Olivia didn't know about what had happened with him out on the dusty road, and Angie intended to keep it that way.

"You're curious. Don't make excuses."

Angie gritted her teeth. "Why must you always talk to me like that? For once, just once, could you talk to me like a sister instead of a mother?"

Olivia blinked rapidly. "I don't know what you mean."

"Now who's making excuses? I need to go."

"Angie..."

Angie hesitated, glancing back over her shoulder.

"Please be careful. Do you even know his name?"

"That will be the first thing I ask him." With that, she turned and stepped out into the cool San Antonio night.

JUST WALK UP to him, say hello, say goodbye, and walk away. No, no, that won't work either. Walk up to him, find out what his blasted name is, take two steps with him, and say goodbye.

That's better. I'll tell him I'm cold.

Angie shook her head. She was being ridiculous. The weather had changed on them again and instead of being cold, it was cool, the light breeze stirring the hair on her neck. Her excuse that she was cold was unbelievable, even to herself.

The town was settling down for the evening, the few homes lining the road placing lamps in the windows. A few children still played with their sticks and rocks, trying to get a few final minutes of playtime before they were called indoors. And among all the normal activities of the town, the soldiers hovered, their bayonets creating a tension that was almost visible. Though most still wore the patched and worn uniforms that had lasted them several months, others had shiny new boots and powder horns.

Several soldiers walked past her, the leers on their faces telling her more than words what was on their minds. She lifted her chin and pulled her shawl tighter around her shoulders. Fortunately, General Cos, who was in charge of the mission Alamo, had issued orders to his men not to harass the townspeople. Considering the increasing unrest of the soldiers, Angie feared the order wouldn't contain the men much longer.

The fountain was around the next corner. Her heart stuttered. She had been an idiot to accept his proposal. She didn't know him. He was a convict, for God's sake! She had no idea what crimes he had committed and she didn't want to know. She could sense danger in him, a barely suppressed anger and, for all she knew, he might enjoy taking it out on women. There were men like that.

She shivered and pulled her shawl tighter. *Stop it. Just stop it. This is getting you nowhere.* She squared her shoulders as she came around the corner, determined to just deal with her mistake, come what may, and keep an eye out for quick exits.

LORENZO WATCHED HER approaching and hoped the surprise he felt didn't show. He honestly didn't think she would come. He had heard plenty of rumors about the sisters, especially the older one, and suspected Angie was merely trying to annoy her sister. He genuinely hadn't expected to see her.

And yet she strode towards him, looking as though she was facing a firing squad instead of a potential suitor. He scoffed at that thought. Potential suitor he was not. Regardless, he was intrigued. She was proving to be more interesting than he had expected and the idea that she could be a pleasant distraction during his time in the city made him more willing to invest an effort into knowing her.

She seemed a bit out of breath when she stopped in front of him, her face flushed. He wondered if she had run down the road to come meet with him. That thought brought a smile to his face.

"What is your name?"

"*Buenes noches* to you, too, *Senorita* Angie."

Her lips pulled into a thin line and her eyes narrowed at

him. Obviously she didn't like him reminding her of her manners.

"*Buenes noches*. What is your name?"

"Lorenzo Delgado Valdez."

"Very well, *Senor* Delgado. Let's get a few things…"

"Lorenzo."

"Pardon me?"

"Call me Lorenzo."

"I don't think that's proper at all, nor do I think it proper for you to address me as Angie. There are certain formalities you seem determined to forget, no matter how many times you are reminded."

"Are you trying to reprimand me?"

"Trying?" She looked like she was about to swallow her tongue.

"Well, first off…" He offered her his arm and stood silently, waiting for her to take it.

It was a long wait, punctuated by her sharp glare. Finally, with a dramatic huff, she slipped her arm through his, her fingers resting lightly on his wrist.

"First off," he continued, guiding her down the road, "you need to put just a bit more indignation in your reprimand. It almost sounds as though you're praising me by the way you reprimand."

She tried to pull her arm free but he lay his hand over hers, holding her to him.

"Then, perhaps you shouldn't look so appealing while you try to knock me down a peg or two. It makes it difficult to concentrate on your words." When she didn't answer,

Lorenzo held his breath. Perhaps he had finally pushed her too far.

ANGIE'S HEART WAS racing from a combination of fear and something else she couldn't identify. "I never should have agreed to this. This is a mistake."

He stopped and turned to look at her, keeping his hand over hers, keeping her linked to him and unavoidably close. His legs brushed against hers through her skirts and she suddenly felt lightheaded. Heat rushed to her face and she tried to take half of a step backwards, tugging unsuccessfully on her hand.

"Why did you agree to walk with me? I have been wondering."

"I—I needed to thank you. I am grateful for what you did, and felt it only fair to agree to this-this meeting in order to properly thank you. Now will you please let me go?"

He released her instantly and she would have stumbled backwards had he not quickly grabbed her hand again to steady her. His fingers held hers for only a moment, before he dropped her hand, deliberately taking a step away from her. "If you don't want to be with me, then please go. I understand."

"You must be the oddest man I have ever met." She clutched her shawl while shaking her head at him.

"Because I do what you want me to?"

"Because you—Well now, if that isn't a lie I don't know

what is!" She put her hands on her hips and thrust out her chin. "If you did what I told you to, you would have stopped calling me Angie and been far more proper."

"Now that is a far better reprimand. I knew you could be taught."

Angie's mouth hung open. Suddenly realizing how she must look, she closed it so fast her teeth clicked. She had the irresistible urge to laugh. She fidgeted with her shawl, trying not to look at him.

"Now, don't do that. It will ruin the whole thing. You can't reprimand someone if you're laughing."

A giggle escaped her and she clasped a hand over her mouth in shock. She looked at him and saw that he was smiling at her, a soft smile that touched her in the oddest places. She gave in, unable to hold back the hysterical giggles that were bubbling up inside of her. There was nothing truly humorous about the situation but, God, it felt good to laugh. She couldn't remember when the last time she had laughed, and now she did, all because of the egotistical man before her she had sworn to hate.

When she finally caught her breath, she found herself smiling at him. His smile in return warmed her and she felt more relaxed than she had in years. Perhaps Grandma had been right, laughter was like medicine.

"Your laughter is wonderful," he said softly. "You should do it more often."

She drew a deep breath. "Don't start that again. You really must be more proper."

He leaned in towards her as though to be confidential.

"More proper for whom?" He glanced around dramatically. "I don't see anyone around that we really need to appease with our knowledge of social ways."

Angie blinked rapidly. "Well, more proper for... for the sake of propriety. There are rules, you know."

"No, I didn't know."

"Well, I suppose I'll need to explain all of it to you so that this will work." She did her best to hold a stern expression on her face.

"So what will work?" He looked confused.

His hazel eyes watched her closely and she found herself fidgeting with her shawl again. "So that we will be able to enjoy our walk," she stuttered, feeling like she had forgotten how to speak.

His eyes sparkled and, for a brief second, he looked like he was going to point out that just moments ago she was going to storm away. But instead he held out his arm to her. She slipped her arm through his once again, feeling the rough fabric of his military jacket on her skin, then the warmth of his calloused hand over hers. It was an odd sensation, and she didn't mind it a bit.

She glanced up at him and his eyes were still sparkling. She tried to act annoyed, but she wasn't doing a very good job at it, because his smile lit up his face.

"Don't gloat," she muttered.

"Gloat? What do I have to gloat about?"

"Because you won. You got your way."

"Ah. Did I really win? Tell me, what did I win?"

It was her turn to look smug. "Why, the pleasure of my

company, of course."

His bark of laughter made giggles bubble up inside of her again as well. "I'm pleased to know I'm in the company of such a humble person."

She nodded regally at him, giving in to the smile that tugged at her mouth. "Seriously, though, you really must behave more properly."

"I have a suggestion. Why don't we behave the way the 'rules' say we should when there are others around to judge us? When it's just the two of us, though, I say we be however we want."

The idea had such appeal she wanted to latch on to it. To be able to feel comfortable, relaxed—free to be herself without the fear of someone watching, scrutinizing—it was almost too much to imagine. Yet, at the same time, it was almost frightening. Who would she really be if she let go of the rules? But he was one she absolutely could not be herself around, no matter who she might be. He was the enemy and she could not forget it. She could not.

HE SAW THE shadow cross over her face and wondered what he had said wrong. He hadn't thought she was so wrapped up in society's rules that his suggestion would offend her, but perhaps he had been wrong. Perhaps she was more like the stern, older sister than he had originally thought.

"Why did you agree to come with me tonight?" He watched her closely, wondering how she would react. All he could remember was the way she had felt in his arms. He couldn't help leaning close to her, breathing deeply of her fresh lavender scent.

She didn't look at him. "I told you. I needed to thank you. I-I appreciate your assistance."

He raised his eyebrows. "Is that what you consider a real thank-you?" He mentally shook his head. He was pushing too hard with her, testing her innocence. "Why were you running out in that road anyway?"

Angie rolled her shoulders slightly, and he wondered if she was trying to shrug off the incident entirely. "I—well, I needed to drop something off at a neighbor's home. So-some jam she wanted. My family makes some wonderful jams, and we have people from miles around asking for some."

"You're avoiding the question."

She frowned up at him. "Are you always so forward?"

"Always."

"It isn't much of a reason. I just thought I would run home."

Lorenzo said nothing for several moments then he pinned her with his eyes, his lips twitching. "So the only reason you are here tonight is to thank me?"

She started to fidget with her shawl again. "Well…" She licked her lips nervously. "I suppose I was curious about you."

"I'd say you've made a poor effort at satisfying your curiosity."

"I'm here, aren't I?"

"So you know everything you want? All of your questions have been answered?" He was opening himself up to her questions and he would be forced to lie to her. Which story should he choose to describe his life? He had made up so many he had lost count. And which story would be suitable for the woman that was drawing him in deeper with every look, every touch, every smile?

"No, I'm still curious. Though I shouldn't be. I really shouldn't have a thing to do with you." She was licking her lips nervously, drawing his attention.

"Why is that?" He needed to focus on what she was saying. This woman was proving to be an unlikely distraction he hadn't imagined possible. But what questions could she have that would make her so nervous?

"YOU'RE A SOLDIER in the army, and I've heard plenty of rumors about your type. Also, you're not from here. You could be dangerous and I wouldn't find out until it's too late." She felt his arm tense, and a genuine fear struck her. What if she was right?

Though his lips smiled, his eyes did not when he looked at her. "Should I be flattered you've lumped me in with a group holding bad reputations and have already decided what I'm like?"

Angie could feel the pulse beating thickly at the base of her neck. "Should I be afraid of you?"

He hesitated and turned to face her, his hand reaching for her hair, but stopped midway. "Yes, *senorita*. You should be afraid of me." A half smile lit his lips. "The thoughts I have about you are far from pure."

She was blushing and couldn't quite catch her breath. Her mouth suddenly seemed to go dry and she tried to work moisture into it so she could speak.

His smile deepened. "But don't worry. I won't do anything you don't ask me to."

Angie felt disoriented. His voice was warm and alluring, but the things he said should have made her run away. Instead, she continued standing so close to him his breath blew across her cheek. But he was a mystery and there was a very strong part of her that wanted to solve it.

"But just in case you were wondering," he said, turning and continuing their walk, "I don't make it a habit to devour beautiful women. Though you are quite the temptation. I'm willing to wager you taste like fresh strawberries and cream." He once again turned towards her, a mischievous smile on his face. "Shall we find out?"

Angie sputtered for a few moments. "I-I—No man has ever talked to me like this!"

"Ah, but they were all thinking it. You should be thankful you have an escort tonight who will talk to you so candidly."

She should be running from him. But the fact that she stayed, her arm still resting on his, her eyes watching him with curiosity, made him bold.

Angie had never been more flustered in her life. His words were intoxicating, bringing out a curiosity and warmth she had never expected. Her skin tingled where his hand covered hers and she had the maddening wish that he would carry through with his motion and touch her. And then he winked at her.

She shook her head, licking her dry lips, breathing deeply to slow her rapid heartbeat. "Are you ever serious?"

"Are you ever not?" He urged her to start walking with him again, and though her mind yelled at her to turn around and go home, her body followed his on its own will.

She blinked. "No. No, I suppose not. I haven't found much lately around me that isn't serious."

"All the more reason to escape it sometimes."

They had walked a long stretch of the road, passing the few remaining homes, moving further away from the heart of town. Only a few townspeople walked the road, and they nodded cordially, though they looked at them with curiosity. Angie knew each of them and hoped they would not come ask her for an introduction. She'd already forgotten his last name. *Por Dios*, she would have to introduce him as Lorenzo!

They had reached the bridge over the river and he paused there, looking down at the gently flowing water. She took the few moments of silence to study him, to get her first really good look at him. His uniform fit him snuggly, though not tight, the brass buttons on his jacket polished to a shimmer. His boots were also shined and polished and it was obvious he took great care in his appearance.

His skin had tanned darkly from days spent marching under the hot Texas sun and the lines at the corners of his eyes told her he smiled often; his lips looked as though they were constantly twitching for a laugh. His shoulders were broad but he was lean and he almost looked too thin and was certain his life didn't give him much chance to get plump and content. He was several inches taller than she, but it was somehow comforting having him near instead of intimidating.

Suddenly, he was watching her just as closely and she felt a blush rise in her cheeks. She turned to look towards the river, shivering as a rush of cold, damp air came from the water and blew over them.

Shrugging out of his jacket he draped it lightly over her shoulders. She grasped a hold of the lapels, wondering if she should wear his jacket or not. Was it proper? Did she really care? The last thought put a smile on her face.

"Have I done something right to earn that smile?"

She glanced up at him. "I was just thinking about propriety."

He raised his eyebrows, but didn't say anything. The silence was pleasant, and both of them enjoyed it for a while. The sun was starting to set, the river catching the orange and purple glow from the sky.

Finally, she turned to look up at him. "So, who are you, Lorenzo?"

THE USE OF his name made him smile. "There are so many answers to that question I don't know where to begin." She made him so comfortable he felt as if he had known her for years; that he could reach to her for such an intimate touch, like brushing back her hair, as he had nearly done earlier. Mentally he shook himself.

She raised her eyebrows at him then turned and began to walk slowly over the bridge. "So pick an answer and start talking."

He followed her wondering exactly what he could tell her. Not much of his life was something he wanted to tell a woman—actually anyone—about. It hadn't been pleasant and he certainly didn't want her sympathy.

"Laredo used to be home. At least that's where I lived as a child. Home right now is where my head rests for the night. You already know I'm a soldier. What else can I tell you?"

She looked at him from over her shoulder, doubt all over her face. "Since you don't believe in propriety, does the same apply to me?"

He wasn't sure he wanted to say yes, but he would be a hypocrite if he didn't. "Of course."

"Hmm." She turned back to her path, her skirts swishing softly as she walked. He liked the view. Then she stopped and turned back to him and he quickly jerked his eyes upwards. Her smug smile told him she knew exactly what he had been looking at. Naïve indeed. He had been naïve to think she was.

"Rumor has it you are a convict soldier."

It was as though she had slapped him, and he was momentarily speechless. "When you ignore propriety, you do an excellent job."

"Yes. It is terribly rude to ask such a thing of you. However, given our history together so far, I'd gathered you wouldn't be offended."

"So we have a history together already?"

"Don't change the subject."

He raised his eyebrows and walked towards her. "I'm beginning to think I liked the prim and proper Angie a little better."

"You unleashed the beast."

"Did I?" he murmured.

She took two steps backwards. "Answer the question."

"I didn't hear a question."

"Are you a convict soldier?"

"Ah. See, you never asked me that. You just alluded to it."

She watched him in silence, one eyebrow raised in annoyance. She was a difficult one to understand. One moment she was flirting with him, the next moment running from him, the next moment ready to do battle with him.

He sighed heavily, wishing there was some way he could avoid the question. He could just lie, but for some reason he was compelled not to. He had been telling lies for too many years, and knew it would continue, but—"Yes, I am a convict soldier."

She remained silent, and he didn't know if she was expecting him to go into any further detail or if she was trying to figure out how to get away from him the fastest. She turned and leaned against the rail of the bridge, clasping her hands in front of her as she watched a leaf floating on the water.

"It must be hard for you," she said, still staring at the leaf.

He didn't say anything. There was nothing he could say. He knew from experience life could be much, much harder. In truth, he was supposed to be dead, but one man had forbidden the prison to execute him. He owed his life to that one man, and he never hated a debt so deeply. He moved to stand beside her, also clasping his hands in front of him, leaning over the water.

A half smile touched her lips. "I suppose I would be severely pushing the limits of propriety to ask you what you did."

Unease slipped down his back. He'd known what she was going to ask. He would be forced to lie.

Sometimes he wondered if his life was just an entire lie as he tried to look amused. "Severely. But you can go ahead and ask. Just remember you are the one that pushed the limits."

She hesitated, obviously uncertain what he meant, and obviously not certain if she wanted to know. Then, finally, "What did you do?"

He had half wished for her not to ask. The other half had reverted to his "I don't care" personality that had gotten him into most of his problems in the first place. He pulled his hat off and ran his hand through his hair, ruffling it into a wild array.

"Many things. Most of them not lawful." He smiled ruefully. "I was a very good thief."

"Do I need to lock up our fancy dinnerware at the

cocina?" She smiled.

His grin matched hers. "I'd say there are other things that are far more valuable you might want to keep under lock."

She was silent for several long moments, and again, he questioned if he had gone too far. Finally, "Do you think you will be in San Antonio long?"

He shook his head, straightened and pushed away from the bridge. "The rebels won't last long, not in this cold. They'll pull out before a single shot is fired. It's a lost cause. And then, God willing, I'll be a free man."

Angie pulled the jacket tighter around her. "What will you do?"

He turned a smile on her. "Haven't I bored you enough? My plans are just that… plans and schemes. Not something you need to worry about."

"I wish I held your optimism that this will all be over soon."

He reached out and he saw her force herself not to flinch. He smiled as he touched a lock of her hair. It was just as silky as he had imagined. "Those are things you don't need to worry about. I'll make sure your *cocina* is safe." If he could. He really had little say in the matter. But it if would reassure her, then he would make the hollow promise.

ANGIE'S HEART SKIPPED a beat then thudded forward. This man was having too strong of an effect on her, and the frightening part was she liked how he made her feel. Wanted, desired... special. But he was a Mexican soldier...

She wondered fleetingly if he really supported the Mexican government, or if he, like so many others, was being forced to march to war.

Anjelica wanted to grind her teeth in frustration, but he was watching her so close he would even see that. She wished he would stop getting so close to her. Every time he did she lost focus, lost concentration, and lost the ability to be strong. Every time he drew close to her she could only see him, not the damnable uniform he wore... or that she now wore. God, she was turning into a traitor. She had to shake herself. She already was a traitor. When he stood so close to her she could see the pulse beating in his neck, any rational thought seemed to scatter to the breeze.

"It is reassuring that you will personally take care of our little *cocina*," she said, unable to keep the sarcasm from her voice.

"I'll convince a few of my fellow soldiers to help, of course."

"Of course."

"May I walk you back?"

She hadn't realized the sun had already dipped below the trees. The air had turned drastically colder and darkness was settling around them.

Her breath plumed in the air. "Yes. I hadn't realized how late it was."

"At least I have been marginally successful in helping you escape."

"What?"

"Escape. Being serious."

"Oh. I thought we were being serious. Weren't you?"

"Perhaps. Perhaps you will never know."

She glared at him as she accepted his arm. "Have you been telling me stories all evening?"

He nodded. "No."

She shook her head to clear it. "You will have me befuddled before the eve is over, I fear."

His grin looked wolfish in the fading light. He glanced down at her hand and her eyes followed his. Her fingers had unconsciously been rubbing his wrist.

Mortified, she tried to yank her hand away. She had been drawn to his warmth, to his strength.

His other hand reached over and once again captured hers, holding her to him. "I don't mind," he said softly.

"It is highly—"

"Improper. Is it? I don't think so." His voice was husky and she felt as though she were being drawn towards a burning flame.

"I-I- didn't realize—I mean, I hadn't intentionally—"

"I know."

He didn't remove his hand from hers and they continued walking, though she made certain she didn't touch his skin again, instead keeping her fingers on the fabric of his shirt.

They walked in silence for several minutes, the sounds of the descending night keeping them company.

Finally, "Why did you ask me to go walking with you?"

He didn't respond for a moment. She watched his face,

though it was blank. Whatever he was thinking, he kept it to himself.

Then he looked at her, his gaze warm. "You intrigue me."

She pulled herself deeper into his jacket. "Exactly what does that mean?"

"Just that. You draw out my curiosity. I want to know more about you."

"I don't think you accomplished that tonight. I was the one asking all of the questions."

"I suppose we'll have to go for a walk again so that I may ask the questions."

Her heart raced. It was foolish. It was madness. He wanted to see her again. God, she hoped the excitement didn't show on her face. She was being naïve. He didn't want to know her. He had known many women. She was certain of it. He was using her. Wasn't he?

"I don't know how my grandparents feel about this." *Liar! Liar! Grandma and Grandpa will be dancing all night if they hear about this.*

"Hmm," he said, his face thoughtful. "I believe it was your grandfather who cornered me as I left your *cocina* today. He told me to be patient with you."

"What? What!" Her face was red. She could feel it. It was as though she had a fever. "Is this one of your stories again?"

He shook his head. He was smothering his chuckles— badly. "No. Your grandfather is a very nice man."

"Unbelievable!"

"So, since I have your grandparents' blessing…"

"But they didn't even ask me!"

"For someone who speaks so much about the rules, you seem to forget I needed their permission before I could take you walking tonight."

"That is absurd. Things are not like it was when they were young."

He stopped and she suddenly realized they were close to her home. "Does that apply to some of the other rules as well?"

She drew a deep breath, suddenly feeling as shaky as she had when she had first walked up to him that evening. "I-I don't know. Such as?"

"There are too many to think of. Perhaps tomorrow evening we should make a list of them. Will you walk with me again?"

He hadn't put his hat back on and his hair was horribly disarrayed. She had the mad urge to touch it, to see if it felt as wonderful as it looked. He was watching her, searching her face for her reaction and she didn't know what to do. He made her feel so much like a woman—and a moment later made her feel like a furious storm. She had never felt so much conflict. Was this what all the other women talked about? Was this why the girls her age were in hysterics over walking with a boy or going on a picnic with him?

And above everything else, he was a Mexican soldier. He represented everything she opposed, everything she was fighting against. But what if she could use him for information...

"Yes. I would like to walk with you again."

His face lit up with a bright smile, the dimple in his cheek making her want to laugh. How could he be a soldier in a war and be so happy? Maybe, for just a short time, he could share some of that happiness with her. She smiled at him in return, feeling warmth spread through her.

She stepped up onto the porch and turned, finding herself eye level with him. She drew a deep breath, a shiver settling in her stomach that had nothing to do with the cold air and everything to do with the man that stood in front of her.

"Tomorrow night, *senorita?*"

"Tomorrow night."

He reached up and this time she didn't flinch. His fingers lightly brushed her cheek and she wondered if he heard her knees knocking together. "*Buenas noches.*"

She watched him walk down the road, waiting for strength to return to her legs. She had never thought a single light touch could destroy a person's body so quickly. She had heard about such power in some of the stories Grandma told. Now she knew they were true. When she could no longer see him, she turned with a sigh and stepped through the door.

Chapter Six

"DON'T EVEN THINK of coming into this house with that thing!"

Angie stopped at the sound of her sister's angry, hoarse voice. "Olivia?"

There was a flash and an oil lamp came to life in the corner of the room at one of the dining tables. Olivia stood there, her back more rigid than usual, her face twisted with anger.

"Don't you dare step into Mama and Papa's house wearing that coat. You make me sick!"

Angie looked down at herself and realized she was still wrapped in Lorenzo's jacket, still wrapped in his scent, in his warmth, in his Mexican Army jacket.

"You are a little fool, Angie. A naïve little fool. I saw you out there with him. I know the types of things he was saying to you. They are all lies. All of it. You are being a fool!"

"How would you know, Olivia? How would you know about any of it? You've never even been touched by a man. Just because you are going to turn into a bitter, old maid doesn't mean that I have to, too!" Angry tears burned behind her eyes, but she wouldn't let them fall. She would never let

Olivia know how much she was hurting her, and how much it hurt to lash back.

"I'd prefer to be a bitter, old maid than fall for a convict soldier, a man who can't even think enough for himself to choose sides! Fool!"

"You don't know. You don't know he's like that."

"And you do? After this one night, do you know what he's like?"

"Of course not! But I'm willing to give him a chance. I'm willing to look past the jacket!"

"Do not come in here with that thing. I won't permit it. Go track down your convict. Give him his jacket back. Then again, he'll probably be shot for not having it when he starts duty. Maybe you should keep it."

"You're despicable."

"And you're a shame to Papa and Mama."

Angie gasped, reeling backwards as though she had been slapped. Olivia's face turned ashen as though she realized what she had said, realized what she had done. "Angie—I-Angie…"

With a sob lodged in her throat, Angie turned and fumbled with the door, desperate to get out, desperate to get away. Blinded by her tears, she couldn't find the latch.

Olivia moved around the tables, trying to reach her. "Angie, I didn't—Angie, wait!"

Angie had finally found the latch and was out the door before she could hear anything more. She ran blindly down the road, not knowing where she was going, not knowing what direction to take. Four houses down, she paused to take a breath, wiping at the tears that were warming her cold face.

Glancing back, she saw that the *cocina* was dark. Olivia hadn't followed her. Angie didn't know if she was glad or if that hurt even more. All she knew was that she hurt, and badly. She clutched the lapels of the jacket and the warm scent of man and leather and the faintest hint of mesquite surrounded her. Lorenzo. She would go to him, give him his jacket, see one of his smiles. Then things would go on.

She turned down the next road, heading towards the Alamo. Surely she would catch up with him before he got within the walls. She knew many of the men were stationed outside of the walls as well. Perhaps he was in one of those groups.

She didn't pause to think about the dangers she was bringing upon herself. A woman walking all alone at night in a town filled with rowdy soldiers was hardly safe. But she wouldn't let herself dwell on that. All she could think about was getting to Lorenzo.

It seemed she had been walking forever when she spotted a clustering of soldiers around a fire. There was plenty of light. Maybe they could help her.

LORENZO WANTED A good, strong drink. He doubted he would find one. The evening had been all that he had expected and more. The *cocina* girl was a challenge all right, but he found himself anticipating their next discussion, the next flash of excitement in her eyes.

He had misjudged her, though. He had expected a woman he would be able to seduce very easily, seeing as how she had been under her sister's strict rule for so long. But she hadn't been that way at all. She wasn't anything like what he had expected. And he was glad.

A part of him was beginning to regret asking her to go walking again. Though he was drawn to her in a way he hadn't felt in a long, long time, she would be more of an investment than he was willing to make. She was already proving not to be the quick and easy conquest he had hoped for. And yet...

He mentally shook himself. He couldn't let himself get too wrapped up in this woman. It could prove disastrous on more than one level. He wouldn't go walking with her again. He couldn't afford the risk.

The men had begun to get restless and the camp was getting lively when he returned. But all stopped to focus on him as he came walking up.

"*Vamanos*! Tell us what happened."

"Did she show up?"

"Did she give you something to remember her by?" That comment brought loud, gruff laughter.

"It is none of your concern." He growled, reaching for the coffee tin that sat on the fire.

"*Nombre*, shut up. He's gone weak on us, *hombres*! Did she cut off your *huevos* with that sharp tongue of hers?"

"I'd take that tongue anywhere!"

Lorenzo shook his head at the bawdy laughter that filled the air. "Don't worry, *hombres*. Everything is exactly where it should be."

"You have to answer us. Did she show up or not?"

"Look at how late it is. Of course she showed up. She had to. Right, Lorenzo?"

"We have a bet going! You have to answer. Did the junior *fria senorita* show up?"

"Don't tease us, *hombre*! There's a lot of money here! My money says the little *puta* didn't show!"

One of the men leaned in close to him, his voice low. "This is our only entertainment. Humor us."

"All right, all right," Lorenzo shook his head, disgusted with all of them. He held up his hands to draw their attention and they grew silent.

"The junior *fria senorita*..." He paused and the men groaned.

"Tell us!"

"The junior *fria senorita*... did show up." Shouts rang through the air in both joy and disappointment. "And let me tell you, *hombres*... she is no *fria senorita*!" More shouts filled the air, but it suddenly became silent, as a hush fell over the group.

Lorenzo looked at them with confusion then turned around to see the object of their fascination. His stomach fell to his feet when he saw the tear streaked face of Angie glaring at him.

She tossed his jacket to the ground and stepped on it to walk up to him. "You bastard," she hissed and he didn't even try to stop her hand when it smacked across his face. The whoops and cheers that followed the crack only seemed to fuel her anger.

She whirled away from him and he tried to grab for her, but she was too fast. "Anjelica! Stop!"

Angie ran as fast as her legs would carry her, unable to stop the tears that poured down her face. Olivia had been right. She had been right. God, Angie had been such a fool. She wanted to scrub her body, scrub his scent off of her, scrub away his touch.

She stumbled on the steps to the house, her tears blinding her. She didn't know how she made it through the door, but she did, and she found warm arms holding her, soothing her, warm fingers wiping away her tears.

"Shh, shh, Angie, baby. I'm so sorry. I didn't mean what I said. I didn't mean to hurt you like that. You know I didn't mean it." Olivia was holding her, rocking her back and forth.

"No—It's not that—No—You were right..."

"You need some warm tea. It will make you feel better."

Angie looked up into her sister's face, shaking her head, trying to make her understand. "No, you were right." She hiccupped. "About him. He—the men—they had bet... over me!"

Olivia's face turned into a mask of rage, then slowly crumpled as she realized the pain her sister was in. "Oh, Angie, baby, I'm so sorry. I'm so sorry." She hugged Angie tightly, rocking her in her arms. "It will all be alright. It's a good thing you found out now before it got any further."

Angie's tears were slowly starting to fade away and anger was starting to take over. "I just can't believe—I can't believe I was such a fool."

"It happens to all of us," Olivia whispered.

They both jumped as a floorboard creaked. Serena stepped into the small circle of light around them, her feet bare as always despite the cold. She looked at them for several seconds, taking in the tears on both sisters' faces.

Olivia tried to straighten and Angie too started to wipe away the tears and get up off the floor. Serena's words made them freeze, though only momentarily.

"Grandma's sick."

THE SENSATION OF falling jarred Angie out of her light slumber. Jerking upright she realized she actually had been about to topple out of her chair. Wiping a hand over her face she straightened stiffly, her body protesting every movement. Slowly she stood and walked over to her grandmother, who had begun to sleep peacefully, unlike the hours of fever and vomiting she had just been through.

Angie touched her forehead and was relieved that it had cooled considerably. She would probably be back on her feet, giving them orders in a couple of days.

Sighing heavily, Angie went to the window and pressed her head against the cool glass, rubbing at the knots in her back. Her eyes felt gritty and dry and that was partly because of her lack of sleep and partly because of her tears earlier.

Her anger at Lorenzo had gradually worn away and now she only felt like a fool. She had let his charm sway her; she had let him lead her to believe there could be something between them when she had always known there could not. Perhaps it had been for the better that he had turned out to be so cruel. She wouldn't fall so easily again.

The palest hint of pink glistened on the horizon, teasing with the promise of the day. Olivia and Serena would be starting the fires and getting breakfast simmering very soon. Angie had volunteered to tend to their grandmother, arguing that Serena couldn't be exposed to the illness, whatever it was, and Olivia was essential to running the *cocina* as soon as dawn arrived. Secretly, she had desired to get away from everyone so that she could cry her eyes out over being so naïve.

Grandma had been unaware of her tears and they had finally dried up by the time Grandpa had come in and checked on them, looking with worry at his wife before settling himself onto the little couch in the corner and falling into a slumber punctuated with loud snores. He continued his baritone song as Angie pulled a blanket over him and kissed him on the forehead.

She envied her grandparents and their love. They trusted each other impeccably, and their love for each other still burned brightly every time they looked at each other. To be so content and happy after so many years was a beautiful thing.

She heard clanging in the kitchen and winced, knowing that it was Serena who was making such a racket. Who knew what kind of mischief the girl would cause in the kitchen?

There was a slight tap at the door before Olivia stepped in, her face drawn in concern. "How is she?"

Angie smiled halfheartedly. "She'll be up and kicking us around in no time. She's got a bit of fever left, but nothing like it was last night. I think the worst is over."

Olivia was visibly relieved. "Good. Has she had anything to eat yet? Any water?"

"I'm taking care of her, Olivia. Don't worry. Go make sure you have enough food to get through this morning. Do you want me to wake Grandpa?"

Olivia hesitated, then nodded. "In a bit. It will take us a while to get the kitchen set, and I can light the pit for him." Olivia hurried out of the room, obviously already making a list in her mind of all the things she needed to do.

Angie went back to check on Grandma and saw her eyes were just barely opening. She sat down on the edge of the bed and took her hand. "How do you feel, Grandma?"

"Like a dog chewed me up and spit me out. Do I look that bad?"

Angie smiled and squeezed the stiff and wrinkled hand she held. "Never. You are still the most beautiful woman in San Antonio."

"Hmph. Don't let that beauty fool you. She can be mean. Real mean. Do you see how much of my *nalgas* she's chewed off? You want to talk about dogs? Like going after a bone, that one."

"Grandpa! Be nice. Grandma's been sick."

Grandpa was swinging his legs over to the floor, groaning

as his body protested, but there was a glint in his eyes. "She was faking. She just wanted attention."

Grandma smiled weakly at him. "You shouldn't make yourself such a tasty target."

"That's enough!" Angie laughed. "I can only take so much of your talk this early in the morning."

Grandpa leaned over the bed and kissed his wife on the cheek, then gave a growling peck on the forehead to Angie. "I suppose you want me to go cook now or something."

"Or something."

Grandpa muttered under his breath good-naturedly as he turned, grabbing his jacket and hat off the couch. He hesitated and looked back at them. "You won't forget your promise, now, will you?"

Grandma smiled. "You have nothing to worry about."

He grunted with apparent satisfaction then walked stiffly out the door, whistling softly.

Angie watched him, then turned back to face Grandma. "What promise?"

The smile on her grandmother's face was soft and wistful. "A long time ago we promised each other that we would never leave each other. So I can't leave him, no matter if God calls my name or not. We have to take that trip together." Grandma's hand came over hers and patted it lightly. "Tell me how it went with the nice soldier, dear. Was he a gentleman?"

Angie's heart sank. "No, Grandma, he wasn't. I will never see him again."

Disappointment was clear on her grandmother's face, but

she nodded. "If they don't treat you right, you just stay far, far away. A man must treasure you. If he doesn't, you don't need him."

Angie nodded, preoccupying herself with pouring a glass of water. She didn't want this conversation. What had happened wasn't something she wanted to relive. She had thought Lorenzo was different, had thought he was more. But she had been wrong. She pressed it into Grandma's hands, unable to quite meet her eyes.

"You like him, don't you?"

"What? Grandma, I think you still have a fever. You need to rest."

Grandma batted her hands away when Angie tried to tuck her back down under the covers. "You do. Angie, *hija*, I can see it on your face. I know because I used to look the same when I thought of your grandfather."

"Grandma, you are confused. I do not care for this man, nor could I ever. He is not a good man. I will never forgive him for what he did." Anger built up in her again as she remembered him laughing with the other soldiers, laughing at her and how willing he had described her.

Grandma was silent for several seconds while she sipped at her water. Then finally, "Men are not always aware of the things they do. They hurt us without realizing it, say things that are foolish and don't know it. Sometimes—"

She wished she could just tell her grandmother the simple answer. Lorenzo was her enemy. Grandma and Grandpa may disagree, but that was how Angie felt. She supported the Texians and their mission to free Texas from the oppression smothering them. But Grandma and Grandpa were loyal to the Mexican government, even when they didn't agree with all of the different things Santa Anna ordered. They would stay true to the Mexican flag.

"You're seeing things that aren't there, Grandma. You need your rest. You're getting too worked up over this. Would you like a tortilla?"

Grandma frowned and shook her head. "No. I just want to sleep."

Angie nodded and took the cup from her, then tucked her into the covers. "I'm going to help Olivia and Serena. If you need anything—"

Grandma waved her away, her eyes drooping as she settled in for a healing sleep. Silently, Angie closed the door behind her.

Chapter Seven

"WHAT ARE YOU doing?" Olivia marched up to her and yanked the apron out of Angie's hands. "Go get some sleep. You need it."

Angie shook her head and grabbed the apron again. "I couldn't get any sleep even if I wanted to."

Olivia frowned with disapproval. "Is Grandma alright?"

"Yes. More than alright. She's already getting her spunk back and I couldn't get away from her fast enough."

Olivia's lips twitched with a smile then she turned back to the *menudo* that was bubbling on the fire. "Well, since you are here, you can start on the *empanadas*. Although you burn them, at least you don't add mystery ingredients like Serena."

Serena wiggled her eyebrows dramatically, half her face covered in flour. She was elbow deep in dough as she tried to roll out tortillas.

Angie headed to the work table to join her, ready to get something else on her mind other than Lorenzo. She didn't care if he had made a mistake. She wouldn't forgive him for humiliating her like that, for using her just to play some stupid game. She refused to be his entertainment while he killed the men she was trying to help.

Angie stirred some anise into the dough and watched the seeds disappear into the fluffy white mixture. He had looked so surprised, so shocked to see her standing there after he had announced to all she had been so willing to meet him.

"Angie, you knead the dough. Not beat it."

Angie looked over at Serena, then back at her hands that had been pummeling the dough on the table.

She gnawed on her lower lip. "Just taking out some frustration."

"Why does it bother you so much?"

Angie looked at her sister with furrowed brows. Serena looked relatively normal, save the bright teal sash she had crisscrossed over her shoulders, down her back, and around her waist. "Will you ever dress sensibly?"

"What's wrong with what I'm wearing?" She looked down at herself, then shrugged. "Don't change the subject."

Her comment reminded her of how Lorenzo had talked to her the same just the night before. It had been so exciting to have a man wanting to talk to her, wanting to spend time with her. Olivia hadn't allowed any men to ever consider the idea before. Rumor of the time Olivia had cut a man in his most vulnerable place when he had made advances had kept most of the men away. If Lorenzo had heard the story, it hadn't scared him.

"You wouldn't understand, Serri." Angie began to roll the dough into the triangular shape she would fill with fruit and more seasoning.

"What's there to understand? So he wasn't what you

were expecting. You weren't expecting much to begin with, were you? You haven't really lost anything, at least not anything worth crying over."

Angie was stunned. Her hands wavered over the dough before she finally shook herself and returned to her work. A laugh suddenly bubbled up inside her, fighting to get out. She couldn't stop it.

Leaning over the table she let loose the laugh, laughing so hard tears came to her eyes. "You're right, Serri! You are absolutely right!"

Olivia frowned at both of them. "Look at you. You're delusional with exhaustion. Go get some sleep."

Angie was still chuckling. "No, I'm just trying to understand how a twelve-year-old—"

"I'm nearly thirteen."

"Knows more about life than I do."

Serena smiled smugly, turning back to her tortillas. She started whistling and shaking her hips back and forth while she rolled. Olivia and Angie both looked at each other, and burst into more laughter.

"*Hola!*" The call came from the other room. They had been laughing too hard to even hear their customers come in.

"I'll take care of it," Olivia said, still smiling as she grabbed the coffeepot and headed to the front of the house.

Angie joined Serena in whistling as they both rolled out dough. When Olivia came back in the room, though, they both fell silent. Olivia's smile was gone and replaced with a deep frown. She marched up to Angie and grabbed her wrists, pulling her away from the dough.

"He's out there, Angie. He's here for breakfast. Of all the nerve—Why, that man deserves to have his—"

"Who? Who is out there?"

"Your betting man."

Angie's brief joy vanished. "I don't want to see him."

"Yes, you do. You are going to go out there and show him how little he means to you."

"That doesn't seem like very good logic to me."

"Just do as I say. Here…" She grabbed a towel and started wiping at Angie's hands. "Clean yourself up a bit. You want to look good."

"Why? I don't want him anymore."

"Did you ever want him?" Serena asked curiously.

Angie straightened her back. "No. I didn't. Now, Olivia, I will go out there looking like I always look when I've been working in the kitchen. I don't care what he thinks. I. Don't. Want. Him."

LORENZO KNEW THE moment she entered the room. The men had been more somber than usual for such a cold morning, having just heard word some of the men would be moving out the next day to make camp closer to the enemy. But they had been talking and joking some. All noise died away, though, as she stepped into the room full of Mexican soldiers.

He had been forced to sit with his back to her with all of the men that were visiting the *cocina* so early, but he still knew it was Angie. The men were all dying to see what would happen next between them. He wished they would all go away.

Her voice carried across the room to him and he fought the urge to turn around to see her. He would only get ribbed from his comrades for showing his weakness. Her voice sounded husky, and he wondered if this early in the morning it always sounded that way.

He could hear her walking around the tables, speaking softly and pleasantly to each soldier as she refilled coffee and took breakfast orders. His buddies at the table started nudging him with their feet. "She's not carrying a knife... you might be safe."

"Think she'll slap you again?"

Lorenzo rubbed his jaw and shrugged, humoring the men. They were the reason he was in this mess to begin with, but there really wasn't anything he could do to them. Not without being alienated from the group and he couldn't afford that. But Angie could hear the comments they were making, the snickers from the men at the other tables, and he wanted to strike down each man. They were only making things worse.

Her skirts brushed against his leg when she stopped near their table and his eyes traveled up her, noting the splotches of flour that covered her dress. When his eyes landed on her face, he wanted to smile, but was afraid that might upset her even more. And she was definitely upset. Her gray eyes were hard and cold, her lips drawn into a thin line. But the smudge of cinnamon above her eyebrow and the pale white flour on her left cheek greatly diminished her angry appearance.

She looked at him with disdain, then turned to the other men at the table. "Coffee, *senors*? Anything you would like to eat?"

They were grinning like fools at her, lifting their mugs for refills of coffee. Some asked for food, others just kept grinning. It was time for him to say something.

"Angie…"

"My name is *Senorita* Torres. You would do well to remember that."

He hesitated, and remembered their conversation the night before as they had walked by the river. "Of course. How forgetful of me. Would you happen—"

"Would you like some coffee?"

Her smile was too sweet, pulling at the corners of her mouth, but not reaching her eyes. Her eyes drew his attention. Dark circles smudged the skin beneath and her eyelids looked heavy. Had she lost sleep over the craziness from the night before? The thought disturbed him.

He held up his cup, slightly away from his body, afraid that she might "accidentally" pour some of the steaming liquid on him. "Can we speak privately?" he said softly, but his group still heard him and snickered.

"I'm afraid that's not possible. You had your chance, you tossed it aside. Too bad for you." She turned to walk away from him, surrounded by laughter and inappropriate comments.

His pride was pricked. She had every right to be angry,

but couldn't she at least give him the chance to explain himself?

"Fine. Then can you at least bring me some *juevos rancheros*? It is the least you can do to soothe my aching heart." He placed a hand over his chest dramatically, imploring her with the saddest face he could pull.

The room erupted in laughter.

Her nostrils flared with anger, her eyes piercing him with a cold stare he could almost feel. Without another word, she stepped back into the kitchen and he actually felt remorse for such an easy victory.

"Don't worry, *compadre*. She'll be coming back to you in no time. These prissy little *senoritas*—they can't get enough of our convict loving. We know how to make them scream for it."

Lorenzo shook his head, aggravated. Things were not turning out like he had planned. He had hoped to catch her off in private, tell her things were not as they had seemed last night. It had only been a game, an innocent one at that, and it was unfortunate she had been drawn into it. But she couldn't be mad at him, not if he could explain that he was trying to protect her virtue, not destroy it.

Now she was ignoring him completely one moment, pretending he didn't even exist, and then giving him the sharp side of her tongue when she did decide to acknowledge him. He wouldn't have it. He was probably better off without her anyway. He liked his women willing and submissive. One that talked back had no place in his life. Absolutely no place. It had all been a mistake.

It wasn't Angie that came out with his food, but Olivia, and she didn't look any happier than Angie when she had walked out. He was going to have the entire family hating him before long, and he hadn't even done anything to deserve it.

Olivia stomped up to him, gave him the most taunting smile he had ever seen, then pronounced, "For your aching heart." She slammed the plate full of eggs and chili onto his chest.

Startled, he shoved his chair backwards and tried to stand, only to find that his boots had been tied together. Flailing his arms he landed on the floor, slimy eggs slipping down his jacket and onto his legs. Watching him from underneath his table sat Serena. She bared her teeth at him, plucked at his tied bootlaces, and gave him a saucy salute.

His laughter shocked everyone. It came from deep inside him, he couldn't stop it, and it felt wonderful. Quickly untying his boots, he stood, trying to brush off some of the food, but it just smeared more. "*Hombres*, a word of warning. Never upset the Torres sisters! You'll never get away with it!"

Laughter joined his as he walked to the doorway, then turned and flipped a coin back to Olivia, who looked absolutely stunned. "For the best food and entertainment a man could ever ask for," he said, though his words sounded a little harder than he had intended.

As he turned he saw Angie standing in the doorway, looking as though she didn't know whether to be shocked or amused. He nodded to her. "*Adios*, Angie." And he was gone.

Chapter Eight

"I DON'T THINK this is a good idea."

"It doesn't matter what you think. It needs to be done."

"I could go."

"No!" Angie and Olivia both yelled at Serena at the same time, then turned back to their task. Serena glowered at both and plopped down on a pile of blankets in the corner. She coughed as dust plumed up around her.

"I should go. I don't think it is safe for you to go alone."

"So, what exactly are you proposing, Vi?"

Olivia wagged a finger at Angie while trying to finish pinning up her skirt. "You know I don't like to be called that."

"You don't like a lot of things. It's never stopped me before."

"That's exactly the problem. You and Serena are going to cause me to have an early death."

Angie looked up at the ceiling, noting the cobwebs. She really needed to come down and clean. They never knew when they might be harboring victims of the Mexican Army in their basement.

"Are you going to answer my question?"

"I should go," Olivia said sternly.

"You think it's safer for you to go by yourself than it is for me?"

"No. No, you're right. We should both go together."

"And leave Serena here with Grandma? That sounds promising."

Olivia sighed heavily. "No, we can't do that. God knows what she would do."

"Me or Grandma?" Serena asked with narrowed eyes. Angie and Olivia ignored her.

"Let me do this."

"You're sick. I don't think it is wise."

"I'm not sick, I'm perfectly fine and you're making excuses. You need to stay here and look after Grandma. I need to get this information to the soldiers. You know it's crucial for them to know that they are sending troops to the west border of the city."

Olivia finally finished fastening the outer layer of Angie's skirt, now filled with a mixture of beef, vegetables and bread. She smelled like the Market Square. Olivia stood with a groan then turned a stern look on Angie.

"You must be careful—"

"As opposed to—"

"You're exhausted. Listen to the way you're talking. This is a bad idea."

"One of us needs to be able to run the *cocina* in the morning, and, Olivia, you are better at it than me. If I sleep thru the morning, then I can help with lunch. I was able to get a *siesta* this afternoon... this is the best way. Besides, someone must stay to take care of Grandma." Angie turned to the ladder and started climbing it, huffing and puffing from the weight of her skirt. She still had enough breath to tell Olivia her opinions. "Once you get past the idea that this is a bad choice, then maybe you'll have some good suggestions on how I'm supposed to fit through this hole!"

Olivia and Serena scampered up the ladder after her, offering advice on how to wiggle her stuffed skirt through the opening. Several minutes later they were through with only squashed bread as a victim. "Next time"—Angie panted—"we attach the skirt upstairs."

Serena was giggling. Olivia was fretting. She pressed the back of her hand to Angie's forehead. "You're warm. What if you're sick? We can't risk you getting the men sick."

"I won't go near them. I'll just drop off the food and information and leave. I'll even let you give me some of that disgusting tea when I get home."

"Garlic is one of the best... don't distract me! Alright, don't go the same route this time. I don't want to take any chances. That crazy soldier might be checking that path even more thoroughly now. Take the route next to the river."

"I don't know that route. And crazy is too kind of a description."

Olivia waved her hand distractedly. "Yes, you do know that way. We took it several weeks ago. Remember, by the tree line. There's a walkway the men built through the water."

"Oh. That way." Angie couldn't suppress her shudder.

She had never really liked water. And the San Antonio River was no exception.

"It's not that bad," Serena said reassuringly.

Angie kissed both sisters on the cheek then headed towards the door, drawing Papa's jacket tightly around her. She looked back at Olivia. "Don't wait up for me. I know how you fret. But one of us needs to be awake enough in the morning to get the *cocina* running."

Olivia didn't look happy, but she nodded. "I know you'll be fine. Just don't take any risks."

With a quick smile, Angie stepped out into the cold night air. She made it past two houses before she bent double and wretched in the shrubs. Shaking, she wiped at her mouth with the damp kerchief she had stuffed in her skirt pocket.

She had lied to Olivia when she had said she was fine. Her sister didn't need to know she was sick, and Angie was in no mood to be coddled over. Besides, she was stronger than her grandmother. Once her stomach was empty, she would feel perfectly fine, and that would be the end of it.

She hadn't known how to react to her sisters' actions with Lorenzo earlier that morning. She hadn't thought she would be so furious just seeing him. But his smug smile and attitude had triggered her anger. She was trying to calm her nerves and get a hold on her emotions when she heard the commotion in the dining room. The rest of the day he had dominated her thoughts. Had he really been playing a game with her the moment he met her? She remembered his gentle caress as she had stood on the porch steps. It had seemed so genuine… it didn't match with everything else.

She was telling herself that she was stronger than her grandmother over and over again as she made her way towards the river. It didn't stop the stomach spasms or the vomiting as easily as she had hoped. She chalked the shivering up to the cold night air.

By the time she reached the river, she felt as though her body were a limp rag. She leaned against a tree and pressed her cheek against the cold, damp leaves. Even now her mind was on him, and she hated herself for it. He was nothing to her, and she needed to remember that. The breeze blowing over her was refreshing, even though it made her fingers feel numb from the chill. She was strong enough. She could make it. She didn't need to turn back.

She took several large gulps of air. Her stomach seemed to calm and she began to feel more clearheaded. It had been a miracle she had made it so far without being seen. She had tried to pay close attention to everything around her, but if a guard had started following her, she probably would have been none the wiser.

Suddenly feeling wary, Angie searched the trees around her, moving slowly to keep from losing her balance. Odd, her grandmother hadn't seemed dizzy while she was sick. There wasn't any sound other than the usual night noises. She was all alone. The thought should have been comforting.

Hugging one of the trees, her eyes searched the river, trying to locate the path that she vaguely remembered crossing with Olivia weeks ago. The third time her gaze swept the bank she was beginning to get frustrated. Her eyes were gritty from not getting enough sleep, and everything was getting blurry.

Finally, she saw it, or at least what she hoped was the path she needed to take. Slipping on the damp leaves that covered the ground she headed towards the river, her palms getting damp. She hated water. She really hated water.

The shadow seemed to come at her from nowhere and she had no time to dodge it. Something large struck her shoulder and she went flying, the weight in her skirts helping to throw her body off balance.

She rolled several feet down the slope towards the river, trying to grab hold of anything to stop. Finally, her roll ended, and she tried to push herself up, but her cumbersome skirts got in the way again.

She looked around, pulling her hair out of her face with her hands, trying to see who or what had attacked her. The sound of heavy breathing behind her warned the attacker wasn't finished.

She turned quickly, staggering as the skirts swayed, but she wasn't fast enough. The man lunged for her but she ducked down, turning and trying to race back to the trees. He caught her hand and yanked hard to stop her, whirling her back around. She slammed into his chest and they both fell, the man cursing fluently in Spanish as they tumbled back closer to the water.

She struggled against him even as they rolled, trying to strike him with her fists any chance she got. He tried to grab her wrists, but the dampness of the air and the nervous sweat on her skin helped her slip from his grasp. When their tumble finally came to a stop, he was on top of her, his breath blowing hotly against her cheek.

Angie refused to let herself panic, though it was bubbling up inside her. She couldn't scream; that would only bring the attention of the army, and they were too close to the Texian camp for her to take such a risk. Anger surged through her, and she decided to aim for the place a man was most vulnerable.

She drew her leg up sharply and was stunned when he easily deflected her attack. Obviously he had expected it. She twisted frantically, trying to escape his weight, and her hand hit something solid.

"Be still!" he snapped in Spanish, his hands tightening painfully on her shoulders.

Her hand wrapped around the hard, lumpy object and she felt immense satisfaction as she lifted the rock. With a cry of rage stuck in her throat, she swung her arm up, slamming the rock into the side of her attacker's face. The man grunted in surprise and pain, falling to his side. She didn't bother looking to see how badly she had hurt him. She scrambled to her knees, but before she could gain her feet, a large hand grabbed the back of her head and yanked.

Gasping, struggling not to cry out at the pain, she tumbled backwards. Fear bubbled inside her as she once again fell to the ground. What did this madman want? Riding right behind the fear, though, was anger. She would be damned if she would let this man stop her from reaching the camp.

Lashing out with a growl, she struck at him, with her fists, with her nails, with her teeth. His skin ripped under her nails and she tasted blood when she bit hard at his neck. Undiluted fury filled her. She wanted to hurt him. She wanted to make him bleed. She wanted to kill him.

He responded to her fight in kind. He grabbed her shoulders and shook her hard, causing her head to snap backwards. She punched him as hard as she could in the stomach. He grabbed for her wrists and she deliberately slammed her head forward into his.

She hadn't thought it would hurt so badly. She had seen a young boy do that one time in a fight, and he hadn't even been fazed. She was seeing spots. She continued striking out at her attacker, even though she didn't know if she was doing him any damage.

The crack of his hand across her face sapped all of the fight out of her. Stunned, her ears ringing, she fell away from him and to the ground. He continued straddling her, breathing heavily, but she couldn't quite focus on him.

"I didn't want to do that, but you gave me no choice," he muttered, as though speaking to himself. His hand buried in her hair again and he yanked her up. "Now, *puta*, tell me— You!!"

Angie gasped as she was released so quickly she fell back again to the ground and her head made a sickening thumping sound. She didn't want to open her eyes. She was afraid if she did she would vomit from the spinning world.

When she finally did open her eyes, she wished she hadn't. Lorenzo was staring at her in disbelief, which gradually faded into suspicion, then rage. His eye was ticking and his lips were drawn into such a thin line they nearly disappeared.

"I should have known," he growled.

Grabbing her by the hair again, he forced her to her feet. Angie cringed, knowing she would be missing chunks of hair in the morning if the pain in her scalp was any indication.

"Let go of me!" she hissed, swinging at him again.

He caught her wrist in mid-strike and held her tight as she tried to yank away from him. "You would just love it if I did that, wouldn't you? You're coming with me."

"You're making a mistake. Wait until I tell your sergeant about this. You have assaulted a local out for an evening stroll. I'm sure you'll be disciplined severely for such an action!"

"I'll be praised for such an action." He pushed her forward roughly. "Walk."

"Where are you taking me?"

"As if you don't know. You play the sweet innocent girl very well, I might add. You certainly had me fooled."

Angie stumbled forward as he pushed her again, directing her towards the path that led across the river. "I don't understand. Where are we going?"

He glowered and didn't answer, just pushed her again. His lip and eyebrow were cut, and she was glad she had at least inflicted some pain on him. To think she had been close to trusting him. What was he going to do with her?

When he pushed her towards the rocky path she turned on him. "Are you out of your mind? What are you—"

"Stop pretending to be something you aren't. I know what you are. Now, move." His sneer should have terrified her.

She was past being terrified. "And if I refuse?"

He shoved her—hard. With a muffled shriek she toppled backwards into the icy cold San Antonio River. The water closed up over her quickly and for a couple of moments she panicked. For those few brief seconds, she was a child again, being pinned under the water by the boys at school. The water trough had looked just as harmless as the San Antonio River. And she had nearly died. Her skirts weighed her down heavily, but her feet touched bottom almost immediately.

Pushing hard, her head burst above surface, and she realized that if she stood on her very tiptoes, she could keep her head above water. Gasping, she tipped her head back, coughing each time her movements caused water to slosh over her face. She was very close to hysteria. If she didn't get out of the water soon, she was quite certain she would drown.

Lorenzo was already near the other side of the river. He looked back at her with little sympathy.

"Aren't you going to help me?" she cried out, swallowing a mouthful of murky water in the process.

He stood on the shore, watching her, arms folded across his chest. She was going to cry. No, she decided. She would make the best of this situation.

"Very well, then," she called to him, giving him one of her tight smiles. She turned and began to paddle and tiptoe as fast as she could—towards the other shoreline.

She heard him curse behind her, heard the splash, and knew she needed to move faster. Gasping and choking, she thrashed through the water, but she was no match. Moments later he grabbed the back of her dress, yanking her backwards. Water sloshed over her mouth and she struggled back to the surface.

Turning around, she grabbed a hold of him, her arms locking around his neck as though her life depended on it. In her mind, her life did depend on him at the moment.

"Swim on your own," he snarled, trying to loosen her grip.

She swallowed more water. "I can't," she gasped.

"You live next to a river. How can you not know how to swim?"

He had almost worked her hands free. *Dear God, let him get me to shore. Then give me the strength to kill him.*

"Afraid!" she choked out.

"You're afraid to know how?"

"Afraid of water!"

Lorenzo's grip on her hands loosened and she once again wrapped them around his neck desperately. As soon as they reached the mud at the edge of the bank, he tore loose from her grip and she fell to the ground, spitting up water and gasping for air.

Lorenzo watched her with a deep frown on his face, before stepping forward. Grabbing her under the arm he lifted her to her feet and started heading through the shallow brush towards the camp lights ahead.

"Have you absolutely lost your mind?" Angie demanded, her voice hoarse from choking on the river water. Fear was starting to grip her again. Why was he headed towards the

Texian camp? Dear God, had the Mexican Army infiltrated the camp? Had they sent out their own spies?

She needed to warn Tom. She had to tell him what was happening and let him know there were enemies in his camp. The future of the revolution depended on it.

Her skirts continued to weigh her down, even though she feared most all of the food was ruined. She faltered and he yanked her forward to keep up with him, his face a mask of rage. She nearly laughed. Little did he know she no longer wanted to go the other direction.

As they came closer to the campsite, several men nodded in acknowledgement to Lorenzo, and her fear grew. How long had he been posing as one of the Texians? How badly had he misled them?

She needed to speak to Tom, and immediately. But she didn't know if she could find him. Sometimes she and Olivia would stand on the outskirts of camp, having sent one of the soldiers in search of Tom. They never knew where he would be, and he never knew when they would come. She prayed that luck was on her side.

Lorenzo turned to someone nearby and spoke to him, but Angie couldn't hear his words. Besides, she was too intent on searching the faces for someone she knew, someone who would believe her when she told them there was a traitor in their midst.

Finally, he turned to her, his face blank. She couldn't tell if he was still angry or if he didn't care anymore. "Sit down." His voice was emotionless.

"I would prefer to just go home," she said sweetly, trying

to keep him from noticing how frantically her eyes searched the men.

He smirked at her. "You won't find any friends here."

"I just wonder what they'll think when I tell them you're a soldier for the Mexicans." She wished she had learned how to keep her mouth shut.

He laughed. "Go ahead. I'm sure they'll enjoy your story."

"It looks like you caught a drowning cat. Just in time, too, it appears."

Angie's head whipped around at the sound of Tom's voice and she tried to yank her arm free of Lorenzo's grip. Tom's eyes widened in surprise. "Ms. Angie?"

"Tom, I must speak with you. It's very important!"

"You know her?" Lorenzo asked, shock on his face. "She's a spy!"

"He's a spy!" They both spoke at the same time. "What?!"

Angie turned around and thrust her face in Lorenzo's, straining up on her tiptoes so she could see his eyes. "I know the game you're playing, and I won't let you get away with it! I'm not letting you leave here with your treacherous intentions!" She turned back to Tom, nearly stumbling as her skirts swung around with her. "He's a Mexican soldier, Tom."

Tom was watching her with a strange look on his face. "I know."

Angie was breathing heavily. "You know? You know and you let this—this filth into your camp?"

Lorenzo had released her arm in the confusion. "What the hell is going on?"

Angie, however, did not feel confused. Before either man could react she had grabbed Tom's knife out of its hip holster and was facing Lorenzo, her knuckles white around the handle.

In Angie's mind, all she saw was the uniform. Perhaps her fever had gotten to her. But she saw the uniform and she felt the loss of her parents. The Mexican Army had to pay. "You might have fooled them, but I know what you are. You can't be trusted. What are your real plans, huh? What kind of thrill are you getting out of this whole thing? Is Cos paying you extra to stab us all in the back while we sleep?"

Lorenzo watched her warily. "You don't know what you're talking about."

"Hah. You don't want me to tell Tom who you really are. You don't want the truth to get out."

"Let's just all calm down," Tom said, watching Angie as though she had lost her mind.

Angie shook her head at him. "He'll stab you in the back, Tom. He's playing you for a fool."

"I can see you're still bitter about last night," Lorenzo quipped.

She lunged for him, hoping she struck his throat with the sharp blade. "You despicable, conniving—"

He deflected her attack, easily turning and letting her fly past him while at the same time giving her a hard shove in the back. She stumbled and nearly fell, but righted herself quickly. She dove for him again and aimed low, hoping to emasculate him the way he deserved.

This time he didn't dodge. Instead he caught her by the shoulders and whirled her around before she could inflict any damage. Grabbing her wrists, he crossed her arms over her chest, pulling her back against his chest.

"Just what do you think you're doing?" he growled in her ear.

She yanked on her wrists, twisting against his hold, furious that he had bested her again.

"Have it your way," he snapped and lifted her, her legs swinging up off the ground. He brought her down hard and fast and she found herself sitting in the mud, her legs splayed out in front of her. "You ready to pretend to be a lady now?"

Fury ignited her. Without a second thought, she bit down on one of the arms that held her, locking her jaw and sinking her teeth into his flesh. He grunted in pain and released her instantly, trying to get away from her. With her hands once again freed, she thrashed at him with the knife.

"Damn it, *puta*, would you just—Ah!"

She finally struck him. Unfortunately it was only his hand. And, even more unfortunate, he was very angry. Growling, he grabbed her wrist in a painful grip, ripped the knife out of her hands and yanked her to her feet.

Whirling her around, he held the tip at her throat, the blade scratching at her delicate skin. "Tell me right now why I shouldn't kill you. It was you I found creeping out there like a thief—or better yet a spy. How much is Cos paying *you*?"

"Just stop. Both of you! This is out of control!" Tom had

pulled off his hat and run his hands through his sparse hair as he watched their skirmish.

He looked as though he wanted to be far, far away.

Angie leaned into the blade. "Go ahead and kill me. I'm sure it won't be the first time you've had innocent blood on your hands."

"Innocent blood. There's a joke if I ever heard one. The only thing innocent about you—"

"I said that's enough!" Tom roared, obviously at the end of his temper. Stepping forward, he grabbed the knife and lowered it away from Angie's throat. "There will be no more of this." He sheathed the knife, all the while glowering at them. Lorenzo still held Angie in a punishing grip.

"Let her go," Tom said sternly, and reluctantly Lorenzo did, though he took a giant step away from her. "Since both of you obviously know each other, introductions are unnecessary. Some things, though, should obviously be cleared up.

"Lorenzo, Angie has been helping us ever since we set up camp outside of town. She and her sister bring us food and information, whatever they can. The supplies they have been able to bring us has helped more than one man not go to bed with an empty stomach."

Glaring at him the entire time, Angie ripped at the pins that held her outer skirt together. It fell to the ground in a wet heap, soggy bread rolling on the ground with mashed tomatoes. Lorenzo stared at it in surprise.

"Ms. Angie, I know Lorenzo is with the Mexican Army. He snuck a message to us about a month ago about the convict soldiers that would be heading our way. He's been sending us information through our network from the day he was pulled out of the Laredo prison. Ever since he arrived in San Antonio, he has brought us information, whatever he can. He has helped us in more ways than I can list."

Angie felt as though the wind had been knocked out of her. She stared at Lorenzo, but couldn't read his expression. She didn't want to believe it. He was the enemy. It made it easier to hate him.

Trying to take deep breaths, she looked down at the ground and saw her skirt full of bloody meat that was mixing with soppy bread. Bile rose up and burned the back of her throat.

"Oh, God," she gasped and whirled away towards the bushes.

As she bent double, she felt an arm around her waist, steadying her, and a hand pulled her hair out of her face. The stomach spasms were hard, but there was very little in her to throw up. She wanted to lie down in the cold grass and sleep it all away. She didn't want to have to deal with being sick. She didn't want to have to deal with her humiliation and, above everything else, she didn't want to face Lorenzo.

Slowly she straightened and turned. "Thank you, Tom. I've just been a little…" Her voice trailed away as she stared up into Lorenzo's face. From the heat she felt in her face, her cheeks had turned beet red.

"You should sit down." His tone didn't imply what he was thinking, though she couldn't imagine why he would feel anything other than anger.

She had insulted him, stabbed him, and nearly thrown

up on him.

"I'm fine," she said hoarsely. God, she didn't want to sound weak in front of him. Her eyes started to burn and she pushed on his chest, trying to get him to release her. "I really am just fine."

He frowned at her, suspicion crossing his face. The back of his hand brushed over her forehead and the hated tears started to slip down her face. "You're burning up. What the hell are you doing out here like this?"

She didn't want him to see her cry. She didn't want him to know how embarrassed she was, how angry she was with herself. She pushed on his chest again, but he was holding her tightly.

"Please, let me go. Just please leave me alone."

He shook his head at her and slowly released his hold. "You're crazy. You're out of your damned head."

She took a couple of steps away from him and then hesitated when the world started spinning. Her head ached fiercely, and the blasted tears running down her face weren't going to make the situation any better. She needed to go home. She just needed to get away from all of them. That was the last thought she had before her world went dark.

Chapter Nine

LORENZO TOOK A giant step forward and caught her before she hit the ground. She was a dead weight in his arms as he lifted her, and the dark smudges under her eyes spoke volumes of her exhaustion.

He looked to Tom for help, not certain what he was supposed to do.

Tom looked frustrated and a bit uncertain himself. "Bring her over to the fire, but don't get too close. I can't afford for any of the men to get sick."

Lorenzo frowned, but knew it was the truth. Several men had become ill lately, and even more had deserted to return to their homes. If they had any more setbacks, it could mean the end.

He headed towards the fire and, as soon as he could feel the warmth, he laid her carefully on the ground. Her eyelashes were dark against her cheeks and she was still soaked through from her dunk in the river. He was torn between guilt and anger.

He was furious at her for the things she had done. Furious at her for being a part of something so dangerous. Furious at her for taking such risks. And angry with himself for completely misjudging her.

He lightly touched the small cut on her neck. Part of him said she deserved it. She had overreacted just as badly as he and he had only been defending himself. But he had been harder on her than if it had been someone else. His pride had been greatly bruised that morning, and she was the source of that bruising.

She groaned and brought a hand to her forehead. She slowly become aware of her surroundings, and he watched her gray eyes settle on him. Confusion clouded her face for several minutes before it was infused with color. He didn't know if it was anger or embarrassment. Maybe both.

She ignored his hand as she tried to push herself to her feet. "I'm fine," she said for the third time. She staggered to her feet, held herself still for a few moments while she drew a deep breath, then finally turned to face Tom.

"I came here tonight with some information." She was speaking slowly and deliberately, as though she were thinking very hard about each word she said.

Lorenzo stood behind her, his arms crossed over his chest, glowering at her. "You shouldn't be here in the first place."

She ignored him. "We heard word some of the army is being moved."

"Yes. To the western border of the town. That's why Lorenzo is here tonight."

"So there really was no need for you to be here. As I have already stated."

Angie turned to look at him, trying to control her anger.

"I had no way of knowing that now did I?"

"Well now you do. So don't come out here again."

"You don't give me orders. Why don't you go run back to your friends in town? Go place another bet."

His jaw clenched. "Just because your feelings are hurt—"

"Believe me, you aren't important enough—"

"Ms. Angie," Tom broke in. "I think it would be wisest if you don't return to the camp."

Angie whirled back to face Tom. "What?"

"It isn't safe. It never has been. I don't think you and Ms. Olivia should risk this anymore."

"You're going to listen to him? To-to this madman? Just exactly who is giving the orders around here?" Tom's dark frown at her made her wish she could draw back her words. "I'm sorry, Tom. You know I mean no offense. I just don't understand."

"Lorenzo has been giving us most of the information we've needed lately, though you and Olivia have uncovered some things that have been extremely valuable. But it would be better for Lorenzo to bring us all of the information, instead of risking the lives of two women."

"We know the risks we take, Tom. We knew that when we started. Remember, we came to you, not the other way around."

"I know. And we have been extremely grateful. But with Cos getting new recruits lately and having more patrols out, I can't take the risk of something happening to you two."

"And how will you get food?"

"What you bring us has been a blessing. But there are

more than four hundred men out here, Ms. Angie. How many men do you think a couple of skirts full of food will feed? If you really want to help us, you will find a way to bring us a larger amount of food. Something has to be better than in your skirts."

Angie ran her hands through her hair, pulling the damp strands out of her face. "We must be able to do more than that."

"Possibly. But I'd prefer if you worked with Lorenzo for now until I let you know further."

"You want me to what?"

Lorenzo stepped forward. "It would be for the best. You'll remain safe and I'll get any information at all to Tom."

"No. Absolutely not. I will not work with you."

Tom shook his head. "I cannot accept you in my camp anymore, Ms. Angie. Nor Ms. Olivia. It is your decision to make if you want to continue to help."

Angie's stomach churned again. She faced Lorenzo and pointed a stern finger in his face. "Do not come near my sisters. Olivia will kill you. She is not as forgiving as me."

"I wasn't aware there was any forgiving that needed to be done. Unless you're referring to me forgiving you for biting me, scratching me, stabbing me—"

"If anything further happens, I'll be the one to speak with you. Not my sisters. That's it." She nodded to Tom, holding herself as proud as she could. "I hope all goes well for you, Tom. Perhaps I will see you in San Antonio soon, when there is peace."

"I hope so, Ms. Angie. I really hope so."

Without any further comment, she turned and headed towards the river, her head held high, trying her best to walk gracefully. She didn't know if she was keeping a straight line or not. She was just waiting until she was far enough away so she could throw up in the bushes.

Lorenzo and Tom watched her weaving her way towards the river. "What's her story?" Lorenzo cringed when she stumbled, but she didn't fall.

"I don't know much. One of the men that defected apparently knew her family and told us their parents died years ago. The girls have been relatively on their own, since, although their grandparents help them a lot. That's all I really know."

"Any idea why she's so passionate about helping you?"

"No. But I have learned not to question it. I'll take what I can get."

Lorenzo gave him a half smile then extended his hand. "I'll see you in a few nights. I think I should head back to town before someone starts to notice I'm gone."

Tom shook his hand and smiled knowingly. "Make sure she gets home safe." Lorenzo nodded solemnly and then turned to follow his new partner.

ANGIE WASN'T ABLE to make it to the river before she fell to her knees and threw up again. Had Grandma thrown up this many times? She couldn't remember. She wanted to laugh at herself for thinking that she was stronger than Grandma. She stood up and suddenly realized she wasn't alone.

"So, why is such a lovely woman like yourself out for a stroll so late?" Lorenzo stood beside her, his arms behind his back and looking entirely like a gentleman who had encountered a lady on a stroll. Except for the fact that he wore a ragged uniform that was drenched with river water and she looked even worse.

She stepped around him and headed towards the crossing. "Would you please just leave me alone? What do you want?"

"It would take me too long to list in detail what I want."

Angie made a sound of disgust. "Do you know how to be anything but a pig?" He caught her arm, forcing her to look at him.

His face was hard. "I don't like things any more than you do. But I make the best of them. And I think the same would help you."

"Good. We seem to be of the same thinking. The best thing for me to do is get away from you and get home. That would certainly be making the best of things." She needed to be angry with him.

It helped her feel more clearheaded to focus on that anger. If she thought about everything else, she would lose her composure completely. She had to remind herself that he couldn't be trusted. Or could he? If Tom trusted him...

"I think you're missing the point."

"Let me go." She had to be strong in front of him.

If he thought she was weak, then he might decide not to

even attempt to work with her for the revolution, and that was completely unacceptable.

"No. You can barely walk on your own. How do you expect to cross that river?"

"This may come as a complete shock to you, but I can take care of myself."

"You're right," he said as he picked her up and threw her over his shoulder. "I'm shocked."

"What are you—Put me down right now! This is outrageous!"

Angie swallowed hard as she bounced on his shoulder. He really was a madman. And he had the nerve to call her crazy!

"Set me down right now. I don't need you. I don't need your help!" Suddenly the ground tilted and she was back on her feet. She was surprised to see that they had already crossed the river.

"That's exactly your problem. You don't realize when you do need help, and you're too damned stubborn to ask for it when you need it! One of these days, when you're all alone and your sisters have gone off to make a wonderful life without you, you'll wish you had asked for help."

She wanted to slap him. She didn't have the energy to lift her arm. She just turned away from him, took a step forward, and slipped in the mud. He caught her and picked her up. "Don't bother asking me. I know how badly right now you want to ask me for help, but I'll just go ahead and take care of things for you."

She watched him with wide eyes. "You really are out of

your mind."

"Yes." He didn't look at her. A large splash of water hit his nose and he glanced up at the sky. "Why not? Nothing else could make this night more miserable." As though having received permission, thunder boomed and the rain began to pour down with earnest.

ANGIE GASPED AND threw her arms around his neck, trying to huddle closer to his warmth as the icy drops drenched them. He wanted to laugh. She did need him—she just didn't want to admit it yet.

"Why do you do it?" he asked, his mouth close to her ear so she could hear him over the downpour. "Why do you take such risks to help the Texians?"

Her hair was plastered to her head and water ran in her face. Even as pale and wan as she looked, she was the most alluring woman he had ever seen.

"I could ask the same question of you."

"I have different reasons. Sometimes I don't understand all of them. I suppose for freedom more than anything." He wouldn't quite look her in the eyes.

She didn't need to know everything that motivated him. He had seen enough injustice to know that the side he had picked would help right some wrongs.

"And you are willing to risk your life for this?"

"Yes."

"So am I." Her voice was stern, her eyes watching him

closely.

He felt a tick in his eye. "Men die for freedom. Women don't."

"So, women shouldn't care so strongly about their home, about their people, to give their lives for it? We can't have the same level of devotion?"

"That's not what I'm saying." He clenched his jaw, wishing the rain wasn't rushing in his face, nearly blinding him. "It's just not something a woman should have to concern herself with."

Her eyes were beginning to droop, but what he had said was making her angry. He would never understand this woman.

"I'm concerned with it, as are my sisters, as are many other women. It is very important to me." She lay her head back down on his shoulder, unconsciously nuzzling his neck as she tried to get comfortable.

"Why? Why is it so important? Why did you come out here tonight, knowing how sick you are? Was it really necessary to risk your life tonight?"

He doubted she was aware her fingers were lazily combing through the hair that curled at the back of his neck. He, however, was acutely aware and it was playing havoc on his concentration.

"I can't trust you," she said softly.

"If that is your answer, it's not good enough."

She was silent for so long he began to wonder if she had passed out again. Tilting his head back he could see her face. Her eyes were half-closed, but she looked up at him.

"My parents were killed by the Mexican Army." She spoke slowly, as though trying to pick the best words. "They were protesting the new taxes. They helped their friends in the ports. They were disloyal, or so it is said, for opposing the will of the Mexican government. And so they were killed."

Lorenzo could read the pain on her face, and just as strongly sense her anger. Now he knew what was motivating her, what was pushing her to put her life at risk.

"You want revenge," he said almost bitterly.

To know that she was being motivated by such an anger, such a hatred, disappointed him. In the back of his mind he realized he was being a hypocrite. A large portion of his motivation was revenge, but he refused to admit it.

"Put me down." She had stiffened in his arms and had slid her hands forward so she could push on his chest. "I said put me down!"

He pulled his arm out from under her legs and she slid to the ground, but he still kept an arm around her, steadying her. She looked pathetic as she tried to face him, her legs quivering beneath her.

"I have no reason to trust you, and you certainly have no reason to trust me. And you obviously have a low opinion of me, so I think it would be best if we just part our ways right here."

"Do you think I'm low enough to just stand here and watch you drown in a ditch?"

"Yes."

It hurt. He couldn't believe knowing she thought so

poorly of him would hurt, but it did. "You're absolutely right. There is no reason for this charade to continue."

Lorenzo turned from her sharply and headed away from her. He should have never thought he could trust her. She was no different than any other woman he had met in his lifetime. Friends and lovers one moment, backstabbers and enemies the next.

※

ANJELICA WATCHED HIM turn and head into the woods. A part of her couldn't believe he was actually leaving her. But another part of her wondered why he had tried to take care of her so far in the first place. She had been nothing but rude and difficult with him, and she feared her actions might have even ruined her chance to work with him as Tom had ordered.

She tried to wipe the rain out of her face, but it just kept coming back. It was so cold her teeth had stopped chattering and her whole body was numb. Pulling her father's coat tightly about her, though it really did no good, she began to slip through the mud towards town. It wasn't too terribly far to go. Lorenzo had carried her a long distance.

She still couldn't grasp the fact that he was on their side. She knew some of the soldiers had defected, but she hadn't known there were any spies actually in the army. She couldn't trust him, though. She had seen him interacting with his comrades the night he had taken her for a walk. They were friends. He was one of them. How could he turn his back on them? Her mind just continued to run in circles. But at every conclusion, it seemed more and more likely that he really was on the Texian side.

Her feet slipped in the mud and she fell to her knees. She stayed that way for a while, the rain pounding down on her as she tried to gather enough strength to push on. She didn't know how long she stayed that way, but finally, slowly, she pushed herself up and continued.

She needed to concentrate on getting home, not the man who might or might not be on their side. She knew what Olivia would think. Olivia would think he was playing both sides, and he couldn't be trusted any further than the rest of the soldiers. But the thought of having someone so close they could trust, a man who could provide the strength they might someday need was terribly tempting.

At the moment, she was actually longing for that strength. Her feet slipped again and she headed closer to the tree line, hoping for less mud. Why had he gone back into the woods? Had he been just so angry with her he had only wanted to get away? She didn't know what he had been so angry about. It wasn't as though she had insulted him. The nerve of him suggesting that she was only trying to get revenge.

She reached the tree line and leaned heavily on one of the trees. She hadn't realized how far it was to town. Maybe he was right. Maybe it was revenge that was motivating her. Maybe she was that shallow of a person. Inside, she shook her head. No. It was the principles that the revolution was fighting for—the freedoms they deserved—that was what motivated her. Wasn't it?

Her legs were shaking so hard she pictured her knees bruised in the morning. Revenge wasn't the only thing motivating her. It couldn't be. She wanted to make things right—she wanted to continue the path her parents had started.

She sat down on the grassy patch near the tree, holding on to the tree while the world spun. She never would have thought it possible, but she wished Lorenzo was next to her. The thought of his warm arms supporting her, holding her, comforting her, warmed her slightly. She started to pull herself up when the world tilted crazily. Gasping, she closed her eyes, but her grip loosened on the tree. As she fell to the ground, only one thing flashed through her mind—Lorenzo's face.

Chapter Ten

❧

LORENZO WEAVED HIS way through the trees, angrier than he had been for a long time. The woman was impossible to understand. Why was she getting so angry? If she was offended that he disapproved of her choices, then she should get mad at herself, not at him.

The weather wasn't improving his mood any. The cold rain pelted his neck and shoulders since he was keeping his head down. Several feet into the trees he found where he had stored his uniform. Cursing and stomping his feet he shed out of his rough and used white, ragged private's uniform, and into his standard red jacket uniform they were expected to wear. The white one had been what he wore on the journey to San Antonio. But General Cos, their commander, expected most of his soldiers to strike an imposing force upon the streets of town.

Damned woman probably wasn't even going to make it back to her house. If she even made it to town, she would be discovered by soldiers easily in her poor condition, and he had no doubt what the soldiers would do to a defenseless female wandering around at night. The thought made him a little ill. An image flashed in his head of her olive flesh being grasped by a group of soldiers eagerly taking advantage of her beautiful body, and he felt as if someone had punched him in the gut.

He wrapped up his clothes and stuffed them back under the tree. He didn't even pause to second-guess himself as he turned back towards the area he had left Angie. He would follow the direction she should have taken. If he didn't find her along the way, he would go to her home. He didn't care how angry she got. He would prefer to deal with her anger at him than let her get hurt. He didn't evaluate why he felt so protective over the woman that was causing him headaches.

He started walking in the direction he felt she would have taken, looking in both directions in case she had diverted paths. The woman was too hardheaded for her own good. He started walking faster. If anything happened to her…

He wouldn't have seen her if it hadn't been for her petticoats. As the wind gusted especially hard, a flash of white off near the trees caught his eye. He continued walking, his eyes narrowed against the rain as he tried to see what it was. His heart began to pound hard in his chest as he realized it was Angie, and she wasn't moving.

Running awkwardly on the rain slicked ground, he raced to her, cursing over and over again. He never should have left her. His pride might have cost her life. He skidded to his knees beside her and leaned over, pulling the long wet strands of hair away from her face. She didn't move and her face was terribly pale. Her lips looked blue.

His hands were shaking as he lifted her onto his lap, rubbing at her wrists, hoping to revive her, wanting to reassure himself that she was alright. Her skin felt like ice.

"Angie, wake up." He rubbed her arms and shoulders. "Angie, wake up now!" He smoothed his hand over her forehead, lifting her closer to him. He placed his mouth at her ear. "Wake up and hit me. I know you want to. Let's just go ahead and get it out of the way."

Her eyes flickered and she winced as fat raindrops struck her face. He leaned over, shielding her face from the rain.

With her eyes half open she smiled at him. "Lorenzo," she whispered, "I was just dreaming about you."

Relief was so intense he nearly had to sit down. He scooped her into his arms and stood, heading in the direction of town once more. "If you weren't so stubborn, you wouldn't get yourself into such a mess." She didn't respond and it appeared she had fallen asleep again.

Lorenzo didn't even want to think what might have happened to her if one of the other soldiers had found her. It was unbearable to imagine. The town was silent; everyone was staying in the warm and dry blankets their homes offered. He only saw two soldiers out on patrol, but they were huddled under an eave, sharing a smoke and were oblivious to everything around them.

Angie hadn't moved since he picked her up. It made him nervous. When they drew near to her home, he gently shook her, trying to rouse her. "Where is your room?" She didn't answer. "Angie, we're almost to your home. I need to know where to find your room in the house."

She made a motion with her hand and he watched her

try to focus on everything around her. "You can't…"

"Unless you want me to get Olivia and ask her where…"

"No, no—I'm fine. Just leave me here. I can make it from here." She tried vainly to push at his chest and free herself from his arms.

"I fell for that before. I'm not going to again. This is your last chance…"

"At the back of the house. My room is at the back."

He nodded and turned at the side of the house. No lights were on; it appeared everyone was asleep. He wished he could be so lucky.

Pausing at the back door, he slipped out of his muddy boots then slowly, slowly opened the door. It hardly made a sound, though the squishing of his socks seemed to make even more noise.

When he spotted the door to his right he took it, praying it was the right one. A familiar scent of lavender greeted him and he knew it was Angie's room. "I'm going to set you down. Can you stand?"

"Yes." Her voice was hoarse. "Yes," she said again, more strongly. "You really should leave now."

He was going to go crazy. He bumped around the room until he found the lamp then lit it quickly. "You're welcome," he said sarcastically, turning back to face her.

A small puddle of rainwater was beginning under her feet and she looked like a drowned cat.

He shook his head at her. "You're a little fool."

ANGIE FELT SLIGHTLY lost, but knew she had to tell Lorenzo something. "You've made that point before." She was afraid to move, afraid if she did she might step into one of the black spots floating before her eyes.

Why was Lorenzo still with her? She didn't even remember him coming back.

"Why?" She was whispering, hoping to God Olivia hadn't heard them enter. "Why did you come back?"

Lorenzo was looking around her room, obviously distracted. "Do you have any extra blankets or towels?"

"Yes, in this chest…" She nearly fell as she took a step towards the cedar chest at the foot of her bed.

He gave her a hard look. "Stay put," he ordered, opening the chest and pulling out several towels and blankets.

He approached her with determination, holding one of the towels in his hand. She started to back up, felt dizzy, and stopped. He reached up for her head and she flinched.

He looked at her with frustration. "Do you really think I would go through so much hell to bring you back safely so I could hurt you?"

She let out her breath slowly. "No."

He gave her a half smile and reached for her again. Gently he began to towel her hair, squeezing the water into the fabric. Finally, he wrapped the towel loosely around her hair and found her staring at him intently. "Why did you come back?"

He turned away and grabbed another towel. "It's not important." The answer to that question was one he couldn't even explain to himself.

He turned back, reaching for her, and she grabbed him.

Her fingers circled around his wrists, holding his hands away from her. "It matters to me."

In the soft glow of the lamplight he watched her, wondering why he was standing in front of her. Any sane man would be far away from her and working on getting even further away. But he wanted to be here with her more than anything else. He wanted to make sure she was safe before he could leave her. The woman was having a devastating effect on his concentration, though.

"I couldn't leave you out there." She didn't release him and continued staring at him. "I felt responsible for you."

"Then your responsibility is over."

He couldn't take his eyes off her lips. They were full and no longer blue but a light pink.

"I know," he said softly.

He moved his hands forward so he could rub her shoulders with the towel, and she slowly released her wrists. He tried to dry her with the towel, and then noticed the puddle of water that was growing larger under her. He was sure he had a similar one around him. "We need to get you out of these clothes."

She blinked. "*Perdone?*"

He turned her around and began to pull at the ties of her dress. "You can't! This is entirely improper."

"I don't care. Be still. I'm going to get you out of these wet clothes." She was starting to shiver, something he felt was a good sign.

"Wh-what about y-you?" she asked through chattering

teeth.

"What about me?"

"Y-your clothes are ju-just as wet."

"I'm fine."

She turned back to face him when her dress began to slip on her shoulders and saw that he, too, was shivering, but was trying to hide it. She made a decision instantly and reached for the buttons on his jacket, vaguely realizing he no longer wore the old patched uniform. Her mind was too foggy to ask him where it was.

"You're not being very sensible right now," Lorenzo said, his voice sounding odd to her. "My clothes have no time to dry, and I'm going back into the rain to return to my company."

Her fingers hesitated, then continued. "You c-can at the very l-least take off your j-jacket. You sh-should be comfortable wh-while you're here."

His hands slid her dress off her shoulders at the same time she pushed his jacket off his. He wore nothing beneath his jacket and she was staring at his chest, at the light scattering of dark black hair against his bronzed skin. She was beginning to feel light-headed again.

※

LORENZO WAS FINDING himself in much the same predicament. Though she was not nude, her chemise did little to conceal the womanly figure he had been admiring since that first day in the *cocina*. Her pale shoulders glistened with moisture and the thin fabric of the chemise clung to her skin. Her breasts formed round globes that pressed against the fabric; her dark nipples taut from the cold, drawing his attention. He desperately wanted to touch her, to pull her against him so she would know what she was doing to him. Her chemise tucked in against her narrow waist and led down to the petticoats that flared out at her hips.

"I-I should wrap your jacket..."

Her words seemed to cut into his temporary immobility and he turned with her. She leaned down to pick up his jacket and nearly fell face-first had he not caught her and supported her.

Holding her, holding her in his arms, his fingers flexed on her waist and he closed his eyes briefly, wishing he could hold her until the sun rose hours later. She took the jacket from him and broke free of his hold, even though he tried to hold on a little longer. Slowly, she walked to the chest and used one of her spare blankets to wrap the jacket and press it, forcing some of the moisture out.

When she looked up, he was standing right next to her and her arm brushed over his bare chest. His heart skipped a beat. She was having the oddest effect on him and he didn't want it to stop. And he hoped somewhere, deep inside, she didn't want him to leave.

SUDDENLY, HE KNEELED in front of her and his hands were on her ankle, unfastening her shoe. Almost as though she were in some sort of dream, she let him take her shoes off as his hand slid up her calf on each leg as he pulled them off. She didn't know why she was still shivering. Her face felt so warm she thought about going outside just to cool off.

His fingers slid further up her leg, gripping the top of her stocking high on her thigh. Her breath caught and her hands grabbed his shoulders for support.

"Lorenzo…" She didn't know if she spoke loud enough to be heard.

He removed her other stocking slowly, then stood, his expression dark and unreadable. Watching her closely, his fingers reached for the tiny laces of her chemise.

She took a wavering step backwards. "You can't. It's—"

"Improper. I know. And I think I've told you before, I don't care."

He stepped towards her, suddenly so close her bare toes touched his wet socks; his breath blowing warmly on her face. Watching her face he reached for the laces again. This time she didn't move.

"I'm not leaving until I have you safely tucked into that bed."

She shook her head and the towel fell off, leaving damp tendrils curling around her face. "Haven't you done enough?"

His fingers slid through the top laces and his skin touched hers. She gasped.

"No," he said thickly.

She caught his hands and held them still, unaware that she was holding them against her breasts, unaware she held him so close he could feel her racing heart.

"You've done more than enough. You've saved my life." Her shivers were quickly dissipating as she watched him. "You don't need to do this."

"I won't look," he said softly.

A faint smile touched her lips. "I don't trust you."

"I know." He watched her and, when he flexed his fingers, she realized he had them nestled between her breasts. "Let me do this for you, Angie."

Very slowly, her hands released his. Their eyes remained locked as he undid the laces. He was determined to let her know he could be trusted, even if it was something like this.

As his fingers slipped between the fabric, they would lightly brush against the sensitive skin on the sides of her breasts, her abdomen, her lower stomach. She was starting to breathe heavily and found it hard to concentrate on anything other than his touch.

Lorenzo was finding himself in a situation that usually was not a problem for him. He had never been more aroused in his life, and she wasn't even naked yet. He pulled the string on her petticoats and they slid to the floor with a wet plop. His fingers were trembling slightly as he eased the chemise off her shoulders.

Knowing that she stood before him completely nude and he couldn't look was an unbelievable torture. His eyes dropped slightly to her chin and in the dim light the unmistakable purple of a bruise was beginning to shine through on her smooth skin.

"Did I do this to you?" he whispered as his thumb lightly

rubbed over the mark.

She winced. "I believe that was after I tried to damage your... well... your... umm..."

"Oh, yes." His smile was a brief flash. "I remember that."

His thumb circled around the mark, and then, impetuously, he leaned forward and pressed his lips lightly against the bruise. She gasped and her nails dug into his upper arms. She was watching him with curious eyes when he pulled back. His thumb dropped to her collarbone where there was another faint bruising.

"And this? Did I cause this?" Not waiting for her answer he dropped his lips to her skin, pressing them lightly against the blemish in her flesh.

She sucked in a sharp breath and arched against him. He moaned softly against her skin as her nipples brushed against his chest. He wanted to haul her up against him. To press his body against hers, to ease the ache she had started within him.

"And here?" he murmured, his lips trailing along her neck where he decided there should be a pattern of bruising—if only imaginary.

His lips came across the small nick the knife had made and he kissed it tenderly, wishing he could take it back. Her nails dug into his arms and his hands slid around her lower waist, pulling her closer to him. God, she was so sweet in his arms. He needed more.

Pulling back slightly, he weaved a hand through her damp hair, tilting her head back. "Sweet little *chula*," he whispered, focused on her parted lips.

"Lorenzo," she breathed and hearing his name used by her husky voice was nearly his undoing.

Crushing her body against his, he let her know how badly he needed her. Her eyes widened, and it was in that moment he realized exactly what he was doing. Though her eyes were heavy with a passion he desperately wanted to taste, they were equally as bright with fever.

He ran his fingers lightly over her forehead and the heat reminded him of just how ill she really was. He hovered over her lips, craving something he couldn't have. Not unless he wanted to be the same as the soldiers he had condemned in his thoughts earlier.

"Lorenzo," she whispered, "what are you doing?"

He buried his face at her neck, nuzzling her ear. "Making a mistake, *chula*. Making a terrible mistake."

Her hands ran up and down his arms slowly. "I thought you don't make mistakes."

He smiled against her neck, then sighing so hard it was nearly a groan, he lifted her into his arms and carried her to the bed. He laid her under the covers and reluctantly didn't follow.

Her eyelids drooped heavily as soon as her head hit the pillow. But she was still aware enough to grab his hand and pull him down to her. Her other hand came up to caress the side of his face, his neck, his chest.

"Stay with me, Lorenzo," she whispered.

His heart lurched. "You don't know what you are asking."

Her eyes were closed. "Don't leave me." Her voice trailed

off slowly and she released his hand.

He ran his hand through his hair with frustration. "I have to get Olivia," he said, hoping she heard him. She was far too ill for him to leave her alone.

Cursing under his breath he turned from her and grabbed his jacket from the top of the chest. He would be lucky if Olivia didn't slit his throat just for being in the house.

"I'll take care of her."

The tiny voice at the door startled him. Serena stepped into the light, watching him cautiously.

"What?"

"You don't have to tell Olivia anything. I'll take care of her."

Lorenzo nodded with relief then turned back to Angie. She was moving restlessly on the bed. He leaned over and pressed a kiss to her warm forehead, not caring that Serena watched.

"I'll walk you out," Serena said as they met in the doorway. She didn't look at him with condemnation as he pulled on his uniform, just curiosity. He stepped out onto the back porch, and much to his surprise, Serena stepped out with him.

He began to put on his boots, then watched dumbfounded as Serena stepped out into the rain, cringing and shivering as her night rail became soaked through. "Are you out of your mind?"

Serena frowned at him as she hopped about shaking her head to get the massive curls drenched. "How else can you explain two sets of puddles in her room? Or did you want to be the one to tell Olivia you undressed our sister?"

He was glad it was dark. Otherwise Serena would see the flush in his face from being reprimanded by a twelve-year-old. "I should have known you were the smart one of the family."

Serena stepped back up onto the porch, hugging herself. "I'm disappointed it took you this long to figure that out."

His lips twitched with a smile then he looked back towards Angie's room. "Take care of her."

Serena's eyes narrowed at him. "Why do you care? Why did you even bring her back? I know about your disgusting bet with your friends."

Lorenzo frowned. "Things are not always as they seem. Is that why she's ill? Did she make herself sick last night because of me?" His guilt would be immeasurable if that were true.

"Hah!" Serena was beginning to shiver. "You flatter yourself far too much. Grandma was sick. Angie stayed up with her all night. Olivia's with Grandma right now, which is probably why she doesn't realize Angie's home. You—you aren't going to—to do anything about her being out tonight?"

Though she stood with her back straight and her chin thrust out, there was a very real fear in her eyes. "I'm going to make sure she never does it again," he said harshly, then more gently, "but I won't report her."

Her relief was visible though she tried to conceal it from him. "Thank you. For bringing her home."

He nodded stiffly then stepped out in the rain. He paused and looked back at Serena. "I know you don't think much of me. But I will never let anything hurt Angie. Anything. That includes Olivia."

A half smile touched Serena's lips. "Your secret is safe with me. Go. Angie needs me."

He smiled and nodded to her and turned back to the drenched town. He wondered what the next couple of days would bring with his new alliance with Angie. He wondered if she would help him like Tom had ordered. He wondered if she would live long enough for him to find out. That thought chilled him more than the icy rain. He decided then and there he would be having breakfast at the *cocina*.

Chapter Eleven

THE FEELING OF a cool cloth on her forehead pulled her out of her sleep. She could see Lorenzo's face before she even opened her eyes, and a smile pulled at the corners of her mouth. Turning her head towards the source of the cool cloth, she lifted her lids.

"Olivia?" Confusion clouded her face.

"You were expecting someone else? Looks like you were having quite the pleasant dream. Care to share?"

"I-I don't remember. It was nice, though, I remember that." What had happened? Her mind was racing, trying to remember everything that occurred. She wasn't grabbing much, and Lorenzo kept getting in the way. Why was he dominating so much of her thoughts?

Olivia ran the cloth across her cheeks. "Your fever is almost gone. You stopped vomiting several hours ago. I'd say it's almost over."

"I don't—How—This isn't making any—"

"Take a deep breath. You've had a rough time. Just start with one question."

Olivia was smiling gently at her. That must mean she didn't know about Lorenzo. What was it about Lorenzo she didn't want her to know about? Things were flashing through her head so fast she couldn't seem to grab a hold of just one.

The sun was up and shining brightly into her room. That was the first thing that confused her. "How long have I been asleep?"

"A couple of hours. You will be blessed fortunate if you have forgotten the past day or so. You were getting very little sleep during that."

Vaguely, she remembered becoming very familiar with the chamber pot and the agony of constantly bending over it. But it seemed as though it had happened a long time ago, in a different life. She remembered Olivia at times and at other times Serena holding her hair out of her face, pressing water to her lips, and pressing cold cloths to her forehead.

"I see you're starting to remember," Olivia said sympathetically. She set the bowl of water and the cloth aside and grasped Angie's hands. "You left for Tom's camp two days ago. You came home that night, and we are very fortunate Serena saw you approaching. You passed out right before you reached the porch. How Serena was able to get you inside and undressed, I'll never know."

"That was two days ago?" Her voice was raspy, her mouth felt like she had been eating a raw tortilla.

Olivia helped her sit up, propping several pillows behind her, then handed her a glass of water. Angie sipped at it cautiously, wanting to avoid any hard reaction from her stomach.

"Yes. We were all very worried about you."

Had Lorenzo just been a dream? Had all of it just been a dream? It had seemed so real; all of it had seemed so real. The feel of his hands on her skin, the feel of his warm lips on her neck—had she just imagined all of it?

"I don't really remember much of anything," she confessed, feeling more confused and disoriented than she had when she was out in the woods.

Olivia patted the blankets around her. "You just need a bit more rest. Then I'm sure everything will be clearer."

Angie leaned her head back on the pillows, fighting against the fog that still surrounded the past few days. "I remember seeing Tom. I spoke with him. And then—well, then I threw up."

"So you did make it to him." Olivia sighed with relief. "I was worried you might not have been able to make it."

"No, no, I made it. But—" Lorenzo's face flashed through her mind, his face stern as he yelled at her for going out to take the information to Tom. "Someone had already brought him the information."

"What?" Olivia froze in her motions of refolding the cloth. "What are you talking about?"

"He has a new contact. He's depending strongly on this person."

"Did you meet him? Do you think he is trustworthy?"

Of all things for Olivia to ask. Angie honestly didn't know how to answer. She instantly wanted to reply no. But that would only generate more questions, and Angie wasn't prepared to answer those just yet. Besides, her skills at lying were terrible.

"I don't know. But he gave Tom the same information that I was going to give him. Perhaps he is trustworthy."

"Hmph," Olivia shook her head. "I think we'll just be extra careful and be sure to get him every bit of info we can."

Angie sipped on her water again, wishing she actually could get sick again so she didn't have to tell Olivia the next thing she remembered. She swallowed hard. "Actually, Tom has a new request for us. He needs us to concentrate on getting them more food."

Olivia's eyebrows rose. "Do we need to start making more trips out there? It will be difficult, but we can—"

"He doesn't really want us to go out there again. He feels it is getting far too dangerous."

"He feels—Well of all the preposterous—That just doesn't make any sense."

"Why? He wants to keep us safe. It's very admirable."

"Admirable? Exactly what happened out there, Angie? Did you anger him?"

"I knew that's what you would say." Angie shook her head, frustrated. Olivia would have a hard time believing she hadn't done something to make Tom no longer want them to visit the camp. "There's nothing wrong with what happened, and yet you're trying to place blame somewhere."

"Something must have happened for him to think he can trust this man over us."

Angie rubbed her fingers over her dry, gritty eyes. "It's not a matter of trust. It's a matter of safety." She sighed heavily. "It's what Tom has requested of us. Believe me, I argued just as strongly as you, but he has his reasons."

Olivia's lips were pulled into a thin line. "Very well. How are we to get food to them, then?"

"I don't know. We'll have to think of something." Angie was growing tired, but hated to see the look of disappointment on Olivia's face.

Defeating the Mexican Army had been Olivia's drive for so long Angie didn't think her sister would know what to do once there was no longer an enemy.

Olivia took a deep breath, shook out the cloth and began to refold it again. "You've been missing a bit of excitement in the *cocina*." Her tone implied the excitement had been unwelcome.

Angie felt guilty for not even thinking about the *cocina*. "How have you and Serena been? You haven't had to turn away customers, have you?"

"No, though Grandpa has been helping more than he would like. And Grandma has been able to help for a few hours here and there."

Olivia smoothed back a piece of hair that had pulled loose from her bun and fixed a suspicious eye on Angie. "That crazy soldier has been coming for breakfast."

"What?"

"The betting soldier."

Angie bit her tongue before she accidentally said his name. "You mean the snake charmer?"

"I mean the low life *bastardo* that bet on your virtue, that's who I mean. Snake charmer. Hah. I'll tell you a few things he can charm. That man—"

"When did he come back?"

"What do you mean 'come back'? He never even stayed gone! The very next morning—right after you fell ill. The nerve. Serena gave him an earful, though. She's going to be tough, just like Papa."

Angie picked at a piece of lint on her quilt. "What happened?"

Olivia shrugged, but there was a glint in her eye. "Not much. Serena told him he had already said his goodbyes, we had acknowledged them, and we weren't interested in seeing his acrobatic talents with a bowl of chili and a chair anymore."

A giggle escaped Angie, and she covered her mouth to stifle it. Olivia smiled also, obviously taking delight in telling the story. "You wouldn't believe what he said. He said that he couldn't stay away from a *cocina* that had the three most beautiful women in San Antonio." Olivia's lips twitched with what could have been a laugh. "Serena offered to help him find the proper restraint."

Angie couldn't help the laugh that bubbled out of her. Finally catching her breath, she asked, "So what happened? Did he leave?"

Olivia's smile dropped. "No. And he's been back every day, asking for you."

Angie's breath lodged in her throat. "What did you tell him?"

Olivia's eyes narrowed. "Exactly what he needed to hear. That it was none of his business and he would do well to remember that. As you would do well to remember what he did to you and not go all breathless when I talk about him."

That was the problem. She was remembering all that he had done to her—with his lips and hands—or at least what she thought he had done to her. It couldn't be a dream. It was far too vivid to have been a dream.

"I can see you're getting sleepy again. Next time you wake up we'll eat some tortillas. I think your stomach can handle it."

Angie nodded as she slid further down under the covers.

"Get some rest," Olivia said, patting her hand.

Angie almost laughed. How could she rest when every time she closed her eyes she saw Lorenzo's face and felt his warm embrace? He was a mystery to her—a complete conundrum. And same as other mysteries she faced, she would solve this one. She just prayed she wasn't the moth being called by the enticing flame.

***

HE SHOULD HAVE walked away. He should have turned his back on the *cocina*, turned his back on her, and never looked back. And here he was, for the third day in a row, standing outside the little house, fighting with himself whether he would go inside or not.

She was a strong woman and he was incredibly impressed with her dedication to the Texian Army. But, had it not been for her illness, he might end up being humiliated, slapped, or insulted for even caring.

He knew she was fine. The little freckle-faced Serena had told him as much. That was all he had wanted to know. He should just walk away. But he needed to see with his own eyes. He needed to see her with color in her cheeks again, with that anger burning in her eyes. Then he would know she was alright—then he could walk away from her.

He watched a few locals step up on the porch and into the bright house. Despite the mud and grime in the road, the porch was pristine, with only the footprints from the recent morning patrons. He had no doubt that Olivia was the one keeping things so spotless.

The hateful looks she had thrown his way the past two days had left him with no doubt as to his welcome. He would endure it once more. He needed to see Angie, know that she was alright. Then he would walk away and never look back.

He heard Serena's nonstop chattering as soon as he stepped through the door and, from the pained expression on the old man's face, Lorenzo had no doubt the conversation was unwanted.

Smiling to himself, he slid into an empty chair at the corner of the room, his eyes watching the kitchen, hoping that today he would see her. Serena, finally having become bored with her victim, walked up to him, her skirts swishing loudly. He leaned over to look at her then raised an eyebrow in question.

"I think it makes a lovely skirt, don't you?"

"I don't even know what that is."

Serena rolled her eyes dramatically. "You aren't a very good soldier, are you?"

Lorenzo tugged at his ear, trying not to smile. "I'm not

sure I follow."

She sighed heavily. "It's a tarp that was wrapped around all of these guns. So I just took it and cut it into strips and made these knots—you see?" She sat down next to him, lifting a piece of her skirt so he could admire her handiwork. His mouth was gaping.

"Then I found these officer's jackets. I tell you, they really should be more careful where they set down things. But the buttons are just gorgeous, and when I tied some together, this clinking sound was…"

"Wait, wait, wait." Lorenzo was shaking his head. "Are you telling me stories?"

Serena frowned at him. "Of course not. I've got quite a talent for creating these beautiful clothes…"

"You've got quite the talent for stealing." Lorenzo glared at her.

Were all of the sisters crazy?

"Well." Serena stood up with a huff. "I'd prefer to think I just have the tenacity to find things others don't see."

"Until you've taken them!"

She grinned and shook out her skirt, the buttons rattling together. She turned towards the kitchen then looked at him over her shoulder. "Angie is doing well."

Lorenzo sat forward slightly. "Is she working the *cocina* today?"

Serena only grinned as she flounced away. He decided all sisters were seriously disturbed and needed to be avoided at all cost. He nearly laughed at himself. Perhaps he was the crazy one. He was doing exactly what he told himself was foolish.

Angie came into the room with a smile on her face, though she looked tired. Lorenzo leaned back in his chair, trying to blend into the corner as much as possible so he could watch her. She had lost weight and her blouse was loose about her; her skirt riding closer to her hips than her waist. But her smile was bright and warm as she placed plates of steaming food in front of her customers. He watched her ask the old man about his wife, watched her put her hand on his shoulder for a friendly expression.

Jealousy bubbled up inside him so unexpectedly it startled him. He wanted her to be smiling at him, touching him. Quickly following the jealousy was anger. This was why he couldn't have anything to do with her. She clouded his thoughts and judgments, something he couldn't let happen.

Working with her as Tom had suggested was the worst idea he had ever heard. The last time he had trusted a woman enough to consider her his partner, he had ended up in hell. Shortly after that he found a close cousin to hell, prison. He was headed in that same direction with Angie, and he would be damned if he let that happen again.

Still, his eyes drank in the sight of her, knowing this would be the last time he ever saw her. Though there were dark circles under her eyes, there was color in her cheeks. He watched her go about the room, watched her graceful movements, watched her hands as they poured more coffee.

He remembered those hands on his chest, remembered her asking him to stay. A part of him regretted his decision, another part was extremely thankful. The complications that could have risen from such an affair were too numerous to count.

She had walked around most of the tables as she turned towards his and, for a moment, she didn't see him, tucked into the morning shadows as he was. She started to turn away, but the slight glint off one of his buttons drew her eye.

She approached with a smile, but it faltered when she saw his face. "*Buenas dias*," he said softly.

Color infused her face and he wondered if it was embarrassment or anger. Probably a little of both.

Her eyes were fixed on his face, watching his expressions closely. "*Buenas dias.*"

They were silent for several seconds, both just looking at each other. It was Lorenzo who broke the spell, lifting his mug for some coffee. She jerked her eyes away from him and focused on pouring the coffee, and he noticed a fine tremor in her hands. Was she still ill? Or was she nervous to be near him? After that night, he wouldn't blame her for having a case of the nerves.

SHE HAD KNOWN she would see him eventually. She just hadn't expected the sight of him to affect her so strongly. "What would you like for breakfast?" She forced a smile on her face.

His hand moved across the table and captured hers as soon as she set the cup down. She couldn't stop the gasp that escaped her as his thumb rubbed over the back of her hand.

"How are you?"

She glanced around the *cocina* but, for once, no one was watching them. Many of the usual bawdy soldiers had already come and gone. She swallowed hard when she looked back at him. "I'm fine. Bit clumsy this morning, but that's nothing unusual." She gave him a shaky smile.

"I've never seen you clumsy... I've been looking for you."

"So I've heard. Do you think that's wise?"

His thumb was still rubbing her skin, causing gooseflesh. "No." He didn't offer any further explanation. She was blushing to her ears.

"I should thank you..."

"I won't accept it."

"Why not?" Her surprised voice was still hushed so the dining customers couldn't hear them.

"Because I did it purely for selfish reasons."

Her eyebrows rose in silent curiosity.

The corners of his mouth hinted at a smile. "I was well rewarded."

If possible, her cheeks flamed even darker. "I didn't, I mean—we didn't..." She smoothed her hair out of her face and licked her lips nervously. "What I'm trying to say is..."

His grin turned wolfish as he slowly released her hand. "Why don't you bring me some of your famous burned *empanadas* and I'll tell you the entire story—every tantalizing detail?"

"Wh—I... Oh." She turned on her heel, hoping no one saw her flaming face.

So it hadn't been a dream. Or was he just teasing her? No, no—when his hand had touched hers, her body had remembered his touch. And it was a pleasant memory.

Olivia was stomping around in the kitchen, slamming down pots and pans. She glared at Angie when she came in. "I don't understand why you're even talking to him."

"What happened to being cordial to our customers?"

"We don't need him as a customer."

Angie sighed and began to put together a plate of *empanadas*, shaking her head. Olivia wasn't going to like anything she said at the moment, so it was best to say nothing.

"Why didn't you just tell him to leave?"

"The same as you have the past two days?"

Olivia's lips pressed into a thin line. "This is not my fight."

"Exactly." Angie turned towards the doorway. "So perhaps it would be best for you to stay out of this." She walked out into the dining area, ignoring Olivia's sound of shock then stopped in the middle of the room. Her eyes darted to every corner, but she didn't find what she was looking for. Lorenzo was gone.

Chapter Twelve

T HE CRACKING SOUND jarred them out of their sleep in the middle of the night. They met in the hall wearing nightclothes and slippers—Serena barefoot as usual. The cracking echoed again and they all jumped.

"That sounded close," Grandma whispered.

Olivia, levelheaded as usual, began to push everyone to the back of the house.

"We've all heard the gunfire before," she soothed. "It will pass quickly as always."

"What if it doesn't stop this time?" Serena whispered. "What if this is it? What if the Texians are attacking the city?"

"Then so be it. We knew it would be coming eventually."

They sat down in chairs around the stove at the back of the house, while Angie arranged the wood to start a fire. It was hard to know how long they would have to wait before they knew something.

Olivia sat ramrod straight in her chair, as though she were hosting a tea instead of trying to get out of range of stray bullets. Grandpa sat with his arm around Grandma as she held her rosary beads and muttered prayers. Serena sat cross-legged in her chair, braiding her hair into several odd clumps.

The fire came to life slowly and the warmth was welcome. Angie sat down in the last wicker backed chair and stared into the flames. The crack of gunfire sounded gain, but it was further away. Angie's eyes clashed with Olivia's and they were both thinking the same thing. Were the Texians alright? The gunfire was sporadic, though, making her think it wasn't too severe—at least not yet. Shivering, Angie hugged herself, wishing she knew what was happening.

"They should just give up." They hadn't noticed that Grandma had finished her prayers and now leaned back in her chair, resting her head against Grandpa's arm. "They're all fools. There's no way they can take this town."

The sisters looked at each other, not saying anything. Olivia's look conveyed a warning—don't argue with Grandma.

Angie ignored the warning. "You don't think things might be better without these soldiers here?"

Grandma turned her complete focus on Angie. "These soldiers protect us. They shield us from the Indians. They shield us from those crazy Texians that would storm through here and destroy us."

"They don't protect us, Grandma. They guard us. We're prisoners. If we don't do what they want us to do, they'll punish us. What kind of life is that? To constantly be afraid to do as we please?"

Angie was surprised by herself. The feelings had been building the last few days as she had reflected on her real motivation to help the Texians. After her argument with Lorenzo the night she had gotten sick, she was more passionate than ever about why she was a part of the revolution. She wanted to carry out her parents' drive and devotion to earn them freedom. She wanted to taste that freedom and not be worried about her every move day and night.

"You sound like your mother. Where have you been getting these foolish ideas?" Grandma asked harshly.

"Grandma, just calm down. I'm sure Angie is just agitated by the gunfire." Olivia's eyes were snapping with anger at Angie.

"Why is everybody afraid to talk about these things?" Angie asked, imploring the faces of her family to listen.

"Because it's not loyal, Anjelica," Grandma snapped. "And if you are not loyal to our government, then we might as well just tell you goodbye now."

"Same as Mama and Papa?"

Grandma's eyes glittered with moisture and her lips drew very thin. "Yes." Her voice was hoarse. "And I'll tell you the same thing I told them. It's not worth it. It will never be worth that price."

Angie sat back in her chair, regretful of the sorrow she had caused. Her grandmother was hurting just as bad as the rest of them—maybe more. Olivia was staring into the flames, her face blank, her hands folded calmly in her lap. Serena had drawn her knees up, resting her chin on them, her expression subdued.

Angie felt like a heel. She had wanted to know why her grandparents were so opposed to the efforts of the Texians, so opposed to the efforts of their parents. She didn't know any more now than she did before, and she had stirred up emotions that could have remained dormant, at least until daylight.

Silence surrounded them, the only sound in the room being the hiss and pop of the fire. "I think they've stopped." Serena's hushed voice seemed loud in the small room.

Grandma shook her head. "No. It hasn't stopped." Her eyes lifted to Angie. "It will never stop."

"WE SHOULD HAVE heard something." Olivia sifted through the pile of garlic, pulling out whole cloves and discarding the skins.

Angie watched her silently, sorting another bin of dried goods that they needed to store for the winter. She knew what was causing Olivia's agitation. There was nothing she could do about it.

Olivia tossed a cleaned clove of garlic into a pile. "Somehow he should have told us something."

"Who?" Angie decided pretending she had no idea the source of Olivia's frustration could cause the conversation to cease all together. She could hope.

"You know exactly who I'm talking about. Why would he just discard us so quickly? Weren't we being helpful?"

Angie closed her eyes and wished she were somewhere

else. Anywhere else. Because the same questions had been racing through her mind. It had been three days since she had seen Lorenzo. Two days since the gunfire had awoken them. Hadn't Tom told them to work together? Hadn't he said they could help each other? "Maybe he doesn't need us."

From Olivia's astonished look, Angie realized she had spoken the words out loud. "How can you say that? We have perfect access to information on both sides! We hear it from the locals, from the soldiers; we can go just about any-where…"

"You don't have to tell me these things, Olivia. I'm on your side, remember?"

Olivia tapped her fingers on the table, her eyes staring at something only she could see. "We need to go see him."

Angie dropped a potato. "He told us not to. We can't go against—"

"He told you not to go. He didn't tell me a thing."

"You're not being rational, and that isn't like you."

"There must be something we can do. I will not stand around meekly and let these men dictate how we live!" Olivia's face had turned red and several strands of her hair had straggled loose from the bun.

Angie watched her sister with disbelief. "It's killing you, isn't it? It's killing you not being in control, not knowing what is going on."

Olivia began to clean up the garlic skins in short, choppy motions. "If you want to sit around and knit while men tell you what you can and can't do, fine. That's you. But I will not be told I am useless just because—"

"Tom never said we are useless. And we're not sitting here like meek, little women. We're collecting food, just like he asked."

"There must be something more!"

"Like what? What do you want to do, take Papa's gun and go attack the Alamo?"

"Yes! If that is what it takes, yes!" Tears glittered in Olivia's eyes as she grabbed a basket of potatoes.

Angie shook her head. "What are we trying to accomplish, Vi? What is it? Is it purely revenge?"

Olivia set the basket down on the table with a thump. "Is that what you think? You think that all we've been doing is for the sake of revenge?" She laughed and it was a harsh, bitter sound. "If I wanted revenge, I would have hunted down the man that ordered Mama and Papa to be killed."

"Then why? Why are you ready to storm the Alamo?"

Olivia looked astonished by the question. "To be free, Angie. To be able to say and do the things we believe in without fear a soldier will shoot us for not being loyal to the government." She narrowed her eyes. "Why all of these questions? You did the same thing to Grandma the other night, but you were arguing my side. Why are you doing this?"

Angie stared at the pile of onions and potatoes in front of her. "I just want to make sure what we are doing is right. Are things really going to be better once the soldiers are gone?"

Olivia put her hands on her hips. "This is about that soldier, isn't it? He's the reason for all of this."

"No. And I won't argue about something as foolish as

that. Sometimes I just wonder when I see you get so passionate about fighting the Mexicans. It makes me wonder what our real goals are."

"What are your goals, Angie? If you are questioning mine, have you looked at your own?"

"Yes."

"And?"

Angie rubbed at her neck, trying to loosen the knots that were building. "At first I think I just followed you. Your enthusiasm for this cause is enough to sweep up anyone. And I think that's exactly what happened to me. But then I wanted the revenge. I wanted to punish every soldier I saw for murdering Mama and Papa. It ate at me. It almost consumed me. But something changed in me as I watched the struggles of our neighbors and felt the burden on us. Now…"

Olivia raised her eyebrows at Angie's pause. "Now?"

"I want freedom. I want it so much I can practically taste it. What kind of life will our children, God blessing us with any, have, if they must play under the boots of a Mexican soldier who could bully them, hurt them, or even imprison them if they feel any provocation? They are the only law we have right now, and they exercise it at their whim. We've been semi-fortunate with Cos. But he won't be here forever." Angie shook her head, looking at the potatoes in her hands. "I don't want to live in fear. I don't want to live by rules that only punish those of us who work so hard while the people in great favor with Santa Anna become spoiled off of his lavish parties and 'gifts' and so many other things. All of those things coming from the taxes he continues to force down our throats."

"You really do sound like Mama now," Olivia said softly. "But exactly what good are we doing? What do you suggest we do to reach this utopia state you desire?"

Angie was silent for several minutes. She realized, suddenly, that something had changed—within herself and in her relationship with her sister. For the first time Angie realized how much Olivia needed this, how much this battle had come to mean to her. And for the first time, Angie was the calm, rational head while Olivia chomped at the bit. "We wait," Angie said finally and firmly. "We give it a couple more days."

Olivia looked appalled. "Wait for what?"

"We just wait. I have enough faith in Tom that if and when he needs to contact us, he will."

"You may have all the faith in the world, but I have little patience."

"So I've noticed."

Olivia pursed her lips but didn't respond. Until… "Fine. We'll wait. But not for long."

"No." Angie smiled. "Not for long."

Chapter Thirteen

ANGIE DID TRUST Tom. She had no doubt if he needed them, he would seek them out. Lorenzo, however was another matter altogether.

It had been three days since he had vanished from the *cocina*, leaving her to wonder what had really transpired between them. He hadn't tried to contact her; hadn't sought her out in any way. Hadn't Tom told them to work together? Though she had been opposed to the thought, she realized now that it was her only way to get any kind of information.

There had to be a good, legitimate reason why he hadn't returned to the *cocina*. Perhaps his duties in the army and his night activities reporting to Tom were keeping him too busy. Perhaps he had realized how foolish it was to continue coming to the *cocina*, raising Olivia's suspicions as well as his comrades', and was trying to think of a better way to contact her.

Or maybe he was a pompous ass who didn't care or even enjoyed making her crazy. And what frustrated her even more was she couldn't tell if she wanted to see him to get information… or if it was because she missed seeing him.

She began to carefully pack a basket full of *empanadas*, keeping a wary eye out for Olivia and Serena. They hadn't noticed her making the extra *empanadas*, and she was proud only a third of them were faintly burned.

Maybe he had been hurt.

Her hand paused over the basket as that thought settled over her. A flicker of apprehension tickled her neck. They had heard the gunshots; there had been fighting. What if he was hurt or worse yet...

She yanked her mind away from her dark thoughts, concentrating instead on finishing her basket. The *cocina* had been relatively quiet all morning, probably due to the dank weather that shrouded the town. It was the perfect opportunity for her to go in pursuit of information, and perhaps find Lorenzo as well. As long as Olivia didn't find out.

She hesitated by the kitchen back door, listening to Olivia scolding Serena in the other room. Serena's new pet squirrel had caused quite the stir when Grandma found it in the hamper that morning. Slipping silently through the door, breath held, Angie tiptoed away from the house and into the neighbor's yard. If her luck held, no one would notice she was missing until lunch. She planned to return far before then.

With her head held high, her back straight, she stepped onto the sidewalk, her basket clasped in front of her. Unfortunately, there were few people on the road and she didn't have much opportunity to conceal herself in groups. She was imagining the eyes that were watching her, the gossips that were racing over to Olivia at that very moment to tell her

Angie was walking towards the Alamo.

Her life would be so much easier if she could just tell Olivia who Tom's new contact was. But it was highly likely Olivia's reaction would not be pleasant and she would confront Tom with his choice. Lately, Olivia's reactions had been surprising, and her determination to be involved in the revolt might outweigh her usual rational thoughts.

Angie wanted to avoid such a thing. The Alamo wasn't far and she could see the clusters of soldiers huddling together against the cold. Papa's thick jacket protected her from the wind, but her face felt stiff and dry from each blast of icy air.

She quickened her step, trying to strengthen her resolve. The men might just laugh at her and tell her to leave. She pasted on her brightest smile as she drew closer and realized that many eyes were on her.

A soldier broke apart from one group and approached her, his step hesitant. "*Buenas dias, senorita.* Eh... the church...*es* that way. You are going the wrong way."

Angie's steps slowed, though barely. Her smile remained firmly in place. "No, *senor*. I came to sell *empanadas*."

His eyebrows shot up. "Sell *empanadas*?"

"*Si*. I made them myself." She hefted the basket up as she stopped in front of him.

Looking at her suspiciously, he flipped the corner of the bright checkered cloth and the sweet spicy aroma filtered up.

A smile tugged at his mouth. "I will buy one."

She didn't get much further. Every step she tried to take she was greeted by a new customer eager for an *empanada*. A crowd began to gather around her and she was starting to feel slightly like the stuffing she put in her pastries.

"What else are you selling today, *Senorita Bonita*? Pretty lady."

Angie ignored the comment that came from the edge of the crowd and continued smiling. Someone bumped her from behind, and another man stood so close to her shoulder she could smell his breath. It wasn't a pleasant smell.

"*Senors*, if you give me a little room, this will be far easier."

"It isn't often we get to be so close to something that smells so sweet and feels so soft." A hand squeezed her bottom.

She jumped and turned, but couldn't tell who had touched her. All of the men were smiling at her lecherously. She started to look for a way out, but she was completely surrounded. This had been a bad idea. A very bad idea.

"Well, if you can't be civil, you certainly don't deserve any *empanadas*." She hoped she sounded stern, like Olivia. The men pressed in closer.

"It's not an *empanada* I want." The man in front of her winked, his teeth bared in a yellow grin. She shivered uncontrollably.

"I'll warm you up!"

"I saw her first. You wait your turn."

Swallowing her fear, Angie slammed her basket into the chest of the man in front of her, temporarily setting him off balance. She shoved past him and the next man before arms circled her waist and yanked her backwards.

Wet lips landed on her neck as a hand roughly grabbed

her breast.

"Let go of me!" she spat as anger and humiliation collided inside her, boiling into a mad rage.

She twisted and she kicked, thoroughly pleased when she heard a grunt of pain. But her disabled pursuer was quickly replaced by another, this one holding her in a tight grip that was difficult to fight. Slimy lips pressed firmly against her and the crowd made whoops of encouragement, followed by multiple suggestions that had her ears turning red.

When her assailant tried to stick his tongue in her mouth she bit him, enjoying his yelp of pain, but disgusted with the coppery taste of his blood. The man's face turned furious and he drew back his hand. Angie cringed and pulled back, hoping to minimize the blow that was to come.

His hand was caught in mid-swing. "She isn't worth it. Trust me."

Angie's eyes flew to Lorenzo's face, but he wasn't looking at her. His eyes were watching the other soldier unflinchingly.

"You can have some of her later. Right now she's mine." He tried to yank his hand out of Lorenzo's grip as the men around them encouraged him.

Angie watched Lorenzo's knuckles turn white as his grip tightened. "You're causing quite the scene. I don't think it will be appreciated." Lorenzo's voice was calm, deadly.

Angie had never seen him like that. The men around her started to back away, their comments slowly fading. Lorenzo didn't look away from the soldier, although the soldier's eyes were beginning to dart about.

Lorenzo continued in that same, soft voice. "There are officers heading this way. I saw them around the corner just a moment ago. You know how they feel about harassing the locals."

The man glared at Lorenzo, then fixed his eyes on Angie. "You were lucky this time, sweetheart. But not again." He yanked away and joined his retreating friends.

Angie hadn't realized she'd been holding her breath until she let it out painfully. Her hands started shaking and she had the frantic need to scrub her body clean. Slowly, Lorenzo turned to face her, and the anger burning in his eyes made her wish she were far, far away.

"Well." She licked her lips nervously, her hands fidgeting with the buttons on her coat. "Thank you, again."

He continued to glare at her. Needing to escape those penetrating eyes, she turned and began to pick up her basket and the spilled *empanadas*. Nervousness made her feel the need to talk. "Though I must say I think you insulted me. What exactly did you mean when you said I wasn't worth it? Worth what? He was about to slap me. I would have thought you could have chosen some different words."

"Such as?" His voice was still cold, same as it had been when he talked to the soldier.

Angie focused on brushing dirt off one of the *empanadas*. "Such as... such as... 'You don't want to hurt this nice young woman. She hasn't done anything to—'"

"Such as go ahead and hit her, maybe you'll knock some sense in her so I don't have to?"

Angie straightened slowly. "That wasn't what I had in

mind," she commented dryly.

She gave up on the *empanada* and tossed it back into the mud. Her tremors were starting to fade.

She focused on him, hoping she looked calmer than she felt. "Besides, you should have shown up sooner. What took you so long?" She fidgeted with her blouse as she noticed the vein sticking out on the side of his neck. "You appear a bit angry. Why is that?" She wasn't prepared for his response.

"A BIT? A bit—" He sputtered. He tried to calm his temper, tried to take a deep breath, but he was furious.

His nostrils flared and a muscle jumped in his jaw. She had no idea just how angry he was with her. Watching the men pawing at her, kissing her delicate skin, touching what belonged to him... She jumped when his hand struck out and grabbed a hold of her upper arm.

He started walking away from the Alamo, and the grip on her arm left her no choice but to follow, half-running beside him to keep up. She was in danger of losing her basket again. The men watched them with suspicious, narrowed eyes.

"What are you doing here?" he snapped, never slowing his pace.

"I wanted to... well... to build up some business. You see, it's been a bit slow..."

"Don't lie to me, *chula*," he growled.

She yanked on her arm, but he kept a firm grip. "I don't

lie. Unlike some people I know."

His laugh was without humor. He was still trying to get a grip on his emotions after what he had just witnessed. "I don't think you know how to tell the truth. Now, let's try this again—What are you doing here?"

"I came to find you, if you must know, though I'm sorely regretting it now. You just vanished from the *cocina* without…" She swallowed her words and took a step backwards, nearly stumbling as he stopped abruptly and whirled to face her.

He gave her a thin smile. "I ordered my burnt *empanadas* three days ago." He picked one of the pastries out of her basket and waved it in her face. "You took an awfully long time to bring it to me, don't you think?"

Angie's jaw dropped. "You left, you conceited…"

He yanked her forward again, cutting off her words. "You're an absolute fool, you know that? There was no reason for you to come here. None!"

"So you just decided that you weren't going to follow Tom's orders?" she whispered loudly.

He stopped to face her once again. "If I remember correctly, you wanted nothing to do with those orders in the first place." He spoke through clenched teeth.

She lifted her chin. "Orders are orders."

"Obedience becomes you. Perhaps you should try it more often." He began to turn from her again but she grabbed his sleeve, forcing him to look at her.

"Are we going to work together or not?"

"No." The word was clipped, final.

Not surprisingly, Angie wouldn't accept it. "Why not?"

"Because I don't trust you."

"You don't—you don't—Me?" He started forward again, but this time she dug in her heels. He looked over his shoulder at her, hoping she could tell he was not willing to play anymore of her foolish games. "There is no reason for you not to trust me. Whatever your game, it is ridiculous."

"But it is my reason." God, it was so good to see her.

He hated admitting it to himself. But to see her with the bright color in her cheeks, her eyes snapping with anger, was something he had longed to see, even though he shouldn't.

"Tell me one thing that I've done to cause you not to trust me."

He looked her up and down slowly, causing her face to color. He leaned towards her until his nose nearly touched hers, his eyes boring into her. "You're a woman."

Angie stepped backwards, stunned. "What kind of reason is that?"

"My reason. Now stop stalling. I'm going to deposit you in your sister's hands before you cause any more trouble."

"I don't think she'll take us working together very well."

Lorenzo raked a hand through his hair. "I'm not working with you. Not now, not ever."

Angie pursed her lips at him then nodded. She didn't fight to get away from him anymore; instead, she looked as though she were out for a stroll. "I'm glad to hear you say that."

Lorenzo watched her closely his body tense. "Why?" he demanded.

"Well, of course it allows Olivia and me to continue our visits to Tom. After all, if you are uncooperative, he can hardly accuse us of not following orders."

"Go ahead and try."

"Who's going to stop us?"

"Tom will turn you away. He won't tolerate it."

"Same as he will not tolerate you disobeying him."

Lorenzo stopped, forcing her to stop as well. "I won't work with you."

She bared her teeth in the semblance of a smile. "I know. I don't care."

He rolled his shoulders, stretching the stiff muscles in his neck. "Why don't you just go back to your *cocina* and practice making your *empanadas*?"

Her artificial, obviously insincere smile stayed in place. "I will as soon as you let go of me."

"And you'll stay there?"

"What I do is none of your concern. You don't wish to work with me; our need for speaking to each other is no longer there."

His lips grew thin, as he looked at the people walking along the road, stopping into shops, emerging with purchases, and gossiping at the corners. Very few soldiers passed down the road, most were further up near the Alamo. "Did you know a woman was killed just the other day?" His tone was low and soft, very different from the agitated growl from earlier.

Angie sighed heavily, shifting her basket. "What are you talking about?"

"She was trying to deliver food to the Texians. Trying to help them. She was shot in the back by a Mexican soldier before she could reach the Texians."

Angie's face drained of color, but she lifted her chin. "What does that have to do with me?"

"That could have been you. Or Olivia. Or Serena."

"You shouldn't care. That's our problem to deal with."

He shook his head in disbelief. He wanted her safe, protected. And with her running wild on her own, she would be neither. "I just don't understand you."

She shrugged. "I need to go. People are starting to look."

Lorenzo slowly released her arm. "I'm going to speak with Tom tonight," he said slowly, his face tight. "I'll tell him you want to help some more. That you want to be included. I think you know what he'll say to that."

"We could avoid that if you just work with me."

"No."

"Then I can just go speak to Tom myself."

"I'll come visit you tomorrow and let you know what he says."

She gave him an amused smile. "Are you going to tell him you don't want to work with me?"

"I'll see you tomorrow."

Her smile grew cold as she dug in her basket and handed him an *empanada*. "*Adios, senor.*"

Chapter Fourteen

S HE COULDN'T REMEMBER the last time she had been so cold. Her toes had gone numb a long time ago, and her fingers were bright red. She leaned against the tree behind her, huddling deep into her father's giant jacket. He should have passed by already. He was taking too long.

As soon as she had walked away from Lorenzo that morning her mind had been racing. She barely knew anything about him, and yet Tom wanted her to rely entirely on him with their rebel efforts. She wanted to believe Lorenzo would be honest with her. But his reluctance to even spend time with her made her think otherwise.

On top of that, he didn't show any of the tenderness she remembered from the other night. Had she imagined it all? It had been far too real for it to have been imaginary. But from the way he acted, there was no sign whatsoever that he felt anything other than anger and distrust towards her.

By the time the sun had faded in the sky, she had decided on a course of action that would anger many people. But she couldn't sit at home wondering what tales Lorenzo could be spouting to Tom to make sure she was no longer part of the rebellion. So she shivered within her father's jacket, hiding just inside the tree line, waiting to follow him out to the camp.

The moon was high, nearly directly overhead. He should have passed by already. What if he took a different route this time? It would make sense; it would be the logical thing to do. She chewed on her lower lip. Or maybe he had already gone to the camp and she had missed him. Or maybe he had lied to her and wasn't going out to see Tom after all. But why would he lie to her?

She had to keep waiting; she couldn't risk missing him. She slid down the tree until she was sitting on the leaf-covered ground, pulling the collar of the jacket high over her ears. It was going to be a long night.

She would have missed him if it hadn't been for the glint of moonlight off one of his buttons. Her eyes had begun to get heavy, and she was nodding off when the faint glimmer drew her attention. In the pale light, she saw a dark shadow moving and had no doubt it was Lorenzo. She knew no other man who walked so confidentially... as though nothing could strike him down.

She pushed her back into the tree, trying to make herself invisible. He walked into the trees, moving slowly and cautiously, pausing every minute or so to listen and watch for movement around him.

She held her breath, her eyes fixated on him. The strength and grace in his every movement made it impossible for her to look away. He passed her only a short distance from her, and she saw his face, intense and determined, focused on what was ahead. His feet barely made a sound, hushed by the leaves and his own stealth movements.

She waited for the count of fifty after he passed her before slowly standing, her knees aching from sitting for so long. She peered around the tree, her eyes searching the shadows. For a moment her heart stilled, thinking she had lost him. But a movement caught her eye and she saw him, standing not far from her.

He was bending, reaching beside the trunk of a large tree and she watched him, curiosity piqued. A wrapped bundle of clothes appeared in his hand. Breathlessly, she couldn't tear her eyes away as she saw him pull off his jacket and begin to unfasten the buttons on his shirt.

Her fingernails dug into the tree as he shrugged out of the shirt, his bronze shoulders rippling in the pale light. He turned then and she saw his chest, covered with a light spattering of black hair. A memory flashed in her mind, a memory of his chest in the pale lamplight, the feel of his muscles beneath her palms. It couldn't have been a dream. The memory was so vivid her fingers tingled.

His muscles were quivering, and she suddenly realized how cold he must be. She, on the other hand, felt incredibly warm. When he began with his pants, she squeezed her eyes shut, her face infused with heat. The palms of her hands began to sweat. Curiosity was beginning to gnaw at her and she tried to keep her eyes tightly closed. It was no use. Her eyes flew open, eagerly seeking the profile of the man who had been haunting her dreams.

The dark, still night was all she saw. Squinting she peered into the darkness, not believing he had vanished in the few seconds her eyes had been closed. Still she saw nothing. Gnawing on her lower lip she took a step away from the tree, heading cautiously in the direction she had last seen him.

Strong hands grabbed her upper arms and she sucked in a deep breath, a scream tickling the back of her throat.

"I wouldn't do that," a voice murmured, lips lightly touching her ear.

She swallowed her scream, nearly choking on it as a warm male body pressed along her back, the hands slowly loosening around her arms so she could turn around.

"Why are you here?" His voice was still hushed, his breath warm against her neck, and she couldn't suppress the shiver that slid through her.

"Lorenzo, I didn't…" She turned and her eyes met his and she forgot everything she had intended to say.

His eyes were dark and intense, watching her closely. His dark hair was windblown, a lock falling over his forehead. Her gaze traveled lower and his jaw was clenched tightly, his lips pressed into a thin, disapproving line. She watched his pulse beating in his neck, the smooth strength of his shoulder, and she realized he was still without a shirt, his breeches halfway unfastened. Her mouth went dry.

She had the overwhelming desire to ask him to kiss her, to hold her the way she remembered, the way she dreamed. She wanted to feel his lips on the pulse in her neck, his fingertips brushing her collarbone. Her heart was racing and she couldn't draw a deep breath, her eyes moving slowly back up to his face.

LORENZO DIDN'T TRUST himself to speak. He had been engrossed in his thoughts as he had left town, and those thoughts revolved around Angie. She was trouble, in more ways than one, but he couldn't deny how pleased he had been to see her that morning, even though she had placed herself in danger once again.

When he had seen the soldiers crowding around her, touching her, feeling the soft flesh that had haunted his dreams every night, fury had surged through him. He had wanted to kill every man that had touched her. But that could cost his life as well as hers.

As soon as he had gotten her away from the soldiers, he had wanted to crush her to him, to give thanks that she was safe and he held her once again. Instead he had released his anger on her, hoping she would get as far away as possible, removing the temptation that she was.

And then—then he had seen her curious eyes peering through the night, watching him as he had been about to strip out of his pants, and desire had gripped him so hard he had nearly doubled over. It still gripped him as he stood so close to her he could smell her lavender soap, could see the flush that was spreading over her face, could feel her chest rising against him with each breath.

"Why are you here?" he whispered, his hands sliding down her arms, slowly, reluctantly releasing her. But he couldn't step away. Not yet.

"I-I…" She licked her lips. "I was worried about what

you would tell Tom. And whether you would truthfully tell me what he said to you."

"In other words, you didn't trust me."

"No." Her answer was in the same hushed tones as his, though there was the faintest sign of remorse in her eyes. Her answer even seemed hesitant. Did she really not trust him? Or was it an excuse she was using?

His eyes bored into hers, and he should be angry. He should yell at her and send her home. But he wanted nothing more than to taste her pale, pink lips, to give in to the temptation gnawing at him. Her full bottom lip had teased his memory since the other night when he had come so close to getting a taste.

Her gaze dropped away from his face to his chest and her brow furrowed. "Where is your shirt? You're freezing." Her hands flew to his upper arms and she began rubbing vigorously, her hands moving to his chest and rubbing there as well.

When his hands wrapped around her waist, her eyes shot to his face. He knew his eyes were dark, his face tense as he tried to contain the desire raging within him. Her hands stilled on his chest, her fingers buried in the crisp, black hair.

"Do you realize what you're doing?" his voice was hoarse.

"I'm trying—Well, what I mean is—I thought I could help warm you."

His fingers tightened on her waist. "You are doing far too good of a job." He leaned into her and her eyes widened as his arousal pressed into her hip. Her eyes widened and he closed his eyes, praying for the willpower not to go any further. But Angie must not have understood exactly what she was doing to his mind and body.

She slowly slid her hands lower, then hesitated, feeling something rough under her palm. Her eyes followed the path of her fingers and she drew a deep breath as she saw the wicked scar just under his breastbone. Her fingers traced it lightly when Lorenzo grabbed her wrists, gently pushing her away from him.

"Lorenzo, I didn't—I mean, I wasn't trying..."

He let his breath out slowly, squeezing his eyes shut. "I know, *chula*. I know." He pushed away from her while he still could and grabbed his worn uniform jacket off the ground. He kept his back to her as he fastened it, trying to calm down. He couldn't remember the last time he had been so close to losing control.

"You need to go home," he said thickly, speaking over his shoulder. His words were spoken with finality. He wasn't willing to argue with her about the subject any further.

ANGIE WAS TRYING to recover her composure as well. Every time he called her *chula*, or pretty girl, it made her lose her concentration. Realizing he was affected by her had taken her breath away and had made her long for things she couldn't identify. She wanted to get closer to him; she wanted to touch him, to hold him. And his scar was a new piece to the maddening puzzle he was turning into.

She tightened her jacket about her, self-consciously

smoothing her hair back. "I won't go back. Not yet. I want to go with you."

Lorenzo turned slowly, schooling his face into a blank expression before facing her. "No. I forbid it."

Angie squared her shoulders. "Then go and I'll follow you later. I'm going to meet with Tom whether you like it or not."

Lorenzo was silent for several moments, his expression hidden by the shadows as clouds passed over the moon. Finally, he stepped forward and caught her arm. "Fine. Let's go."

She stared up at him in surprise then concentrated on not tripping over the uneven terrain. She hadn't expected him to agree. She was fully prepared to go on her own at another time if so needed. But he was taking her, though he didn't seem too thrilled about it.

He held her close to him, his grip on her arm strong, but not hard. She couldn't see his face clearly, but he didn't look happy from the few glimpses she could get. She remained silent, hoping to avoid a confrontation that would make him change his mind. Yes, they had quarreled some. But it was nothing like it had been in the past. And, she was almost reminded of when he had first taken her walking through the streets of San Antonio.

"Are you gloating?"

Angie looked up at him, surprised to see him watching her closely. "No. Why?"

"You were smiling. Considering you just got your way—again—I assumed you were gloating."

"Oh." Angie was a bit distracted. They were approaching the river, and the recent rains had caused it to swell. Her palms began to sweat.

"So what were you smiling about?"

"What? Oh, nothing. Just a memory."

"Must have been pleasant." Lorenzo's voice was dry, becoming irritated with her evasive answers.

She looked up at him again and the corners of her mouth twitched. "Yes. Unfortunately, it was about you."

His eyebrows shot up. "A pleasant memory about me? Ah, yes, when you slashed me with a knife."

She couldn't see the pathway anymore; the water was up over the rocks. Had he not been holding her arm she would have turned around and headed back for the trees.

She wouldn't let him know how scared she was. "Yes, yes, that was a pleasant memory, but it wasn't the one I was thinking about."

Lorenzo frowned down at her, but her attention wasn't on him.

"I don't see the path," she said slowly. "How will we cross?"

"The water is barely over the rocks. Our feet will get wet, but we'll be fine."

Angie's heart was thudding loudly in her ears and she was having a difficult time swallowing. "Well, I'll let you go first then since you can see the path."

"Are you going to tell me what this pleasant memory is or leave me guessing?"

She looked at him, finally tearing her eyes off the river. "I think I like the thought of you guessing."

He shook his head at her and released her arm, heading towards the water covered path. He didn't hesitate before stepping out into the water and onto the hidden rocks, his stride confident of the path that should be there.

Angie stood on the bank, staring into the inky water with a sense of dread. It was shallow, and she wouldn't drown if she did fall in. And the water was icy cold and it could quickly fill her mouth and nose; quickly replace the air in her lungs, quickly smother away her screams for help, quickly pull her into the inky darkness and never let go.

"Don't tell me you're turning back now."

Angie jumped, her heart leaping into her throat, her body tingling from a rush of adrenaline. Lorenzo paused, halfway across the river, and from her peripheral vision saw that he watched her hesitantly place a foot in the water, fishing for solid rock.

"Of course I'm not turning back." She laughed nervously. "I, unlike you, believe in being cautious." The water swirled around her foot and she wondered madly how she had ever made it across the path before.

Her lips pursed together with determination. Her other foot found a rock and she let out a small sigh. First steps completed. Only a hundred more to go and at the pace she was setting, it would be daylight before she crossed.

"What's wrong with you?"

She had been so intent on crossing she had forgotten Lorenzo was even there. Finding him directly in front of her startled her and she wavered on her precarious footing. He caught her by her shoulders and steadied her, peering down at her intently.

"What's wrong with you?" he asked again. "Are you starting to realize how foolish it is to go with me?"

She lifted her chin, rubbing her sweaty palms on her skirts. "Not at all." She swallowed hard. "I just—well, I just don't care much for water, if you must know." And she prayed that would be the end of the conversation. Because she needed to concentrate as hard as she could on the next steps—literally.

⚜

"YOU DON'T CARE—YOU..." Lorenzo took a step back so he could see her clearly, certain that she was trying to play a trick on him. Her lips were pulled into a thin, tight line, her skin so pale it was nearly translucent. She really was afraid. "So you weren't lying to me. Huh. I was certain you were trying to trick me."

Angie fidgeted with her collar. "Well, now you know... as you should know very well by now, I'm terrible at lying."

Lorenzo shook his head in disbelief. "You continue to amaze me. Give me your hand. I'll help you across."

"Just go on," she pleaded, staring at the water as though transfixed. "I'll catch up in a bit."

Lorenzo's eye ticked. She was going to be the death of him. "Look at me. Angie, look at me."

Slowly, cautiously, she raised her eyes and looked into his. The fear in her gaze made remorse wash over him as he remembered the dunking she had taken in the river the last time they had taken this path.

"You're coming with me." His hands dropped from her shoulders to her waist and her eyes narrowed in suspicion.

"What are you…" Her question ended in a gasp when he hefted her off her feet and turned, aiming her towards the opposite bank, her back to his chest.

Her nails were digging sharply into his wrists and he would be very surprised if he wasn't bleeding.

"What are you doing?" Her voice had risen a notch in fear and its quavering made it difficult to understand her.

"I'm not going to let go of you. If you fall, I'll catch you. And if not, I'll fall right along with you and we'll both get soaked."

"As comforting as that is," she began, her fearful voice sarcastic, "I would greatly prefer to remain dry."

"As would I. So don't fall."

"Now look, I'm not the one…"

He chuckled, knowing he had taken her mind off the water lapping over her feet. Keeping his hands on her waist, he leaned forward. "I know, *chula*. Just walk."

She took a deep breath, then let it out very slowly. "I can't see the path."

"It's there. Just feel with your feet."

She took a hesitant step, then another, her toes searching for the rocks she knew were there.

"So, why are you so afraid of water?"

"I never said I was afraid. I just don't like it that much."

"Ah." His hands tightened on her waist as she wavered,

then regained her balance. "So why is that?" He was torturing himself being so close to her, and he really wanted her to talk, to give him something to think about other than the feel of her waist between his hands, the scent of her hair where it lay so alluringly against her neck.

"It's foolish, really." Her voice wasn't shaking as much anymore, and her steps were more certain. "There was a boy in school that didn't like me much. I think it's probably because I beat him in a race one time. He never forgot."

She was silent for several seconds while her foot probed for another rock, and the slight trembling in her body made his fingers tighten on her. She found her footing once again and continued.

"So, one day, he and his friends decided it would be a great trick to throw me in the cattle trough at the back of the school. It wasn't much fun."

"And that has frightened you this badly?"

She didn't say anything for a moment. Finally, "I've never told anyone what happened. I don't think the boys ever did either."

"It seems a harmless enough prank."

The tension in her body told him she did not agree. "After they threw me in, they grabbed a branch and pushed me down. You know, those troughs aren't very deep. But when they pushed me to the bottom—I felt like I was miles underwater."

Lorenzo could almost picture her fighting the stick that dug into her, keeping her from the air above.

"They would let me up sometimes, just to tease me with

a breath of air. I don't know how long it lasted. I swallowed a lot of water and I guess I just passed out."

"In the water?"

"Yes. I woke up coughing so hard I thought my throat would rip out. The boys were gone but I was out of the trough and the teacher was with me. The boys told her I had fallen in."

"And you let them get away with that?"

"I suppose I felt protected by the knowledge. They never bothered me again, probably because they knew I could tattle on them."

Her foot slipped and she gasped, grabbing his hands on her waist. He steadied her quickly, pulling her back against his chest. Her hair brushed against his face and her rump settled at the vee of his legs. His skin tingled and his hands flexed, feeling her delicate hip bones beneath his fingers. She stood very still, her hands still clutching his. He lowered his head slightly, breathing deeply her scent, her warmth.

He wanted her. He wanted to feel her pressed against him, wanted to hear her soft gasps of discovery—same as when he had held her in her room so few nights ago.

"Lorenzo."

Hearing his name whispered huskily was nearly his undoing. There was nothing to stop him from easing the ache, and she appeared willing—more than willing. But he couldn't. He wouldn't. He would never let a woman control him like that again.

"Are you alright?" he said, his voice sounding as though he hadn't used it in days.

"I'm fine. I think I have my balance now."

"Good, good." It took him a moment to lessen his hold on her, and he noticed that she moved away from him just as slowly.

They were silent for the remaining several steps to the other side of the bank. When their feet touched solid ground, Angie turned to him. "I want to—about the other night—I just didn't know…"

"It was a mistake." He spoke in a clipped tone, looking towards the direction of the camp. He had to withdraw from her, physically and emotionally, or he would become vulnerable, a risk he couldn't take.

Angie blinked. "Well, then…" She smoothed her skirts awkwardly. "I suppose it was a mistake." She started towards the camp, then stopped and faced him. "Exactly what was a mistake?"

He looked astonished at her question. "The whole thing."

"Ah." She nodded thoughtfully. "So, was the mistake coming back for me or taking me to my room?"

His eyes searched her face and he took a step towards her. "I don't regret getting you to safety. I will never regret that."

"What do you regret?"

A cynical smile crossed his lips. "Many things in my life. But that night…" He paused, his eyes narrowed on her face. "You don't remember, do you?"

She fidgeted, not quite meeting his eyes.

He ran a hand down his face, a humorless laugh causing his shoulders to shake. "You don't even remember. How perfect."

Angie's face went from curious to furious. "I'm beginning to think it's good I don't remember. But I did dream—I dreamed that you were kind and gentle with me, that you made me feel like a woman. I should have known it was just a dream. You don't have a kind bone in you!"

She turned and stomped away, anger clear in the rigid line of her body. Lorenzo was stunned. So she did remember, only she thought it was a dream. He should leave her thinking that way. He didn't need the complications that could arise otherwise. Shaking his head at himself and Angie, he followed her, hoping to avoid any further anger from a safe distance.

But a part of him wanted to tell her. He wanted her to remember the few moments they had together in her room when she hadn't looked at him as though she would slice him with any weapon available. His pride demanded she know it wasn't a dream; he really had held her and caressed her and, more than anything, he wanted her to know she had asked him to stay.

Both jerked to a stop when a man suddenly emerged from the undergrowth, his rifle set on Angie. "This isn't the best place to be, miss. If you're lost, you'd best turn back and take your fellow with you." The thick, Southern drawl was difficult to understand.

Lorenzo squinted through the darkness and recognized the slightly heavyset man with the bushy blond hair. "Sam, it's me, Lorenzo. I've come to speak with Tom."

The man looked towards Lorenzo, still keeping the barrel on Angie. "Step closer."

Lorenzo obliged and Sam grinned as he recognized him.

"Haven't seen you in a while. We're all getting a bit jumpy here lately. Is the little miss with you?"

"Yes. She's insisting on talking to Tom."

Angie hadn't moved but, at his words, she looked over her shoulder and glared at him. He gave her a thin-lipped smirk and nodded to her.

"Not going to be easy to find Tom tonight. He went to the other end of camp earlier today. Hard to say when he'll be back or where he even is."

"We'll look for him."

Sam leaned on his rifle. "I would leave the little miss here. The men haven't seen a woman in quite some time. Might not be safe."

Angie made a scoffing sound and began to stride forward. "I can take care of myself just fine, thank you very much."

With a curse, Lorenzo took off after her and caught her arm. "If you're going to continue to be so naïve and foolish, I'm going to let you find out just how much trouble you can get into."

"I will find Tom. I'm not about to sit here and twiddle my thumbs while I wait for you. I might as well not have come at all."

"It's a little too late to have a flash of common sense. If you want to go look for him, fine. But you stay by my side. Do you understand?"

"I'm not a child."

"Angie, by God…"

"Fine. Let's just go."

Chapter Fifteen

S AM ESCORTED THEM into camp and pointed them in the direction where Tom was most likely to be found. Surprisingly enough, Angie stayed close to Lorenzo, matching her strides with his. She didn't look at him, just searched the faces of the men as they passed them, occasionally asking if they had seen Tom. Many of them didn't even know who Tom was.

"They seem restless," she commented softly, watching the many men that paced and cleaned weapons already clean.

Lorenzo raised an eyebrow. "I would be too if I had been sitting around a camp for months away from my home, waiting for someone to make a decision."

Angie looked at him curiously. "What did you do while you were in prison, then?"

His expression became shuttered. "I went crazy. Same as most of the men out here." He rolled his shoulders as though they were tense. "Let's look this way."

He turned between two tents and Angie followed. "So what exactly did you do that sent you to prison?"

"I've already answered that question."

"Were you telling me the truth?"

Lorenzo stopped and turned to face her, his eyes hard and cold. "I don't know what I did to make you think so low of me, but your constant accusations are getting a bit tiresome."

"You are a convict, and it seems you received a harsh sentence if you just stole a few things. What exactly did you steal?"

"My past should be none of your concern. I haven't done anything to you to make you think..."

"You don't know what you did? You bet on my virtue! I'd say that was low enough. You played with my emotions—you used me to get something you wanted."

"If I used you to get what I wanted, you would be flat on your back and there would be no further discussion about your virtue—or lack thereof."

"You disgust me," she snapped, feeling the flame in her cheeks.

But what shamed her even more was that there was a part of her that wished he would act upon his desires.

"Good. But know this, *chula*. I never bet on your virtue."

"I saw you. I heard you. You can't lie your way out of this one."

"Things are not always as they seem. There was a bet, yes. Over your virtue, possibly. I had no knowledge of it. All I knew was I had better provide them with a story or we would probably have an unpleasant brawl on our hands. And over you of all things. Over whether you were as cold as your older sister. Believe what you want to believe."

His eyes scanned her face for a reaction before he finally

turned away from her. Gradually she realized the entire camp was watching them, that several men grinned at her with intent in their eyes she didn't want to know about. A blush climbed from her neck and across her entire face and she wanted to turn away from all of them. Lorenzo, unfortunately, seemed unaware of the attention they were drawing.

Turning back to her, his expression dark, he pointed a finger in her face. "And if you want to make accusations about using a person—exactly what did you expect when you accepted to go for a walk? Were you trying to use me to anger your sister? Or did you think you could get information from me to give to Tom? Or were you hoping for a quick and hot toss in the hay? All three maybe?"

"That's enough. This conversation is over."

"Why? Because you're having to face the truth?"

"What's going on? Lorenzo? Ms. Angie! I thought I told you not to return."

Angie's head whipped around at the sound of Tom's voice and she felt relieved that attention would be diverted from her and Lorenzo. "Tom, I didn't mean to disobey you, it's just that..."

Tom held up his hands to silence her, his eyes snapping with anger. "Whether you meant to or not, you disobeyed me. I wouldn't tolerate if from my men. Why should I tolerate it from you?"

"I asked her to come with me." Lorenzo spoke from behind her and she quickly turned to look at him, unable to hide the astonishment in her face.

He didn't look at her, just continued staring over her

shoulder at Tom.

Tom still looked angry, but it was beginning to fade into confusion. "Why? I specifically told her not to return here."

"I know. But since she came with me, I hoped you might be more understanding. I asked her to come with me to get a better clarification on the task you asked her to complete. I thought perhaps you could help."

Tom's eyebrows rose. Angie glared at Lorenzo. He was putting her on the spot, and he knew it. She turned slowly to face Tom, who was watching her closely. She licked her lips nervously. "We've been able to gather a lot of food for your men. We've got an assortment of vegetables we've been able to get from our neighbors, and we make extra flat bread every day. The meat, however, is going to be a bit of a problem."

"Why is that? You've always brought us some in the past."

"We have no way of carrying all of this. We only have a mule, and he's not very strong. Our wagon was destroyed"— she cast a glance at Lorenzo—"by the Mexican soldiers when they first arrived at the city. If we start gathering meat now when we don't even have a way to transport it, it will go bad. Even if we can get dried meat, we have no way of getting all of this to you."

He was silent for a moment, a deep frown on his face as his eyes darted back and forth between Angie and Lorenzo. "You needed to come out here to tell me that? Why didn't you just tell Lorenzo?"

Angie fidgeted with her skirt and glanced back at Lorenzo. He quirked an eyebrow at her. She wanted to spit on him. She narrowed her eyes and turned back to Tom. "If you must know, I wasn't certain that the message would get to you."

Tom looked at Lorenzo. "Is there a problem?"

Lorenzo shrugged. "Not that I was aware of."

Angie whirled to face him. "Why don't you tell him the truth—although I know that is a difficult thing for you to do?"

Lorenzo gave her a tight-lipped smile. "Ms. Angie here feels like we are keeping things from her—thinks that we aren't allowing her to help you enough."

Angie pursed her lips. Put that way, it sounded like she was behaving like a child.

"You haven't even been able to complete the task I assigned you. How can you do anything more?"

Angie's jaw dropped, then she shut it with a click. "We can do more. We are trying to find a wagon, but..."

Tom turned towards Lorenzo. "Have you been able to locate a wagon for them?"

It was Lorenzo's turn to look uncomfortable. Angie turned towards Lorenzo, folding her arms over her chest. "Yes. Have you been able to locate one?"

"Not yet."

Tom shook his head. "I don't know what's going on between you two, but I expect you both to help us, whatever your disagreement."

Lorenzo ground his teeth together. "Sir, I don't think it is a good idea to have these women involved."

"And your reason for thinking that is…" Tom began.

"We can't count on them." Lorenzo cast a scathing look towards Angie.

"Just exactly what have I done to make you think that? I haven't done anything to—" Angie's words were cut off by Lorenzo's angry voice.

"Exactly. You haven't done anything except put yourself in danger." Lorenzo ran his hands through his hair, wanting to grab a hold of Angie and shake some sense into her.

"Are you always going to tell lies? It would be nice to hear you tell the truth for once," Angie fumed.

Tom addressed Lorenzo, his tone irritated. "Just work with Olivia from now on. Obviously you two are going to cause us more trouble than good."

Angie turned back to face Tom. "That might not be such a good thing."

Tom shook his head. "I've had enough of this. I'm not going to deal with your childish spats anymore. Either you help each other or never return to this camp again. Either of you."

Angie and Lorenzo looked at each other, both of them furious. "I'm willing to do this," she hissed. "You're the one with all the problems."

"Hah. You *are* the problem."

"Then we aren't going to be any help to anyone."

Angie turned back to Tom. "I'll find a way to get that food to you. I understand if you expect no further help from me."

Tom nodded solemnly, then looked at Lorenzo.

Lorenzo's whole body was tense and he glared at Angie. "May I speak with you for a moment?" He spoke through clenched teeth.

Angie smiled sweetly at him. "Of course."

Tom turned away from them towards a group of soldiers, obviously eager to get away from them.

"What are you doing?" Lorenzo demanded, his voice low to keep from drawing even more attention.

"What needs to be done. You're going to continue to be an ass about all of this, so I will take other action."

"You heard him, either we help each other or we don't help at all."

"Illogical thinking, if you ask me, but I can understand him not wanting to put up with your tantrums anymore." Angie appeared so irritated her foot was tapping a tiny hollow into the ground.

"He needs our help. Mine at least. I don't understand why you are so important."

"Good. I'm glad to see you are growing from this experience. I'm going home now to finish getting the food they need."

He caught her arm when she tried to brush past him. "If this is going to work, we will establish a few rules."

"What makes you think I want to have anything to do with you?" She glared at him.

"Because, whatever your reasons, you don't want to see the Mexican Army succeed any more than I do."

"Working with you isn't going to guarantee their failure." She tilted her head as she watched him for his reaction to her comment.

"But it won't help its cause either."

She stared at him for several long seconds, as though measuring him, her foot still tapping madly. "Go ahead and tell me your rules. Then I'll give you some of my own."

He released her arm and took a step back, his face tense. "First, you don't do anything without me. I don't want to see you putting yourself in the position you did this morning."

"You mean you want to keep me under your thumb."

"Think of it however you want. It's rule number one." Why the hell was he trying to work with her?

"Does the same rule apply to you?"

He raked a hand through his hair. "No. And you shouldn't ask such a foolish question. There are places I can go without arousing suspicion. A woman would create havoc."

Angie was silent, and he knew he had hit a strong point with her that she couldn't fight.

"Second, I don't want you to keep things from me. Any information—you are to share."

"That rule definitely applies to you as well." She raised her eyebrows, waiting for him to disagree.

Lorenzo nodded. "Agreed."

Angie sighed heavily. "How is this going to work if neither of us can trust each other?"

"We need to put that aside. Both of us. We have a priority."

"Fine. I agree to your rules. All I ask is for you to be

honest with me."

Lorenzo only nodded. "One final rule." He raised a hand to stop Angie from speaking. "Don't ever converse about me to anyone in the army."

Angie shook her head at him. "Really, do you think I am that foolish…?"

"No one. Regardless the topic. Even if they are commenting on something I've said that is totally irrelevant. Do you understand?"

Suspicion crossed her face, but she nodded her agreement. "I agree," she said softly, when he still didn't appear satisfied with her silent answer. Her eyes searched his face. "Why, though? What are you afraid of?"

His eyes became shuttered. "You," he said finally. "You don't think before you speak, before you act. I won't risk my life because you have some crazy idea."

"Will you always answer a personal question with an attack? If you want to make this work, you're going to need to tell me more—about you."

"My life has no bearing on our success. Now, can you agree or not? I won't negotiate on this." It was their make or break moment. And he couldn't believe how much he wanted her to agree, if for no other purpose than to have a reason to keep her in his life.

"Fine."

"I'll speak with Tom. Wait for me here, then I'll take you home."

He could tell she wanted to protest, but she didn't say anything and finally nodded at him.

"I'll wait," she said softly, and Lorenzo gave her a half smile.

Lorenzo turned from her and went to Tom, wishing he could break something. He was being forced into a position he had never wanted to be in again. "Why is she so important?" he demanded when Tom turned towards him. "I can get you the same information she can—more even. All you're doing is placing her in further danger."

"I'm not seeking information from her. It's supplies I need, and I need you to help the sisters get them."

"They're already getting them. If all you want is for me to get them a damned wagon…"

Tom turned and started to walk, leaving Lorenzo with no choice but to walk beside him. "How have things been in camp?" Tom asked, studying his men as he passed them.

Lorenzo frowned at the change in subject. "Quiet. Still. Not much has happened at all."

Tom nodded as though he had expected that. "The tension has been getting thick lately. Austin planned an attack a couple of days ago, but it fell through."

"Why didn't you tell me?"

"It was too hard to get any information out. Things were moving too fast." He shook his head. "But it fell apart. I think the Mexican Army knew, because they moved some troops towards our attack point." He cut a sideways glance towards Lorenzo. "Know anything about it?"

Lorenzo's look was hard. "I would have told you if I did. You know that."

"It's a time of war. No one can be trusted."

"Glad to know you're so confident in me."

Tom sighed. "You wear the Mexican uniform. You've just been recruited to fight for something and we don't really even know what that is. The Mexican Army is paying you right now... they're giving you food to eat. It wouldn't surprise me if you would be more loyal to them."

"I have told you from the very beginning where my loyalties lie..."

Tom clasped a hand on his shoulder. "I'm not accusing you of anything. I'm letting you know what runs through my head every time something goes wrong around here. I've got men deserting left and right. It makes me wonder if there's going to be a strong enough man to defend my back when the time comes."

Lorenzo couldn't reply. The same things had run through his head every time he came to the Texian camp and saw the dwindling numbers. He wondered if the Texians were just going to leave, as many had suggested for them to do.

"Has Houston corresponded with you lately?"

Tom frowned. "He sends letters to the officers weekly. Always saying the same thing. He doesn't think San Antonio is important."

"Maybe he's right. But the Mexican Army seems to think it is."

Tom nodded, a half smile on his lips. "That's what I keep saying." He watched the men for a few minutes then turned to face Lorenzo. "The food the sisters are getting for us will help, but we need more."

"I'm not too sure how much they've gathered so far, but…"

Tom shook his head. "That's not what I'm talking about." He pulled a rumpled, dirt stained piece of paper from his pocket. "I met with our officers today. These are things we need, or we will have to abandon San Antonio."

Lorenzo scanned the list quickly, his eyebrows climbing. Finally, he looked at Tom, trying to conceal his disbelief. "How soon do you need this?"

"A fortnight is the latest. A week would be best."

Lorenzo glanced back at the list. "There are so many things—so many different items…"

"That's why we still need the sisters."

Lorenzo felt a slight chill go over him. The women would be in a lot of danger if they tried to get some of the items Tom was asking for. It was inevitable. If they were going to help the Texians at all, he would have to work with the women. He didn't look forward to what lay ahead. He refolded the list and tucked it in a pocket. "We'll take care of it."

"Are you going to be able to work together?"

"If I must."

Tom didn't appear pleased with the answer, but he didn't push further. "I expect a report as soon as you can." He half turned then looked back at Lorenzo. "Next time, don't bring her with you." He nodded in the direction of Angie who stood by one of the campfires, arms crossed and angrily tapping her foot as she watched them.

A smile tugged at the corner of Lorenzo's mouth. "I'll do my best."

Chapter Sixteen

ANGIE WATCHED THE two men talking, watched them shake hands and part ways. She tried not to stare at Lorenzo as he walked back to her, but she couldn't resist. He revealed nothing on his face, his eyes shuttered as usual, his lips a hard line. As always, he walked with confidence, nodding to the men who spoke to him as he passed.

His jacket was snug across his shoulders and a bit short at his wrists. She wondered if it was a hand-me-down or if he had stolen it. Obviously it was not his. His breeches, however, fit him well, though snugly, and her mouth went dry. She couldn't take her eyes off him.

When he stopped in front of her, she raised her eyes to his face, hoping her cheeks weren't red. There was a glint in his eyes that told her he knew exactly where she had been looking.

"What did Tom say?" she asked, hoping to avoid any comments he might make.

Lorenzo pulled his hat off and ran his hand through his hair, watching her closely. "First, he said that you can't come out here anymore."

Angie's eyes flashed. "What? If we are to continue working together like he wants—"

"We must trust each other." He caught her arm and began to lead her away from camp. "Which means, you need to trust me with this side of things, and I'm to trust you with the other things."

"What other things?" Angie didn't try to pull free of his grip, instead trying to concentrate on his words. Was there finally something she and Olivia could help with?

"He needs some more supplies."

"We haven't even brought him the one's we've already accumulated."

He sighed and pulled a paper from his pocket, handing it over to her silently. Angie wished he would let go of her arm. The constant brush of his fingers against her breast was driving her to distraction and she couldn't concentrate on the list he had handed her. She tried to take a deep breath to calm down, but that only succeeded in pressing against his warm hand even more. Her stomach felt as though someone were tickling it from the inside out. What made it worse was that he seemed completely oblivious to what he was doing.

"So, when do we start? Tonight?"

Lorenzo looked down at her with an astonished expression. "What?"

"I think tonight it will be a bit difficult for us. I'm exhausted and won't be able to focus well." She looked back at the list, trying to concentrate. "I should be able to get the supplies they need for the horses. The guns will be a bit more difficult, and I think the ammunition is best left in your hands…"

He pulled the list out of her grip. "All of this stuff is going to be difficult to get. We can't just jump into this. It will take some planning."

Angie looked up at him, trying to read his expression. He looked irritated above anything else. "Are you going to hold to your word and be honest with me about everything?"

He cut her a sharp sideways glance. "Trust, remember, *chula*. It's all about trust."

They came upon the river quickly and he didn't slow his stride.

Angie began to gradually dig in her heels. "Lorenzo, I- ah!" He had her nestled against his chest before she could take another breath. "What are you doing?" she demanded, her arms wrapping tightly around his neck.

He shrugged. "Seems like a good idea. I'm not going to cure your fear of water in one night, and I would very much like to get back to my bedroll before dawn."

"Are you planning on curing my fear?"

"Perhaps. Would you like me to?"

Her lips twitched. "I don't know."

He looked away from her and towards the path, focusing on the path. As soon as he reached the other side he set her down, even though that was the last thing she wanted him to do. She felt incredibly safe in his arms. And it had to stop. She couldn't get close to this man. She couldn't risk her heart.

SHE FELT TOO damn good in his arms. And it needed to end. She was a beautiful woman and he looked forward to her quick thinking. But he had fallen for that once before, for a woman who had seemed to be everything he needed and wanted and more. He had trusted and loved, and he had a bullet wound in his chest to remind him daily of her betrayal.

They walked in silence up to the tree line, both lost in their own thoughts. Angie hesitated when he stepped into the trees and undergrowth and he glanced back at her. "I'm not leaving you out here, if that's what you're thinking. You already took a peek once before, don't be bashful now."

She lifted her chin, and stomped into the trees behind him. He retrieved his uniform quickly, chuckling softly as he watched her turn her back on him.

"What's wrong? One glance was too much for you to handle?"

"Hardly. I don't know if I've told you this before, but you think far too highly of yourself."

"You've never said that, but your sister did."

"Who? When?"

"Serena. When she helped me sneak out of your room the other night."

"It wasn't a dream!" She whirled around to confront him then gasped.

His body tensed and he looked over his shoulder at her.

He had been about to pull on his shirt when he had heard her gasp. "Just had to have another peek?" Though he tried to sound sarcastic, he hurried to pull the shirt down.

No one had ever seen his scars. He hadn't wanted them to.

She stepped towards him, shaking her head. "What happened to your back?"

He turned back away from her, slipping his other arm into the jacket. "An accident. Nothing to worry about."

His muscles went rigid when her cool fingers lifted his shirt and touched his back, and his heart was thundering so loudly he could barely hear any sound around them.

Her fingers gently traced his scars, following the angry pattern. "What kind of accident caused this? The scar on your chest—did you get it at the same time?"

"It's not important," he said thickly. "We make many mistakes in our youth." He began to pull up the jacket, but her hands were in the way, her fingers still tracing the dark lines.

"I can't imagine… it must have been terrible," she whispered. He nearly lost all self-control when he felt her lips press against one of his deepest scars. "Did it happen in prison? Did they do this to you there?" Her lips hovered over his skin, and he could feel the warmth of her breath wafting over his damaged skin in its own type of caress.

Lorenzo sucked in a deep breath, feeling her body pressed against him, the warmth of her lips touching several places against his back. The woman was either completely unaware of the affect she had on him, or she was using her skills with devastating ability. Her breath blew over his cool flesh again as she slowly pulled away, and the loss of her touch was nearly painful.

"My time in prison is not something I talk about," he

said, his voice hoarse.

He couldn't allow himself to trust her, couldn't allow himself to believe she actually cared. With concentrated effort, he shrugged the rest of the way into his jacket, giving himself several moments to fasten the buttons and encourage his body to calm down. He wanted nothing more than to turn and grab her and make certain she knew just what she was doing to him.

When Lorenzo turned to face her, he did his best to hide his emotions and physical reaction to her incredible caresses.

"I-I should thank you," she stammered. She nervously rubbed her hands over her skirt and gave him a hesitant smile. "It seems like I am always thanking you."

Lorenzo didn't trust himself to speak. Feeling her hands on his skin had sent all of his nerve-endings into shock. He still tingled. He just watched her, waiting for her to continue.

"You didn't need to tell Tom that you had asked me to come with you."

He wanted to hold her. The desire to do so was overwhelming, and he needed to get away from her. "No. I didn't need to. But I wanted to."

"Oh." The tension between them hung thickly in the air. She drew a deep breath. "So, what types of plans did you have in mind for getting these supplies?" She turned from him, walking towards town.

Lorenzo raked a hand through his hair before slapping his cap onto his head and following her. "I don't have any yet. That's why I said we need to plan."

"What's there to plan, really?" she said over her shoulder. "You get the items that are easily accessible to you, I'll get the items that I have access to."

"That's the problem. Neither one of us has access to any of those items. Almost everything will need to come from the locals."

Angie stopped and faced him. "You do realize that the locals that support us have already given most everything they have."

He pulled a dramatically shocked face. "Really? I had no idea."

Angie frowned. "Your attitude isn't going to help."

"I'm being realistic in the face of lunacy. Of course, you would say it's attitude. Now you see why we need to think about this a little more." Lorenzo followed her closely, his eyes probing the moonlit surroundings for any trouble.

Angie waved her hand in the air. "Why can't we just get most of these things from the army?"

"And you thought the locals would be unfavorable to our cause…"

"I mean steal from them. We'll take what we need."

"Now there's a brilliant plan. I wonder why I didn't think of that." His tone was dry and sarcastic.

"Well, why not? You're the expert thief."

Lorenzo stepped forward and caught her arm. "We're getting close to town. It would be best if you keep quiet." His eyes searched their surroundings.

She didn't need to know his history. Yes, he had been a thief, but a petty one. His expertise lay in something far darker, something he didn't want to share with anyone.

Angie stared up at him. "You're ashamed for people to know you're a convict, aren't you?"

He shook his head, but kept his eyes on their surroundings. "I'm not ashamed. I never will be. It's part of who I am and, if someone has an issue with it that's their problem to deal with."

"Then what are you ashamed of?"

"Lower your voice. It's an absolute wonder you and your sister haven't been caught yet."

"Do you always avoid questions you don't like?" Angie whispered.

He ignored her.

Several minutes went by and they were moving between houses when she finally spoke again. "Are you going to tell me when we're going to start gathering the items for that list, or am I going to need to do it on my own?"

Lorenzo stopped and turned towards her. "The first thing you need to learn is patience. We're in a war, Angie, and you need to think before you go plowing into something."

"I absolutely agree," Angie said, raising her chin. "But, being a time of war, we can't sit around and wait for an idea to smack us in the forehead."

"Like this morning? Did your idea of selling *empanadas* to women-hungry soldiers smack you in the forehead, or did you take the thoughtful, planning route and still decide to do something simply because you thought it would gain you what you wanted? Did you even consider the possible consequences?"

Angie felt a blush creeping up her neckline.

Lorenzo continued in an angry, clipped voice. "No. You didn't consider the consequences and that's why I had to save you from a group of randy men who didn't care about your virtue, didn't care if they hurt you. Now, is that the type of 'smack us in the forehead' ideas we want to work with?"

Angie met his glare without flinching. "I got what I needed this morning. That's all that matters."

Lorenzo pressed in on her and she took a step back, then another, as he continued to step closer to her, a muscle jumping in his jaw. "That's not all that matters. You were about to be raped. Do you realize that? Those men were going to rape you. And no matter how loud you screamed, the other soldiers would look away. If I hadn't been there…" He shook his head. "I don't even want to think about what all they would have done to you."

"Thank you for reminding me of this delightful morning. I would like to go home now. Let me know when you've come up with your plan."

His arms struck out on each side of her, pinning her between his body and the wall behind her. "In a hurry?"

"You were the one rushing to get back to your bedroll," she scoffed.

The road was only a few feet away and across the next road was her home. He had come to know the path to her house well.

He ducked his head to catch her attention. "We need

Olivia."

That statement drew her attention more than anything else could and her eyes flew to his face. "Absolutely not."

"What are you afraid will happen? Someone else will get to have all the fun?"

Angie shook her head, clearly agitated. "You don't know a thing about me. Don't put your own twisted way of thinking into my head."

"Then give me a good reason. A believable one at least."

"I don't need to explain anything to you. Now, good night." She pushed on his arm to gain her freedom then tried to duck under it. It only succeeded in bringing him closer, more effectively trapping her.

"Give me a good reason." He wasn't going to let her be until he had the answers he needed.

ANGIE, FLUSTERED, BRUSHED her hair off her forehead. "Fine. Olivia hates the Mexican Army and anyone associated with them. If you think I don't trust you, wait until you have Olivia deciding whether you are who you say you are."

"I'll win her over," he said, a half smile on his lips.

"You don't understand what I'm saying. Olivia hates the army with a passion. She will probably try to kill you."

The thought of the thin, tight-lipped woman trying to do him harm nearly made him laugh. "So why does this concern you? Wouldn't you be thrilled if that happened? Or have you come to care for me after all?"

Angie glared at him. "Hardly. But it wouldn't surprise me if Olivia disowns me for having anything to do with you."

"You're going to need to get past those fears. We need her help and Serena's too."

"Absolutely not! You will not bring her into this. She's just a child."

"She's nearly a woman, in case you haven't noticed. I've already seen her sneaking around the Alamo. She can help us. In fact, I'm quite certain she already knows more than we do about everything that's going on."

Angie looked towards the road again, wondering how she could escape him—at least temporarily. As though reading her thoughts, he pressed closer.

"You could at least give me space to breathe," she snapped.

He shook his head. "Not a chance. Every time I ask you something you don't like, you bolt. I'm not going to let that happen." He was silent for a moment, looking out towards the moonlit road. Finally, he returned his gaze to her. "We need your sisters' help. There's no way we can get all those items in a fortnight by ourselves. It will be damned difficult even with your sisters' help."

"A fortnight?" Angie's eyes were wide.

"And you thought this was going to be easy. Tom would prefer to have everything in about a week."

Angie slumped back against the wall. "A week," she whispered in astonishment.

The sound of footsteps on the road made both tense and

Angie's eyes flew to Lorenzo's face. The unmistakable sound of men's voices and the clacking of rifles knocking against belts told them it was soldiers coming closer every second.

Angie felt frozen to the ground. She had never been caught before. And what would they do to Lorenzo? Lorenzo grabbed her by the shoulders and captured her eyes with his. "It's the only thing we can do," he whispered. "Just play along."

"What are you…mph—" Her words were cut off as Lorenzo's mouth came down on hers, pushing her back against the wall. Startled, she pushed against his chest, trying to free herself. His grip tightened and his lips pressed harder against hers, silently reminding her this was to protect both of them.

She squeezed her eyes shut tightly and forced herself to relax, forced herself to allow the kiss she had been craving for so long. As soon as she began to loosen her stiff muscles, he gentled his hold on her, his hands softly rubbing her shoulders as his lips moved teasingly over hers.

HE HADN'T REALIZED how desperately he had needed to kiss her, to hold her in his arms in an embrace for lovers. She sighed softly and her body melted even further against his, melting against him, fitting him in a way that made him wish the kiss was legitimate, not for the sake of tricking the soldiers.

His hands moved around her shoulders, slipping down her arms, pressing her into the wall. Her lips were sweeter than he had imagined, and he couldn't get enough of them. His hands continued down her torso and he clasped her waist, lifting her slightly, holding back a groan as she matched his body perfectly.

Her hands, which had been shoving against his chest, now tugged on his shirt, trying to draw him closer. His lips slanted over hers and she lifted her chin, both trying to match the urgency of the kiss.

The sound of snickers broke through the haze surrounding them, and Lorenzo pulled back sharply, turning his face to glare at the soldiers whom he knew had been watching them for some time.

"Looks like you've got a live one, *compadre*," spoke one of the three men. "Want to share?"

"Find yourself another woman. This one's mine," Lorenzo growled.

"None of the other *putas* are as pretty as yours," he whined.

When they saw her, though, they took a step backwards collectively. "One of the *fria* sisters," one of the men said in awe, and they looked at Lorenzo with admiration.

"Get out of here," Lorenzo snarled. "She's mine."

The men nodded distractedly, very slowly walking away, though their eyes remained riveted on the couple.

Lorenzo caught Angie's chin between his fingers and turned her face towards him. Her eyes wouldn't meet his. "Angie. Angie, look at me." ₊

Slowly she raised her gaze to his, confusion and apprehension clear in hers.

"*Chula*," he whispered huskily before his lips come down hard over hers.

SHE DIDN'T FIGHT him this time. Instead, she arched up against him, flinging her arms around his neck, her fingers burying in his hair, tugging him closer, closer. Angie couldn't catch her breath. In her dreams, while she had worked, while she had done chores around the *cocina*, she had fantasized about what it would feel like to kiss him. Now, locked in his embrace, she felt light-headed and only craved more.

His hands cupped her face, holding her, his fingers light-ly rubbing behind her ears, along the sensitive skin of her neck.

Her fingers moved restlessly in his hair, wanting more, but not knowing what or even how. Slowly his hands moved down her neck and brushed delicately over her collarbone. His lips became insistent and she tried to follow his example, but was afraid she was doing a terrible job.

Cautiously, curiously, she parted her lips and felt his groan as much as heard it. His tongue traced her lips slowly, and she shivered, learning for the first time the power a man's kiss could have on a woman. He pressed her back against the wall of the house and she became very aware of the effect the kiss was having on him.

Knowing that she was not alone in the rush of feeling pouring through her fueled her desire. The kiss became more urgent, more powerful, and when his tongue touched hers, a quiver settled in the pit of her stomach that needed soothing, a soothing that somehow she knew only he could provide.

Instinctively her body lifted to his at the same moment his hands peeled open her heavy jacket. She gasped against his lips as the cold air washed over her, and he slanted his mouth over hers, silencing her.

His warm hands soon took away the cold she felt as they caressed her ribs, his thumbs rubbing on her stomach. She moaned softly, tugging on his hair and standing on tiptoe, trying desperately to get closer to him. His hands drifted upwards, and they groaned together as he cupped her breasts, her nipples forming hard pebbles that stabbed his palms.

Breathing heavily, he pulled his mouth from hers and went down her neck, his warm lips finding her rapid pulse and suckling at it gently as his fingers plucked at her nipples. She arched her neck to give him better access, her fingers digging into his shoulders.

"Lorenzo," she gasped. "What are you doing to me?"

She was released so quickly she had to brace herself against the wall to keep from falling. Dazed, she blinked rapidly, only to see Lorenzo's back as he strode towards the corner of the house.

"Wh-what…" Angie was too stunned to form a complete thought, much less a question.

He held up his hand in a gesture for silence as he peered around the corner. He stood there for several moments, then turned and walked leisurely back to her, appearing calm and unruffled. "It looks like they're gone. I thought for a moment they were going to stand there all night."

Angie was suddenly very self-conscious and pulled her jacket tight about her still tingling body. "Who are you talking about?"

His grin was slow and all male. "Don't tell me you're flustered? The soldiers, *chula*. Remember… the one's we were trying to trick."

Angie felt her face flush. The soldiers. How could she have forgotten? It had all been a trick. She began to push away from the wall, but Lorenzo's body suddenly blocked her movement.

"We must speak with your sister now."

Chapter Seventeen

ANGIE WAS STILL trembling. Having Lorenzo so close, smelling him and remembering the way his body felt against hers made it difficult to focus. "Why? I still haven't decided that she needs to be involved."

"Because by tomorrow morning half the town will be discussing how very intimate you were with a Mexican soldier in the alley. How are you planning to handle your sister's reaction?"

"I didn't ask you to start pawing me."

His eyebrows shot up. "Pawing you? I thought I was protecting you. And, if I might point out, you were doing a fair amount of pawing yourself."

"Hah." Finally beginning to clear her head, Angie pushed him on the chest, trying to get him to move out of her way. "You took it too far," she huffed.

He took a step backwards, giving her a small bit of room. She slipped past him, squeezing her eyes in humiliation as her still very sensitized breasts brushed over his chest. When she looked at his face, his expression said he knew exactly what she was feeling. "You used me. Again."

She turned on her heel and began to stomp away from

him, her head held as high as she could. She was drawn up short when his hand clasped around her upper arm and whipped her around.

"For someone acting so righteously, you weren't complaining when you rubbed that little body all over mine."

"You told me to play along. As disgusting as it was, I endured your kisses." She wanted it to have been real. Because it had been real for her. "Will you let go of me now?"

He released her instantly. She stared at him hard for several moments, then turned and headed quickly towards home. She had never been more thoroughly embarrassed in her life. She had been a fool to let his charms, to let his embraces, to let his kisses affect her so. But at least she knew it had affected him, at least a little. His body couldn't lie the way he could.

"So, when you kissed me back, were you just enduring then as well?"

She jumped at the sudden sound of his voice next to her. "Will you just go? You need your rest, as do I."

"We need to speak to Olivia."

"Fine. You go speak to her. I'm going to get some sleep. If she kills you, too bad."

"I would have thought you would enjoy watching me die," Lorenzo quipped as he fell into step beside her.

"No. I would not enjoy such a thing. Watching my sister lower herself to kill the likes of you would not be enjoyable."

"I think I'm supposed to be hurt."

"No, you're supposed to leave. There is no reason to drag my sisters into this danger."

"Ah. Are we really coming to the heart of the matter now? You're afraid for them, aren't you?"

"This conversation is over. I will let you talk to Olivia—briefly. Then we can plan further tomorrow."

Lorenzo nodded, but he didn't say anything. Angie worried what he would tell Olivia. She worried about everything that involved Olivia.

Instead of being relieved when they arrived on the steps, Angie's tension had grown to consume her. "Olivia won't like to be awoken," she whispered, trying desperately to sway Lorenzo.

"I'm already awake." The clipped voice at the doorway made Angie jump. Lorenzo watched Olivia closely.

Olivia stepped out onto the porch slowly, her gaze fixed on Lorenzo. She gripped a pistol tightly in her left hand... pointed directly at his crotch. "Give me a good reason why I shouldn't shoot you right now."

"Olivia, stop, you don't—"

Olivia made a sharp gesture with her left hand before quickly bringing it back up to help support the heavy gun. "No. Obviously you have lost all good judgment." Olivia never took her eyes off Lorenzo as she spoke to Angie. "I won't hear another word from you."

"That's the first thing we agree upon," Lorenzo said slowly, his eyes locked with Olivia's. "I think she's lost all good judgment, too."

Angie snorted. "You would be the authority on such a mater."

Olivia cocked the gun, refocusing their attention. "Other

than the obvious, what are you doing with my sister?"

"Discussing the Texians for one thing."

Olivia's stunned expression and the slackening of her grip on the gun was the opportunity Lorenzo had needed. His hand darted out so quickly neither woman had a chance to react before the gun was out of her hands and tucked in the back of his pants. He stood there calmly, his hands folded over his chest, appearing as though nothing had happened.

Angie and Olivia were stunned at his quick movements, and Olivia seemed shocked to the point that she couldn't stop blinking. She turned her rage on Angie. "How dare you bring him here. How dare you do something this foolish!"

"If you would just slow down and stop judging everyone around you..." Angie's words trailed off under Olivia's fierce glare.

"I know what I see with my own eyes. You're flouncing around like a tramp with this man and now—now he wants to talk about the Texians? You're a fool, Angie."

Lorenzo stepped forward, his face blank, revealing nothing that he was thinking, but Angie could tell by the taunt lines of his body that he was furious. "It would be best for all of us to step inside. It wouldn't be good for anyone to overhear this conversation."

"You will not set one foot into my house. Just leave. I don't care that you've ruined Anjelica's reputation. She deserves it. But she will have nothing more to do with you and neither will the rest of this family."

Angie's irritation had reached its limit. "You two can battle this out for as long as you want. I, for one, would like to see an end to this night and all the unpleasantries it has brought." She cut a sharp glance towards Lorenzo. "But to do that, Olivia, I strongly suggest you step aside."

Grabbing Lorenzo's coat, Angie pulled him past Olivia, physically pushing her sister to the side when she wouldn't move.

"I won't allow this!" Olivia spat, trying to push in front of them and block the doorway.

Angie glared at her sister. And suddenly she saw the fear and desperation that filled her eyes, hidden so well by the angry and bitter expression on her face. Instantly, Angie felt remorse. Her sister was just trying to protect them, same as always. And she was scared to death, probably also something she had always felt.

"He's on our side," she said softly to Olivia. "I know you don't want to believe it, and I know you're angry at me for going behind your back. But Tom needs our help, and we need Lorenzo to do that."

Olivia's eyes widened, either from the information Angie had just given her or from the soothing, understanding tone she had used. Regardless, Olivia stepped aside, her hand trembling as she smoothed her already slick bun over and over. She didn't meet Lorenzo's eyes as he walked past her and into the house. Following them inside, she quickly took up her role as commander again.

"Down to the basement. We can't risk someone seeing the lantern."

Angie nodded and followed Olivia, her hand still gripping Lorenzo's coat. She could let go of him, and that he was also aware of her unnecessary grip, but she wouldn't let go. She didn't want to. And she didn't want to examine the reasons why.

When Olivia leaned down to lift the small door leading to the basement, Lorenzo stepped forward, breaking Angie's grip. "If I may?" he asked, but didn't wait for Olivia to reply as he lifted the heavy door for her. Olivia descended the stairs quickly, not sparing either one of them a glance.

Lorenzo moved back, giving Angie the room to turn and head down the stairs.

Angie shook her head at him. "This is a bad idea," she whispered.

His eyes bore into hers for several seconds, long enough for Olivia to light a lantern and stand at the foot of the stairs, impatiently waiting for their descent. "For once, have a little faith in me." He reached up and pushed her hair away from her face, hooking it behind her ear.

The touch was so intimate, so personal, she didn't know how to react. It wasn't the fierce caress of a lover she had experienced in his arms earlier. This was the caress of a man who cared—of a man who wanted to touch her just for the sake of being close.

Suddenly extremely flustered, she turned from him and descended the stairs quickly, not daring to look back up at him, knowing he was watching. She didn't want to evaluate the feelings coursing through her veins, the confusion that was clouding her mind.

"What is going on?" Olivia hissed as soon as Angie's foot

hit the basement floor.

"Just listen to Lorenzo," Angie said softly, turning to catch Olivia's shoulders. "I believe he's on our side. Can you please just give him a chance?"

Olivia's eyes were hard. "You never should have…" Her words trailed off as the ladder creaked and Lorenzo descended. She turned away from Angie and stood in the corner of the room, her arms crossed over her chest, the picture of an iron wall. Angie could only pray that Olivia didn't have another gun hidden somewhere in the room.

LORENZO FACED THE women, thinking it would be easier to face the entire Mexican Army. Angie looked at him with a combination of confusion and frustration on her face, and Olivia glared at him so hard he could nearly feel her hate.

He took a moment to glance around the small basement, noting the cot in the corner, the collection of blankets and rags, the stacks of bagged vegetables, and the small heap of cured meats and cheeses. The women had obviously been busy.

"Have you seen enough?" Olivia snapped.

Lorenzo refocused his attention on the agitated sister and mentally debated what would be the best possible way to handle her. He decided honesty was probably the best—and only—sensible route to take with her. But he was going to need to throw her off her "shoot now, ask questions later" attitude.

Slowly, so as not to startle her, he pulled the gun from his waistband and placed it on the edge of a table—closer to Olivia than himself and took a step backwards.

Olivia eyed the weapon while gnawing on her lip, obviously tempted by the opportunity he had just placed in front of her.

"I stand in front of you as a Texian wearing a Mexican uniform," Lorenzo said softly. "I have been a Texian for many years. Up until I was placed in a Mexican prison and all of my rebellions were quickly put to an end."

Olivia's eyes were slowly pulled off of the weapon and drawn to his face. Lorenzo gave a silent prayer of thanks. "When they began to pull the prisoners for duty in the army, I was placed in service. At first, I thought it could be a chance to escape. But then I heard rumors of some Texian activities that I might be able to help with—as a Mexican soldier. That is how I met Tom."

Obviously thrown off by so many things suddenly being tossed at her, Olivia shook her head, a confused expression on her face. "You know Tom? How? I don't understand."

Lorenzo's eyes clashed with Angie's. He couldn't read the expression on her face, and briefly wondered if she were going to be angry with him for a long time over their passionate kiss. Quickly, he pulled his eyes away. It shouldn't matter. *She* shouldn't matter.

Angie spoke up, answering Olivia's questions. "I didn't believe it either, Vi. That night I last went to see Tom, Lorenzo caught me at the river. I thought he had discovered the Texian camp and was spying on them. Seems he thought the same of me." Olivia wouldn't make eye contact with Angie, but Lorenzo watched Angie and saw a faint blush touch her cheeks. Was she remembering everything from that night? And, more importantly, was she remembering it with disgust or with pleasure? "But Tom knew him and confirmed his story," Angie continued.

Olivia turned towards her. "Why didn't you tell me? How could you have kept this a secret from me?"

Angie clasped her hands in front of her, and Lorenzo could tell she was battling her guilt. "I-I didn't…" She drew a deep breath. "I don't know. Tom didn't want us involved anymore. I had thought—I had hoped that I could handle things on my own and you wouldn't have to be involved anymore."

"You thought… you—" Olivia was shaking her head so much a couple of strands came free of her tight bun. "How could you think—" Her face was becoming red and she paused to take a deep, steadying breath, having for the moment forgotten Lorenzo was even in the room.

Lorenzo watched Angie, one eyebrow raised.

"I know you're angry, Vi, but…" Angie's words trailed off when Olivia made a sharp gesture with her hand to silence her.

"You know," she began slowly, as though trying to pick the right words, "that this revolution means everything to me. I have fought this battle long before you were even aware of what was going on—" Her voice broke and she swallowed hard, a vein standing out on the side of her neck. "And now you think you can just cut me out, do things on your own…"

"It's killing you, Olivia," Angie said softly. Olivia pulled back in surprise. "I've seen you, Vi, pacing the hall at night, looking out the windows, jumping at every sound. You're terrified of Grandpa or Grandma finding out what we are doing, so terrified of the Mexican Army finding out…You're strung so tight you snap at Serena for tiptoeing past you in the kitchen."

"That's not—"

Angie stepped forward and grabbed her sister's hands. "When was the last time you slept, Vi? When?"

Olivia tried to turn away, but Angie's tight grip wouldn't let her. The sisters faced each other, the tension between them thick enough to see, and Lorenzo felt terribly awkward witnessing their argument.

"I have to finish this," Olivia said harshly. "Mama and Papa—"

"Papa and Mama were killed for following their beliefs. You're going to kill yourself trying to prove they were right."

Olivia began to shake. "They *were* right."

"I know that. You know that. Lorenzo knows it. But you can't prove it to the Mexican Army by yourself. And no matter how many nights you stand guard, you aren't going to stop this revolution from affecting all of us."

A tear slid down Olivia's cheek. "I didn't want you involved. I still don't. This is my fight."

"If you don't mind me saying so," Lorenzo broke in softly, "this is a Texian fight. And there's a whole army out there ready to get to it."

Olivia looked at Lorenzo for several long seconds, then back at Angie. She spoke to Lorenzo, though her eyes never left her sister. "For some reason, Angie has decided to trust you. I'm inclined to trust her judgment. What do we need to do?"

Chapter Eighteen

OLIVIA STUDIED THE list for several minutes in silence while Angie did her best to look at anything but Lorenzo. It was difficult. He had a way of dominating the room, of filling the small space with his presence completely. He leaned against the far wall, his legs crossed at the ankles, his face expressionless as he waited for Olivia's reaction. He hadn't looked at Angie once since handing over the list, and she didn't know whether to be annoyed or relieved.

"How soon?" Olivia's voice was hoarse as she lowered the crumpled paper.

"A week. Fortnight at most. It appears they're getting anxious—ready to get this over with."

A wry smile touched Olivia's lips. "We all are." She drew a deep breath, obviously still trying to adjust to a Mexican soldier standing in their basement.

"We've got a few things gathered already. The food shouldn't be much of a problem. It will take longer for some of the other items, but we can do it."

Angie saw the determination in her sister's stance and knew that Olivia was actually relieved to finally have a mission again.

"You can't do it without help, not in a week."

Olivia opened her mouth to object when she saw Angie's face. Eyebrow raised, Angie waited to hear if her sister would argue Lorenzo's point.

With an angry narrowing of her eyes, Olivia folded her arms over her chest, turning to glare down Lorenzo. "Very well, then. What do you suggest?"

Lorenzo ran his hand down his face, and Angie wondered when he had last gotten a decent night's sleep. "It's going to take several different things for us to get all of this together. Obviously, you're going to have limited access to artillery and army provisions."

"Obviously," Olivia said dryly.

Lorenzo gave her a tight-lipped smile, making Angie cringe. They had to get along with each other if they were going to accomplish this task. "I have obligations to the Mexican Army that I can't shirk without raising some unwanted attention. But I am given reprieves, on occasion, such as tonight. I can gather weapons and stockpile them for us to get at a later date. I'll also work on getting us a wagon. Is there any barn—any type of shelter we can use in the meantime?"

Angie exchanged concerned glances with Olivia. "There is a shed behind us—but the soldiers check it frequently. That's how we lost our first wagon," Angie said softly.

It was the first time Angie had spoken to him since descending to the basement, and she hoped her cheeks were not as hot as they felt. She couldn't look at him without remembering his hands on her breasts. From the direction his eyes took, he was remembering, too. She had no doubt how red her cheeks had become.

"Then the wagon will have to be one of the last things we get. How difficult would it be for you to look for help at some of the farmhouses outside of town?"

"Very," Olivia said quickly. "The soldiers have blocked off most of the major roads and are inspecting anyone that comes or goes. On top of that there are troops that usually are on patrol around the town. Besides, Tom says he has already made attempts at several of the farmhouses."

Lorenzo nodded. "Most, yes, but not the ones to the north. I walk the patrol most nights…" He glanced at Angie before resuming, "and I could arrange for you to sneak through. There are a lot of things you can get at those farmhouses that are on that list."

"If the owner is a supporter."

Lorenzo gave Angie a hard look. "Even if they aren't. We've reached the point that we can't accept no for an answer anymore. So we won't even ask."

"Are you suggesting we steal?" Olivia said her tone thick with indignation.

Lorenzo's smile was all teeth. "Absolutely, and you've got the best thief-in-training in this room."

Lorenzo reached behind a stack of vegetables and both women jumped at the soft squeal. Holding a fistful of curly, copper hair, Lorenzo pulled Serena to a standing position. She wouldn't look in the direction of her sisters, merely glared at Lorenzo.

Olivia was shaking her head frantically. "Absolutely not.

Serena, you go to your room right now! I don't even want to know what you were doing down here in the first place."

Serena raised her angry eyes to Olivia and walked out from behind the vegetables. She was wearing one of their mother's old shawls. "I came down here because it still smells like Mama and Papa. You aren't the only one that misses them. How was I to know that you would have some crazy meeting down here tonight?"

Angie watched Olivia's eyes soften, but her voice remained firm. "Regardless, you don't need to be a part of this conversation. Go to your room."

Serena turned her back on her sister, facing Lorenzo. "I want to help. Tell me what you need of me."

"No." Olivia stepped forward, placing herself between Lorenzo and Serena. "I won't have you corrupting her, turning her into some pickpocket, even if it is for the good of the Texians. There are certain lines we just won't cross."

Serena grabbed Olivia's arm, turning her around. "He won't be corrupting me. He'll be teaching me how to help our cause without getting caught, right?" Serena raised her eyes to Lorenzo, and Angie saw a look of desperation in them. What was Serena trying to hide from them?

Lorenzo nodded. "Absolutely. You understand she was down here the entire time and neither of you noticed. She's small enough to—"

"This is not your cause," Olivia interrupted Lorenzo, addressing Serena.

"Like he said"—Serena nodded towards Lorenzo—"all Texians are fighting this cause, and I'm a Texian…"

"You don't even know what you're talking about."

"I think she knows a lot more than either of you want to believe." Lorenzo stood with his arms behind him, shaking his head. His insinuation that they didn't know their own sister irritated Angie, and she glared at him for a few moments, but he looked like he could care less about her thoughts at that point.

Olivia and Angie looked at each other, their dark scowls revealing their disapproval.

"I am as much a part of all of this as either one of you. You already told me you understood I should be a part of things. Are you turning your back on that statement?"

"Letting you be a part of things is one thing. Letting you be in danger is another altogether."

Serena tried to maneuver so she could see Lorenzo on the other side of Olivia. "I want to help. Please let me help."

Lorenzo looked at Angie. "Serena could be a valuable asset. But I well understand if you don't want to expose her…"

"I need time to think on this," Olivia said, again talking over Lorenzo. "We all need our rest. We'll be able to think much more clearly with fresh minds."

She faced Lorenzo, her face tight. "When do you plan to—visit us again?" She hesitated over the correct word, making it obvious he was not yet welcome, not to her at least, and Angie cringed. At what point would her sister trust her judgement?

"Tomorrow's noon meal. At that time I will make a point of asking Angie to go walking with me again."

"What?" The trio of voices ranged from confusion to indignation.

Angie was ready to throttle him. How dare he suggest such a thing after what had just happened not more than thirty minutes earlier? Lorenzo continued his explanation. "The best possible way for us to exchange information and make plans is if we act a part—act as though I am pursuing one of you. Angie, considering the gossip that will be flying tomorrow—Hell, even by tonight—you are the most logical choice."

Angie's cheeks flamed and she was thankful Olivia didn't turn around, but from the sudden rigidity in her back, she knew her sister wasn't happy. Worst of all, Angie wasn't certain why her own hands clenched into fists with anger. She couldn't tell if it was from rage that he was summing her up as a means to an end, or if she was flustered by the knowing in his eyes as he looked at her.

"I don't know that your logic is very sound, but I am willing to give it some thought. However, don't be surprised if I say no tomorrow."

A slow, very male smile crossed his lips, letting her know he had no doubt what her answer would be.

Olivia's face was pinched as she watched them. "We will see you tomorrow, then." She started to turn, then spun back to him. "What do we call you?"

"I've had many names in the past. But I would very much like it if you call me friend."

"I THOUGHT I had made myself clear."

"You have also put me and my sisters in a dangerous position."

"Regardless, I told you not to come out here again. You are deliberately disobeying me."

"You have asked me to trust a man that I know nothing about—to trust him with my family. I can't just blindly accept that."

Tom shook his head, looking up at the sky, still deep black in the early hours of the morning. "You don't know anything about me either, do you?"

Angie clasped her hands together tightly. She had convinced herself her need to question Tom was for the safety of her family. She had convinced herself it was a good enough reason to risk Tom's wrath and also make the dangerous trek by herself out to the Texian camp. After Lorenzo had left she had snuck out of the house to find Tom, needing answers. "I don't know anything about him," she said again.

"Then ask him," Tom said harshly, crossing his arms over his chest, his stance angry. "What is really wrong?"

What was really wrong? The question was almost humorous. What was wrong was that her body craved his touch; her eyes craved the sight of him; her ears craved the sound of his voice.

And she couldn't trust or believe a single thing he did without wondering about his real motives. "I need to know more about him."

Tom sighed heavily and ran a hand over his weary face. Angie was thankful he had been on patrol and not asleep.

She didn't want to think how angry he would have been if she had woken him. "I know he's a convict. I need to know what crime he committed."

"Most of the men in this camp have committed crimes. Some worse than others. I can't be picky about who fights on our side."

"You haven't sent those men into my home to work with me and my sisters. But you did send Lorenzo." There was an apprehension clutching at her chest.

She didn't know what had her more afraid—what Tom would say—or what he wouldn't. *What do I really want to hear?*

"Do you think I would deliberately put you girls in danger?" Tom turned from her, stomping towards the nearest campfire. He turned back, angrily pointing a finger at her. "Hell, I don't even know if you are what you say you are. All I can go by is what I'm told and what I see."

Angie clutched the lapels of her jacket tightly, shocked by his outburst. She had never thought about the situation Tom was in; his decisions on who to trust could affect the lives of hundreds. "I'm sorry. I shouldn't have come."

"Tell me why you don't trust him. Why are you so certain you can't work with him?"

Because I can't think when he is near me. Because he makes me want to be someone he would want as much as I want him.

Her silence made Tom frown. "Has he hurt you? Has he tried to take advantage of you?"

The vivid memory of his hands on her breasts, his lips on her neck, flashed through her mind. "No." She shook her head. "No. I just—he just..." She grasped for something to say, something to make Tom understand why she had to know more. "He has scars. Terrible scars."

Tom studied her face and she hoped it wasn't crimson. She prayed he wouldn't ask her how she knew about the scars.

"He said he was a thief." she blurted out, hoping to avoid any awkward questions. "Is that true? Is that why he went to prison?"

Tom didn't answer her for several long moments, staring into the fire. When he looked up, his expression was frustrated. "I don't know much about his past, and I don't make a habit of asking. But when he sent a letter to us a month ago, I needed to know whose side he was really on." He shook his head, looking back at the fire. "He was in prison for murder."

Angie felt as though a bucket of cold water had been dropped on her. "Murder? Who?"

"I don't know. And I really don't care. Found out he's been helping the Texians for a long time. He probably killed a Mexican soldier. Least, that's what I figure."

Angie was finding it difficult to breathe, but she grasped Tom's logic almost desperately. "Yes. Yes, I'm sure that's what it is."

"I trust him, Miss Angie. He's done nothing but good for us since he first sent word. I'm asking for you to trust him, too. If we can get those supplies..." He looked out towards the sleeping town of San Antonio. "I don't think I need to tell you what it will mean."

Angie nodded solemnly, but her mind was racing. "Thank you for telling me this."

He nodded, pinning her with a dark gaze. "I'll give you one piece of advice, though. No matter how much I trust a man, I never turn my back."

*

OLIVIA DROPPED THE griddle with a loud clang. The usual afternoon clamor from the dining area didn't even dim. Angie picked up the cast-iron griddle with a towel and placed it back on the countertop. "Being so skittish will draw more attention than you want."

Olivia snorted as she busied herself with dicing onions. "You are one to talk. You've been preening all morning."

Angie self-consciously smoothed a hand over her hair. "That's absurd. You're the one dancing around as though you expect a solider to attack any moment."

"Would you please lower your voice?" she snapped.

She scraped the onions into the pot bubbling over the fire and turned back to the cutting board, her motions quick and efficient. "There is no guarantee that he didn't just run off and tell the highest officer what he found out."

Angie pulled tortillas off the griddle and threw on two more. "I'm glad to see that a night of rest has lessened your paranoia," she said wryly, watching her sister's sharp movements.

Olivia stopped chopping long enough to glare at Angie then refocused on the onion. "It would do you some good to have a bit of my paranoia. You can't trust everyone you meet. Being cautious is not a bad thing."

Caution with Lorenzo was probably the wisest approach. But if he got his way, she wasn't going to get an easy escape. She yanked the tortillas off the griddle just before they burned. The sharp look from Olivia was a warning to pay attention. Damn Lorenzo. He was occupying too many of her thoughts lately. And last night he invaded her dreams.

She blew a wisp of hair out of her face. The feel of his hands in her dream had been so real—her skin was still tingling when she awoke. For several insane seconds she had wanted to fall back to sleep, to fall back into the passionate, yet gentle arms of Lorenzo. But that had been a dream. In reality, everything about him was cold and calculated, taking advantage of every situation available.

"He's here." Serena ran in breathless, her cheeks flushed with excitement.

"You might as well announce it to everyone," Olivia snapped, wiping her hands hastily on her apron.

Angie's heart skipped a beat. How would he act towards her? Was he going to be formal, politely asking her to go walking with him? Was he going to pretend the previous night had never happened? Impossible. As he had predicted, the rumors had been flying before they had even crawled into bed that night.

Every gossip in town found it "scandalous" that a soldier and one of the "ice sisters" had been seen in an intimate embrace during the wee hours of the morning. The stories that were flying around were ridiculous and embarrassing.

Some said she was pregnant by the soldier, a good three months along. The notion was laughable, considering Lorenzo had only been in San Antonio for a few weeks. Some said that she met a different soldier every night, offering them comfort between her legs to keep the morale of the Mexican Army strong. That suggestion had her red to the roots of her hair. Another said that she and Lorenzo had been a match from the very first time they met.

She desperately hoped Lorenzo hadn't heard that one. All of the stories, though, said that Olivia's cold, man-hating attitudes had driven Angie to him. From the tight look on Olivia's face all morning, Angie could only assume she had heard the stories. It was almost a given that Lorenzo had heard them, as well as many more. And yet, in spite of, or maybe because of, all the gossip, the *cocina* was busier than ever.

"Are you going to go out there or not?"

Angie looked up from two burned tortillas to see her sisters staring at her intently. "Of course," Angie scoffed, dusting her hands off. "I just didn't want him to think I'm anxious or anything."

Olivia frowned. Serena grinned. Trying to draw as deep a breath as she could without being obvious, Angie headed towards the dining room.

"Oh, for the love of…" Olivia caught her arm and put a pitcher of water in one hand and a glass in the other. "It's not as if you've never met him before. From what I've heard, it would appear you two know each other very well."

Angie groaned. "You're not helping, Vi."

"We'll just save that lecture for later." She gave Angie a tight-lipped smile. "But for right now, it appears he is on our side and I'd like to keep it that way. As much as I hate to admit it, he could be very useful."

"I feel like a toy stuck between two children. He wants to use us to get ahead with whatever his agenda is. You want to use him to accomplish your goals. I'm stuck in the middle."

"You can gain from this as well, and you know it. Now go be your usual charming self."

The slight bite of sarcasm in her sister's voice was not lost on Angie as she stepped into the dining room. As had happened that morning, all eyes turned to her with speculation and curiosity.

All eyes except his. He sat in the corner as usual, smiling at something one of his comrades had just said. Though his comrade was watching her, a leer on his face, Lorenzo leaned back in his chair, watching the others and chuckling good-naturedly at the jokes and suggestions they threw his way.

Angie's heart was thudding so loudly in her ears all of the loud conversation around her was muted. Determinedly she strode towards him, weaving her way in and out of the tables. When a hand reached out and pinched her, she jumped, but ignored it. The number of times she had been pinched so far that morning was too many to count. But when she looked at Lorenzo again, she nearly tripped over her own feet. His glare at the man who had pinched her was hard enough to make her wish she were in another room.

She didn't look back to see how the obnoxious man was reacting to the glare. She concentrated on walking to Lorenzo. She forced a smile to her face as she greeted the men at the table, looking at Lorenzo last. Before she could say hello, he spoke. "Are you all right?"

She made a nervous sound that could have been taken as an affirmative. "I'm fairly used to the grabs."

He arched his eyebrow at her comment, and she wondered how he would classify their embrace the previous night. It certainly was far more than just a "grab." She tried to contain her nerves as she set down the glass and poured the water. She had fought off the embarrassment all morning, but now, face-to-face with him, she could feel the heat of her blush creeping up her neck and to her face.

"I meant about everything. Are you all right?"

Angie cut him a sideways glance as the other men at the table studied her reaction. "I am perfectly fine, thank you. What would you like for your dinner, sir?"

He gave her a full smile, one so bright she was startled by it. She nearly jumped out of her skin when he caught her free hand. "I would like to order a nice, long walk with you this evening."

The dining room fell into an absolute hush. Angie wished the floor would open up and swallow her.

"I—I…" She licked her lips nervously. How did she answer without sounding like she was falling at his feet?

"You don't have to answer me now. I know I angered you last night. I'll come around this evening, and if you do decide to walk with me, I'll be greatly honored."

The man was a genius. And she hated him for being so smooth and making her feel the way she did.

She pursed her lips tightly, trying to mimic Olivia's fiercest look. "I'll need to think about it."

She nodded to the other men at the table and, with her chin held high, she returned to the kitchen.

Chapter Nineteen

"I CAN'T BELIEVE you didn't answer him." Olivia sat in the now empty dining room, her feet propped on another chair as she watched the road outside their home. She lazily fanned herself with an old fan she had owned since she was a child. Despite the chill outside, the front of the house was warm with all the cooking they had done and the sun streaming through the windows. Yet, outside, everyone had their scarves and mittens on.

Angie sat on the just-swept floor, her head resting against the wall. She wanted to take a *siesta*. They would all need it, considering the work that was ahead of them. They had several long nights to come.

But she was too fidgety, too jumpy, to relax long enough. "It was the best way to handle things. He gave me any easy way to avoid embarrassing myself further."

"And whose fault is it you were embarrassed to begin with?"

Angie sighed heavily and opened her eyes slowly. Olivia was half slouched in her chair, rubbing at her temples, her face pinched in frustration and concern.

"You should go rest," Angie said softly. "He won't come

by for quite some time and, even when he does, there is nothing for you to do until sunset."

Olivia shook her head and rubbed her eyes. "No, no. I can get things organized downstairs. I can—"

"You'll be no use to us if you are too exhausted to be alert," Angie's calm words struck a cord in Olivia and she nodded.

"Only for a moment. And you as well. Fretting about things isn't going to help."

Angie almost laughed. When Olivia learned how to stop fretting, water would run uphill.

Olivia stood with a groan. "Do you really feel like you've stopped your embarrassment, or do you think you've added fuel to the fire?"

Angie let her eyes slide shut again. "My gut tells me this town has never had so much fun. I really could care less."

"And Grandma and Grandpa?"

Angie cringed inwardly. She knew the gossip was hurting her grandparents. Grandpa hadn't spoken to her all day, and Grandma looked flustered and out of sorts. But there was no way she could change things. All she could do was face all that was to come, the good and the bad.

She heard Olivia's steps drifting to the back of the house and breathed a soft sigh of relief. Her sister's constant pacing, constant worrying, constant "what if" questions were making Angie want to climb the wall.

Lorenzo had been pleasant during his stay for a meal, and had completely played the part of an innocent beau. From kissing the back of her hand to watching her with intense gazes, he had the entire room believing he was at her mercy instead of the other way around. And the entire time her conversation with Tom ran thru her mind. Who had he killed? Had it really been a Mexican soldier? Or was there really a dangerous man behind his charm?

Angie threw an arm over her eyes, blocking out the sunlight that streamed through the window. She wondered if he was going to be all business when he came to see her. Or was he going to continue to pretend, at least for a little while? The man made her blood run hot and cold at the same time. One minute she fantasized about how to kill him in inventive ways. The next she was wondering how to get one of his sweet caresses again. But, she reminded herself, every one of his caresses had been fake.

The warmth of the sun on her skin was making her lethargic. Her muscles loosened slowly as she tried to put Lorenzo out of her mind.

The sound of footsteps on the porch jarred her awake in a rush. Disoriented, she shoved her hair out of her face and blinked her eyes into focus. The sun was far lower in the sky than she had remembered before closing her eyes. A light knock at the door spurred her into motion.

Surging to her feet in an ungraceful flurry of petticoats and skirts, she righted her bodice and rubbed at her face, praying it wouldn't be too obvious she had just awoken. Where was everyone else?

With a last attempt to make her hair obey her, she yanked open the door, prepared to tell whoever it was the *cocina* didn't serve supper, never had and never would.

Lorenzo raised his eyebrows, his eyes taking a very slow and a very thorough appraisal of her. Heat infused her cheeks. "I wasn't expecting you so early." She swallowed, trying to work moisture into her suddenly dry mouth.

"Have I caught you at a bad time?" His voice was warm, even though it was tinged with sarcastic humor.

"No, not at all." Angie's hands twisted in her skirts for the lack of anything else to do. "I was just... that is, Olivia and I..." She stopped talking, counted to five and drew a deep breath. "No. Your timing is perfect as always."

"I'll give you a few moments to arrange yourself before we go for our walk."

His clipped tone took her by surprise. His husky, warm voice had lowered her defenses, something she had vowed she wasn't going to let happen. "I haven't said I want to go walking with you."

Lorenzo's eyes narrowed dangerously and she nearly took a step backwards. "Fair enough. I'll wait here for a few minutes. When and if you want..." He shrugged and turned away from her, making it obvious the decision was entirely up to her.

Frustrated, Angie closed the door forcefully, but stood there for several moments, her hands still on the knob.

"Was that him?"

Olivia's voice so close to her made Angie jump. She turned to face her sister, hoping her expression didn't give away her emotions. It wasn't to be. Olivia's eyebrows raised as she dried her hands on her apron.

"I see it was. Why didn't you go walking with him?"

"He suggested I freshen up," Angie snapped.

"You do look like you just tumbled from your bed."

"Yes, thanks to you." Angie brushed past her sister, hurrying towards her room. "How could you have let me sleep so long?"

"I didn't," Olivia said, following her. "I just awoke a few minutes ago myself and started preparations for tomorrow's meals. I thought you were in your room until I heard someone at the door."

Angie went to the shallow bowl and pitcher on her nightstand and quickly splashed the cool water on her face. "His manners are in perfect form tonight," Angie muttered as she blotted a towel over her face.

Olivia began quickly braiding Angie's long, dark hair. "He has a point. You really need to look presentable if you are going to go walking with him."

Angie yanked the braid out of Olivia's hands. "If you'll recall, I am not a very willing participant to this idea."

Olivia sat down on the bed, her lips pursed. "I thought your original plan was to take care of all of this on your own and leave me completely out of things. Don't you think you would have had to spend some time with that man if you had?"

"That man has a name. It's Lorenzo. And, no, by my plan, I wouldn't have had anything to do with him ever again."

"You're lying." Olivia's comment echoed Angie's thoughts so closely for a moment she thought she was the one who had spoken. Olivia continued relentlessly. "For some reason, you're letting that ma-Lorenzo, get to you. You need to stop it now. He can only hurt you."

"You don't know what you're talking about." Angie smoothed some of the wrinkles out of her skirts and turned towards the door, but Olivia's cool hand caught her arm.

She looked at Angie with concern. "I know all too well what I'm talking about. Don't trust him. No matter what, you can never trust him."

Angie looked at her sister's intense face and a cold chill shivered up her spine.

She whispered so softly Olivia nearly didn't hear her. "I know. I know."

Chapter Twenty

"GLAD TO SEE you accepted my offer." Lorenzo extended his arm and she lightly laid her fingers on his forearm.

"Given the lack of choices in good men around here lately," Angie said flippantly, "I decided I could settle for you."

The corner of his mouth twitched, but it came and went so fast she wasn't sure if she had even seen it. "Usually when a woman goes walking with a man she looks a little happy. Make an attempt."

"The same could be said for you," Angie spoke through teeth clenched in a fake smile. "Your glare has people crossing to the other side of the road."

Lorenzo said nothing and for several long moments they walked in silence.

Angie's curiosity finally got the better of her. "Might I ask what has inspired your gracious mood?" She could feel the muscles in his arm tense then slowly relax.

"This is not a position I care to be in," he said bluntly.

"Well that makes two of us. At least there's something we can agree upon. It wasn't my idea, if you remember, to put us in this position."

Lorenzo glanced down at her and felt remorse at the tension in her face. "You don't have to do this," he said finally.

"Really? You made a pretty strong argument about it last night. What other options do we have?"

Lorenzo stopped and turned towards her. "There is a small group of soldiers that are planning on defecting. I can get them to assist me."

Angie stared at him for a few moments, trying to understand what he was saying. She couldn't. "So, are you planning on taking one of them for walks with you?"

Her sudden dry humor surprised him, creating a spontaneous smile, then a chuckle. "It wasn't on my mind, though now that you mention it…"

Angie fought against the smile tugging at her lips then shook her head. "I don't see what those soldiers have to do with us. Weren't you going to have them help you regardless?"

His smile slipped. "They can help me get everything we need without putting you or your sisters in any more danger."

Angie suddenly realized what he was suggesting. "You don't want us to help with anything."

"There's no reason. I know Tom feels like you are an advantage, but it's too big of a risk."

Angie pulled her arm away from his. "Just what is so risky about it?" she demanded. An older townswoman walked past, openly watching them with speculation. Angie lowered her voice. "Olivia and I are always going around town to get supplies for the *cocina*. No one notices when our baskets are heavier than usual or we have a few extra items. No one…"

"Angie, you don't…"

"We are known in this town as a family supportive of Mexico. Our grandparents don't hide their loyalty, in fact they flaunt it, and everyone assumes my sisters and I feel the same. People don't even think twice when they see us. And now you think…"

"You've been fine until now since you haven't had to get anything large. A few onions here, a steak or two there." He shrugged. "Of course no one's going to notice. But now it's much more serious. What if you get caught?"

She shook her head. "Not going to happen."

"What if you get caught?" he growled.

She glared at him. "I've received several fine lessons in lying, thanks to you, so I think I'll be just fine."

"You really are naïve," he said through clenched teeth. "I've seen what men do to women—especially women who have sabotaged them. You have no idea what they would do to you."

Angie's fingers trembled slightly as she clutched her shawl tighter, but she kept her eyes focused on him, her face determined. What had he seen? Had he been a witness or a participant? What crimes had he really committed? She forced the thought from her mind.

"Then so be it. My sisters and I are well aware of the risks we take. There's no reason for you to be concerned. If we get caught, then we're out of your hair."

"No reason—" Lorenzo stopped and drew a deep breath.

A couple of busybodies of the town were watching them intently from one of the stores, peering from behind the curtains.

He had a stiff smile on his face as he turned back to Angie. "So, when they break you and you tell them all of our plans, all of the people involved, and everything that has happened, you think I shouldn't be concerned then?"

Angie put on an equally fake smile. Damn him for pretending to care. All he was really worried about was the cause. And, she admitted to herself reluctantly, it should be her only concern as well. "I won't break. Neither will my sisters. We won't say a thing."

Lorenzo gave such an ugly laugh Angie took a step away from him.

He took a step towards her, bringing himself so close to her their bodies nearly touched. "The things that will be done to you will have you telling them every secret in minutes. They'll cut your skin off of you in inches. They'll beat you with a whip you wouldn't even use on an animal. They'll—"

"Is that what happened to you? Is that why your back has all of those scars? Did you break?" She tried to divert his attack and bring it around to a subject she knew he didn't like.

She watched his face closely, hoping for a clue to his thoughts. But as usual his eyes became shuttered, his face emotionless. Except for the muscle ticking in his jaw, revealing at the very least his frustration.

"There are some things you do not need to know." He

took off his hat, raked a hand through his hair, then forcefully slapped the hat back on. "Obviously, there's no getting through to you," he said in a clipped voice. "I was offering you a way out."

He stepped away from her and held out his arm again, staring down the road. Very slowly she placed her hand on his arm. "You've been opposed to working with me from the very beginning. Were you offering me a way out—or yourself?"

Lorenzo started walking, his face tense. "You willingly put yourself in danger. Your choice. Whatever happens from here, just remember it was your choice."

"You're saying that as if I don't already know. It would be the same as me saying it is your choice to be an obnoxious ass. But you already know that."

He glanced sideways at her. "I'm glad you've resorted to a rational argument. It helps your cause greatly."

Angie was beginning to feel ill. "You need to make a decision. You either accept the fact that we have to help each other or you don't. And if you don't I don't ever want to see you near our *cocina* again."

"And what would you do? You don't have the list. You can't get the things Tom needs."

"We can do our best, which is what we've been doing for years. And there's nothing you could do to stop us."

There was something he could do, but Angie prayed he either hadn't thought of it or had dismissed it altogether. He could bring the Mexican Army down on them so fast they wouldn't know what had happened, and it would only take a few words to the right person. But he wouldn't do that. It would put them in the very position he was trying to stop.

"I made a promise to Tom that I would try to make this work," he said, shaking his head.

"You're doing a miserable job of keeping that promise if you ask me."

"I had hoped you would finally come to your senses."

"Is that why you decided you would take me walking? Is that what's behind all of this? Talking me out of doing something that could help so many people? I suppose you saw last night that Olivia is just as passionate about this as I am so you decided to work on me again. You don't even have a plan, do you?" They had reached the small bridge over the river and she once again turned to face him, forcing him to stop. "What really is going on here? Are you trying to help the Texians or not?"

From the look on his face and the way he clenched his fists, Angie realized she had pushed him too far. "You know nothing about me, Angie, so don't begin making assumptions."

"You've made an awfully poor attempt of sharing yourself. Other than stating the obvious, you haven't told me anything. You know nothing about me, either, yet you have no problem judging me all day long."

"I know that you don't really know what this war is all about. I know you are naïve enough to think you can do anything you please because there's always someone else behind you cleaning up your mess. I know that—"

"You know nothing about me," she whispered in a

choked voice. Her hands were clenched into fists and she looked like she was ready to punch him.

His eyes burned with an anger she had never seen in him before, but she was too mad herself to be afraid. "Either you help us with this list or not. Either way, the sooner you are gone, the better."

"You're like every woman I've ever known. You focus on what you want and to hell with anything else."

"Fortunately we want the same things in this instance, right? Or is there something you aren't telling me?"

Lorenzo shook his head at her and turned back towards town. She laid her hand on his arm, though she didn't even want to touch him. He walked quickly, his tone all business. "Tonight, Serena will get her first lesson in being a thief. There's a house on the edge of town that has a stash of weapons. Mostly rifles, but I heard the old man that lives there bragging about his collection to some of the men this morning."

"When?"

"I'll come in through the back door of the house a bit before midnight. Make sure your grandparents are tucked away."

"I'm going with you."

"No. You'll be a hindrance."

"I'm not letting you take my little sister out to commit crimes without me being there to protect her."

"So what happened to the agreement of trust we made?"

They were getting close to the *cocina*. It was obvious Lorenzo was eager to be free of her presence.

She looked up at him. "Are you saying you trust me?"

Lorenzo looked down at her with a raised eyebrow and stopped in front of the white porch. "If I said yes?"

"I wouldn't believe you."

"Then it doesn't matter what I think, now, does it?"

He leaned in towards her and his tightened grip over her hand kept her from pulling back. "Your neighbors are watching," he whispered, watching her expression. "We don't want to give them the wrong impression."

She opened her mouth to tell him just what she thought about impressions but her words were cut off by his mouth over hers. Her sound of protest never escaped her throat as his lips moved over hers, rough at first, then slowly gentling. Her heart was racing as she stood on tiptoe, hating herself for enjoying his embrace so much.

The wolfish smile on his face when he pulled away from her told her just how much he knew of her warring emotions. She wanted to slap him. Then she wanted him to kiss her again. She decided she hated him.

"Until tonight," he said as he turned, never once looking back as she stood trembling on the porch.

Chapter Twenty-One

LORENZO STOOD IN the dark corner watching and listening. His mind screamed at him not to trust, not to hope that this time would be different. But she was different. Everything about her was different, and she made him feel stronger and a better man whenever he was around her.

He would never forget the beautiful face he had loved so much, the way she would smile at him. And he would never forget that same smile twisted in a sneer as the whip had torn through his flesh. He would never forget the look on her face as she embraced his enemy, all the while seeing him witness her treachery. And he would never forget watching the beautiful face he loved so much convulse in surprise as her last breath left her body.

But he wasn't watching a soft, rose-scented blonde walk across the room. He was watching a hardheaded woman with dark hair and smooth skin telling her sister not to be afraid.

"I know there's nothing to be afraid of. Stop saying that." Serena pushed her auburn curls up under a cap, making her look more like a twelve-year-old boy than a blossoming young woman.

Angie kneeled in front of her, buttoning her sister's jacket. "I know you think this is going to be exciting, but it's dangerous stealing from people. You know that Olivia and I would never want you to do this under different circumstances."

Serena rolled her eyes and adjusted her cap. Lorenzo smiled to himself. He wondered how many times Serena had actually stolen things.

Olivia sat at one of the tables, her hands folded tightly in her lap, her foot jiggling madly.

Quickly, she stood and began pacing. "I still think this is a bad idea. This is a very bad idea. Why Serena? Why have her do this? Why doesn't he just do all the stealing himself? He is the thief, for God's sake."

"Because Serena can fit in places I can't." Lorenzo's voice, though soft, filled the room.

Serena squeaked and jumped so hard she stumbled backwards. Olivia whirled to face him, nearly falling as she tripped on her skirts. Angie fell flat on her rump.

Shaking, she shoved her hair out of her face. "A little warning would have been nice!" she hissed. "How long have you been standing there?"

He shrugged, stepping into the flickering candlelight so they could see him. "A few minutes. Not very long."

Olivia folded her arms across her chest. "Obviously you are skilled at sneaking in. Why do you need Serena?"

"I already answered that."

"Angie's small. Use her instead."

Angie was struggling to get to her feet but hesitated and cast a surprised glance in her sister's direction. "You're small, too."

"Not as small as you."

"And neither of you are as small as Serena." Lorenzo walked over to Angie and held out his hand.

She looked at him for a couple of moments, her eyebrows raised, before finally accepting his offer. He pulled her to her feet quickly, bringing her against him, and her eyes clashed with his. Her cheeks stained pink and she quickly stepped away from him.

Olivia frowned at both of them. "Where are you taking Serena that's so small only she can get in?"

Lorenzo looked over at Serena and she smiled eagerly at him. He returned the smile.

Angie glowered at him. "If this place is so tiny, kindly tell me how you were going to get in and out of there when you used your soldiers for help."

Lorenzo looked at her and his smile slipped. "It would have been difficult. I would have had to make different plans."

"Then make those different plans and leave Serena out of this." Olivia was tapping her foot angrily.

"Have you forgotten I'm right here?" Serena snapped. "I want to help, and if this is something I can do, I'm going to go." She had her hands on her hips, clearly unhappy with the direction of the conversation.

"How about I let you make the decision?" Lorenzo spoke to Serena. "Because where I'm going to send you, things could be... unpleasant."

A wary look crossed Serena's face. "What do you mean?"

"There's an old building from the mission. It was built a long time ago, probably the same time the Alamo was built. But it's been abandoned and most of it has collapsed inwards. I had heard that some of the missions had been built with underground storage. I was suspicious when I saw that the Alamo didn't have any. So while on patrol today I explored the old building. Through one of the collapsed walls I can see a hole that looks to go farther down than the rest of the floor."

Serena was pale. "I don't see what you'd want to steal from there."

"Nothing. But we can store the supplies there. It's not safe to take all of the weapons back here."

"So you would need me to… to climb through there and go below…"

All of them could see the fear on her face. "You've been out there before, haven't you?" Lorenzo asked.

Serena fidgeted with her cap. "Well… yes. It's very dark and there are so many animals that hide in there."

He nodded. "That's all I needed to know." He turned to Angie and Olivia. "So which one of you want to help me? Or should I ask someone else?"

"I didn't say I wouldn't…"

"Serena, you've already shown me you're afraid of this place. I can't have you hesitating at the wrong moment."

Serena looked as though she were about to cry. "I can be a good thief. I can help."

"You're too young. Your sisters were right. Concentrate on helping them with some of the other tasks." He looked back at the other two sisters. "Well?"

For a moment, Angie wanted to tell him to get one of the soldiers to help him. The problem was she knew he would do just that. And she wanted to help.

"I'll do it," Angie spoke up, lifting her chin as she watched his face for a reaction. He nodded and turned his back on her, starting towards the back door. "Wait!" Angie whispered to his dark back. "Give me a few minutes."

Lorenzo clenched his teeth as he looked back at her. "Are you beginning to understand why I don't like working with women? Indecision and wasted time."

Angie glared at him as her fingers flew over the laces of her skirt and felt an ounce of satisfaction as his jaw dropped along with her skirt.

"Anjelica!" Olivia gasped as Angie stepped free of her skirt, wearing an old pair of her father's pants, rolled at the ankles and belted at her waist with a dark piece of leather. Her chemise fell to reveal one of her father's darker work shirts that was rolled to her wrists and straining over her breasts.

"You forgot to add that we are prepared for anything," Angie snapped, tying her hair behind her head. She gave her two wide-eyed sisters kisses on the cheek then hurried down the hall past Lorenzo. "Hurry up," she said over her shoulder. "You're wasting time."

LORENZO COULDN'T TAKE his eyes off of her. And it was

making it damned hard for him to watch out for any danger. Watching her step out of her skirt wearing those snug pants had been the most desirable thing he had ever seen. And every step she had taken since had been as equally the most desirable thing he had ever seen.

They paused for a moment against the side of one of the stores, listening for anything that didn't fit with the cold November night. "If you were going for shock, I think you accomplished your goal," Lorenzo spoke in a tense whisper.

Angie looked up at him. From the anger in her eyes he could tell she was still mad from their argument earlier. "Would you prefer me tiptoeing around in someone's home, wearing several layers of skirts?"

"You won't—"

She took off dodging to the next home across the road, light on her feet, her movements smooth and graceful without the hindering layers of skirts. He cursed under his breath and followed her.

"You aren't going into any houses," he said angrily when he caught up with her.

"So you plan on clunking around in there on your own?"

"I'm the master thief, remember?"

She looked at him intently. "Really? For some reason I don't think you know how to steal any more than I do."

On that surprising statement, she took off again.

When he caught up to her he grabbed her arm and forced her to face him. "Just exactly what are you getting at?"

She yanked her arm free of his grip. "You don't act like any thief I've ever known."

"You've known a lot of thieves? Glad to know I'm not ruining your standards for the company you keep."

Angie put her hands on her hips, tilting her head back to glare up at him. "There are a couple of pickpockets in town. They can't stop themselves. Every time there is an opportunity for them to take something, they do. You've had plenty of opportunities, and you haven't done anything."

He visibly drew within himself. "People change," he said through tight lips.

"That's good for you, but it doesn't help our cause much right now, does it?"

He grabbed her arm again when she tried to turn from him. "Just because I don't do it anymore doesn't mean I've forgotten how this game works."

"How reassuring. Was part of your plan to stand here talking all night or did you want to go get some guns?"

He shook his head in frustration. "There's no winning with you, is there?"

"No," she said, her voice rough, "and there never will be."

They stared at each other in silence, each lost in their own thoughts before he quickly released her arm and they continued heading towards the outskirts of town. Finally, they were in the field next to the house, moving at a crouch among the tall weeds.

"So what did you steal?" Angie asked from behind him.

Lorenzo felt his eye tick. The woman was relentless. "Money," he said blandly.

"Just money, huh? Why not jewelry? You could have

found more reward that way."

"I'll take your advice into consideration."

ANGIE GLARED INTO his back. It was probably unrealistic for her to expect him to confess his crimes to her. What man openly admitted to murder? But knowing he continued to lie without a second thought made her question what else he was lying about.

Ever since they had parted that afternoon, she had gone over and over in her mind the things he had said to her and could only reach one conclusion. He didn't want to have anything to do with her. Which made his caresses and kisses all the more embarrassing and humiliating. For him, it had all been a performance. For her, it had been amazing, the awakening of awareness she had never dreamed of—and she craved more. She hated herself. She wanted to hate him even more. But she was finding it impossible to hate him, and she didn't want to examine the reasons why.

They stopped at the edge of the tall weeds just before the dusty yard of the obviously wealthy homestead. "So you must have been a pretty lousy thief to have been caught." Angie tried to catch her breath, watching Lorenzo from the corner of her eye.

"Must have," he said dryly, not looking at her, his eyes focused on the house.

Angie shrugged. "Either that or someone sold you out."

His eye ticked and she knew she had struck a cord.

"We should go in through the window on the east side," he said, pointing to the right side of the house. "I'll hand the guns back to you through…"

"So, was it your partner?"

His hand slowly dropped to rest on his knee and he tilted his head to the side to look at her. "What are you talking about?"

She noticed the beads of sweat on his forehead despite the cool wind blowing and hoped he didn't catch a chill. "You had a partner, didn't you? I've always heard that thieves work together, especially when they're robbing homes?"

He rolled his shoulder, joints popping loudly. "Why the sudden curiosity, Angie?"

She hated it when he spoke her name. It rolled off his tongue so smoothly, so gently, it felt like one of his caresses. She had to remind herself that it, too, was fake.

She shrugged. "If you are the one guiding me in the arts of being a thief, I've got to know what I'm getting myself into. Did your partner get caught, too?"

He smiled at her, a slow, condescending smile that made her want to throttle him. "If you follow what I tell you to do, there won't be any problems at all."

She mimicked his smile. "How very vague of you."

He turned back towards the house. "Paying attention will also keep us from having any problems. The last thing either one of us wants right now is to have an enraged farmer chasing after us through these fields." Once again, he pointed towards the right side of the house. "I'll go in through there. You stay outside the window and collect the guns as I hand them to you. I trust you know how to handle a gun?"

If he could be obscure in his answers, so could she. "I never quite made out which end was which, but I'll make do." She stood and headed towards the house but was yanked back by his hand on her wrist.

His gaze was intense. "Be careful."

For a moment, a sharp comment lay on the tip of her tongue.

But the sincerity in his eyes confused her. "You, too," she responded just as softly.

Then together they headed towards the first crime.

Chapter Twenty-Two

S HE HAD COUNTED to nine thousand by the time he reappeared at the window. It didn't matter she was counting as fast as her heart beat within her chest. It had seemed to be an eternity. The butt of a rifle slid through the window and she grabbed it with sweaty palms. Two more rifles followed, then nothing. She peered in the darkened room and saw a table and chairs, but no Lorenzo. He could have at least told her…

She smacked her hand over her mouth to stifle her scream when he reappeared directly in front of her. He gave her a stern look, then quietly handed her two pistols. Awkwardly holding their large treasure, she stepped backwards as he gingerly climbed through the window, wincing with him at each bump and clunk.

He grabbed the three rifles from her as soon as he was through the window and led her back through the field. "What took you so long?" Angie snapped when they were several yards from the house. He cut her a sideways glance but said nothing.

"Alright, then, where are we going?"

"Back to the *cocina*, where else?"

Angie stopped walking and didn't move until Lorenzo stopped and looked back at her. "I want to go to that old store room."

"No." He turned and started walking again.

"You might as well take the chance that—"

"It would just be a waste of time," he threw over his shoulder.

Angie gritted her teeth and charged after him. "Look, I'm admitting that for once you had a good idea. It would be much safer if we could store things there."

Lorenzo stopped and she nearly crashed into his back.

Stepping around him she placed herself in his path and looked up at him. "You obviously feel it is a good place to keep things. It would remove some of the chances of us being caught taking things to our home."

"I am well aware of the benefits. I'm also all too aware of how small that hole is, and from my most recent feel of your bottom, I'd say you won't fit."

Angie's cheeks flamed. "Then we'll just make me fit, one way or another. I'm going. You come if you like."

She turned west of town and began walking quickly, her head bent so that she wouldn't be seen above the tall weeds and shrubs.

She could hear him cursing women in general and Angie in particular, but Lorenzo followed. It wasn't long before they reached the dilapidated building and Angie shivered as a pair of glowing coon's eyes watched them approach.

"We haven't much time," Lorenzo said, glancing around the rubble in the dim moonlight. "There will be a roll check in the next hour."

Angie looked at him curiously. "Roll check?" He nodded, his eyes still focused on the building.

"Bed rolls. An officer comes by to make sure no bed rolls are empty."

Angie's eyebrows shot up. "How have you been able to get away from those before?"

"I haven't. Cos ordered the checks to start last night. I just barely made it back in time."

"Wouldn't it make sense for those checks to be a surprise?"

He gave her a half-hearted grin. "They are." He headed towards the building, and Angie noticed how intense his eyes were as they probed the darkness.

Angie stayed close on his heels. Two walls had collapsed inwards, probably from poor construction. Angie had seen several similar structures outside of town. The buildings had been built to provide quick shelter against the harsh Texas weather and little thought had been given on how to make it stable. The shadows seemed to move as they got closer and Angie's grip tightened on the pistols. Perhaps insisting that they make this detour had been a bad idea after all.

One of the walls that had collapsed had originally been the front entrance. Jagged fragments of a wooden door and a slab of limestone that might have been the front step was all that was left. Dried clay, rocks, and wood were scattered on the ground, but most of the debris was within the last two remaining walls.

"Do you think this used to be someone's home?" Angie

whispered.

Lorenzo stepped over the former threshold and turned to help Angie do the same. "Possibly. I doubt it, though." He held two rifles in one hand and had another tucked under his arm.

With his free hand he took Angie's wrist and guided her over the rubble. The beating of Angie's heart doubled. She wondered if he could feel it through her wrist.

He glanced sideways at her. "There's nothing to be afraid of."

He thought her pounding heart was due to fear. Best for him to think that than realize it was the touch of his hand that was creating such an irrational reaction.

She ducked beneath a low beam. "What do you think this building was for, then?" Conversation would keep her mind off his touch.

"Hard to say. Whatever used to be inside this building has long been removed."

"Or stolen. If someone had to leave here in a hurry, it wouldn't surprise me if others came to pick it clean."

A rock beneath her foot slipped away and she stumbled, trying to regain her balance. His hand tightened on her wrist, pulling her upright.

"Thank you," she muttered, not looking at him. "I don't see this mysterious hole you mentioned and we've nearly walked the whole mess."

"You're not very patient, are you?"

Her smile wasn't pleasant. "You should know me well enough by now to know that."

They were at the corner of the house, where the two walls that collapsed overlapped each other. Lorenzo propped the rifles against some debris then bent down and pushed several rocks aside. A small, very small, hole appeared. Angie leaned in, struggling to see against the dim light.

"Now you've seen it," Lorenzo said with finality. "Let's go."

She leaned in closer. "How far down does it go?"

"Same as your cellar from the little I could see of it. It's small, though. Probably five foot by five."

Angie set her pistols to the side and leaned in further, kneeling on her hands and knees to get a better look, effectively shoving Lorenzo out of the way.

"There's nothing more to see, Angie. Let's go."

She ignored him as she shifted a rock out of her way. A timber groaned and several rocks shifted, pelting Angie with tiny fragments and dust.

"Alright, that's enough," Lorenzo grabbed her under the arm and hauled her to her feet. "You're going to get hurt if you keep messing with things you shouldn't."

Angie yanked free of his grip and nearly stumbled on the rocks in the process. "If you didn't think this place was safe, why were you so willing to bring my sister here?"

He opened his mouth, then shut it with a click. Finally he said, "If you don't move things around that you have no business moving around, the area is perfectly safe."

"And you think a curious twelve-year-old wouldn't touch anything?"

Lorenzo frowned at her. "We're wasting time. Let's go."

"I can fit."

Lorenzo had started to turn from her but stopped, looking back over his shoulder. "What?"

"I can fit through that hole. I'll need a bit of light, though. Do you think we can risk it?"

"You're not going down there."

Angie turned from him and once again got on her hands and knees, pulling the loose rubble away from the hole. Dropping to his hands and knees beside her, he began to wedge broken chunks of wood under the larger rocks that hung over the hole.

When Angie looked at him curiously, he gave her a tight smile. "As much as the thought of you being trapped down there and dependent on my help appeals to me, I'd prefer to not deal with the wrath of your sisters."

Angie quirked an eyebrow at him. "There is a very dark side to you."

His smile was genuine. "You have no idea."

Before she could start asking him any more questions he probably wouldn't answer, he turned away from her and grabbed a thick twig off the ground. "This is as much light as you can have," he said, carefully lighting the twig on the ground, avoiding setting fire to anything else in the area.

Angie didn't take the twig from him when he offered, but grabbed his wrist and guided his hand towards the hole. She could feel his pulse beneath the skin on his wrist and wished her heart was beating as slow and even as his. Instead, it raced and her mind yelled at her to let go of him and regain her sanity.

Holding his wrist over the hole she peered down, trying to gauge how far she would drop before hitting ground. A foot, maybe, if she dangled from the lip of the hole. She breathed a sigh of relief when the only sign of animals inhabiting the small room were a few spider webs. The remnants of an old ladder lay on the floor, along with a few other items she couldn't quite make out.

She took a deep breath and released his wrist, then turned so that her back was to the hole. "Let's see how small I can make myself." Angie lay on her stomach and began inching her way backwards, her feet and legs quickly disappearing down the hole.

Lorenzo watched her with a dark frown on his face, and she knew he still doubted whether she would fit. When her rump hit the entrance, she flashed him a quick smile. "Now's when we find out if your evaluation of my, er—bottom – is correct." She wiggled and twisted, struggling to get through the hole. She was determined she would prove him wrong.

"There!" she said triumphantly when her rump made it through, then gave a breathy squeal as her weight began to drag her downwards. Lorenzo jumped forward and caught her hands, but it proved to be unnecessary. Her breasts had stopped her quick descent.

Red streaks covered her cheeks as she realized her dilemma and knew Lorenzo was aware of it. "Perhaps I measured the wrong thing," Lorenzo said, the humor in his voice not helping her embarrassment. Angie twisted slightly, wincing as the rocks dug into the tender underside of her breasts.

"I can help—"

"No! Don't even think about it." Her eyes shot sparks at him. "It would be best for me if you would just turn your back—"

"You can't be serious."

She made a twirling motion with her finger and, with a sigh, he released her hands and turned his back to her. Slowly releasing her breath, Angie pushed down on her breasts, trying to force herself through. It worked better than she had planned and she was suddenly through with nothing to hold onto except herself.

She fell like a rock.

The ground was not a gentle place to land and she gritted her teeth as her legs gave beneath her and she landed hard on her rump. Surrounded completely by darkness and clouds of dust, she was relieved when Lorenzo's face appeared at the hole.

"Are you all right?"

Angie coughed and waved her hand in front of her face. "Never been better," she choked out. "But I'll give you the full report later."

His lips twitched in a grin then he tossed the twig down to her. The room lit up under the flickering light and Angie took in her surroundings quickly. The area had obviously been a storeroom a long time ago. Completely dried bunches of onions lay in one corner, barely recognizable. Jars of canned goods lined one wall, some shattered on the floor, the contents completely gone, probably devoured by a hungry animal. Crosses hung on every wall. A couple of leather pouches hung on one wall, and a box stood in the other corner.

"Are you ready?"

Angie jumped at Lorenzo's voice, having temporarily forgotten their real purpose. "Yes, yes." She stood under the hole, refocusing on their mission.

One by one, the rifles descended, then Lorenzo leaned far into the hole, one shoulder dipped within and he carefully dropped the pistols into her outstretched hands.

She piled everything neatly against one of the walls, then headed back towards the hole. She stood under if for a few moments, then started laughing, softly at first, then more hysterically.

Lorenzo leaned into the hole, his face alarmed. "What's wrong?"

Angie struggled to catch her breath. "We were so damned worried about me getting down here, we didn't think about how I was going to get out!"

Lorenzo's face registered shock and surprise at first, then frustration as he peered down at her. Angie, her hysteria past, rubbed her forehead, wondering how she was going to get out of her newest predicament. It didn't help that her mind kept screaming that Lorenzo needed to get back to his camp and soon.

She turned around the room, looking for rope or twine, anything that she could use. The old ladder cracked and snapped in pieces when she tried to pick it up. Shaking her head, she kept looking. Lorenzo did the same above her, digging through some of the rubble in hopes of finding something.

"I've got something!" Angie cried from below.

She began tugging a crate from one of the corners out to where the hole was. After several grunts and curses, the crate moved and a wall shuddered. "Angie, I don't think..."

"This is the only..." She paused to catch her breath. "This thing sure is heavy."

She tugged again and the crate creaked along the floor. A beam above her made a menacing sound.

"I might be able to reach you. Just..."

"I've almost got it."

The crate was away from the wall now and things seemed to have settled. Dust covered Angie from head to toe and her sweat on her face was leaving trails. Breathing heavily, she gave the crate one last shove and it was beneath the hole.

Lorenzo reached his arms towards her as she scrambled on top of the large wooden box. Stretching on tiptoe her fingertips brushed Lorenzo's. "You need to grow another two inches," Lorenzo said sarcastically.

"I'll do my best to make that happen," Angie panted, her tone just as sarcastic. Bending her knees slightly, she jumped.

Her palms slid over Lorenzo's and she landed back on the crate. The wood beneath her feet creaked. Three attempts later, she was beginning to get frustrated.

"One more time," Lorenzo ordered from above.

Gritting her teeth, she leaped and heard the wood crack under her as Lorenzo's hands locked onto hers. Looking down at the crate, the dwindling twig clenched between her teeth, Angie saw bright red cloth peeping through the slats of wood before her head was through the hole and she was face-to-face with Lorenzo.

He leaned towards her and his teeth clamped the twig right next to her lips and he pulled it away from her, flinging it aside with the toss of his head. Angie couldn't catch her breath for more than one reason.

"Now," he said, looking down at her body wedged in the hole. "Do I get to help this time?"

Angie blew a wisp of hair out of her face. "Just stand up and pull."

"Is that going to work?"

"If they get left behind, I won't complain."

His smile was all male. "No, but I will."

Angie's mouth was still agape when he stood and began to pull. The difference in positions must have helped, because she was through the hole with only a few wiggles and grunts, and leaning against Lorenzo.

The expression on his face was hard to read as she tried to step away, but his grip held her close. "You did good, *chula.*"

She stared up at him with perplexed eyes. "Why did you ever kiss me? Why me?"

Chapter Twenty-Three

Five days. Five days had passed since she had asked him that question, and he still didn't have a good answer. His answer at the time hadn't been one of his best moments.

Caught off guard he had shrugged nonchalantly and said, "Soldiers get lonely. And you were there."

At least the comment had given him a reprieve from all her questions. She had shoved free of his hold and remained silent for the rest of the night. After concealing the hole with several large, well-placed rocks, she turned and headed towards town.

He started after her. "I can—"

"I'll make it home just fine on my own, thank you."

Her back was ramrod straight, her nose lifted in the air. If she hadn't been wearing men's trousers and covered from head to toe in dust she could have been mistaken for royalty.

With a grunt Lorenzo lifted his end of a log. Cos had gotten wind again that the Texians might attack and had ordered the men to strengthen the fortress. Lorenzo prayed every day he could find the man leaking the information and slit his throat.

Sweat beaded on his forehead despite the cold air. Temperatures had dropped drastically in the past few days and the nights were bitterly cold. The non-stop drizzle wasn't helping to improve conditions either.

Finally shoving the log into place, Lorenzo took a step backwards, rolling his stiff shoulders. The exhaustion that pulled at him was beginning to wear him down. Each night he went with Angie and pillaged homes. People were beginning to talk about the thefts, prompting Cos to be even more cautious.

The drizzle picked up again and the men around him cursed. Their feet hadn't been dry in days. Lorenzo took a moment to drink from his canteen. Every night they gathered more things, and every night Angie remained distant, aloof.

He almost preferred her endless questions to the long moments of silence. It gave him too much time to think. It gave him too much time to watch her. He couldn't stop himself. The way she moved mesmerized him.

He told himself it was only because she continued to wear those damned trousers, but he had been watching her long before then. He hadn't stopped watching her since he first laid eyes on her. And he felt more protective of her than ever. He couldn't bear the thought of anything happening to her. She had become a part of his life, despite how much he had fought.

"One more log and we should be done here," he commented to the other men around him. They nodded their consensus, looking as tired as he felt.

Angie had remained polite to him, answering when he

spoke to her, but there was a distance about her he didn't like. Leaning down, he caught the end of the heavy log, watching some of the soldiers milling around the well. Something had captured their attention. He shook his head at them. Most were only boys, too young to realize all they had to risk.

He had been that age once. Long before he had received many bitter lessons in life.

The wood was slippery and he almost dropped it. Cursing, he told himself to concentrate. Angie wasn't worth his thoughts. And yet she was there, consuming him, making it impossible to think of anything else. What if he had misjudged her? What if she was everything she said she was? His comment shouldn't have upset her as much as it did unless his answer had been important to her.

He cringed every time he remembered what he had said. He had meant it to hurt, to make sure she fully understood the nature of their relationship. The problem was he didn't know if he even knew.

Feet slipping in the mud, the men shoved the last log into place. Lorenzo closed his eyes for a few moments, wishing he could rest, if only for a short while. Pushing himself away from the wall, he headed off with the rest of the men, ready for whatever they would be assigned next.

He glanced back at the well and saw the men still standing there. Curiosity piqued, he started towards them then froze, his heart beat becoming a thick, dull thud.

A woman stood to the side of the group, her long cloak hem brushing over the mud. She looked up at the soldier in front of her, a smile on her lips. The soldier's hand reached out and gently touched her face within the hood of her cloak. He turned halfway, looking around him, not paying any attention to the young bucks who clamored for her attention.

Lorenzo watched with narrowed eyes as she slipped her hand along his, as though in a caress. But Lorenzo saw the white parchment that passed between them and his fists clenched at his sides. The soldier turned away from her and Lorenzo memorized his face.

The soldier would be the second to die.

He finally knew who it was passing on the Texian's secrets. It wasn't a man's throat he would slit. It was a beautiful pale one. *Trust.* He watched Angie pull the hood over her face, glance around, and head back towards the *cocina. Trust that I will set things right.*

⚜

LORENZO WAS CORDIAL to Olivia and Serena that night and even managed a glance or two at Angie that weren't necessarily hateful. All of the sisters were too busy to pay much attention.

Olivia was ticking things off the list, talking out loud while Serena and Angie folded blankets and rags. Their secret basement seemed all the more confining that night as Lorenzo stood against his usual wall, waiting for Angie to join him on their nightly excursions. Only this time, she wouldn't return. He wondered if he should ask her why, ask her how she could stab him in the back.

His eyes searched Olivia's face as she gnawed on a finger-tip, still studying Tom's list. Did she know what Angie was doing? Was she part of the treachery, too? His eyes fell to Serena. He had no doubt the young girl just followed what her sisters told her to do. He lifted his eyes to Angie and found her staring back at him, a concerned expression on her face.

She had every reason to be concerned if she knew what he was thinking. He wanted to know why. He wanted to grab her shoulders and shake her till her teeth rattled and demand to know why she had deceived him.

He pulled his eyes away from her. He couldn't look at her without seeing the soldier's hands caressing her face, the smile she had given him. And he had almost trusted her. Almost.

"That should do it." Olivia sighed heavily, jerking Lorenzo back into the moment. She stood with a smile on her face. "If you and Angie can get the ammunition tonight, we should have everything from Tom's list, plus some."

"We're done?" Angie's voice rang with the disbelief that Lorenzo felt. How could they have already gathered so many items?

Olivia nodded. "Now it's up to you to get us a wagon."

Lorenzo rubbed a hand down his face. Of course they weren't done. The most challenging part lay ahead of them. But he would enjoy their momentary success. "By tomorrow night I'll have one. But once we get it filled, what do we do with it?"

"This was your plan, remember?" Angie said dryly, walking over to Olivia and peeking over her shoulder to see for herself that they really were done.

"So far the plan has worked rather well, wouldn't you say?" Lorenzo rolled his shoulders, trying to loosen the tension. The best thing he could do was get as far away as possible. But he had been given an assignment that wouldn't let him do that. He had to get those supplies to Tom, and killing Angie would defeat his chances of making that happen. But he couldn't let her leak any more information either. She might have even told the army where all of the supplies were being hidden. That thought gave him chills.

All three sisters were watching him, waiting for an answer. He'd be damned if he gave Angie any more information to turn against him. "I'll think of something."

Chapter Twenty-Four

"THE SOONER THIS is over with, the better," Angie muttered, rubbing at the scrapes on her stomach.

Lorenzo looked over at her and for a moment gave in to the thought of kissing each of her scrapes, of soothing away her pain. He squeezed his eyes shut. If only she was a different woman. If only she wasn't like every other woman he'd ever known.

With resolve she stepped towards the hole, turned, twisted, wiggled, and slipped through. "I'm ready," she called up to Lorenzo. Lorenzo lowered the last of the supplies to her with a rope they had wisely brought their second time, and within minutes the last of the supplies had been stacked with everything else.

Lorenzo stood at the top, looking at the rope in his hand and the thought of leaving her down there crossed his mind. He immediately dismissed it as an idea from a madman. That was what he was becoming because of her. A madman.

He gathered the rope to drop down to her when something caught his attention out of the corner of his eye. Thinking he had missed a box of ammo that Angie had been carrying, he turned.

His eyes opened in surprise, then narrowed in suspicion as he saw that it was just a white parchment paper fluttering in the cold breeze. Kneeling, he grabbed it before it could blow away already certain he knew what it was. Several lines of handwriting filled the page, but it was the most bizarre writing he had ever seen. The first line was definitely written by a woman. The clean lines and soft swirls were all feminine. But as the lines went on, the handwriting became drastically more and more masculine. And it was the same line over and over. "The Texian Army grows in number. Solidify your walls."

ANGIE BEGAN TO tap her foot impatiently. Lorenzo had been in an odd mood all night. It wouldn't surprise her if he completely forgot she was waiting for him and went back to his bedroll.

Sleep sounded magnificent at the moment, and she wouldn't blame him if that was what he had done. Even standing on top of the crate, she felt like she could fall asleep. The endless night journeys with Lorenzo were beginning to grind her down.

She covered a yawn. In the back of her mind, she wondered if she would ever feel rested again. At the same time, she wondered if all the supplies they had gotten were really going to help their cause. If the Texians never attacked, there wasn't much point to any of it.

The rope hit her on top of the head. Startled, she nearly

fell, but she grabbed the rope and wrapped her leg around it, the way Lorenzo had taught her.

Her skin still tingled where his hand had held her calf, showing her how to support her weight on the rope. Of course, it didn't seem to faze him a bit, which only added fuel to her already raging anger with him.

The rope pulled and slowly she began to move to the top. Lorenzo had certainly known how to fuel her anger. She had been foolish to ask her question that night in the first place. She didn't know what had inspired her to ask, and she regretted it. Since that moment, she had done everything she could to avoid him. Olivia had been right. He wasn't to be trusted, and she had let her emotions cloud her thinking.

She had thought—she had hoped—that he was as breathless by her touch as she was by his. She was naïve. He had been right about that. She was horribly, terribly naïve.

Her head cleared the opening and she grabbed the ledge with one hand, quickly released the rope and began shimmying her way up. Twisting at the shoulders she looked up and saw Lorenzo watching her. She suddenly wished she were back in the small room.

The look on his face terrified her. "Did a bug sting you?" She laughed nervously, wondering if she should finish climbing out or duck back inside and grab a gun.

"Too cold for bugs," he said softly.

Angie shivered, though not from the chill in the air, but from the ice in his eyes. He moved quickly, too quickly for her to drop down, but she tried. His hand wrapped around her forearm so tight she felt her bones shift.

"What is wrong with you?" She tugged on her arm but it only made him tighten his grip. "If you're trying to help me out, you're going about it the wrong way."

She was afraid, and she knew he could see it on her face. His actions were unnerving, and she didn't know what she should do, or even could do to escape him.

He held up a folded parchment between two fingers, waving it slowly in front of her face. Her eyes widened in recognition then shot back to his face.

"Where did you get that?"

"Why? Is it yours?" He smiled at her, a cold smile that wasn't meant to soothe.

"Obviously you think it is or you wouldn't be so angry."

He yanked her up and out of the hole with such a force tears came to her eyes and she heard fabric rip.

He held her up by her arms, his nose nearly touching hers. "Why did you do it?" He shook her. "Why?"

"I haven't done anything." She spoke quickly, trying to calm his temper. "I just wrote those sentences tonight while I was waiting for you. I haven't done a thing."

Lorenzo let go of her so quickly she stumbled backwards and landed hard on her rump. He was shaking his head in disgust. "Do you even know how to tell the truth?"

"I just told you—"

"I saw you today!" His voice was nearly a shout and she saw him visibly attempt to calm himself. The last thing they needed was for the army to come see what was wrong. He lowered his voice. "I saw you today."

Angie suddenly realized why he was so angry, and felt her

fear escalate. "Lorenzo, you don't understand…"

He squatted down in front of her, the parchment clenched in his fist. "You almost had me," he said, looking at his clenched fists, his eyes avoiding hers no matter how hard she tried to get his direct attention. "I almost believed you were who you said you were. A naïve woman wanting to help the revolution any way possible…"

"I am! I mean, I'm not naïve, but…"

"You lied to me," he growled. "Everything was a lie."

"No it wasn't! Now if you would just—" She tried to push herself to her feet.

"Does Olivia know what you're doing? Is she part of this, too?"

Angie shoved herself to her knees and leaned towards him, her face a scant inch away from his. "Shut. Up." Her words were hard and clipped, but they quivered slightly with a fear she couldn't hide. "You've made a lot of assumptions about me, and you have no facts to base them."

"I saw you—"

"Yes, I was at the Alamo today. Yes, I spoke to a soldier. But that doesn't—"

"You gave him one of these." He waved the paper again. "Remember?"

Angie looked at the paper, her face tight. "Yes. I gave him one of those."

"Did you decide you needed to cover all bases so that no matter who came out the victor you'd be on the right side?"

Angie was appalled that he would even suggest such a thing. But if she looked at things from his perspective…her gut clenched. "Do you want to know what that note said?" Angie demanded harshly.

"The *cocina* menu?" he suggested sweetly.

"It said the Texians have shifted west. They have laid ground for an ambush. Be aware."

"Why would you give—" Lorenzo's voice trailed off and his brow furrowed. "The camp hasn't shifted in weeks. If anything they would move east." Angie was watching him closely, her lips pressed into a thin line. "Why did you tell them that?" Lorenzo's face was full of confusion.

"Because it would confuse them, much as it has you. Because it would make them look in the wrong direction."

Lorenzo glared at the white parchment he held in his hand and then back at Angie. "Am I supposed to believe that you are deliberately misleading the Mexican Army?"

She gave him a shaky smile. "I'm doing my best."

"How can I believe you? You could be lying to me about this whole thing."

"We agreed to trust each other." Angie clung to a thin thread of hope that he would listen to her, reason with her, and by the grace of God, believe her.

"We also agreed to tell each other everything that happened. Considering that you kept this from me, I'm inclined to doubt you."

"We made our agreement after I was already involved in this." She sat back on her heels, watching him intently.

Lorenzo stood slowly, looking down at her. "I want to know everything. From the beginning."

Angie also stood, cringing at the pain from her quick exit

from the storage room. Lorenzo was looking towards town, his face tense. "When did all of this start?"

Angie rubbed her arms, wondering how to tell him everything. No matter what she said he was going to get mad. It was unavoidable. "Before I came to offer the men pastries— remember? When you had to…"

"I remember what happened," he snapped.

Angie chewed on the inside of her cheek then continued, realizing getting angry with him would only worsen the situation. "A couple of days before then, when I realized you weren't going to help me, I decided to take matters into my own hands."

Lorenzo said nothing and kept staring towards town, his back to her. "There was an officer that had lunch at the *cocina* one day. I saw the opportunity and took it."

"To sabotage the Texians? Why now?"

Anger made her tremble. "I have never sabotaged the Texians and I never will. I believe in independence and I want to fight for it along with the others."

"Then what opportunity did you take, Angie? What?" He glared at her over his shoulder, still gripping the parchment in his fist.

"To sabotage the Mexican Army," Angie said, her tone just as angry as his. She stepped forward and snatched the parchment out of his hand and he turned to face her, his expression dark. She held the paper in his face. "All of the notes I've ever given him are just like this one. All of them. There's no truth to them. If anything, we're losing the volunteers, not gaining them."

"What did you tell the officer?" His expression hadn't changed.

"I wrote a note, just a little scribble that said the army had received a line of volunteers. That's it. I caught the officer outside as he left and gave him the note. Since most men find it impossible that a woman can read, much less write, I told him one of our regular customers gave it to me and had me deliver it."

Lorenzo's eye ticked. "How many times have you done this?"

"Today was the third time. But I intend on continuing until the war is over."

Lorenzo looked at the paper she held and shook his head. "How can I trust you? How do I know you aren't lying about the whole thing?"

Angie saw that most of his anger was gone, but not all of it. He believed her, or at least wanted to. "I'm telling you the truth. The only reason I've not told you is because you would make me stop. If my little notes are helping in any way, I won't stop."

"What if they hurt?"

"How could they?" Angie waved her paper in the air again. "All they do is mislead."

"What if Cos becomes afraid that the militia is growing too strong? What if he decides to attack to stop them from getting any larger?"

Angie's face paled. "That would be a foolish tactic. I'm sure he is too afraid to attack because he thinks they are getting larger."

"You're playing a dangerous game. And either way you look at it, it's the Texians lives you're betting."

"I'm helping," she said with firm determination.

For the first time since they had started their argument, his eyes met hers, and she prayed he didn't see the hot, angry tears building in her eyes.

"I'm helping. I'll continue helping however I can." Her voice was raw.

"Who is the officer?" he demanded.

Angie wiped at her eyes with trembling fingers, turning away from him so he wouldn't see her hurt. "Zapeda. That's all I know. I don't even know what rank he is. I just ask for Officer Zapeda."

She drew a shaky breath, trying to regain her composure.

"Are the notes all that you have given him?"

⚜

IF SHE TURNED around and slapped him, he would have deserved it. But he wanted to know. He wanted to know if another man had held her, kissed her, been lost in her intoxicating scent. He had been haunted by the memories of their embrace for a week. He couldn't bear to think another man had enjoyed what was his.

"What else could I…" Angie's voice trailed off and he saw by the sudden tension in her shoulders she realized what he was implying.

Squaring her shoulders, she turned and started past him, not quite looking at him. "It's getting late. I need to get home."

He grabbed her arm as she passed, forcing her to stop. "We're not done, Angie."

She looked up at him, and he hated her for deceiving him. He hated her for making him hope again. He hated her for making him feel again. He hated himself for wanting her to care, hated himself for wanting to be with her even when she so obviously didn't want to be with him.

"I have nothing more to say to you. Obviously you already have an opinion about what kind of person I am. You believe I could sabotage people who mean so much to me, you believe I could... could..." He could see how hard she was struggling not to cry, and he wanted to pull her into his arms and soothe her.

"I saw the way he touched you."

Angie shook her head. "Then you must know everything."

"I want to know. I want to hear you tell me that you let him..."

"Let him what? Paw at me like you did? Use me like you did? No. He hasn't. He wants to—" She was shaking with the power of her emotions, and he knew he had pushed too hard. "He has asked..." Her voice betrayed her, and she swallowed hard.

Relief washed over Lorenzo, and he felt regret at the tears in her eyes. "Angie, I..."

"Why do you think the absolute worst of me? What have I done to you? What have I done—" She started yanking on her arm, trying to get away from him.

Lorenzo released her arm but only to cup her face in his hands, his thumbs brushing away her tears. He didn't know what to say to her. He didn't know the answers to her questions. She grabbed his wrists, tugging on him.

"Let go of me. Just let me go!"

"No." He spoke with such finality she looked up at him in surprise. "I won't. I won't let go." Her nails dug into his wrists, but he still held her. "How could I think anything else, Angie? If you had seen me do the things you did… if you had seen me giving notes, even just talking in confidence to an officer, what would you have thought?"

She opened her mouth but he placed his thumb on her lips, silencing her. "And if you had seen me being touched by a woman the way that man touched you, what would you have thought?"

She tried to speak and, annoyed by his thumb, bit it. It surprised him so much a quick smile crossed his lips.

"I would have given you the benefit of the doubt," Angie said, sticking out her chin.

"Would you?" he asked softly, his bitten thumb wiping away a stray tear.

She was silent for several seconds. "I would have been suspicious," she said slowly. "Very," she added at his raised eyebrow. "But I wouldn't have hung you before you got to speak."

"I didn't."

"Tell me this. What were you planning to do after you found that paper? What were you going to do?"

He didn't want to answer her. He knew what he should

have done. He knew he should have waited to confront her, waited until the time was right and they wouldn't be in jeopardy of being discovered. And then he would show her the proof he had of her treachery. And then... Then he should have killed her before she could try to convince him otherwise. But instead his emotions had taken over and he believed what she had told him and prayed to God he hadn't made a mistake.

His thoughts must have shown on his face because Angie was trying to get away from him again. "I can't believe you! You didn't even care about what really happened. Why didn't you just do it? Why don't you just go ahead and kill me if you think so little of me?" Her next question caught him completely off guard. "Is that what happened before? Did you kill someone who betrayed you?"

$$\textit{⊱}$$

HE PULLED BACK from her, releasing her so quickly she stumbled to regain her balance. "What?"

Angie shoved loose strands of hair away from her face, watching the familiar closed expression cross his face. "I know you were sent to prison for murder. I've known for a long time."

His stance had become rigid, his eyes focused on something in the distance. His silence made her more nervous than his angry accusation had earlier.

She took a step towards him then hesitated, unsure of what more to say. "What happened?"

The eyes he turned on her were cold and aloof. "I killed someone. I murdered her… I watched her die." He took a step towards her and she couldn't stop her body from instinctively moving backwards. The smile on his lips was without humor. "Isn't that what you want to hear? Every little detail?"

"Why? Why did you do it?" Damn her voice for shaking.

He took another step closer to her and she forced herself to stand still. He didn't stop until his legs brushed her, until her breasts touched his chest. His hands reached for her and she flinched. His smiled turned even colder as he gripped her arms, his gentle touch conflicting with the hard expression on his face.

"At first, I thought you were just like her. She was beautiful, same as you. And smart. And she claimed to be a Texian."

Angie's heart was pounding as his hands moved up to her forearms. "What-what made you think she wasn't?"

"She was supposed to be helping me. She was supposed to be getting information for the Texians. A lot like you." His hands were on her shoulders. "But one day, I went to meet her and she had a handful of Mexican soldiers waiting for me. They took turns whipping and beating me while she watched. They thought I was dead by the end of it."

Angie shivered, her hands reaching up to cover his. "You don't have to tell me…"

"You wanted to know what happened, didn't you? You wanted to know why."

"I didn't know—"

"But you already thought the worst of me, didn't you?" He shook his head. "I escaped. They had thrown me into prison, thinking I was good as dead. They ignored me." His eyes weren't focused on her, and she knew he was remembering what he had gone thru. "I didn't even wait until my wounds had healed before I went after her."

Tears built up in her eyes as she watched him. For once his face was unguarded, and she saw pain, guilt, and anger warring within him. "Lorenzo..."

"And still I wanted to believe her." His laugh was a harsh bark. "I wanted to believe she had been forced... I gave her a second chance." His eyes refocused on her. "Same as you."

She should have been afraid. But instead anger coursed through her veins. "I am nothing like this woman!"

His fingers caressed the pale skin of her neck. It seemed as though he hadn't heard her.

"And when I gave her another chance, she shot me." Angie's eyes dropped to his chest, remembering the wound she had seen before.

"I strangled her even as I thought I was dying." He shook his head, looking at Angie with haunted eyes. "I've had to kill before, Angie. This wasn't the first time. I've had to fight for my life, and more than once it meant the other man had to die. But this was... this was different."

"Why did you stop with me? You believed I had betrayed you... why did you give me a second chance?"

His fingers were still caressing her neck, his eyes watching her face closely. "I wasn't going to. I didn't want to. But I can't do it again." He stepped back and raked a hand through his hair. "I wanted you to show me I was wrong."

"Did I? Or are you still thinking about killing me?"

"I don't understand you, Angie. I don't understand why you do the things you do. But I want to believe you. And if you are lying to me, you better pray to God you kill me before I find out."

"I could never do that."

"Lie to me or kill me?"

Her laugh sounded like a sob. "Either. I've never lied to you Lorenzo. I never will."

She knew he would realize it as the truth. She hadn't always told him everything she was doing, but sometimes she told him more than he wanted to know. And there could be no doubt she had never lied.

"I want to trust you," he whispered.

The pain was still in his eyes and she couldn't stand seeing it anymore. She closed the distance between them and caught his face in her hands. "I will never betray you."

He only shook his head and leaned towards her. She felt like a flower reaching for the sun as she rose on her toes, a sigh escaping her as their lips met. She had craved his kiss from the moment their last heated embrace had ended.

His lips moved lightly over hers, tasting, teasing. His hands buried in her hair, dislodging the knot that held it all together. His lips moved more urgently, pressing, nibbling. When she cautiously bit his lower lip he moaned, one arm sliding down around her back to pull her closer.

She had wanted this for too long. She needed it. His lips moved over hers, urging them apart, tasting her lips with his tongue. She slid her hands against his chest, her fingers slipping through the gap in the fabric of his shirt until she touched the warmth of his skin. He sucked in a deep breath and her lips moved down his chin to his neck. The rapid pulse she found made her bold—encouraged her to continue. Her fingers came across the scar and his body tensed.

She looked up at him and his eyes were hooded, his hands tight on her hips. "I won't betray you."

His hands moved up slowly over her ribs, over the sides of her breasts. A sting of pain jolted her. She pulled back, remembering how he had yanked her from the storage room, how he had accused her of sleeping with the officer.

He shook his head, stepping away from her. "I never should have... You didn't deserve..."

Angie felt at a loss without his arms and the shock of the whole night weighed on her shoulders.

She reached up and placed her fingers on his lips, silencing him. "I—we both need some rest. Let us know when you have the wagon." She gave him a weak smile. "Good night, Lorenzo." She was thankful when he didn't try to stop her, thankful that no one would see her tears.

Chapter Twenty-Five

"DO WE JUST sit here, twiddling our thumbs, waiting to hear from him?"

Angie rubbed the shirt up and down the washboard, singing a song in her head to tune out Olivia.

"He should have told you last night what the plan was. How can he expect us to be prepared?"

Down, up, swirl around... Angie practiced a dance in her mind, matching the rhythm of her scrubbing to the rhythm she tapped with her toe. Olivia finished pinning the sheet to the line and grabbed a wet garment from the stack Angie had washed.

"For all we know, he could take everything to Tom himself and we'd never know."

Angie let the towel fall into the water. "And wouldn't that be just great?" Angie demanded, sitting up and trying to work the knots out of her back. "How many times are you going to have this conversation with yourself? One moment you're saying he has no way to pull this off on his own, the next you're complaining because you think that is exactly what he's done."

"There are just several possibilities..."

"And none of them have him leaving the supplies in that room to rot. Serena and I got everything we had left over there this morning. It's all there. If he can get someone small enough to do it all, then more power to him. If not, we'll see him soon enough. One way or another, the supplies are getting to Tom."

"You seem very confident in him."

Angie returned to her wash. "He's devoted to the Texians, Vi. He would do anything to help them." *Including kill me.*

Olivia watched her silently for a few moments, then returned to the laundry. "I still think he should have—"

"Yeah, already!" Angie threw up her hands. "That's enough! We're going to know something—"

The sound of gunfire exploded in the air, making both sisters jump and turn towards each other. Three shots. Angie grabbed Olivia's hand and they stood silent, breathless. Another series of shots erupted, this time so many they couldn't count.

"Dear God, it's begun," Olivia whispered. "Quickly, go find Grandpa. I'll get everyone else downstairs."

Angie took off around the side of the house, her heart pounding. It had begun. How? How already? They hadn't gotten the supplies to Tom yet. A chill shivered down her back. What if Cos was attacking because of her notes?

She hurried down the road, knowing her grandfather was playing cards with his friends several blocks away. The gunshots filled the air, making her blood pop with each loud crack. Townspeople raced past her, doors slammed shut on each side of the road, children scurried towards their frantic mothers.

She nearly collided with her grandfather as she dodged around a wailing child. "Anjelica!" He caught her by her shoulders. "What are you doing?"

"I came to find you. The gunshots—"

"I know, I know. Let's go—quickly now."

She couldn't remember ever seeing her grandpa move so fast. In no time, they were going down the stairs into the basement. Grandpa went to Grandma instantly, pulled her in his arms, and held her gently.

Olivia grabbed Angie's hand and squeezed it reassuringly. "We'll be alright," she said softly. Angie nodded and gave a shaky smile as the gunfire continued. But she wasn't reassured. She knew, somehow she knew, Lorenzo was in the heart of the battle, not able to fight for his side.

THE SILENCE WAS more frightening than the gunfire had been. Smoke clung to the air and stung the lungs. Angie and Olivia stood silently on the front porch, looking towards the large field where the battle had been. Slowly Mexican soldiers walked back, their clothes dirty, their faces long and weary.

"I suppose we didn't win," Olivia said softly.

Angie saw two men carrying a man that was either dead or about to be. "I'm not too sure we lost, either." She searched each face that passed, praying to see Lorenzo, praying that he was alright.

"He's fine, I'm sure," Olivia said softly.

Angie shrugged. "I'm just worried for Tom's supplies."

Olivia made a scoffing sound and turned towards the door. "I don't think we need to be afraid right now. I think whatever fight there was is over."

"For now," Angie replied.

The door closed behind Olivia and Angie leaned against the porch post, her eyes still searching faces.

"Are you looking for someone, *senorita*?"

Angie turned quickly and her heart leapt into her throat when she saw him. She stepped off the porch and walked to him quickly, wanting to touch him, wanting to feel that he was real, wanting to know he was alive. She pulled herself up short before reaching him, uncertain how she should really act towards him. She clenched her hands in her skirt to stop herself from touching him.

"Are you all right?" Her voice was thick.

He gave her a weary half-smile. "Why, *senorita*, I just might think you were worried about me."

A couple of soldiers walked past, smirking at them. "Fight all day and still feel like going at it huh, *hombre*?" One laughed.

Lorenzo never took his eyes off her.

"I have been a bit concerned, yes," Angie said stiffly. "If we lose you, we have no way of getting the supplies to Tom."

Lorenzo pushed his cap back on his head. "That sounds more likely."

His movement revealed a jagged cut on the side of his

head. "You are hurt!" Angie gasped, stepping forward quickly, her fingers searching the wound, trying to see how bad it was.

"It's only a scratch," Lorenzo muttered, though he didn't object when she pulled his hat off and her fingers searched his scalp for any more scrapes.

"It's not very deep," she observed, realizing it looked worse because of all the dried blood. Her hands moved to his chest. "Where else are you hurt?"

Lorenzo caught her hands in his and her eyes rose to his face. "I would love nothing more than having you soothe away every ache and bruise I have." His eyes were dark and she recognized the flame in them.

"I-I..."

"You don't know what you do to me, Angie, and that makes you dangerous." He leaned forward and she could feel him breathing in her scent, and she was the one who became lightheaded. "We won today," he whispered in her ear.

"We as in the Mexicans or we as in..."

"The Texians. They were amazing."

Angie smiled up at him. "So, we're alright?"

"I don't know how many died. But I know most that fell today wore red jackets."

Her fingers plucked at the red jacket he wore. It could have been him. "Was it my fault?" she asked, her eyes searching his face. "Did my notes cause this?"

He smiled and shook his head, pushing her hair away from her face. "No. Don't even think that." He leaned in and she pulled back.

"Are you doing this for their benefit?" She nodded towards the soldiers passing them, watching them.

He didn't look at them. His eyes remained locked on her lips. "No. I'm doing this for me."

Chapter Twenty-Six

ANGIE FINISHED BUTTONING her father's shirt and bent to tug on her boots.

"Why isn't he coming here first?" Olivia leaned against the doorjamb, her arms folded across her chest.

Angie didn't look up. She had waited until only minutes earlier to tell Olivia she was leaving. Lorenzo's kiss the night before had been short, but so tender she had nearly pulled him back for more. The crude suggestions coming from the men as they walked by didn't even make her blush. She was paying too much attention to Lorenzo.

He gave her a wary smile and brushed his thumb over her tingling lips. "Meet me tomorrow night?"

She didn't hesitate. "Where?"

"The old house." His smile deepened at her nod and he leaned forward once again, the quick kiss doing nothing but tease her more. And then he was gone, leaving her counting the minutes till the next night.

Now she finished lacing her shoes as her stomach did tiny flips and Olivia asked a thousand questions.

"Did you hear me? Why isn't he coming here first? He always—"

"I didn't ask him." Angie sighed.

Olivia cocked her head to the side. "Why didn't you tell me this last night?"

Angie grabbed her thick jacket and started to walk past Olivia. "Because I didn't want to endure a whole day of your questions."

Olivia blocked her path. "We don't even know what the plan is."

"If he's figured something out, he'll let me know to-night." Olivia frowned, but nodded. "You still don't trust him, do you?" Angie's question deepened Olivia's frown.

"No. And if you do, you're a fool." Angie didn't respond and Olivia finally stepped out of her way.

It didn't take long for Angie to make it to the old, ruined house, and her heart was racing every step of the way. Had Lorenzo thought of a way to sneak all the supplies to the Texians? Or did he have another reason for asking her to meet him? That thought had her in turmoil more than anything else. Because she didn't know if she could tell him no.

The rational part of her mind said the only reason she wanted to hold him and be held was because she was so happy he was alive. The emotional part of her replied back that the reason she was so happy was because she loved him.

She stumbled on a rock and barely caught herself. It was not possible that she loved him. It was a completely foolish notion. They were in an odd situation caused by the odd events surrounding them. Of course she would gravitate towards him for comfort, but it was only because of the unusual circumstances. The rational part of her brain had taken over once again and she felt more confident with each step.

The cold wind whipping around her made it difficult to hear anything, forcing her to be even more cautious as she approached the house. She didn't see any movement and she supposed Lorenzo hadn't arrived yet.

Shivering, she climbed over the collapsed wall and moved towards the two remaining walls, hoping to get shelter from the wind.

"Angie..." He spoke softly so as not to startle her and moved slowly out of the shadows.

The pale moonlight shone down on him and, as soon as Angie saw him, her rational mind went numb. Weariness was etched in every line of his face, and the small jagged cut on his forehead looked black against his tan skin. But his smile was real and it was all for her.

She desperately wanted him to kiss her. The thoughts racing through her mind must have shown on her face, for she was instantly in his arms and she couldn't remember who had reached for whom.

His mouth came down on hers with an urgency she matched. She rose on her toes, her arms wrapping around his neck, cursing her gloves that prevented her from touching him. With a groan he pulled his mouth from hers and pressed his lips to her forehead.

"Angie," he breathed, kissing her temple, her jaw, her neck. "We can't... we can't do this..." With visible effort he pushed himself away from her. "There's too much to do tonight. I want…" He raked a hand through his hair. "God, if I told you what I want you would run home and never look back."

Angie wasn't so sure. The thoughts running through her mind were far from pure. Why did she lose all reason when she came close to this man? "No, no, you're right. I shouldn't have…"

His lips cut off her words and she couldn't make him stop. She couldn't make herself stop.

"Don't say that," he murmured against her lips. "Don't say you shouldn't." His lips brushed lightly over hers again. "This is too damned good to be wrong."

Angie felt the same way. Which scared the hell out of her. He stepped away and she was relieved. When he was close she couldn't think.

He caught her shoulders and turned her, pointing towards a shed that was probably used by the owner of the house for a mule. Now it looked like it wasn't fit to hold a bale of hay.

Angie blinked, trying to see whatever it was Lorenzo wanted her to see. Finally, the dim lines of an object came into focus.

She whirled to face him. "You got a wagon? How! Without anyone seeing you taking it?"

He grinned. "I have a few tricks up my sleeves. I got one of the farmers to help me. He butchered one of his hogs and left the meat in the sun for a couple of days. Then he lined the wagon with it. We loaded up one of the soldiers that died in the battle yesterday—just in case anyone peeked—and I just walked into town. Not a soul bothered me."

"That's incredible," Angie whispered.

"I'm going to get a mule again tomorrow and we'll do the same thing."

"How? How are we going to take it out of town?"

"You're going to get really good at lying."

Angie's eyebrows shot up. "Excuse me?"

He pulled her back towards the walls, getting them both out of the wind. "One of your cousins died on that field yesterday."

Angie blanched then shook her head. "That's not possible. None of my—"

"Those soldiers don't know that."

Angie's eyes widened as she realized what he was saying. "So I want to give my cousin a proper burial—"

"And put him in the community cemetery outside of town."

"Of course I'll need an escort—"

"Not me. Too many people know our relationship."

Angie's face dropped. "Then who…"

"Your aging uncle, father of your deceased cousin."

Angie looked at him and shook her head. "If this works, it will be a miracle. And if it doesn't, at least we'll die laughing."

A corner of Lorenzo's mouth twitched. "I've sent word to Tom that we're burying the supplies in the cemetery. Best hiding place they'll ever have."

"So I suppose I'll be spending most of tonight down below."

Lorenzo nodded. Angie drew a deep breath and tried to put on a bright smile. "Then let's get to it."

ANGIE'S JACKET WAS tossed over a stack of bagged potatoes and she was fanning herself with her hand. With narrowed eyes she watched the dust streaming down from the ceiling. Every time Lorenzo took a batch of supplies to the wagon he walked across the storage room. And every time he did, wood creaked and dust and dirt fell.

Angie wiped at the sweat on her forehead. She would be glad when she finally climbed out of the room for the last time. With resolve she turned back to the task at hand. Though they had made a big dent in the supplies, there were still several stacks left.

Using a flat piece of wood they had tied the rope to, Angie loaded blankets and bagged vegetables till the stack was a foot tall. She secured it with another rope then tugged on the main one to let Lorenzo know it was ready. Slowly it drifted upwards.

Angie didn't envy Lorenzo's job. Not only was he contending with the terribly cold wind and carrying so many bulky things, he had to look at a dead man every time he put things in the wagon. She had wanted to bring the wagon closer so he wouldn't have as much work, but they couldn't risk making so much noise. With the wind blowing as it was, sound would travel far, and they couldn't take such a chance.

The wood lowered down empty and she bent to her task,

cringing as the beams to her side groaned loudly. *Just a few more loads and we'll be done.* She had the thought over and over. *Just a few more loads.*

⚔

LORENZO WIPED AT the sweat on his forehead, cursing the weather that had him shivering the moment he stood still. The wagon was halfway full. He was arranging everything to be as flat as possible so it would be believable it was just a body under the tarp, but it was getting harder. And he knew it was impossible for them to make two trips.

He stepped over the crumbling wall and his footing slipped. He righted himself quickly, but the ground shifted slightly under him. A cold sweat broke out down his back. He rushed back to the hole, skidding to his knees in front of it and leaning as far in as he could.

Angie was working diligently on stacking another load for him, her back turned to the dirt falling from the ceiling. "Angie, you're going to need to get out."

Angie didn't look up at him, but waved a hand in his direction. "I'm alright. The air isn't that bad down here. I'll be fine until we're done."

"No, you need to get out now."

Angie hesitated loading a bag of onions and looked up at him. She blinked in surprise at seeing him leaning so far inwards. "I'm fine, really."

Lorenzo pointed behind her at the dust that still clung to the air. She looked over her shoulder and shrugged. "It's been doing that for a while. Maybe you shouldn't jump around so much up there."

She gave him a smile that would have caused him to fall through the hole if his shoulders hadn't stopped him. He couldn't remember the last time she had smiled at him like that. The first time he had ever taken her walking, he supposed. When things had been simpler.

As he had stood out on the battlefield recently, firing randomly in an effort to miss hitting a Texian, and dodging any fire that could hit him, all he could think about was Angie. She was chipping away at the wall he had built against all women, and he could feel himself needing her, wanting her. He had never thought it possible to feel this way towards a woman again.

Covered in dust and sweat she was more appealing to him than ever. And his mind screamed to run away from her as fast as he could, but his heart thundered with the desire to hold her tight. "It's not safe, Angie. You need to get out."

"As soon as we get everything. Not until then."

"Damn it, Angie, if you don't grab that rope right now I'll—"

"You'll what? Come down here and make me?" She placed the onions on the stack then gave the rope a tug, shaking her head at him. "I'd like to see you try."

Lorenzo's eye ticked. "It's not worth—"

"It only shakes like that when you walk over the room. If you're really concerned, walk a different way."

With a curse, Lorenzo pulled himself back up and the recently loaded wood began to creep upwards. He moved as fast as he could, his heart racing along with him. He knew the roof could collapse on her at any second. And he couldn't bear to think about what that could mean for Angie.

Lorenzo came and went quickly with the stack, but while he was gone a clump of dirt fell on her head and she winced, looking warily at the ceiling. The plank dropped down quickly and Lorenzo's head appeared. He eyed the ceiling and shook his head, then frowned darkly at the dirt he saw in her hair. "It's time to get out. Now."

A beam creaked.

"This is the last load. They'll need this." Another clump of dirt hit her head.

"Angie, get over here, now."

Angie glanced up at him. "Just one more—" The stack completed, she backed away.

"Grab the rope, Angie."

"You can't lift me too."

"Damn it, Angie—"

A supporting beam cracked and bent. Lorenzo yanked the plank up quickly, nearly tipping the supplies off. He was frantically untying the rope when the ground shifted beneath him.

"Angie!" he yelled, moving to the side, trying to see her. The ground gave way.

With the final angry groan of the beams, his floor and Angie's ceiling collapsed. He barely grabbed a secure hand-hold before the spot where he had been sitting vanished beneath him. The silence that surrounded him in the wake of the crashing collapse was worse than the noise.

Dust plumed in the air, but he wasn't worried about anyone coming to find them. There was more on his mind. He couldn't see Angie.

Scrambling down the rocks, dirt, and broken wood, Lorenzo entered the store room for the first time. The collapse had snuffed out the small light Angie had, making it even more difficult to see anything.

"Angie," he called softly, though he wanted to yell for her at the top of his voice.

What if she was pinned beneath all of the debris and he couldn't see her? The thought terrified him. His eyes probed the corners, hoping that somehow she had escaped a majority of the debris. She was not to be found.

He turned back to the rubble, frantically searching. Dropping to his hand and knees he began to dig, his heart racing, refusing to think of what he might find. A small sound to his left drew his attention and he turned quickly to the shadowed corner, afraid to hope.

The dust made it nearly impossible to see, but he took it as his best chance. Feeling his way in the darkness he felt something soft. "Angie!" Her hand twitched in his. A broken beam blocked him from getting to her.

Cursing more fluidly then he ever had, he shoved on the wood, pushing it out of the way with a grunt. Moonlight pushed through the dust and he could finally see her.

"Angie, Angie." He pulled her to him, suddenly realizing her legs were beneath all the dirt. "Talk to me, *chula*." His fingers searched her face, trying to find any cuts. "Say something." His hands ran along her ribs, her back.

"You're crushing me," she moaned.

Relief rushed through him in such a wave that laughter bubbled up inside him.

"I see nothing funny about this. Would you please get off of me?"

"It's the ceiling that's crushing you, remember? The one that I warned you was going to fall?"

She groaned and tried to move, discovering for herself how thoroughly pinned she was. "So what are you going to do about it?" she asked wryly.

He smoothed her hair out of her face, unable to believe that she had escaped injury. He felt along her side to her waist and over her hips. She held her breath, watching him with wide eyes.

"I'm tempted to leave you in this position."

The seductive smile she gave him was one he had never seen before. "It limits your… access."

Lorenzo's eyes darkened dangerously. "Maybe you should get knocked on the head more often."

She tried to frown at him. "Don't even think about it."

The dirt was piled up around her hips and covered her the rest of the way down. He began to scoop the debris away from her legs before her fingers suddenly wrapped around his wrist, her nails digging into his skin. He glanced at her in surprise, but her eyes were fixed above them.

Lorenzo turned quickly and his blood ran cold. A Mexican soldier stood above them, his eyes searching the rubble until he spotted them. He began slipping down towards them, and Angie's hand tightened on Lorenzo's wrist.

He glanced at her sideways. "It's alright. Don't worry. It will be alright."

He continued trying to pull her free as the soldier approached, completely ignoring him. A couple of tugs and she was free of the dirt and staggering to her feet beside him just as the soldier came to a skidding stop in front of them.

"What happened here?" he demanded in clipped Spanish.

"The ceiling of the room caved while we were finishing," Lorenzo answered.

"Did you get everything out?"

"One thing was left," Lorenzo nodded his head towards Angie, a half-grin on his face. "But I was able to dig her out."

"You're lucky I was on patrol. I told Jaime I would come look."

Lorenzo glanced back at Angie. She was pale and shaking. "Angie, this is Mando. He's one of the soldiers I told you about."

"You mean he—you—he's on our side?"

Mando answered, "I'm all for the revolution, if that's what you mean. Are you alright?"

Angie didn't answer. She had passed out cold in Lorenzo's arms.

Chapter Twenty-Seven

A NGIE CAME TO in a rush, her heart racing, trying to push herself to her feet.

"Slow down, slow down." Lorenzo caught her flailing arms and pulled her against his chest.

She looked at him with wide eyes. "What happened?"

He smiled reassuringly at her and tucked one of her curls behind her ear. "You fainted, *chula*."

"What? That's ridiculous. I've never fainted in my life." She glanced around and realized they sat in the store room that was nearly full of dirt and rocks and she suddenly realized she was in his lap. Her cheeks reddened as she looked at him. "Where did your friend go?"

"He had to get back to the post and report what he found before they sent someone else out here."

"Do you trust him?"

"You should know me well enough by now to know that I don't trust anyone."

"Oh." She began to push away from him. "Then I suppose we're finished here tonight."

He caught her chin and turned her face towards his. "Not yet," he said softly.

His mouth slanted over hers and her body melted into his. Her arm slid around his neck and her fingers sifted through his hair slowly. She sighed against his lips and turned more fully into his embrace.

He moaned and his arms moved around her, rubbing her back, pressing her closer. His hands shifted restlessly from her neck, to her shoulders, to her waist. Her breath caught as his hands moved lower and cupped her bottom.

"Have I told you," he murmured, trailing kisses down her neck, "how much I hate these damn pants?"

Angie struggled to concentrate on what he was saying as he nibbled lightly on her collarbone. "I do recall... you mentioning something... along those lines." She bit her lower lip as his fingers flexed on their new hold.

"I'm considering changing my mind."

Angie's hands tightened in his hair as he lifted her, turned her, and positioned her legs around him. Straddling him, she watched him with a combination of passion and unease. She had no idea what she was supposed to do next or even if what she was already doing was right.

Lorenzo ran a hand through her hair, tugging her towards him. "You are beautiful. You could make a man go crazy."

She raised her eyebrows, her fingers slowly exploring his face. "Sweet nonsense from you. I never would have thought it." Her fingertips traced his eyebrows, the line of his nose, and felt his smile rather than saw it.

"I wouldn't call it sweet nonsense. It's the truth. They'll carve on my gravestone—Beautiful woman drove him mad."

Her fingers explored his cheekbones. He seemed perfectly content allowing her exploration as he rubbed circles on her back. Then she leaned forward and pressed her lips firmly to his.

HE ENDURED HER sweet, innocent assault for as long as he could. Then he took over, changing her chaste kiss into the more thorough taste he craved. His tongue traced her lower lip and, when she gently bit him, he nearly lost all control.

Tilting his head, he took her mouth more fully, his tongue sweeping inside. She gasped in surprise, her hands tightening in his hair. When her tongue cautiously rubbed against his he was certain he heard whistles.

His hands ran along her sides, down her waist, over her hips, and cupped her rump, pulling her against the hard evidence of his desire. Straddling him as she was, wearing those obnoxious slacks, he could feel her heat, feel her softness pressed against him.

Lorenzo's hands moved up to her waist and tugged on the shirt, pulling it free from her pants. A sigh escaped her as his hands reached beneath and brushed over her camisole, the warmth of his skin seeping through to her skin.

SHE COULDN'T SEEM to get enough of him. She needed... something. She tugged on Lorenzo's hair and wiggled in his lap, trying to get even closer.

He pulled free of the kiss, but before she could get the breath to protest, his mouth was on her neck, kissing, nibbling. She let her head fall back, giving him better access and vaguely heard his murmured sound of appreciation. There was a tug on her arm and then his lips were on her shoulder... her bare shoulder. Slowly, as though her head weighed hundreds of pounds, she looked down at his dark head. Her shirt was opened halfway, her camisole nearly completely unlaced, and, barely, the tips of her breasts were kept from the moonlight.

A quivering settled low in her stomach as she watched his tan fingers move over her skin, lightly caressing her other shoulder, her collarbone. Slowly his hand moved down and she watched in desperate fascination as his fingers skimmed her full breast. She bit down on her lower lip when his finger brushed her nipple, but she couldn't contain the small whimper of pleasure.

His eyes lifted to hers and he leaned back, his eyes dark as he watched her. His fingers flicked over her nipple again.

"Lorenzo," she gasped, closing her eyes and arching her back, pushing her breast into his hand.

His hands were gone quickly and she wanted to cry at the loss. But then they were back, at her waist, lifting her till her breast swayed before his face.

Using his teeth, he gently pulled away what was left of her camisole and looked at her in the moonlight. Angie gasped when she felt the warmth of his mouth touch her skin and she dropped her head forward, pressing kisses into his dark hair. Her hair fell forwards, creating a dark curtain around them and they were surrounded by her scent, by her warmth, by her silky skin.

He kissed the side of her breast, moving towards her pouting nipple slowly, teasing her. Her fingers tugged on his hair restlessly, asking him for something, not knowing what it was. When he took her nipple into his mouth, she shuddered, her fingers clenching tightly in his hair.

He pulled back, looking up into her face. The desire in her eyes was reflected in his. He touched the side of her face gently and she turned, kissing his palm, doing nothing to calm the burning flame.

"Angie, you don't know what you do to me."

She smiled against his palm. "If it's anything like what you do to me, we're both in a lot of trouble."

He gave her a very masculine smile as he let her slowly slide down him, and he watched her eyes widen as she realized just how strong an effect she had on him. Her eyes slid shut and she shivered, moving against him instinctively.

"Oh, God," she moaned, balancing herself by placing her hands on his chest.

Lorenzo suddenly wrapped his arms around her and held her close to him, his breathing ragged. Angie touched his face and he opened his eyes, giving her a half smile. "If we don't stop, I'm going to take you right here and to hell if anyone walks by. And that's not what either one of us wants."

To know that he had as little control as she did at the moment sent an odd thrill through her. A part of her wanted to push him to the point where he lost all control. But at the same time she had completely lost control of herself and straddled him with her shirt opened to her waist.

His hands moved up over her back and around her shoulders, caressing her bare skin. His grin turned into a scowl. "Your skin is like ice."

"Is that what you say to all the women you try to seduce?" she asked wryly, absently playing with the buttons on his shirt.

His grin returned. "I thought you were the one trying to seduce me."

She looked down at her bared skin and a blush stole over her cheeks. "From current appearances, you'd probably be right." Angie began to tug on her camisole, but Lorenzo's hands stopped her.

Watching her, his hands lifted her breasts, weighing them, measuring them with the span of his fingers.

Her breath caught in her throat. "I-I thought you said—" She couldn't remember what she was going to say.

With a heavy sigh, Lorenzo released her and pulled her camisole over her breasts. "You are far too much of a temptation, *chula*."

Her fingers replaced his and quickly laced and buttoned herself back into order. At least on the outside. On the inside, she was a chaotic disaster.

"I-I suppose…" She cleared her throat, smoothing her hair out of her face, trying awkwardly to move off his lap. "I suppose I'll see you tomorrow. When do you—"

He caught her hand and helped her stand with him.

"Nothing has changed, Angie. Nothing. Don't start getting fidgety and nervous around me. It won't help us."

Angie looked at him and wondered for a moment if he had lost his mind. Nothing had changed? She had just come close to being as intimate with him as any woman ever is with a man and nothing had changed?

"You're going to freeze to death. Where is your coat?"

Angie vaguely realized she was shivering. She glanced to the corner where she had tossed her coat and only saw piles of dirt. "It's gone. Funny"—she shook her head at herself—"I hadn't realized I was cold."

He pulled his jacket off and wrapped it around her shoulders. "You did a great job warming me up, too."

Angie returned her gaze to his face and called herself ten thousand times a fool. "That's all this was to you, wasn't it? Just a little bit of fun while you could." She laughed at herself, a sad, bitter laugh. "It's like you told me before, you haven't had a woman in a long time and I was available. And like the naïve nitwit you've pointed me out to be, I was actually willing. Willing! Hah, I nearly attacked you." She shrugged off his jacket and handed it back to him. "I'm sorry. I got carried away and nearly caused something to happen we would both regret."

He caught her arm as she tried to turn from him, his face a dark mask. "I will not let you cheapen what we just had. I wanted to hold you, I wanted to feel you. You. Not any woman available, Angie. I want you. And I think you wanted me, too. I know I sure as hell enjoyed what we had and don't regret a single moment of it!" He leaned in towards her.

"And, if I can, I'm going to do that as often as I can while I'm with you. Once you realize you want it too, we'll both be happy."

He released her quickly and began to climb out of the storage room, pausing occasionally to help a speechless Angie climb up as well. "Tomorrow, be here as soon as you've served the last customer," he said when they'd reached the top, not quite looking at her. Then he turned and looked at her, his eyes conveying that his next words held more than one meaning. "I'll be waiting."

⚜

THE CHILL THAT had settled over the town made most everyone stay indoors. As sleet began to fall, the *cocina* became silent. While the rest of the family sat around the fire in the back room, Angie rifled through the supplies in the kitchen. She didn't want to do what she was about to, but she had to.

Finally, she pulled out a jar of freshly ground peppers that Grandpa used when he was making the *picante*. Usually it was so hot it numbed her tongue. She opened the jar quickly, hoping to get it over with before she changed her mind.

The dust rising from the powder made her cough, but determinedly she stuck her hand inside, made sure some of the residual powder was on her fingers, and brought her hand to her eyes.

"What in the name of God are you doing?"

Angie heard Olivia, but she couldn't see her. The moment the powder had touched her eyes she had wanted to scream. She had known it would hurt. She just wasn't expecting the agonizing burn that consumed her whole face.

"I'm supposed to be grieving, remember?" Her nose started to run.

She pressed her clean hand to her eyes, wiping at the tears that kept overflowing.

Olivia took the jar out of her hand and gave her a towel. "Well, that's certainly one way of doing it. You'll be lucky if you haven't blinded yourself."

Angie pressed the towel into her face and sighed heavily. "If we end up losing after all this…" She chuckled softly, speaking into the cloth. "Well, at least we'll have stories to tell."

"It will be a long, long time before we can tell any stories."

Slowly, the pain was easing up and Angie pulled the towel away. Through blurred eyes she saw Olivia's frown.

"Well, I hate to admit it, but you look like you've been crying for days." She shook her head. "Lorenzo probably won't be interested in pawing you today, looking like that."

"What are you implying?" Angie straightened, gripping her towel tightly.

"Oh, stop pretending to be so innocent, Angie. I've seen the way he looks at you. I see the way you look at him. You two have been intimate—it's as plain as the nose on my face. If this is the route you choose to take, fine." She started to turn then looked back at Angie. "I will give you one piece of advice, and you can take it for whatever you want. Don't pin your hopes on him. Don't give him all you have thinking he'll reciprocate in kind. I can promise you, as soon as this battle is over, he'll be gone. He won't even stay to watch the smoke clear." Olivia tried to give her a smile. "With that said, please be careful today. This is a crazy idea, but it just might work."

Angie said nothing, only pressed the towel back to her stunned face.

Chapter Twenty-Eight

"WHAT DID YOU do to your face?"

"Me? Look at you! I can barely tell it's really you."

Lorenzo wiggled his bushy gray eyebrows. "And who do you think I am? I'm an old man following a pretty little lady around. Maybe she'll put a little pep in my step."

Angie took a step away from him, wagging a finger at him. "You're my elderly uncle who's trying to protect me." She couldn't believe his transformation. She didn't know how he had done it, but the hair that peeped out from under his tattered farmer's hat was salt and pepper gray, and something had been smeared on his face, making him look wrinkled and... old.

"How did you do that?"

His wrinkles shifted in a smile. "Secrets of the trade, madam."

She quirked an eyebrow. "So you played dress-up when you were stealing?"

"It made it more fun. So, why is your face so red?"

Angie accepted the change in topic. She had come to the realization that his past was too painful for him to talk about. She still had so many questions, but knew what little he had told her would need to appease her curiosity—for now. "I'm grieving the loss of my cousin, remember?"

Together, they turned away from the small shelter they had in the dilapidated house and headed towards the shed where a mule waited impatiently, ears pinned to his neck to avoid the annoying sleet.

"How did you get him over here without being seen?" Angie couldn't help looking at him, staring at him, trying to convince herself that the "old man" walking beside her was truly Lorenzo.

He glanced sideways at her and pulled the collar of his coat up around his ears. "You know, we might not be very convincing if you keep staring at me."

Angie jerked her eyes away quickly. "Sorry. It's just so— Good Lord!" Angie stopped and placed a hand over her nose and mouth, trying not to gag. Lorenzo calmly handed her a kerchief scented with a strong herb she couldn't quite distinguish. She pressed it to her face and was relieved when it cut the odor.

"I was afraid it would be bad," Lorenzo sighed, tying his own kerchief around his face. "The good thing is it will certainly keep any nosy soldier away."

Lorenzo made short work of connecting the wagon to the mule and in no time Angie was being hoisted up onto the wagon seat. When his hand patted her bottom before she sat down, she had no doubt it was Lorenzo in the old man she saw.

He settled in next to her, his leg pressing intimately along hers, his arm brushing hers with every move he made.

She tried to scoot away, but she was already pressed against the rail. The man certainly took up a lot of space.

As soon as they were moving, the odor dissipated some as the sleet and wind diluted it. For several minutes they rode in silence, Angie tense with worry about what was ahead, and Lorenzo seemed to be lost in thought.

Angie's hands twisted in her skirts. "So what happens once this is over?" She asked the question that had been on her mind ever since they had stored enough supplies. Their mission was almost at an end. Would she ever see him again?

Lorenzo pulled the collar of his coat more tightly around his ears. His disguise was starting to get messy. "We return the mule and the wagon."

Angie gnawed on her lower lip. "I know that. I'm talking about once we've finished this… this assignment Tom gave us."

For several moments it seemed as if he wasn't going to answer her. He glanced over his shoulder, watching a small group of soldiers lounging against one of the stores. As the wagon rolled past they turned up their noses and gagged at the unpleasant scent. She watched the smile that made some of his mask crack.

Eventually, he turned back to Angie's question. "I can't plan any more than what we're doing right now. Why are you worried? You know that if Tom needs anything further from you, he'll tell you."

Angie's fingers were going to worry a hole through her skirt. Forcing herself to relax, she adjusted the shawl around her face to keep out the sleet. After many long moments,

"And where will you be?"

He cast her a sideways glance, his lips twitching. His fake wrinkles seemed to smile, too. "Are you asking me to stay?"

"I'm asking where you will be. If something happens and Olivia or I need your help…"

His smile faded slowly. "I'll be leaving soon. It's not safe for me at the mission anymore. Too many suspicions."

Angie tensed. "You think someone—"

"No," he interrupted. "No, but questions are being asked. I can't take any chances."

Angie looked down at her hands in her lap, casually smoothing wrinkles out of her skirt. Questions swirled in her mind. Questions she couldn't ask. When was he leaving? How much time did she have left with him? After it was all over would he return to her? After it was all over, one or both of them might be dead.

She shivered uncontrollably. He was right. There was no reason to look too far ahead. They just needed to get through this situation at hand and then plan.

And the situation at hand was the cluster of soldiers ahead of them, blocking their path to continue. Angie's heart thudded so hard she was afraid it would beat out of her chest. Her palms began to sweat and she rubbed them nervously on her skirt.

Lorenzo turned towards her and the look in his eyes was one she had never seen before. Beneath all the makeup, he looked upset, and slightly afraid. That didn't help calm Angie's nerves at all.

"You need to speak to them."

Angie wiped at the sleet on her face. "What? Are you out of your mind? Shouldn't…"

"Trust me. If you've never trusted me before, now would be a good time to start."

"I don't understand. You're supposed to be…"

"A grieving father." He finished her sentence for her. "Remember, it's supposed to be my son in there." He glanced back at the soldiers. They would reach them in moments. "You can do this, Angie. You must."

Angie searched his eyes for several moments and saw there was no chance for compromise. Turning from him, she did her best to still her trembling. As the wagon slowly rolled to a stop, several feet from the soldiers, she began to step down. Lorenzo was hunched over in the seat, his head bowed, looking for all the world like a grieving, old man.

The soldiers watched Angie slip through the mud towards them, none of them making any effort to come her way. She despised all of them. And yet their chances of success depended on her being nice to them. She was within a couple of feet of them when one of the soldiers acknowledged her.

"No one leaves town."

Not one for pleasantries. She stopped, trying to put a grieved expression on her face. "Please, *senor*, I need to…"

An older man stepped away from the cluster, bringing himself within inches of her, a hint of a smile on his lips. He was a distinguished looking man, his skin bronzed, his black mustache lightly flecked with gray. Under different circumstances they would probably be friends. But as it was, he was her enemy, and she wanted to end her time with him as quickly as possible.

"What is it that you need, *senorita*?"

Angie gave him a wavering smile. "My cousin... he... well, he..." Her smile faltered and she wiped at a nonexistent tear. "He was killed in the battle."

The soldier gave her a sympathetic look and caught one of her hands in his, his thumb rubbing over her knuckles.

Angie wanted to jerk her hand away and slap him. "My uncle and I want to bury him in the old cemetery."

He raised his eyebrows. "I thought the only cemetery was the one next to the church."

Angie shook her head. "There is an old family plot across the river. My mother's side of the family is buried there. It is her nephew we wish to bury."

His thumb continued rubbing her knuckles, but he was looking past her towards the wagon. "And the old man?"

Angie sniffled and turned to glance behind her, hoping Lorenzo had overcome whatever it was that had caused him to withdraw and that he was coming to help her. He still sat in the wagon, his head hanging low. "That is my uncle," she said, wondering if the man had listened to anything she had said so far. "His son..."

"Yes, I see. Perhaps you won't mind if I take a look?" He was walking towards the wagon as he spoke, his attention no longer on her. "I might have known the poor man."

"Yes, yes, of course," Angie stammered, following behind him quickly.

"What was his name?"

Angie's mind froze. If the soldier had actually known the dead man and recognized him, all would be lost. "Gerardo," she said quickly, realizing her long pause could be just as damaging.

Lorenzo didn't look up as they approached, didn't even seem to be awake. "How are you going to bury your cousin with that old man helping you? He's practically got one foot in the grave himself."

"My uncle is much sprier than you would think." Angie gave him half a smile.

As they got closer, the stench floated to them faintly on the breeze.

The soldier wrinkled his nose, but didn't hesitate as he reached in and pulled back the tarp. "Good Lord," he turned and walked several paces away, trying to find fresh air.

Angie stepped forward to pull the tarp back in place, and wished she hadn't. The dead soldier stared back at her blankly, his body bloated and pale in death. The stench was overwhelming and her eyes watered. For a moment she thought she would pass out.

Then suddenly the tarp was yanked out of her hands and she was pushed away from the wagon. She looked up into an old man's face with Lorenzo's eyes. He said nothing and she couldn't tell if he was angry or not.

"I have been around many dead men before, but none smelled like that."

Lorenzo turned slowly at the sound of the soldier's voice behind him. "He was not a healthy boy."

Angie didn't recognize Lorenzo's voice as he spoke. The

slight quaver, the rasp, no one could possible doubt that it was an old man they were speaking with.

The soldier cocked an eyebrow. "Disease?"

"We don't know. Never will, I guess, now. He was always ill. Wife and I tried to talk him out of joining the military, but he wouldn't hear of it. Not even when the fretting put his poor mama in the grave."

Angie hoped that she wasn't staring at Lorenzo in disbelief. The story he was creating right in front of her was incredible and very believable. She wondered, distantly, if she had been victim to similar creations from him in the past. Had he lied to her? Could she believe anything he had ever told her?

The soldier nodded absently. "Perhaps I should send a few men with you. The young *senorita* can stay with me." He smiled over at Angie.

Before Lorenzo could reply, Angie took a step forward, placing herself between Lorenzo and the soldier. "That is so kind of you." She spoke softly, doing her best to give him a sad smile. "But my cousin and I were very close, and I want to say my farewells."

"Understandable. I shall accompany you, then."

Angie's heart skipped a beat. "I don't need your help," Lorenzo snapped, sounding just like an angry old man. "This is my son and I'll be burying him. I don't need you retching on him while we try to shovel dirt."

Angie turned towards Lorenzo, thankful for his quick thinking, but knew she had to continue the charade. "*Tio*! That's no way to talk to an officer."

"Don't reprimand me, girl. Now, sir," he continued in his rough tone, "are you going to let me bury my son or not?"

The officer eyed Lorenzo for several long seconds, making Angie's heart pound in her ears. Finally, he shrugged. "If you get stuck out there in the mud, remember you said no to my help."

And with that, the officer left them, allowing Angie and Lorenzo to pass and head towards the river.

Lorenzo was silent for a long time after they had passed, glancing over his shoulder every few seconds. Angie was trying to calm her nerves. She knew it was over, but she still couldn't stop shaking. "Do you think they're going to follow us?"

"No, I think *he's* going to follow us, hoping to get some of what you kept offering him."

Angie shook her head, her shawl sending sprays of icy drops around her face. "What are you talking about?"

Lorenzo glared at the muddy path ahead of them. "Are you planning on offering yourself to every man in the Mexican Army before this thing is over?"

Angie recoiled as though he had slapped her. "I don't know what is going on in that head of yours, but—"

"First you throw yourself at me. Then you threw yourself at the officer who believed your foolish notes. Now you throw yourself at that pathetic excuse for an officer. Are you just padding all bets?"

He hadn't looked at her yet; otherwise he would have seen the angry red blush creeping up her cheeks. He glanced over his shoulder again and nearly fell out of the wagon as she shoved against him hard. Grabbing hold of his seat he turned as she drove into him again, her shoulder striking into his ribcage.

"You think I threw myself at you?" she panted, rearing back. "I'll throw myself at you. And throw you right off this damned wagon!"

She lunged forward and he caught her under the arms, locking her hands behind her back and holding her against his chest. "Let go of me," she snarled, hating the old face that hid Lorenzo from her.

"You threw yourself at me."

She kicked him in the shin and his eye ticked, but he didn't release her. "I'm sure the soldiers are enjoying watching you wrestle with your uncle," he said through clenched teeth.

HAVING FORGOTTEN ABOUT them, Angie gasped and looked over his shoulder. It was the distraction Lorenzo had hoped for as he flipped her over and settled her on his lap, his arms wrapped tightly around her, still gripping the reigns in one hand.

Angie seethed. "The soldiers can't see us anymore."

"You're going to disturb the mule. Sit still." It wasn't the mule Lorenzo was worried about. It was his body's irrational reaction to her wiggling bottom.

Angie sat still, her body tense. She was silent for several

long moments, moments that Lorenzo was glad to have. He knew the silence wouldn't last.

Finally, "You had no right to imply such things."

He grunted.

"I have never done the things you're accusing me of…"

"The bridge looks icy. You better hold tight."

"To what?"

"Me." He spoke with a wolfish grin she couldn't see. When the mule's hoof slipped, she grasped his thighs tightly.

"Are there any other…"

"We have to get over the river. Unless you would like to swim with all of this…"

"Just go slow."

"If we go fast, whatever happens, it will be over in a blink."

"Lorenzo!"

A smile tugged at the corner of his lips. They had made it past the guards, and it didn't appear anyone followed. The relief was exhilarating. And at the same time he felt remorse for the way he had spoken to Angie. The woman had the ability to pull out the worst in him. And moments later she could pull out the best in him.

He had seen the way the soldiers had been watching her every move, speculating what her curves would feel like in their hands. The anger that had boiled up inside him was surprising, but he hadn't stopped to analyze why. And it hadn't helped to see Angie smile warmly at them.

Her nails were digging into his flesh through his thick pants. "Relax. We're almost across."

Angie nodded, but didn't say anything. Her nails still dug deep with each jolt of the wagon, and each time the mule's hooves slipped. If the mule fell, the wagon would tip, probably fall in the river, and they'd be treading water with a dead man's body. He could understand her fear as she shivered when the wagon jolted again.

"We're across." Lorenzo's lips moved against her ear and her eyes snapped open.

They had crossed, the mule's ears plastered flat against his neck, obviously displeased with their journey.

With renewed vigor, Angie pushed on his arms. "Will you let me go now?"

He released her instantly and she threw herself into the small space left on the seat board. She pushed her wet shawl away from her face and glared up at him. "You had no right to accuse me of—"

"You're right."

His comment left her mouth dangling open in mid-sentence. She closed it quickly. He knew there was no way for her to read his expression through the mess on his face, and he chuckled inwardly. It was probably driving her crazy. "That's it?" she finally said, her voice an octave higher than usual.

He glanced sideways at her. "What more do you want?"

"An apology would be a good place to start."

"What makes you think I'm sorry? I told you that you were right. That doesn't mean I'm sorry for what I did."

She turned away from him. Then, suddenly, she whirled back. "Are you just determined to find a reason to hate me?

Is that why you accuse me of such things?"

It was Lorenzo's turn to squirm, and he didn't like it one bit. "I don't hate you." He concentrated on the vague path ahead of them, not looking at her.

"You want to, though."

He forced a tight smile on his lips while his hands pulled on the reigns, bringing the wagon to a stop. He finally turned to face her, doing his best to control his frustration behind his old man face. "Glad you've finally figured that one out. That's, of course, the reason I've been trying to toss your skirts over your head ever since I met you."

❦

ON THAT SHOCKING statement, he stepped down from the wagon and offered his hand to her. Angie blinked and focused on the hand in front of her. Slowly, she put her hand in his.

She recovered quickly as she stepped down. "Then what's the reason?"

He pulled a shovel from its hook on the side of the wagon and handed it to her. "You best save your breath while you can."

She snatched the shovel from him and began to stomp away from him when he caught her arm and turned her quickly, his head dipping down to catch her lips in a soft kiss that had every fiber tingling.

He smiled down at her dazed face. "You really should stop throwing yourself at me."

Chapter Twenty-Nine

"THAT'S IT, THEN?" Angie clutched her shovel with blistered hands, looking at the mound of dirt in front of them. Despite the chill, sweat slid down her back and between her breasts.

Lorenzo looked over at her, a weary smile on his face. "That's it."

To their left, far to the corner of the cemetery, lay another fresh grave. It had seemed only right to give the soldier a burial after the help he had given them, albeit unknowingly.

The sun had slipped further in the sky, still mostly hidden by the gray clouds. "I'm surprised those soldiers didn't come looking for us," Angie said, speaking softly.

She had practically whispered from the moment they stepped into the cemetery. It seemed appropriate, standing in the midst of so many grave markers, to speak in respectful tones.

Lorenzo glanced back towards town as though expecting to see soldiers ride up just at the mention of them. "They're not concerned about us. At least not right now."

Angie looked at him quizzically as he grabbed a piece of wood and jammed it into the ground, creating a grave marker for their new "grave."

"If we don't return, they'll think we're victims of the Texians. If they even remember us." He dug a piece of chalk out of his pocket and drew a ragged line across the wood.

Hope blossomed in Angie. "So tonight Tom will come to get his supplies, and all will be well."

He looked at her in disbelief. "Just because they get their supplies doesn't mean things are over, Angie. It is only the beginning."

Angie was beginning to feel the cold again and crossed her arms over her chest. "I know. But it will be better, right, once they have their supplies?"

Lorenzo came to her exactly when she needed him, pulling her into his arms and holding her gently. She leaned against him willingly, her arms wrapping around his waist. "I can't tell you how soon it will be over, *chula*. I can tell you these supplies have helped. Where things go from here, I don't know."

Angie closed her eyes briefly, breathing in the warm scent of him, and wondered if he spoke of just the war or of things between them as well. Their immediate mission was over. It was highly unlikely that Tom would need her to continue assisting—he had made it all too clear the last time they spoke that she was no longer necessary. Would Lorenzo continue to visit her at the *cocina*? To ask her to walk with him? There would be no other reason than because he wanted to be with her. She wasn't sure she wanted to know the answers.

But it wasn't safe for either of them. As soon as the battle was over, no matter what the outcome, he would put San Antonio and Angie far behind him, and she would continue her life at the *cocina*.

"It will be dark soon," he said softly, pulling them both back to the present. She pulled away, gazing up at him with a half smile on her face.

"One thing is for sure, you will make quite a handsome old man."

He had nearly forgotten the mud and plaster he had worked on to his face so early in the morning, and was instantly itching. "Doubtful," he said smiling at her, smoothing her hair away from her face. "But I'm glad that your red eyes are gone. I don't care much for that."

"Then don't ever make me cry."

The statement was met with an uncomfortable silence that was finally broken by the sound of sleet once again falling to the saturated ground.

Lorenzo glared up at the sky that had given them a reprieve for a majority of the time they had been digging, but it wasn't finished yet. "Let's go."

The wagon rolled away quickly, no longer encumbered by its heavy load, a pile of rotted pork sitting outside the leaning, rusted iron fence of the cemetery.

They rode in silence, the sleet creating a gray curtain between them. All too quickly they came to the bridge and Angie's hands locked onto the seat.

"It would be safer for you to walk across." Angie looked at him in disbelief. He saw her reaction out of the corner of his eye. "The wagon is much lighter now, so there's a greater chance it will slip on the ice."

"Then shouldn't I stay and add my extra weight?"

He smiled. "*Chula*, your weight isn't going to make much of a difference." When he saw her frown, he shook his head. "Alright. If you really want to help, climb in back and try to sit as close to the back wheels as you can."

Nodding, Angie turned and climbed over the bench seat, quickly placing herself over the wheels. As soon as she was settled, Lorenzo clucked to the mule and they slowly began over the bridge.

THE SLICK ICE hadn't gone away during the day and in the approaching twilight it shimmered darkly. Angie began humming to herself, her eyes sealed tight. She didn't want to see or hear their progress over the bridge. Her plan didn't work.

Not when the wagon suddenly lurched. Her eyes flew open and her hands gripped the side of the wagon.

"Easy, now," Lorenzo was saying softly as the mule yanked on the reigns, trying to regather his hooves beneath him. It wasn't working. Each time one hoof had found stability, the other three were going opposite directions. The wagon lurched again and slid towards the edge of the bridge.

"Lorenzo…" Angie's voice was strained.

"Easy, boy, nice and easy…" He glanced over his shoulder at her. "Get out."

Angie hesitated, her knuckles turning white from their

grip. The wagon slid further.

"Damnit, Angie, I said get out!"

"You, too."

"God help me. Angie, if you don't…"

The left back wheel slipped off the side and the wagon tipped, pitching Angie to the side, hanging over the water. Her weight, combined with the imbalance of the wagon, created an inertia that wasn't going to stop.

The mule was in hysterics as it was pulled backwards and to the side. Within seconds, all of them were in the icy water.

ANGIE SURGED TO the surface of the water, sputtering and gasping, her muscles protesting the frigid water. Her feet found the bottom of the thankfully shallow river, allowing her to keep her head above the water. She was gasping for air, trying to push back the fear that clutched at her. She could breathe. She wasn't under the water. There was nothing to be afraid of.

At the sound of splashing behind her, she turned quickly, seeking the comfort and protection she knew Lorenzo's arms would provide. She narrowly dodged the flailing hooves of the mule.

Pushing herself quickly to the side, she watched the animal madly paddle towards the bank, the broken harness of the wagon trailing behind him. Angie turned in the water, her eyes hunting for Lorenzo. He was nowhere to be seen.

A small piece of the side and front of the wagon stuck up

in the air, one wheel still spinning. A chill settled around Angie's heart, one far colder than the chill of the water.

Lorenzo was in trouble. She knew it in her heart and didn't hesitate to question herself how. He was in trouble and he needed her help.

Forcing back the panic, Angie drew a deep breath and for the first time in years, willingly ducked her head under the water. She blinked rapidly in the murky water, trying to see. It took several moments but finally she could see some of the weeds that waved back and forth and the vague outline of the wagon. When she saw Lorenzo, her heart stopped beating then rushed forward in a painful rhythm.

He was stuck. His leg was caught, pinned beneath the corner of the wagon that rested on the river floor. She pushed herself towards him, a new fear pulsing through her veins. She couldn't lose him.

When her hands grabbed at the side of the wagon and pulled where he was pushing, he looked at her in surprise, then shook his head frantically, motioning for her to go away. She shook her head just as vehemently and pulled harder on the wagon.

It shifted slightly, and he winced in pain. He didn't have much more time. Angie's lungs were beginning to burn. The frigid temperature of the water was making her muscles slow, and he was in even worse shape. She tugged on the wagon and he shoved and it moved a little more. But not enough.

Lungs screaming, Angie pushed herself to the surface and gulped at the air. He was only a couple of feet under water. So close to the air, yet so far. She plunged down again and her cry was muffled by the water. Lorenzo wasn't moving. Anger surged through her. He wasn't going to die on her like this! She refused to let it happen.

With renewed strength she attacked the wagon, pushing and pulling until it shuddered, falling completely on its side. Lorenzo still hadn't moved. His body was limp and pale. Grabbing him around his waist, she pushed upwards, both of them bursting above the water. She gasped and gulped in the air. He didn't move.

She pulled him towards the bank, unaware that she was yelling at him. "You will not die on me, Lorenzo. Do you hear me? We've come too far to lose now. I forbid it!"

They fell together on the bank and she rolled him over, tears filling her eyes at the sight of his dark hair against his far too pale face. "Open your eyes, Lorenzo," she cried, beating on his chest with her fists. "Damn you, don't do this." A sob tore from her throat and she struck with both fists.

His gurgled cough was the sweetest sound she had ever heard. He turned on his side, retching out the water that had so nearly taken his life. Her relief was so overwhelming she sat back with a thump, not caring that she was sitting in the mud. She couldn't let go of him, though, her hands clenched on his shirt.

He turned towards her, his face still pale, but it was no longer lifeless. She never wanted to see him look like that again.

A half smile touched his lips. "I told you I would cure your fear of the water."

A sob escaped her and she threw herself against him, burying her face against his neck, unable to control the onslaught of tears. His arms wrapped around her tightly, pulling her close, his hands running soothingly up and down her back. Warm tears slid down Angie's cheeks. *Thank God he was alive!*

He said nothing, and Angie just enjoyed hearing the beat of his heart and the feeling of his arms around her. Her sobs had turned into hiccups and she pulled away from him, unable to look him in the eyes. "Don't you dare ever scare me like that again," she said in a voice still raw with emotion.

His hand smoothed her damp hair off of her face, his thumb wiping a stray tear off her cheek. Slowly, she raised her eyes to his and his soft smile warmed her in places she didn't know existed.

"I've never been rescued by a woman before. How can I repay you?"

An image flashed through her mind of his dark, tanned hands on her pale skin in the moonlight and her heart doubled its beat. Her thoughts must have shown on her face because his eyelids lowered over his darkening expression.

She straightened quickly, pulling free of him and adjusting her soggy dress. "We really need to hurry. Though I don't know how you expect to get past the guards now that all that goop is off your face."

Lorenzo reached up and felt his face, though he wasn't surprised his disguise was gone. "We can't go back that way."

Angie raised her eyebrows, then looked at their nearly submerged wagon. "The mule's probably already run past them."

"Which means they might be sending guards this way any moment." Lorenzo pushed himself to his feet. "We better move if we…" His words trailed off in a grunt and he gritted his teeth as he placed weight on the leg that had been pinned under the wagon.

Angie was on her feet next to him instantly. "Is it bad?" she asked, looking down at his leg as though she could see through his muddy pants.

"Not at all," Lorenzo said, though his voice was strained. "I just need to walk it off."

Angie slipped under his arm, forcing him to lean on her. She looked up at him and smiled into his glare. "We're in this together, remember? Every now and then we need a little support."

HE HAD NEVER wanted to kiss a woman as badly as he wanted to kiss Angie at that moment. And it was for that reason he turned away from her tempting lips, from the warmth in her eyes, and began walking, leaning lightly on her. He had really thought his life was over. In the past, he hadn't cared when his life was at risk, and had usually been the first to volunteer for the most dangerous missions. But when he had been pulled under the wagon, he cared. He didn't want to die. The reason why had him more shaken than anything else. He hadn't had near enough time with Angie.

As he had predicted, within several steps the pain had lessened and he wasn't depending as much on Angie's support. They stayed along the river, though far enough away that the low shrubs and moss-laden trees concealed their movements.

"How are we going to get back to town?" Angie asked, slightly out of breath from trying to support Lorenzo and avoid stumbling on her own icy feet at the same time.

"We'll sneak back in as though we were returning from Tom's camp. It should be completely dark soon enough. That should give us more than enough cover."

"You don't think they'll start looking for us when they find the wagon?"

Lorenzo didn't want to answer that question. Odds were high that the soldiers would conduct some sort of search. How soon and how thorough they would be was questionable. But if they didn't get back to town soon, their chances of being caught increased with every passing second.

He began to walk faster, cringing at the protest from his leg. It would be sore and bruised for a while to come. Angie kept pace with him, understanding the urgency. Everything that could have gone wrong had. He just prayed that God would get them through in one piece.

﹅

SAN ANTONIO WAS silent. There wasn't even the sound of soldier's marching. But she could hear Lorenzo's heartbeat, feel his chest rising and falling beneath her cheek. They had made it back, and she knew he needed to hurry to his bedroll to make sure he was counted. But she couldn't let go of him.

Lorenzo seemed to feel the same way. His arms were wrapped tightly around her, his chin resting on top of her head. And for several minutes they stood like that, content to hold and be held.

It was Angie who finally pulled back. Her smile trembled. "Is this goodbye, then?"

"Would you be sad if it was?"

Angie watched him for several seconds, as though trying to see a hidden motive. "Yes," she said slowly. "Yes, I would be sad. I loathe to admit it… but I've grown rather—accustomed to you."

His mouth turned up in a smile. "Accustomed. That is very flattering to my ego."

A blush stole across her cheeks and she wanted to stomp his foot. Didn't he understand how difficult this was for her? "What about you?" she demanded.

"What about me?"

"Would you be sad?"

"Devastated."

"You're mocking me."

"Destroyed."

"I can't believe you. I—"

"Emotionally destroyed."

She yanked free of his embrace. "I can't believe I said I would be sad to say goodbye to you! I rejoice at never having to—mmph!"

His mouth sealed over hers, cutting off her words and

literally making her melt back into his arms. A contented sigh escaped her as she wrapped her arms around his neck and leaned into him, her lips parting for the sweet taste of his kiss.

He groaned. "I will miss you," he said softly against her lips.

"Me or this?" she asked dryly, and he chuckled.

"Both. I can't have one without the other." He trailed kisses down her neck, but she slowly pushed him away, obviously battling with herself on whether she wanted to pull him closer or escape his enticing arms. "This really is good-bye, then?"

"No, but soon. I won't come to the *cocina* anymore. But I'll come let you know when I'm leaving." He glanced at the cloud-shrouded moon, then back at Angie. "Go home, *chula*. Get warm. I don't want you ill again."

She smiled at him gently. "The same for you. I-I will miss you." She drew a deep breath, obviously steadying herself. "Well, until I see you again…"

"If you think you're getting off that easily, you're crazier than I thought."

He grabbed a hold of her again and hauled her in for a deep kiss, one that left her lips burning and her body craving more.

Chapter Thirty

S HE FELT HOLLOW. Ever since she had walked away from him two days ago, she had felt empty, as though she had left a part of herself with him. She scrubbed her rag over a greasy pot, not really paying attention to what she was doing.

It was ridiculous to continue fighting her feelings for him. She had known as soon as she had thought he was dying. She scoffed at herself. She had known before then, but hadn't wanted to admit it to herself.

She loved him. Completely and totally, and there was nothing she could do to change it. He brought a warmth to her she had never known existed, and an anger she hadn't known she was capable of. The man had the power of drawing out all of her emotions from one spectrum to another.

"What a foolish grin. Must be a happy thought." Grandmother came to stand beside her, a knowing look on her face.

Angie's cheeks flamed. "I was just…"

Grandma patted her hand affectionately. "Usually that kind of smile is only brought on by a man. Are you thinking about that handsome soldier?"

Angie blushed, this time all the way down to her toes. "Grandma…"

"You don't have to say a thing. I can see it all on your face." She pulled the pot out of Angie's suddenly useless hands and took over the scrubbing. "I haven't seen him around for a few days. Did you fight?" She shook her head before Angie could even answer. "Lovers fight all the time. It's just what happens. Oh, but when you make amends…" She winked at Angie, her wrinkled face smiling brightly.

"Grandma, it's not like that."

She paused in her attention to the pot and looked at Angie. "Oh? You didn't fight then?"

"No. I mean…" Angie shook her head. "No, we didn't fight. We don't have any relationship."

Grandma looked confused. "Then why was he always coming to see you?"

Angie grabbed a towel and began to vigorously dry dishes. "It's complicated, Grandma."

Her grandmother looked relieved and turned back to her chore with a chuckle. "Love always is, my dear. It always is."

)⅄⅋

TWO DAYS LATER, Angie felt as though her nerves were tight strings that were about to snap. She had wondered a thousand times over if he would come to her to say goodbye. And then she had wondered if it would be goodbye forever, if he was walking out of her life, never looking back.

When she had finally accepted the fact that she would

never see him again, he surprised her on the back step as she was carrying in a basket of laundry. The feel of strong arms locking around her waist startled her, but instantly she knew it was Lorenzo. Only he smelled so wonderful to her. Only he had the knowledge of how to hold her just right. Only Lorenzo. No other man could make her feel so good. And no other man ever would.

She dropped her basket, not caring if she had to wash all the clothes again and turned in his embrace, throwing her arms around his neck and holding tight. His soft chuckle warmed her.

"I hope you don't greet all strange men who come to your back door this way."

She pulled back and frowned at him. "Of course not. I make most of the strange men go through the front door."

His bark of laughter made her smile as she ran her fingertips over his eyebrows, his nose, his cheeks.

Her smile slowly disappeared as she looked into his eyes. "This is goodbye, isn't it?" and she braced herself for Lorenzo's reply.

Lorenzo's gaze ran over her face, trying to memorize her every feature. He needed to just say goodbye and step away. But the grip she had on him was around more than just his neck. "One last walk?" he heard himself ask her and wondered what possessed him. He needed to leave, and soon. The danger of being discovered had escalated to a high probability, and he needed to get out of town as fast as he could. And yet, here he stood, wrapped in the arms of the woman who tested his will with every breath, asking her to go walking with him. He was endangering both of them. But he needed to be with her, if only a few more minutes. After that, he would never see her again.

"I would love to go for a walk with you," she said softly, still touching his face with light, feather fingers. "Let me get my shawl."

She was gone for only the space of a couple of breaths, but it was long enough for Lorenzo to wonder at his sanity and consider just leaving. But the smile on her face when she came through the door to join him was enough to make him throw caution to the wind.

She laid her hand primly on his arm as they started towards the road, her shawl pulled tightly around her to keep out the chill. "People will think we are crazy, going for a walk when it is this cold." Her breath plumed as she spoke.

"Good thing for us we already know we're crazy."

"I didn't think you would come," she said softly, watching his face.

"I promised you I would," he said, returning his gaze to the road. Few people were outside since the air was so cold.

"You didn't have to," Angie spoke, though she no longer looked at him.

Lorenzo gave her a sharp glance. "Didn't you want me to come?"

"Yes," Angie replied quickly, then shook her head. "I mean no." She licked her lips. "What I mean is I wanted you to come only because you wanted to. Not because you felt obligated."

Lorenzo was silent for several seconds. Then his hand

came up and covered hers, pressing it against his arm. "I wanted to come. I wanted to see you."

A faint blush stole over her cheeks. "A week ago, I never would have thought we'd be having this conversation."

Lorenzo chuckled. "Just a few days ago I wouldn't have thought we'd be having this conversation."

They walked in comfortable silence until they reached the bridge. Then Angie brought up what they'd both been dreading. "Do you leave tonight, then?"

He sighed heavily. "As soon as night falls."

Angie gnawed on her lower lip. "Do you have everything you need?"

"I'll make by. Besides, I'm sure Tom will have anything I don't have."

"Is that sarcasm I hear?"

Lorenzo shook his head while laughing quietly. "I'll be surprised if he hasn't given away his own shirt to keep those boys happy."

Angie smiled at the image that created. "So you will be with Tom until this is all over?"

"I'll be working for Tom in some form or another for quite some time, I'm sure." He watched her face closely to see how she would take this information.

Does that mean he won't be coming back? Was he trying to find a polite way to tell her? Feeling chilled, they both turned and headed back towards the *cocina*. "Once this is all over, what are you going to do?" She had convinced herself she didn't want to know. She had convinced herself that it was fine if he walked away from her. But now that the moment had come, she was no longer convinced. He had changed her, made her desire things she had never thought of before. She was no longer able to accept him just walking out of her life. But she didn't know if she was prepared for whatever answers he gave her next.

Lorenzo had hoped she wouldn't ask such a question, for he feared she was hoping to hear mention of herself in his plans for the future. She was in his plans—she was the reason he wanted to get as far away from San Antonio as possible. He felt things for her that he no longer wanted to feel for any woman. Even a woman as pure as Angie.

"I'm going to get some land. Build a cattle farm. It's what I've always wanted to do. I'm hoping my brother in Laredo will help."

"I didn't know you had a brother."

"There's a lot you still don't know about me." He spoke slowly, his concentration shifting towards the soldiers that were marching down the road. Something didn't feel right.

"Perhaps one day I will know you better. Until then, I'll just pick up the details you let slip."

"Mmm-hmm," he replied, his body tensing. No, something definitely was not right.

Angie frowned at him. "It appears your mind is already miles away. Are you that eager to leave?"

He glanced down at her and decided he had prolonged the inevitable long enough. "Yes. I need to go, Angie. It's no longer safe for me here." A sideways glance told him the soldiers were still walking towards them.

She unlaced her arm from his and took a step back, with

a fake bright smile to her face. "Well, I wish you the best of luck. And please be careful." It was a goodbye. It was the best she could muster as a goodbye.

This wasn't how he had wanted to say goodbye. He had known she would be angry with him for giving her such vague answers. He had known she would be angrier still when she realized he had no intention of returning. But he had hoped he could hold her just one last time, kiss her one more time. He had wanted to create a memory of her that he could cherish forever. But the quickly approaching Mexican soldiers were ruining his plans. He hated them more than ever.

Disregarding what polite society would say, he took a quick step towards her and caught her face in his hands, shaking his head as he looked down into her startled eyes. "This is the way it must be," he said, wondering if he spoke for her benefit or his own. He pressed his lips to hers, a quick, passion-filled kiss that left her dazed and clinging to his arms. He pulled back, his face masked against whatever he was feeling. "Go home, Angie. Go home as fast as you can. And don't look back." He turned away from her and walked down the road, his back ramrod straight as he faced the soldiers he was unable to avoid any longer.

ANGIE STOOD STUNNED on the side of the road for only a moment before anger coursed through her. Did he think she was that easy to toss away? Did she mean so little to him?

Her fingers curled into fists around her shawl as she glared at his back. She wasn't about to be tossed away like used bath water. He had toyed with her heart, and she would hold him accountable. How, she didn't know. She would figure something out by the time she reached him.

Storming forward, she trudged through the churned up mud of the road and was out of breath by the time she reached him. Not thinking about who could be watching, she shoved his shoulder, forcing him to turn and look at her in surprise.

"Angie! I told you to—"

"I will not be dismissed so easily!" Her voice was shaking and she cursed herself for letting her emotions get to the best of her. "You can't just—"

"Angie, go home. Now." He spoke through gritted teeth.

He was obviously getting angry. Good. Maybe he would begin to feel a little of what she had been feeling.

"My emotions are not something to be played with. It's fine for you if you can kiss me the way you just kissed me and feel nothing… but I can't just turn my feelings on and off like that! I feel something when you touch me, when you kiss me, when you talk to me. And now you're just going to walk away? And you tell me not to look back? What kind of—"

"Go. Home."

"Are you daft? Are you not—"

"Lorenzo Delgado Valdez!"

The loud voice calling his name startled her and she looked around him, completely surprised to see four soldiers standing not far away. Lorenzo's face was tense, and from the look he cast her, he was none too pleased with her. He turned slowly, saluting the man who had called his name.

Angie barely held back her gasp. It was the man who had spoken to them outside of town the day they had buried the supplies. Had they been discovered? Fear slivered down her spine. Instantly she worried for Olivia and Serena. What if the soldiers had stopped at the *cocina* first? The tension in Lorenzo told her he was worried too.

The man who had spoken smiled, though it wasn't a pleasant smile. He walked towards them slowly, an arrogance in his posture that Angie did not care for.

"Well, Lorenzo, I never thought I would get the pleasure of seeing you again. I had hoped of course… but you have certainly done your best to avoid me."

Lorenzo said nothing, his body rigid, his arms forcing Angie to stay behind him. The man stopped right in front of them, still smiling, though it didn't reach his eyes. "No hello for your dear friend? Aren't you just as happy to see me? No?" He made a tsking sound. "What a shame our friendship has been reduced to this." He glanced over Lorenzo's shoulder and his eyebrows lifted. "And who might this be? Really, Lorenzo, you should try to find a coconspirator who doesn't stand out so much. Her beauty must attract the attention of every man in town."

"Leave her out of this," Lorenzo growled.

The man chuckled. "So you can speak. I was afraid perhaps you had bitten your tongue too many times over the years and rendered yourself incapable." He reached around

Lorenzo and caught Angie's arm, pulling her towards him.

Lorenzo's hand gripped the man's wrists tightly. "I said to leave her out of this. There's no need."

"You know I can't do that. You of all people know I can't."

Breaking free of Lorenzo's grip, he pulled Angie towards him, then took his eyes briefly off Lorenzo to glance at her. He did a double take and his eyes narrowed. "Do I know you?"

"I don't believe so, *senor*. Though it is possible we have seen each other in passing. I apologize for not remembering." Her heart was pounding so hard she was afraid it would come thru her chest.

His brow furrowed as he tried to remember. When his eyes lit up, she knew all was lost. "Outside of town, just the other day!" He snapped his fingers. "And you were with that hideous old man—" He turned back to Lorenzo, a large, mocking smile on his face. "That was you! *Mi Dios,* you get better and better. You can still amaze me."

"I'm afraid you're mistaken. I'm certain I would have remembered such a meeting."

He turned back towards her, the look on his face no longer pleasant, his smile just a thin barring of teeth. "He has taught you how to lie, I see. What else has he taught you to do?" He reached up and caressed the pulse racing at the base of her neck.

"You filthy bastard!" Lorenzo lunged at him but was instantly grabbed by the other soldiers, his arms pinned behind him. A solid punch to his stomach brought him to his knees in the mud.

"Stop it!" Angie yelled, desperately trying to yank free of the soldier's grip. "Stop it!" She looked at him imploringly. "What has he done? Why are you treating him like this?"

The soldier looked at her for a long time, his eyes studying every inch of her, making her feel the need to scrub her skin clean. "What were you doing the other day? Why did you have that dead soldier in the back of your wagon?"

"I don't—"

"Leave her out of this, Armando. This is just between you and me."

Armando laughed dryly. "You flatter yourself, my friend. As much as I would love to claim this as my personal mission to bring you to justice, I am here by order of our general. He wishes to squash this puny rebellion. What a delight to see that you are a part of it. We will start with you."

"He is a loyal soldier to Mexico," Angie stated firmly. "How dare you accuse him otherwise!"

Armando smiled, and Angie wanted to pull away from him in revulsion. "He used to be. He was a great soldier for Mexico. His loyalty, however, was easily swayed."

Confused, Angie glanced over at Lorenzo. He wasn't looking at her. He was glaring at Armando.

"Ah, such a look. He didn't tell you about his past, then. Would you care to hear a very entertaining story? It starts with an amazing Mexican soldier and ends with his tragic execution for the crimes against Mexico."

Angie didn't want to hear any more. She wanted to get away, she wanted to get Lorenzo to safety, and then they could sort it all out. But it didn't look like they would be free of the soldiers any time soon. A few of the townspeople had stepped out onto their porches, straining to hear what was being said. She forced a haughty expression on her face, hoping she looked thoroughly annoyed to the officer. "Sir, it is quite cold out here, and you obviously are confusing this man with someone else. Now, if you'll please—"

"Did he tell you about the innocent man he killed so that he could sneak into our ranks? No? It's a fascinating story, though you might find it a bit gory. Or perhaps he told you of the woman he killed? She was beautiful—and innocent. He didn't believe she was. He thought she had betrayed him. He squeezed the very life out of her, watching her die. Personally, I think it was jealousy." His eyes searched her face, watching her expression. "Why did he say he was a convict?"

The tremor within her had nothing to do with the cold. She would not let this Mexican officer sway her belief in Lorenzo. He was a good man who had been forced into terrible situations. Her eyes slid to Lorenzo, but he wouldn't look at her.

Armando's grip on her arm tightened. "Answer me!"

"He-he said that he was a thief, that he—"

Armando's laugh cut her off. "A thief? That was the best you could do?" he spoke to Lorenzo. "Couldn't you come up with anything better?"

Angie shook her head forcefully. "No, he is a loyal, Mexican soldier…"

"He is a liar!" Armando snapped, yanking on her arm.

"You claim him to be a soldier. I know you think he is a Texian. He is neither! He sells information to both sides." He stepped forward and grabbed at Lorenzo's jacket, patting at the pockets until he grinned with satisfaction, pulling forth a bag that jingled with the sound of coins.

Angie felt as though someone had squeezed all the air from her lungs. Lorenzo finally looked at her, but his eyes were cold and aloof, not filled with warmth and care she had seen just moments before.

"I'll tell you whatever you want to know." She spoke softly, her voice dejected. "I just don't want to see him ever again." Angie's mind was racing. If she could convince them that she was on their side and that she had given up on him, maybe they would release her. Only then could she try to rescue him. And then—then she would make the man answer the thousands of questions running through her mind.

Armando studied her face, skepticism etched on his. It wasn't hard for her to will the tear out of her eye, the final touch to her sorrow and disappointment at discovering the true nature of Lorenzo. Armando's lips turned up smugly. "Very well, then."

He made a sharp motion with his hand and a rifle was raised, its tip pressed against Lorenzo's temple.

"No!" Angie screamed and ripped her arm free of Armando's grip, throwing herself forward. She covered Lorenzo with her body, wrapping her arms around his head. She turned hate-filled eyes to Armando and didn't have to force the tears this time. "You kill him and you will get nothing from me!"

Armando made a tsking sound again. "I thought you said you never wanted to see him again. You are leading me to believe you were lying."

She hated this man. She didn't know what Lorenzo's past was with him, but she could see why Lorenzo didn't like him. "Just because I don't want to see him again doesn't mean I wish him dead. He has hurt me and I can no longer trust him, but he shouldn't die."

"We will have to see about that."

A soldier grabbed her arms and pulled her away from Lorenzo. He wouldn't look at her. When Armando made the sharp motion again, Angie's heart leapt into her throat. The man raised his rifle, quickly flipped it and struck Lorenzo with the butt. The sound of the gun cracking against his head made Angie's stomach turn, and she watched helplessly as he fell to the ground. Forcing herself to look away from him, Angie didn't resist as the guards led her forward. She hoped she had learned enough from Lorenzo to be able to lie convincingly. His life depended on it.

Chapter Thirty-One

"HE WAS SO sincere—"

"You were deceived—"

"But I thought—"

"You are a beautiful woman. He used you."

"I hate him."

Lorenzo tried to lift his head and felt like he would vomit.

"I was a fool to trust him."

The sound of Angie's voice pulled at him and he slowly opened one eye. His head pounded mercilessly.

"You mean all those things he had me do did not help the Mexican Army?"

Lorenzo's other eye opened. What the hell was she talking about?

"Why did you think you were helping the Mexican Army?"

"Because he is a Mexican soldier. Or at least that is what I thought he was. I never knew he was stealing all of those things to help the Texians! Oh, I've been such a fool!"

Lorenzo was fairly certain he was going to throw up. She was betraying him, the same as before. He shouldn't have trusted her. He had been tricked again, and this time he had no doubt he would be executed. He had known she would believe Armando, and even her expression in the streets had told him so.

He couldn't really blame her. Armando had done an excellent job of destroying him in front of her and he couldn't defend himself without putting her at a greater risk. Yet it still hurt to know that she could give up on him so easily, that she could turn her back on him after a few well-chosen words.

Armando's voice carried to him. "Why would I believe that you wanted to help the Mexican Army?"

"My family has always been loyal to Mexico."

"Except your parents."

There was a stunned silence. Then, "I do not believe in speaking ill of the dead, especially when they are my own parents."

"So you stole all of those things with him. If you thought it would be for the Mexican Army, why did you think you needed to take it away from the soldiers?"

There was a soft sniff. "He said that when you finally attacked the rebels, you would need supplies readily available. He said the army couldn't afford to go back to base to replenish."

The fog was beginning to lift and Lorenzo felt a rage building in him, eating at him. He had wanted to believe she was naïve and innocent. He had wanted to believe she was everything she had appeared to be. He had been a fool. The lies she spoke, the words tumbling so easily from her lips were just nails in his coffin and she didn't even care.

He took in his surroundings and recognized the inside of a tent. They must be near the Alamo. The tent was divided, the thin fabric that partitioned it off, though, not concealing the movements of the occupants on the other side. Angie's form was hard to miss—he felt her image would be branded in his mind forever. As would the look she gave him when she told Armando she never wanted to see him again. He had thought himself incapable of feeling such pain again. But he hadn't gotten away from her soon enough—hadn't stopped himself when he began to trust her, to feel things for her.

But why, then, had she risked her own life when they nearly shot him? The question rang at the back of his mind, but he deliberately ignored it. She was just like the women of his past. And she would be his last.

He was tied to a low-backed chair, his arms behind him, his feet anchored to the leg of the chair. He wiggled his wrists, testing them. There was a small amount of give. Small, but enough to give him hope as he started turning his wrists back and forth.

"You didn't think it odd you concealed yourselves from the soldiers outside of town… the very soldiers you were supposed to be helping?"

Lorenzo squinted against the pain in his head as he watched Angie's silhouette. Her head drooped. "Yes," she said softly, "I thought it very odd. At the very least they could have helped us. You remember I wanted you to go with us. I thought we could trust you."

"Trust me? Why wouldn't you?"

Lorenzo tugged on the rope harder. If he got free, he would strangle her. He saw her wringing her hands. She was nervous. Good.

"He said... well, he told me... oh, I'm too embarrassed to even say."

Lorenzo gritted his teeth. Sweet and innocent. He wiggled his thumbs, trying to rejuvenate his circulation. He was the one who had been naïve. She would go to any end to make sure she saved herself.

"There, there, my dear, there's no reason to get so upset. Just explain everything the best you can."

Even Armando was being sucked in by her ploy, Lorenzo thought with disgust.

Angie nodded. "He told me there were some people in the army who weren't all they seemed. He said they were secretly working for the Texians. How was I to know he was really talking about himself?"

The tent flap opened and a young officer walked in. He looked at Lorenzo for several long seconds, his face expressionless. Lorenzo wanted to spit on his feet. He recognized him as the soldier Angie had been taking the notes to.

The man turned and stepped around the partition, drawing the attention of Angie and Armando.

"Daniel!" Angie's soft cry of relief made Lorenzo cringe.

She had told him she didn't know the soldier's name. Another lie. He didn't want to watch, but he forced himself to twist in the chair, forced himself to watch her rush into his arms. He had to see it to make her betrayal final in his mind. And having seen it, he closed his eyes and hoped the execution would be swift.

ANGIE KNEW SHE was shaking and hoped that Daniel didn't get the wrong idea from it. His arms wrapped around her and she felt tears building. God, she prayed she was doing everything right. She looked up at him, wishing she didn't have to lie to him.

Even though he was the enemy, he was a good man, and she knew he had developed feelings for her, though she had tried to discourage them. But now he might be her only way to save Lorenzo. She just didn't know how.

"I've done something terribly foolish," she whispered.

Daniel attempted to reassure her. "It can't be as bad as all that." He looked over at Armando, who was a rank below Daniel. Angie knew Daniel wouldn't tolerate the actions that Armando had taken without his permission. It was Daniel's strict obedience to propriety and order that was both his strength and his weakness. Angie hoped, in this case, it would be both.

Armando stood at attention, but his face was splotchy, obviously unhappy to be forced into the position he was in. Daniel nodded to him, indicating it was all right for him to relax. "I would like to know your purpose in my tent, soldier." Daniel's voice was stern, different from anything Angie had ever heard from him.

Armando lifted his chin. "I have orders from General Santa Anna to oust the Texians. I had received rumor that one of our more disreputable traitors had infiltrated your camp. I am interrogating him and his companion."

Daniel looked over at Angie, his eyes kind and under-standing, then glanced back at Armando, obviously needing further clarification. "How is *Senorita Torres* involved?"

"Pardon me, sir, but you know her?"

Daniel frowned darkly at Armando. "Yes. She has been supplying me with information on the Texians movements."

Armando blinked. "What?"

Daniel looked annoyed with the lack of formality on Armando's part. "Where are your orders, soldier?"

Angie wondered how Armando felt, being addressed in such a manner from a man several years younger than him. She hoped he hated it. Armando pulled some parchment paper from within his jacket and handed it to Daniel, who briefly glanced at it. He handed it back.

"Again, why are you interrogating *Senorita Torres*?"

"She has confessed to helping the traitor you saw when you came in."

Daniel raised his eyebrows and looked back at Angie. "Tell me what is going on."

"I was such a fool, Daniel. I-I trusted him. I thought he was helping the army. I didn't know he was a Texian."

Daniel nodded as though he expected as much and looked back at Armando. "She is loyal to Mexico. She has supplied us with much valuable information. The last note she made sure to bring to me helped us to be prepared for a minor ambush from the Texians just a few days back. As for the soldier, I would like to be a part of the interrogation. I want to know how many other traitors are in this camp."

Angie had felt the blood run from her face at the mention of the Texian ambush. So it *was* because of one of her notes. Dear God, what had she done?

Daniel took hold of her arm. "Come along. I will walk you home. I know this has been very traumatic for you."

Armando's face was red and Angie thought the vein in his neck was going to pop. He was obviously furious at the interruption by Daniel. But things had worked in her favor. Daniel glanced over his shoulder as he began to lead Angie out of the tent. "When I return, we will interrogate your prisoner."

Angie hadn't known that Lorenzo was in the tent. When she walked around the partition, Daniel's arm wrapped tight around her waist, she saw him, strapped to the chair, and her breath caught in her throat. Slowly he raised his eyes to her, and the hatred she saw made her want to cry.

He had heard everything she said, saw the way Daniel held her. Surely he must know that she was only doing it for him. Surely he wouldn't believe... but the look on his face told her otherwise. For a second, she wondered if she should try to orchestrate his escape. She feared if she did, he would kill her as soon as his hands were free.

LORENZO ROLLED HIS shoulder, trying to work out the ache. He could barely see out of his right eye, and his ribs were burning. But they hadn't taken the fight out of him.

As soon as Daniel had left to escort Angie home, Armando had vented his fury. With the assistance of a couple of his soldiers, they had untied him and told him to defend himself. At least they had attempted to be fair about it. They could have just left him tied to the chair.

Instead, they had freed him and forced him to stand ground against three other men. It was close to fair. And he was pleased that the soldiers left with just as many bruises as he had.

When Daniel had returned and witnessed what was transpiring, he had been infuriated. Armando said Lorenzo had nearly escaped and attacked the men, and that they were doing all they could to defend themselves against a man who obviously had nothing else to lose.

After rebinding Lorenzo to the chair, Daniel had ordered the men from his tent, and now stood facing him, his fists clenching and unclenching. Lorenzo wondered if this man was about to beat him, too, and be unfair about it.

Finally, Daniel turned from him and busied himself at his small desk, reaching for his small flask of brandy. He took a long swallow from it then glanced over his shoulder at Lorenzo. "You realize what kind of danger you have put her in."

It was a statement, not a question, but Lorenzo refused to acknowledge it. "So Cos has you doing his dirty work for him?"

Daniel swirled the liquid around in the flask, staring blankly at the papers scattered over his desk. "Cos doesn't have time to deal with someone as insignificant as you."

Lorenzo spit blood onto the dirt floor, narrowly missing Daniel's feet. "Glad to hear it. Since I'm so insignificant—"

"You're lucky I don't order your execution immediately," Daniel said tightly.

Lorenzo tilted his head and his neck popped. He restrained his groan of pain. "Then why don't you just do it?" he spat, irritated by the man Angie had thrown herself at.

"Armando certainly dislikes you," Daniel continued in the flat, unemotional voice that was scraping at Lorenzo's nerves. "What did you do that made him hate you so?"

"You'll have to ask him. He's the one with the grudge."

"He says you killed his wife."

Lorenzo lifted his head, trying to see the officer though one eye. "You're only going to believe him. Why are you even asking?"

Daniel turned to face him, and Lorenzo got the first good look at the anger on his face. "I want to hear from you. I want to know what crimes you have committed."

"It doesn't matter. It shouldn't matter. Aren't you more curious about what I've supposedly done to help the Texians?"

Daniel took another drink from the flask. "I already know. I know you work for the Texians. I know that you got those supplies for the Texians. And I know you have several friends within our ranks who help you. And I know that you pulled Angie into all of this."

"If you know all of this, you were certainly quick to let her go without any punishment."

"She doesn't deserve to be punished. You do."

Lorenzo gave a hard laugh then groaned at the pain that radiated through his ribs. "Wait until she stabs you in the back."

"Is that what happened with Armando's wife?"

"What happened with Armando's wife doesn't concern you."

Daniel sighed heavily. "This afternoon, twenty of my men defected to the Texians. This evening, on my return from the *cocina*, I was told another fifteen had defected. I'm losing my men to this rebellion but, even so, I know the Texians don't have near enough men to fight mine. You are nothing but a thorn in Armando's side, and I won't waste useless time on you, when I could spend it trying to rally the morale of my troops."

This was it. Lorenzo felt his palms begin to sweat. This was where he would be killed, executed in the name of the Mexican government. He had known it was coming, but he still wasn't fully prepared for it. Daniel continued speaking.

"Why she has fallen for you, I don't understand. I suppose I never will. The odd workings of the female mind. But she doesn't deserve what you have put her through. Armando filled her head with stories of the things you have done, and yet she still fights for you."

Lorenzo's eyes narrowed. What was he talking about? He blinked several times. Had he passed out and was in some hellish nightmare?

Daniel stepped forward, pulling his knife from its sheath. No, it was no nightmare. It was real, and he was about to die. He pulled himself up straight. He would not cower from death.

The blade sliced cleanly through the binds around his wrists. Lorenzo nearly fell out of the chair, but Daniel caught his shoulder, keeping him from toppling.

Lorenzo looked up at him in complete confusion, wondering if he was going to have to fight again. Perhaps a fight to the death. He was severely hindered to Daniel's fresh strength.

"Every fiber of me wants to see you stand before a firing squad," Daniel said, his voice strained. "But she begged me not to. She begged for your life. I don't understand why. I have no doubt you have killed the people Armando spoke of. I can see it within you. But she can't. She refuses to believe you are capable."

His blade slid through the ropes at his feet and he stepped back, almost as though he anticipated Lorenzo would strike out at him. "It is only because of her that I am letting you live. It is the only reason."

Lorenzo looked at him with unbelieving eyes. Angie had done this? But why? She had said she hated him. She had said she never wanted to see him again. She had said... that she cared for him. He remembered her words that she spoke as she had covered him with her own body, shielding him from the bullet that would have ended his life. But just as clearly he remembered her throwing herself into Daniel's arms.

"What do you gain from this? There is nothing for you out of this."

Daniel shook his head. "There is Angie. I hope that, with

you gone, she will come to see how I can care for her."

Anger infused Lorenzo. "So I leave to join the rebellion and you take care of her. You would be better off killing me. You never know what I might be capable of on the other side."

"I have taken that into consideration. But Angie's plea for your life means more to me. I made a promise to her, and I won't back out of it. But I expect you to leave, and to never enter this town again."

"I'll be back with the rebellion."

"I don't think they will make it this far. Even with my men joining them, they are weak. I have ways of gathering information, same as you."

Lorenzo stood slowly, unable to pull himself to his full height due to the pain in his ribs. "I—I respect you for what you are doing." It was difficult to say, and it was even more difficult to understand. He had been given a reprieve, and he didn't know how to handle it.

Daniel stood before him, a half smile touching his lips. "I am glad to be rid of you, no matter what it costs me. If I were you, I would leave immediately by whatever way you choose. However, Angie is waiting for you, outside the *cocina*, if you choose to see her one last time. I wouldn't recommend it, though."

"Why?"

Daniel gave him a hard look. "Don't you think you've caused her enough pain as it is?"

Lorenzo had no way to respond. He was torn in a thousand directions and couldn't think clearly. "If we should meet again on the battlefield, I will not fire on you."

Daniel looked at him for several seconds, his expression somber. "I cannot say the same."

Lorenzo knew how difficult it was for the officer to be turning his back on him. He didn't know that he would be able to do the same. He nodded slowly and turned away, still not fully believing he was leaving with his life.

"Leave through the flap at the back. I have made arrangements so that you have the greatest likelihood of escaping without notice." Lorenzo turned, but stopped at Daniel's next words. "There is one more thing I must ask of you."

Lorenzo's chest tightened. After everything that had happened, he didn't know what to expect.

A half smile touched Daniel's lips. "I can't let you leave without putting up a fight."

Lorenzo understood and drew back his fist. He had to give credit to Daniel, he didn't flinch or cringe; he stood firm as Lorenzo's fist crashed into his jaw. Without a sound, he crumpled to the floor, and Lorenzo slipped out the back flap of the tent.

Chapter Thirty-Two

ANGIE STOOD ON the back porch, her arms wrapped tightly about herself, trying to stay warm. She was chilled from the inside out.

The odds were high Daniel would not hold true to his word. At this very moment they could be standing Lorenzo in place to be shot. They might not even give that much formality to him. She shuddered, thinking of all the things they could do.

But if Daniel remained true to his word, Lorenzo would be a free man, and was probably halfway to Tom. It was foolish to hope that he would come see her, that he had realized all the lies she had told were just lies, and that he wanted to let her know he was alright.

She would probably never know what really happened to him, nor get answers to all the questions running through her mind. If Daniel had freed him, she was never going to see him again.

She sat down on the bottom step, pulling her legs close to her chest, staring at the moon. It would give him enough light to find his way easily to Tom's camp. She couldn't stop the tear that slid down her cheek. She would never see him again, and she had herself to blame for the emotions that were tearing at her.

Olivia had warned Angie what type of man he was. But she hadn't listened. She had been too caught up in his moments of strength, his laughter, his kindness. He taxed her sanity more than anyone she had ever known, and yet she would miss their arguments. She would miss him, regardless.

"Are you already regretting the deal you made?"

Angie drew in a sharp breath of air, her eyes seeking and finding Lorenzo standing at the corner of the house, his stance tense, his eyes hard. There was no warmth in him; there was no appearance that he was pleased to see her.

Angie's hands clutched her skirt as thoughts raced through her mind. She didn't know what to say to him first. Finally, "I see Daniel held to his word."

"What kind of deal did you make with him to make this happen?"

Angie shook her head. "No deal. No pact of any kind."

"A man such as he wouldn't do something like this without promise of something to gain in return."

"I've already promised what he wants to another man."

Lorenzo's body tightened. "Why did you do this? Why?"

Angie avoided his question, not having a clear enough answer in her own mind. "I thought you would be halfway to camp by now."

"I should be. But I had to speak with you first. I had to know."

"What? What did you need to know?"

"Why you betrayed me."

"Why I what?" Angie's voice rose and she bit down on her lower lip to keep from shouting. "I saved your sorry hide, if you haven't noticed!"

"By getting your lover to set me free so I can witness what the two of you have together. You deceived me, Angie."

Angie rose to her feet and stomped forward, not caring that he looked more dangerous than she had ever seen before. If he strangled her, fine. She wasn't going to have him speaking about her before knowing how she felt, even if it meant going nose to nose with him. "If anyone did any deceiving, it is you, Lorenzo Delgado! You lied to me about the reason you were a convict. You deceived me into believing you have been on the Texians side from the beginning. You..."

"I told you why I was in prison. You didn't even need to know that much. You don't need to know everything about my past."

"You were an officer. One of them. You don't think that might have been important for me to know?"

"Why? So you could fling it in my face when you thought I did something wrong? There has been no reason for you to know anything about me. If I had told you about my past, it wouldn't have helped our situation. It is completely irrelevant."

"It would have been nice to know these things before I agreed to work with you!"

Lorenzo leaned forward, and they were almost nose to nose. "If you'll remember correctly, I never wanted to work with you. You forced the whole thing! And you want to know why I didn't want to work with you? Because I knew you would stab me in the back, just the way you did tonight!"

Angie was close to slapping him. "I saved your life tonight. I made sure to free myself—"

"At my expense!"

"Are you a complete fool? Armando knows you. He was going to find a way to kill you no matter what I said. And, if his story is true, he might have a legitimate reason to kill you."

Lorenzo visibly withdrew. "So you saw no point in trying to help me? You figured it was best to cut your losses and get away while you could?"

Angie gritted her teeth. "With both of us being held captive, there was no way either one of us would escape. But if I could get free, I could find a way to free you."

"By using your lover."

"He isn't my lover. He never has been. But, yes, I used his affection for me to my advantage to save your life. But if he hadn't agreed, I was going to go back myself and help you escape."

"How?"

"I don't know! But I was going to do something, even burn down the whole Alamo if that was what it took to get you to safety!" Tears were brimming in her eyes and she wiped hastily at them. "They were going to kill you, and I couldn't bear for that to happen. Regardless of what you have done in the past, I love you, and I wasn't about to let them hurt you." The tears fell now, completely uncontrollable, but she didn't care.

He took a step forward, and his face came into the light. Angie gasped as she saw the bruises, his swollen eye, his purple jaw. "What did he do to you? I never thought him capable..."

"It was Armando, not your beloved Daniel. What did you promise him?"

Angie's fingers curled into fists. "For the last time, I promised him nothing. I have nothing to offer him. He already knows my heart belongs to you."

Lorenzo was silent for several moments and Angie wasn't sure if it was a good thing or not. She wiped at her tears, hating herself for revealing to him how much he hurt her.

Finally, he spoke, his voice low, hoarse. "I used to be an officer in the Mexican Army. I was damned good at what I did. And I thought our government was right, no matter what anyone said."

Angie watched him, her heart pounding in her chest.

"A couple of years ago, information came across my desk about activities of the Texians. I thought, in my inexperienced youth, I could handle the problem on my own. It was far more than I expected it to be and I was captured." He shook his head. "And they opened my eyes to the cruelty of General Santa Anna's ways. I hadn't known... I hadn't seen the things that were being done to the people in the name of Mexico. They freed me, but I made a promise to them. I would work from the inside towards the cause of the Texians."

He was silent for several moments, and Angie could tell that what he was about to say was painful for him. "I had some contacts on the inside of the Mexican government. Together, we began to help the Texians, to provide them with information, to sneak things to them that would help the cause. Armando and his wife became my closest friends."

Angie was visibly shocked by this statement. "You mean they were…"

"Yes. They were Texians. Or so I believed. They continued helping me, and I became very—fond—of Armando's wife. She was seductive; I was young."

Angie closed her eyes, not certain that she wanted to hear anymore. The pain in Lorenzo's voice spoke volumes of the difficulty he was going through. "She was the one? His wife was the one who betrayed you?"

"Yes. She had been misleading me all along. She pretended to be helping me with the Texian cause, while all along she was informing the Mexican government of our every action. Because of her, many Texians were arrested. Many more were killed, though most of the time it was presented as an accident."

Angie's face began to burn. They had been told by the Mexican government that her parents' deaths had been an accident. She squeezed her eyes shut, afraid to hear anything more. But Lorenzo kept speaking, and she had to know the truth.

"I WAS KEPT in prison for many months. I suppose they realized they couldn't get much information on the Texians without me, so they released me, not saying a word as to why. But I knew they expected me to lead them back to the Texians." He turned and looked at Angie, his eyes cold. He wanted to be sure she understood what he said next. "Instead I killed Armando's wife." He shook his head at himself. "She had taught me most of what I knew. She taught me how to follow people, how to disguise myself. A long time ago she had been an actress. I thought she was..." He hesitated, trying to find the right word. "Magic." He shook his head again, looking down at the mud caked on the side of the house. "So I used the skills she had taught me. I found her and I killed her. I strangled her after she shot me." His eyes rose to hers. "They sent me back to prison. I think they all hoped I would die from the wound. I should have been executed. But Armando wouldn't let them. I never knew why and I hated being in his debt. Now... now I think he had intended all along to use me to get to the Texians."

"You think he was following you all this time?"

Lorenzo shook his head. "I killed a man to get here. They weren't going to let me leave Laredo. They knew who I was—knew I would help the Texians as soon as I got the chance. There was another man in the prison. The crimes he had committed... the only reason he hadn't been executed was because they needed him as a soldier. So I killed him and took his place while they marched out. No one noticed... at least not for a while. The other prisoners were too afraid to say anything."

The silence that followed was complete. Neither of them even seemed to breathe, nor did the wind stir. For a few moments, their world was devoid of sound.

Finally, Lorenzo spoke, his voice rough. "I am not proud of the things I have done. I don't expect you to understand."

"Were you really going to kill me when you thought I had betrayed you?"

He looked away from her again. "I wanted to. The anger in me was something I haven't felt since the day she watched me get beaten. Looking at you, I felt I was looking at her again. But then... then..." He looked back at her. "Then, saner minds prevailed."

SHE HUGGED HER arms around herself. "Why did you come here tonight? Why didn't you just go to Tom's?"

"I needed to tell you these things... and I needed to know that you hadn't really betrayed me."

"Do you still feel like I did?"

"No. Though I'm not too crazy about your methods. And you? You now know the truth."

"You're still the man I believed you to be."

"I'm a murderer, Angie. I'm not a thief... well, I did a bit of that, too. But I'm not the man you thought I was."

Angie looked at his face for several long moments. "I can't change who I love."

"Don't say that."

"Why not? It's the truth."

"No, it's not. You're in love with a man that doesn't exist."

Angie reached up and caught his face in her hands. "I'm in love with a man who believes in something so strongly he's willing to risk everything for it. I'm in love with a man whose strength gives me a security I never thought I would feel in my life. I'm in love with a man whose heart is good, but he's had to face decisions in his life I would never, ever wish to make. I'm in love with you, Lorenzo, and there is nothing you can do to change that."

Lorenzo closed his eyes, his face anguished. She leaned forward and kissed his lips softly, then more firmly, her hands threading into his hair. Groaning, he caught her around the waist and pulled her against him, taking control of the kiss.

Angie's hands ran frantically over his back, through his hair, and down his arms. She could barely believe he was alive and that she was back in his arms again, if only for a short time. He was leaving soon, and in her heart, she knew she would never see him again.

He deepened the kiss, turning and pressing her back against the wall of the house, lifting her so she was at the same height as him. Nibbling on his lower lip, she drew her legs up and wrapped them around his waist, pulling him tight against where she ached the most.

He moaned and pulled back, placing kisses down her neck. "Don't love me, Anjelica," he whispered. "Don't love me. You can't."

She dropped her head and placed tiny kisses along the

collar of his jacket. "I love you. I think I have from the moment you picked up that snake." Lorenzo chuckled against her neck, then she gasped as his teeth bit gently on her collarbone. "I don't want you to go," she whispered softly, and instantly regretted her words.

It was as though cold water had been splashed on him, and he slowly pulled away from her, letting her body slide down his. "I'm not the man you want, Angie. As much as I hate to say it, Daniel would be a better man for you. You can depend on him."

"I've been able to depend on you so far."

He shook his head and took a step away from her. "You're wasting your love on me, Angie. I can't—you can't…" He ran a hand through his hair in frustration. "I have to leave, Angie."

"I know." And she did. In her heart, she had always known he would leave. It was her mind that had created the false hope that he would return. "Whatever happens—" Her voice caught on the words and she couldn't continue. Drawing a shaky breath, she wiped at her tears. When she looked up, he was gone.

Chapter Thirty-Three

A NGIE WAS AT the market the morning it began. The sound of gunfire seemed to explode all around her and she dropped the winter lettuce she had been scrutinizing. A woman yelled, "They're attacking! God save us, they're attacking."

Angie heard the sound of running feet and realized there were Texians pouring from every corner. She was too stunned to move. Those around her, however, were shutting the booths rapidly and racing to safety, shoving Angie out of the way.

She dropped her basket when a woman stumbled into her, and quickly kneeled to gather up her purchases. She couldn't comprehend that the battle had finally begun. In the early morning light, the town took on a surreal look, and the gunshots and startled shouts seemed to echo distantly around her.

A gun fired close to her, so close the smell of burned gunpowder stung her nose and her eyes watered from the smoke. It snapped her out of her daze. Pulling upright, her ears ringing, she turned and collided with a Texian soldier.

He was a rough looking fellow, his plaid shirt so worn

the pattern was nearly indiscernible. He looked just as startled as she felt. "You shouldn't be out here, miss," he said in a soft Southern drawl. "It isn't safe."

She didn't know what inspired her. Maybe it was because looking at him she realized how alone Lorenzo probably felt. She stood on tiptoe and placed a quick kiss on his cheek. "God be with you," she said quietly, before racing up the road, leaving a stunned soldier behind her.

She was out of breath and her heart was pounding when she reached the *cocina*. The combination of fear, excitement, and adrenaline had her trembling from head to toe and uncertain whether she wanted to laugh or cry.

The battle they had been preparing for was finally upon them.

The *cocina* seemed to be a moving sea of people and Angie didn't recognize any of them. Pushing past men she could only assume were Texians, she made her way to the back of the house.

Olivia nearly collided with her as she came out of one of the bedrooms. "Angie! Oh, thank God!" She glanced upwards and crossed herself, muttering a quick prayer. She quickly returned her eyes to Angie and grabbed her shoulders. "Where have you been? My God, you've had me worried sick!"

The confusion must have addled all their brains, Angie thought. "I went to the market, remember? We needed—"

"Oh." Olivia gasped, remembering. She pulled Angie into a fierce, quick hug, before stepping back, regaining her typical cool composure. "As you can see"—Olivia gestured to the chaos around them—"the Texians are using our home as a shelter." She ran her hand over her unusually disheveled hair. "I need you to get everyone to the far end of town. We can use that big barn. They'll be safe there."

Angie's mind still felt like mush as she tried to comprehend what Olivia was asking of her. A lamp crashed to the floor, and Olivia stormed over, waving her finger threateningly. "If you continue to behave like heathens, I won't cook any dinner!"

The men looked properly chastised, though it was obvious they were more concerned about living to eat dinner than whether it would be cooked or not. They were clustered together, discussing what they would do next, where their next point of attack would be.

Angie grabbed Olivia's arm, pulling her away from what obviously held her interest. "Who am I taking to the barn?"

Olivia looked at her as though shocked she hadn't left yet. "The family, of course."

"Then you're coming as well."

"No, I will—"

"You're in this family, and I won't see any harm come to you while the rest of us hide!"

Olivia shook her head. "This house is my responsibility."

"It is our responsibility. I will get everyone to the church. But then I'm coming back."

Olivia's look became stern. "No. And that's final. I won't hear any more discussion on the matter." She looked behind Angie and nodded. "Besides, they need you. You can't abandon them."

Angie ground her teeth together as she turned around and saw her grandparents, obviously frightened, but refusing to let it control them, and Serena, who looked like she would break down into a screaming fit at any moment. Olivia always had a way of making the choice for Angie that she didn't want.

But her family was depending on her. And she wasn't about to let them down. She turned back to Olivia. "Don't do anything foolish, Vi."

Olivia's cheeks flamed. "I'm not you, remember."

"Thank the Lord for small things," Grandma muttered and Angie shook her head, gave Olivia a quick kiss on the cheek, and hurried her frightened family out the back door.

Regardless of what anyone said, she wasn't going to hide in a barn while everyone else fought the war.

THE SOUND OF church bells seemed odd amidst the gunfire. Lorenzo leaned back against the side of a house, reloading his gun as he listened to the deep troll of the bells. A priest must be warning the citizens to get to safety. He prayed to God they were listening. Especially the stubborn-willed woman who had haunted his dreams every night since he had left her.

He glanced around the side of the house. The roads were clear. Everyone had taken up positions that offered them the most protection, firing at anything that moved in a red jacket. He shook his head and settled back into his spot, sharing a look of momentary relief with the men near him. It seemed that as soon as they had set foot into town that morning they had been fighting, ducking behind wagons and homes, racing through the roads as pellets kicked up dust and gravel at their feet.

He blinked as sweat rolled into his eyes, surprised to see the sun beginning to dip in the sky. It had seemed only moments earlier he had been standing in a field, watching in admiration as Ben Milam had rallied the men, challenging them to join him as he went into San Antonio. And they had met the challenge. The men, hungry and cold, had raised their weapons and let up a roar that he knew even the soldiers fortressed in the Alamo could hear.

And then they had charged. The adrenaline rushing through each man showed on their faces. As did their determination. After months of sitting in wet, cold fields and listening to others doubt their cause, they were determined to end the stand-off. And they would not go home losers.

So far he knew they had captured at least two houses north of the plaza, and he had seen several of the men taking refuge in other homes. He tilted his head back, letting it rest against the cool stone. He was fighting a battle with himself, trying to convince himself just how foolish it would be to go to the *cocina*. But he desperately wanted to know that Angie was safe and that she hadn't gotten another one of her foolish ideas.

He cringed, ducking his head down in reflex as a cannon exploded nearby. So much for a reprieve. Nodding to the men with him, they pulled themselves together, and once again charged into the fight.

"THEY DESTROYED ONE of our cannons."

Olivia slowed her stirring of the stew as she strained to listen to what was being said. The men rotated in and out of the house, covered in mud from the roads and the soot and smoke from discharging their weapons. Having found a sympathizer, they were fully taking advantage of Olivia's hospitality and the warm food she offered.

After the fifth time of trying to clean the mud off the floor, she gave up and moved anything breakable down to the basement. The rest of the day had been spent cooking and cleaning whatever she could. She was thoroughly exhausted. But when the Texian had entered describing the state of their attack, a new surge of adrenaline burst through her.

"They keep firing on us, but I think we've got them scared."

One of the men who had sat down on the floor and was reclining against the wall spoke over the din the men were causing. "Those cannons of theirs are causing too much damage."

"It hasn't stopped us yet!" another voice spoke up.

A loud boom rocked them and dust shuddered down from the rafters. A silence fell over the men, each of them watching the dark roads outside.

"Stew's ready," Olivia announced, her voice seeming

loud in the silence, but it stirred the men again, and they eagerly pushed forward for the warm food.

As Olivia served them, watching their weary faces so grateful for the small bowl of soup, she made a decision. She would not stand around cooking and cleaning while these men risked their lives for their freedom. She wanted to do more.

BEN MILAM WAS dead. The news brought a somber mood to the group, but they had to press on. They had been in San Antonio for two days. Lorenzo had slept during that time, he just couldn't remember when or even where he had lay down.

By the end of the second day, he had made his way far enough north in the city to join Tom in the Garza house. Several buildings had been destroyed and they were still digging trenches to connect the houses, offering them protection from the continuous onslaught of musket fire and the occasional cannon fire.

The injuries had been at a minimum, but Lorenzo kept hearing a story repeated over and over that had his skin chilled. As evening grew on their third day, Lorenzo ran into a man with a bandaged arm moving through the trench between the homes. The man, despite his injury, was grinning. "The angels are on our side," he chuckled as he passed Lorenzo.

He whirled to face the man, struck by the comment he

had heard from another injured soldier earlier that day. "What do you mean?" he demanded, wincing inwardly at how harsh his voice sounded.

The man was still grinning. "An angel came and treated my wound."

"Who? What was her name?"

The man shrugged. "I don't know. I was so surprised to see her... I doubt I spoke two words the entire time she wrapped my arm."

Lorenzo looked at the petticoat strips around the man's arm and felt a growing anger and fear building in him. "What did she look like?"

The man was beginning to look impatient to leave. "Dark hair. Gray eyes." He shrugged again.

Lorenzo muttered his thanks and let the man leave. In his gut he knew it was Angie. Three other men that day had talked about an angel that moved among them, giving them water, fetching more ammunition before they even realized they were low, tending to their wounds. They said she walked through the flying bullets, never once getting scraped.

It sent a chill through him that wouldn't go away. But he couldn't concentrate on Angie. They had been ordered to capture the buildings on Zambrano Row, a stretch of homes near the Alamo. Easily one hundred men that had been creating distractions on the other side of town had rejoined them, and their chances of success were high.

Despite the chill that caused his breath to plume in the air, sweat rolled between his shoulder blades and on his forehead. They moved quickly through the dark town, every man on his toes, prepared to see the enemy jump from any shadow.

A shout startled all of them, and it seemed all hell broke loose around them. Pouring onto the road from within the homes came dozens of Mexican soldiers, their bayonets drawn, and fire in their eyes.

With a fierce yell, the Texians plunged forward, guns becoming clubs as their usefulness failed at close range. Lorenzo fought as though a man possessed. Holding his gun as a club in his left hand and his knife in his right, he slashed and struck, feeling the warmth of blood on his hands and knowing his enemies fell.

A blow to his shoulder knocked him off balance and he spun, knife plunging into the Mexican soldier's stomach. His eyes widened as he looked into the face of one of the soldiers he had worked alongside while he had pretended to be a Mexican soldier.

He was just a boy, barely strong enough to carry his pack and supplies. Lorenzo pulled the knife from his body, gripping his shoulder, seeing the look of startled betrayal in his youthful eyes.

The sound of the battle faded away around him as he stared at him, wanting to apologize, wanting to change the course that had led them to stand face-to-face on a bloody battlefield. But there was nothing he could say. They had chosen different sides, and it was war.

Lorenzo suddenly needed Angie. He needed her in his arms, beside him, wrapping him in the innocence of her love that shielded him from the pain of the real world. He needed her.

With a final gasp of breath, the boy fell to the ground, and the sound of the battle exploded around Lorenzo. He forced himself forward, forced himself to continue in the battle. The cause he fought for was just and death was an inevitable part of it.

But none of it seemed important anymore. All he could think of was getting back to Angie, and by whatever means possible.

ANGIE MOVED QUICKLY among the men lining the trenches, bringing them water and encouragement. Many of them were so exhausted they no longer looked up at her in surprise. A woman walking in the battlefield was a strange occurrence, but most just nodded at her and gratefully accepted the water she offered.

As soon as she had gotten Serena and her grandparents secure at the other end of town and surrounded by their neighbors, she had raced back to the *cocina*. Olivia was running about, trying to clean up mud off everything and keep food from burning at the same time.

Angie knew she needed help, but Vi would only send her back. Her sister was too stubborn for her own good.

Knowing she needed to do something, but still not certain what, Angie grabbed canteens from their place on the porch wall and snuck in the back door into her room.

Working quietly, praying every moment Vi didn't discover her, she stuffed an old bag full of torn petticoats and one of her grandfather's hidden bottles of whiskey.

When she ran back outside, she was startled by the smoke that clung to the air. The cannon fire and gunfire had become so heavy the residual smoke was creating a blanket over the town.

As she walked in the trench, she shook her head. She didn't even notice the smoke anymore, though it was still hanging heavy over them. If anything, it was becoming thicker from the increase in fighting.

The men suddenly moved, like the shifting of a wave, and Angie moved quickly to stay out of their path.

"We captured Zamborno Row!" a soldier called excitedly, moving through the trench, proclaiming the exciting news.

Angie's breath caught. Could that be where Lorenzo was? She had searched for him the past couple days, looking at every face, hoping to catch a glimpse of him, hoping to be reassured that he was alive and safe. Alive at least. None of them were safe until it was over.

She watched as a couple of men came stumbling through the trench, their legs bloodied, their arms bloodied, leaning on the shoulders of their comrades, and she squared her shoulders and drew a deep breath. She was needed.

LORENZO FOUND A spot on the floor of the house that

wasn't occupied by a man trying to catch a few winks of sleep. Clenching his teeth he peeled back his shirt from the fresh bayonet wound on his arm. He hadn't been able to dodge the blow fast enough, though it hadn't struck his heart like had been intended.

A man, leaning against the wall, his arms crossed over his chest and his eyes half lowered in sleep nudged him. "You ought to get the angel to patch you up."

Lorenzo's heart skipped a beat at the thought. "Is she here? Have you seen her?" If he found her he would kiss her until he fell asleep in her arms. And then he would shake her until her teeth rattled in her head and she agreed to never put herself in such danger again.

"She was here not too long ago. I haven't seen her in a while, though."

It was all that Lorenzo needed to hear. Pushing himself to his feet he made his way across the room once again and back into the trench. If there was even a small chance Angie was nearby, he would keep looking for her. The thought of her walking among all the men, placing herself in the onslaught of bullets, made knots form in his stomach. He was going to make sure she was safe as soon as everything was over. And then he would leave. He was certain that once he knew she was safe, once he knew she was alright, he would be able to leave. He just needed to find her first.

Chapter Thirty-Four

IT SEEMED IT would never end. Angie rubbed at eyes that had become grainy from lack of sleep. She wasn't exactly sure how many days it had been. Sometime in the past day she had gone back to the barn to make sure Serena hadn't caused too much trouble and to reassure Grandma and Grandpa that she was alright.

She had barely gotten away. She hated lying to them, but the only way she was allowed to leave again was by claiming she was going to help Olivia. She had looked in on her as she headed towards the Alamo and was relieved to see her sister looked none worse for wear. She still hurried about the house, still lectured the men on manners in her home.

Now evening was closing in on them again, and Angie could feel herself nodding off where she sat in one of the captured houses. Even the sound of bullets striking the side of the house and men shouting was unable to disturb her exhaustion. When hands gripped her shoulders she jerked in surprise, her eyes flying open.

Tom kneeled in front of her, his face covered in soot and grime, a weary smile on his lips. "My dear, Ms. Angie, this is no place for you to be. Why aren't you at the other end of town where it is safe?"

Angie straightened, smoothing her skirt and blinking rapidly, trying to snap out of the sleepiness that pulled her down. "I-I want to help. I just dozed off for a moment."

Tom helped her to her feet. "You are exhausted. No matter how good your intentions, you are no good to us if something happens or you get in the way because of your exhaustion."

Though Angie wanted to argue, Tom was right. She could be a hindrance instead of the help she needed to be. She nodded slowly and turned towards the door.

She hesitated, her eyes looking back at Tom hopefully. "Lorenzo. Have you seen him? Is he alright?"

Tom gave her an understanding smile. "The two of you became quite a good team, after all."

Her cheeks flamed, but she was too tired to care. "I saw him yesterday, and he looked fine. You don't need to worry about him. He's quite the fighter." He hesitated, looking at her speculatively. "Does he know you're doing this?"

Angie lifted her chin. "No. And he doesn't need to know, either. I don't need his permission."

Tom chuckled and shook his head, but his gaiety quickly vanished when a cannonball exploded nearby. "You get to safety, Miss Angie. I have a feeling it's going to be a rough night."

LORENZO RUBBED HIS arm across his face, wishing he had

gotten more sleep. He felt sluggish, and the jagged cut in his shoulder was a constant irritation.

They had built up a short wall in front of the trench, and they were staggered across the line, facing the Mexican soldiers who kept trying to break through. He didn't know how many men they had lost yet, but he had seen several Texian bodies being pulled away from the battle. He wondered how many more he hadn't seen.

Still, it appeared the Mexicans were losing more. They might be a rough bunch, but the Texians were some crack shots, and few bullets missed their mark.

He no longer flinched at the musket shots flying around him or jumped when he heard the whistle of an approaching cannonball. It had become such a common thing his motions stayed even and his eyes didn't even blink. His nerves were numb.

Wiping at his eyes again, he focused on the men that were gathering themselves hundreds of yards away—just far enough away that any shot would be a waste of ammunition.

It was the third time the Mexican Army had regrouped. Rumor was spreading that several troops had abandoned the cause and fled as Cos began to pull back into the Alamo. The Mexicans were definitely on the defensive. And as long as they didn't receive any more reinforcements, victory was in sight for the Texians.

To Lorenzo's left and right, his fellow Texians, looking as weary as he felt, prepared for the next attack, checking to make sure weapons were primed and loaded. A young man not far away was loading his gun, his fingers shaking slightly, and Lorenzo wished there was something he could say to comfort him. But when they were so close to killing or being killed, words didn't help much.

Lorenzo's eyes narrowed as he watched the boy. He wasn't as dirty as the rest of them, and he wondered if he had joined later, perhaps escaping from his protective family so he could join the fight.

But something wasn't right.

The boy's hands were slender and pale and, despite the slight tremble, moved smoothly in preparing the gun. The boy was skinny, obviously not having filled out yet into the man he would be, but he appeared to be tall.

The boy cast a glance in his direction, looking over and past him, and Lorenzo felt as though someone had just punched him in the gut. That "boy" looked way too feminine. In fact, he looked like—

Lorenzo was scrambling to his feet when the attack came, and he quickly dropped back down with a curse, taking aim with his rifle, and firing into the soldiers that were beginning to march on them.

Trying to prime his rifle as he crouched down and worked his way around the other men in the trench, he cursed the day he had walked into that little *cocina*.

He watched her fire a shot and fall on her rump as the kick of the gun slammed the butt into her shoulder. Without batting an eye, she was up again and reloading, her face filled with steely determination.

He fired off two more shots before he finally reached her. "What the hell do you think you're doing!" he shouted.

She looked over at him in surprise, her eyes wide in her face, and was slow to recognize him.

She shook her head firmly at him. "This is my fight, too." She turned back, took aim, and fired.

This time she didn't fall down, but she did rock backwards before regaining her balance. Her target fell to the ground, never to move again.

Lorenzo fired another shot and they both ducked down to reload their guns. "I thought your sister was the only one stupid enough to go traipsing around in men's clothes."

Olivia didn't look at him. "Obviously, you've misjudged me as well as my sister, for neither of us is stupid." She glanced at him as she braced the rifle against her shoulder once again. "Unless you confuse stupidity with determination. You might find yourself called stupid."

She stood to take aim, and it took him a moment to snap his mouth shut and take aim alongside her. The soldiers had moved in quickly, and they were close enough now that he could see the face of his enemy as he shot him. Olivia could, too, for her trembling increased, but she didn't waver, and pulled the trigger. A soldier yelled in pain and fell to the ground. Olivia was as pale as a sheet.

"If you want to continue this craziness, you should at least learn how to shoot."

She glared at him. "My father taught me. I know how to shoot just fine."

"If you were still a child aiming at leaves, yes. But you're not, and you're going to tear up your shoulder if you keep doing that."

Olivia was reloading the gun, her fingers beginning to fumble with her trembles. "I'll be just fine."

"I can—"

"No." She looked up at him with angry eyes. "I don't want anything from you. I don't need anything from you. Unlike my sister, I don't want anything to do with you."

The sisters must have been born for the purpose of being a plague on a man's patience. He turned his back on her and fired off two rounds while she continued trying to load her gun.

"Where's Angie?" he finally asked, unable to hold back.

"She's safe at the other end of town."

Lorenzo raised an eyebrow as he started to reload. Olivia stood and took aim.

"Are you sure about that?"

Her eyes narrowed on her target and she pulled the trigger. "There's nowhere else for her to be."

"And she probably thinks the same of you."

Olivia opened her mouth, then shut it quickly and took aim again. Her gun fired loudly. She turned to face him. "Have you seen her?" she demanded angrily.

"No, but I've heard many soldiers talking about a woman helping them, and it sounds very much like Angie."

"I'll kill her," she growled as she primed her gun with quick, angry motions and reloaded.

A whistling in the air drew Lorenzo's attention. It sounded different this time. The hair on the back of his neck rose and he grabbed Olivia's arm.

"Move!" he shouted when she looked like she was going

to fight.

He nearly threw her out of the trench, jumping after her, scrambling right alongside a dozen other men who were trying to escape the falling cannonball. It exploded behind them and Lorenzo felt himself being propelled in the air, the fire from the explosion heating the soles of his feet. He struck the ground with a grunt, rolling several times until he finally came to a stop.

He pushed himself to his hands and knees, thankful that all pieces appeared intact, his eyes searching through the smoke for Olivia. He finally saw her several yards away from him, also slowly trying to push herself to her feet. She looked disoriented. He could understand why. His ears were still ringing from the explosion.

He hurried towards her, his pace quickening as a new fear was realized. The Mexican soldiers were advancing, and one was headed straight for Olivia. He raised his rifle, but remembered he hadn't reloaded before the cannonball had struck.

Cursing, he ran around the debris of the destroyed homes, but he wasn't going to get to her before the soldiers did. The man raised his bayonet as she finally gained her feet, and he charged forward. He stopped before he reached her though, as though a rope had yanked him from behind. He swayed for a moment, then pitched forward, directly on top of Olivia.

Lorenzo pulled his knife from the sheath on his calf, anticipating more soldiers to turn in their direction, but the Texians were coming at them with a vengeance and they were falling back.

Lorenzo grabbed the man's jacket and hauled him back. Blood was everywhere, and Lorenzo felt sick. Until he realized the blood belonged to the soldier. His eyes were glassy in death and his chest was soaked through with blood.

She had shot him. Her rifle lay at her side. Tossing the man off of her, he leaned down and caught Olivia's shoulders. She began fighting madly, her fists flying, her legs kicking.

"Olivia! Open your eyes. It's me, Lorenzo." She continued to struggle. He hauled her to her feet and shook her lightly and her fist struck his jaw. "Olivia!"

Her eyes flew open and she saw him, but she still tried to push away. Around them the battle waged on and they were standing in the middle of it like two perfect targets. Grabbing her flying fists, he half dragged, half carried her away from the battle and around the corner of a home where they would be shielded from any stray musket fire.

He grabbed her chin and forced her to look at him. "Are you hurt?" He was surprised to see tears running down her cheeks, leaving trails in the dust that covered her.

"What?"

"Are you hurt? Did he hurt you?"

She shook her head and shouted, "I can't hear you. Speak up!"

Lorenzo's ears were still ringing from the blast, but he could hear, though muffled. He turned her face to the side and pulled her hair back, checking her ear. It looked fine. But when he turned her face the other direction, he frowned darkly.

Blood ran from her left ear and there was too much of it as well as dirt from her fall for him to see how badly the damage was. But it was highly possible her hearing would never be the same again.

He spoke loudly into her right ear. "Get out of here. Find Serena and get her to take care of you."

She pulled away from him and looked at him as though he had lost his mind. "I'm here to fight and that's exactly what I plan to do." She was still yelling. She was still crying.

She was completely unaware of the tears that spilled down her face. Had she known, she would have been mortified. As hard and tough as she wanted everyone to think she was, she wouldn't have wanted to be seen like this. Especially by Lorenzo.

She stepped away from him quickly and grabbed her rifle and clasped it tightly in her hands, looking at the blood as though she had no idea where it had come from.

Slowly she looked back at Lorenzo. "He was going to kill me."

She was in shock, Lorenzo realized belatedly as he nodded at her. She was beginning to shake as the violent rush of adrenaline slowly faded from her. "But I killed him instead."

"You did what any good soldier would do," he said loudly into her good ear. She blinked and her knees gave out on her.

He caught her and propped her up against the wall of the house, sticking a threatening finger in her face. "Go, now, Olivia. You're hurt and you need help, and none of us here can do that right now."

"I can fight just as—" She winced suddenly, her hand reaching up to her ear.

He was about to stop her, but decided against it. Perhaps finding that most of her ear was torn off from her injury would jolt some sense into her.

The expression on her face was nearly comical in its severity as she pulled her hand away covered in her own blood. "But he didn't get to me. I shot him before he reached me."

She thought the soldier had done this to her. Lorenzo gave her a hard look. "It was the cannonball, Olivia. Something must have struck you and cut your ear. It's probably why you can't hear. Now, go get someone to help you."

She looked up at him as she realized what had happened. She was pale, but she seemed to have better control of herself as she nodded.

She began to turn around then caught his shirt sleeve, not quite looking at him. "I believe I misjudged you."

Lorenzo was startled by her comment. Startled, and humbled. "I think we've all done our fair share of that."

She looked as though she wanted to say more, then slowly shook her head and turned, walking quickly away, her hands out to her sides to try to keep her balance.

Lorenzo shook his head as he watched her, marveling at the strength of the woman. Then, with a deep breath, he turned back to the battle.

OLIVIA HAD HER back to the battle as she headed back towards the safety and security outside of town. But it wasn't where she wanted to go. She wanted to return to the fight—to see it through to the end, whatever that might be.

Determination began to build in her once more and she turned to tell Lorenzo her place was in the battle. Her words died on her lips.

She watched, frozen in disbelief, as a cannonball came through the darkness, headed straight for Lorenzo. He was running back towards the battle, unaware of the danger he was in.

"Stop!" she screamed at the top of her lungs, finally able to get her voice to work.

He hesitated, glancing back over his shoulder at her, and the ground exploded.

He was tossed into the air as the building he had stood next to crumbled all around him. She forced her feet to move, though she felt like she was trudging through water. Dust and smoke clung to the air, making it difficult to breathe or see. By the time she got to the rubble, Lorenzo was nowhere in sight and some of the men had paused in their attack on the Mexicans to try to pull large chunks of rock away from the building.

She shoved her way forward, pulling at the rocks around her, digging with her hands where she had last seen him fall. Fragments of conversation passed through Olivia's hearing, and she couldn't stop the tear that rolled down her cheek.

"Leave him—"

"Too late…"

"Get the body later—"

"No," she said, still digging. And then she felt flesh and, through her tears, she focused on the bloody hand protruding from the rocks. The rest of his body was hidden by the pile. The realization was like being punched in the gut. Lorenzo was dead.

She turned from the rubble and hurried up the road as fast as she could, wanting to escape it all. Dear God, how was she going to tell Angie?

Chapter Thirty-Five

"IT'S OVER!"

"Did he say it's over?"

"Cos surrendered!"

"Sweet Mother Mary! Cos has surrendered?"

"What does this mean?"

"It means we're free!"

The barn doors opened and slowly, the people of San Antonio walked out onto the roads, looking around their town, all of them wondering what they would find. Those that had stayed in their homes also wandered out into the roads, everyone hesitant and curious at the same time.

Smoke clung to the air in the midmorning sunlight, but there was no longer the sound of gunfire, no longer the horrible sound of cannonballs exploding, no longer the agonized cries of men in pain.

Angie grasped Olivia's hand as they walked out into the road. Serena had her arms wrapped around Angie's waist, one of the few times Angie had ever seen the girl calm and tame. Grandma and Grandpa were behind them, holding on to each other, as they had through the entire time they had been cooped up in the temporarily converted barn.

"It's finally over," Angie said in awe.

Olivia said nothing, just stared down the road towards the Alamo. Angie watched her sister for a few moments, wondering what she was thinking. The previous night she had come to the church, pale and quiet, greeting the family only briefly before retreating to the loft, staring out at the smoke close to the Alamo. Angie wondered if something had happened at the *cocina*. She was even wearing her hair differently. The severe bun on top of her head they were all so accustomed to seeing had been replaced with just as severe a bun settled low on her neck, pulling her hair lower.

Olivia turned to look at her, catching her stare. "What?" she demanded.

"There's something different about you."

Olivia shook her head. "I'm just tired, that's all. We're all just tired." She glanced back up the road. "What do you think is happening?" She turned back to face Angie.

Angie shrugged. "I don't know. Do you think they're going to take the Mexicans as prisoners?"

Olivia shrugged, then looked at Serena. "It's over now."

Serena smiled, though she kept her arms tight around Angie's waist. "And we won," she said proudly, drawing an odd look from those around her. "What happens now?" she asked.

Neither Olivia nor Angie had the answer for her. A new government was being born. So many things would be changing, and it was impossible to know what was next. But there was one thing they could be certain of. "We celebrate."

THOUGH THEIR GRANDPARENTS were disappointed with the outcome of the battle, they were relieved the fighting was over and a peace settled over San Antonio that had long been missing. Though several spontaneous celebrations broke out, a large one was planned for the eve of the fifteenth.

The Torres family was doing all they could to ensure the *fandango* would be one to remember. Angie and Olivia threw themselves into the task of making dozens upon dozens of *tamales* while Serena helped their grandparents prepare sweet pastries full of cinnamon and vanilla creating a delightful aroma in the kitchen.

Though it had been four days since the fighting had ended, Angie still clung to the hope that at any moment Lorenzo would walk through the door. He had said he wouldn't return, but she didn't want to believe it. Surely, he had felt the same need as she, the need to be together.

She was smoothing the *masa* onto the cornhusk when the front door opened and a blast of cold air came rushing in. Angie looked up at the plainly dressed man who was pulling off his hat. "I'm sorry, *senor*, but the *cocina* is closed. But you can come back in the…" Her words trailed off as the man looked up and smiled at her.

"Tom!" Olivia and Angie said in unison, stepping forward to greet him.

"I had to see for myself this wonderful place for breakfast that my men have been talking about. I knew it must be yours."

Olivia smiled and offered him coffee, which he gratefully accepted. "It's a mite cold out there," he said, warming his hands on the mug. "I'll be surprised if many come to the celebration tonight."

Angie smiled. "One thing about San Antonio, we're always ready for a *fandango*, no matter the weather."

Tom smiled at her, then slowly turned somber. "I'm sorry about Lorenzo, Miss Angie. I know you two had become rather close."

Angie blinked. Had Lorenzo told Tom he was leaving her forever? The thought was disturbing. "What did he—"

A motion from Olivia drew her attention. She was fidgeting with her collar the way she always did when she was nervous, and her face was terribly pale. "Angie, I didn't know how to tell you…"

Angie's hands began to sweat despite the cold in the air. "Tell me what?"

Tom looked beyond flustered, and forgetting his manners, crammed his hat on his head. "No one told you?"

Her heart was beginning to pound and she felt vaguely ill. "Tell me what?" she demanded again, her voice tense.

Olivia caught her hand, watching her with a sorrowful expression. "Angie, Lorenzo was… there was a cannonball and…"

"Lorenzo didn't survive the battle," Tom said, finishing what Olivia couldn't bring herself to say.

Angie felt as though the floor had been yanked out from under her and she sat down hard in a chair, staring disbelievingly at Olivia and Tom. "It's not possible. It's just not possible. He is an excellent soldier…"

Olivia kneeled in front of her, looking at her with concerned eyes. "I tried to tell you a hundred times, but I couldn't. I didn't know how."

Angie focused her eyes on her sister, trying to make sense of a suddenly very confusing world. "But how did you… I mean, who told you?"

A flush crept up Olivia's cheeks. "I wanted a peek at the fighting. I know it was foolish, but I did it. I saw Lorenzo fighting. He was very brave, but nothing could have protected him from that cannonball."

Angie was strangely numb, and their voices seemed to be coming from very far away. "I want to see him."

Olivia and Tom both looked shocked. "I don't think that's a good idea," Olivia said gently.

Angie focused her attention on Tom. "You haven't buried him yet, have you? I want to see him."

Tom shook his head and shifted his hat back. "I don't know what's been done, Miss Angie. I just got word about what happened. Everybody's so scattered right now, I don't know if they've even been able to find him yet."

The image of his lifeless body buried under a pile of rocks was more than Angie could bear. "If you'll excuse me." Her voice was strained. "I have many *tamales* to make before tonight." She stood and walked to the kitchen with her back ramrod straight.

OLIVIA AND TOM exchanged glances, then Tom, obviously uncomfortable, stood and took a step towards the door. He hesitated, looking back at Olivia. "Why did you lie to her?"

Olivia fidgeted with her blouse. "What are you talking about?"

"I saw you out there, fighting with us. You didn't come out there for a peek."

Olivia licked her lips. "I don't want them to know. I constantly lecture them about being cautious—about not doing something foolish…"

"Hmm." Tom watched her for several seconds then shrugged. "What you do is no business of mine. But I appreciate everything you ladies did for us."

Olivia walked him to the door and received his promise that he would be at the *fandango*, before reluctantly returning to the kitchen. Angie was working furiously on the *tamales*, slapping the *masa* on the husks and smoothing it out in a speed that made Olivia tired.

"How many do you think we should make?" She didn't look up from her work as she spoke. "I'm sure everyone will eat at least three apiece since it will be cold."

"Angie…" Olivia didn't know what to say. "Angie, you should rest for a moment. Step outside to get some fresh air."

Angie ignored her, though her rhythmic movement became choppy. Olivia's hands caught Angie's, forcing her to stop. When Angie finally looked at her, Olivia wanted to cry for the anguish she saw in her sister's eyes.

"He's not dead."

Olivia shook her head. "What?"

"He's not dead. I would know it. I would feel it. He's not dead." Angie's hands began to shake and tears welled up in her eyes.

Olivia drew a deep breath, at a loss for words. "Angie…" she began hesitantly, "I saw… I saw him. I tried to dig him out of the rubble. It was too late. He didn't—he's dead, Angie. I know he is because I saw him, I-I held his hand and it was cold. He's dead. He fought very bravely. There was just no way he could avoid that cannonball."

Angie was shaking her head, the tears flowing down her cheeks now. "No. You don't know what you saw. It was a battle. It was chaotic. There's no way you can be certain…" Her lower lip trembled. "I would feel it," she said, pressing a hand against her heart. "Wouldn't I?"

"I should have been there! I should have been with him…" Olivia's arms tightened around her as she finally gave in to her anguish.

Chapter Thirty-Six

T HE MUSIC WAS lively, the drinks were intoxicating, and the joy of the people was infectious. Regardless of which side had won, the battle was over and San Antonio was free of the Mexican Army that had crowded their roads for so long.

Cos had surrendered to Edward Burleson, the leader of the Texians, early in the morning and had relinquished most of his supplies. Burleson allowed him to take his men south only after Cos signed a document stating Texas was free of Mexican rule. Though the future looked promising, there was a fear that Santa Anna would retaliate, angry that his brother-in-law, General Cos, had been defeated by a group of farmers and ranchers.

The rest of the day half the town had worked on repairing all the damage the homes near the Alamo had sustained while the other half prepared for a *fandango*. It was time to celebrate.

The party had sprung up in the middle of the road, the men bringing out their guitars and singing tunes that were only occasionally off-key. The women had come out dressed in their finest, beautiful silks and brocades in every style and color. Yet they did not seem to mind the dirt in the road getting on their fine dresses as they twirled around happily in a lively dance.

Angie didn't want to have anything to do with it. She stood on the side of the road with Olivia, a fake smile plastered to her face as she handed out warm *tamales* to the revelers. The impromptu dance made it glaringly obvious the shortage of women in the small town, and Angie and Olivia were barraged with pleas for dances. Olivia coolly declined; Angie numbly followed her sister's example.

"At least it isn't too terribly cold," she said, thankful for her warm, yet fashionable dress. Olivia said nothing, just watched the dancers. "Why don't you go join them? I can take care of things." Olivia still said nothing. "Are you listening to me?" Angie asked, catching Olivia's arm. Her sister jumped.

"What?"

Angie looked at her through narrowed eyes. "Your mind must be a thousand miles away."

Olivia's smile was hesitant. "I was just watching the dancers. They seem to be having a good time."

"Then go join them."

"No, no. I don't want to have anything…"

"Miss Olivia, I insist that you honor me with this dance."

Both sisters looked up in surprise to find Tom standing in front of them, his face clean-shaven, his wild hair slicked back under his hat. "And after that dance, I'll be wantin' some of those *tamales*."

Angie nudged Olivia. "You can't say no."

Olivia hesitated, glancing back at Angie. "I'll be fine." She reassured her and Olivia joined Tom in the milling mass of dancers.

Angie kept a smile on her face as she handed out the *tamales*. Her cheek muscles were beginning to hurt. At least she had finally stopped crying. She didn't think she had any tears left. Yet as she watched the dancers, as she watched the smiling faces, she felt a burning in her eyes. Lorenzo should be a part of the happy crowd. He should be there, enjoying what he had worked so hard to achieve.

Her throat grew tight and she turned from the crowd, busying herself by checking how many *tamales* were left. She might have to go back to the *cocina* and get the extras she had set aside. It would be a welcome reprieve.

Glancing back to make sure Olivia was still with Tom, Angie tugged her shawl tighter around herself and headed up the road, away from the noise and into the silence. Everyone in town was at the *fandango*, the rest of the road was empty—ghostlike. She shivered and quickened her step. Even though everyone she knew was celebrating, there were soldiers who might be looking for entertainment elsewhere.

She stepped into the welcome warmth of her home and quickly lit a small lantern, thankful the kitchen fire hadn't gone out yet. She had counted on it to keep the *tamales* warm in case she needed them. The food was covered with a towel and sitting on the ledge near the fire, the scent of the *masa* and seasonings filling Angie's nostrils. For a moment, she stopped in the kitchen and leaned against the counter, trying to gather the strength to go back and join the happy people of the town. She didn't know how much longer she could smile.

"*Hola*, Angie."

Angie's heart leapt in her throat and she whirled towards the dining room, her eyes searching the darkness. Her hands felt along the counter for the knife she knew was close. "Who is there?"

There was a sound from a table at the corner of the room and her eyes focused on the outline of a man reclining in one of the chairs. "What do you want?" she demanded, feeling slightly reassured as her fingers circled the handle of the knife.

"I've come to say goodbye."

Angie's heart was racing. "Step into the light. Who are you?" What kind of man sat in the darkness of a woman's home, waiting for her? Not a man she wanted to know.

The man in the corner leaned forward and he barely entered the circle of light. A dark lock of hair curled on his forehead and his hazel eyes were hard in the faint light.

Angie's eyes narrowed, trying to see more clearly as he leaned forward a little more. She gasped, her knife clattering to the floor. She took a step backwards until her back hit the counter, a hand over her mouth, shaking her head.

A smile lifted the corners of the man's mouth, but it didn't reach his eyes. "I'm not one of Serena's ghosts, I promise."

Angie didn't know what to say. She didn't know what to think. It wasn't possible. Or was it? "How—" Her voice broke and she swallowed hard. "I thought… they told me…"

Lorenzo watched her with a dark expression, his emotions hidden. All she could see of him was his face, he wouldn't step out of the darkness, and she was afraid he was exactly what he had said he wasn't. Her heart was pounding so loudly she couldn't hear her own thoughts.

"I didn't know if I should come or not."

She shook her head, trying to form a complete thought. "Why? Why wouldn't you want me to know you're… you're alive?"

Saying the words out loud made her realize he really was sitting in front of her, that she could reach out… Tears filled her eyes. But he was more distant from her than ever and she didn't know if she could touch him or not.

Lorenzo was silent for a while, obviously trying to think of what to say. "I didn't know if anyone had told you what had happened or not. I thought it would be better for you if you thought I had just left and never returned."

Angie drew a slow breath and grabbed the lantern, taking a step towards him. She stopped when he shook his head. "I shouldn't have come."

"And let me believe you were dead?"

"I didn't know you thought that. I didn't know anyone had seen what happened."

Angie was in so much turmoil, nothing made any sense. Every fiber of her wanted to run to him and hold him, kiss him, know that he was alive and in her arms again. But there was a wall in front of him, blocking her out, keeping her away, and she didn't know why. "How did you… What happened?"

"I didn't see the cannonball coming." He shook his head. "I just didn't see it. The next thing I knew the building was coming down next to me. I couldn't move fast enough."

Angie's hands began to shake, thinking of what had happened to him. She could only imagine how terrifying it had been. She had seen the buildings exploding during the battle.

But she hadn't been close to any of them. "Olivia said she saw you... she said it was too late to save you."

His eyebrows lifted and he was silent for a moment. "It should have been," he said finally. "The rocks came down all around me. I don't remember much after that. When I woke up, it must have been daytime, because I could see some light through the rocks."

Angie wiped at the tears on her face. "I... I didn't want to believe you were dead. I didn't want to think that you..." Her voice trailed off.

She didn't want to tell him how much it had devastated her to think that she would never see his face again.

"I told you I wasn't coming back."

Angie blinked. Then suddenly their conversation from days ago came back to her. It seemed it had been a lifetime since that moment. "I know. But I didn't want to believe you."

"Why?" He looked angry, and there was another expression on his face she didn't understand. "Why didn't you believe me? I meant everything I said."

Angie searched his face, looking for any nicks or scrapes. He was alive, and there was nothing more she wanted. "I had to hope."

"I'm still leaving."

"I know."

"Then don't look at me like that."

"Like what?"

"Like you want me to stay."

A soft smile touched her lips. "Only minutes ago, I thought I had lost you forever and there was no chance that I would see your face again. I thought you were dead. It was…" She tried to control her tears. "It was unbearable to think that you were gone. But you aren't dead. That's all I need."

"I can't stay."

She swallowed hard, trying to decide what to say. "Why did you come back?"

"I wanted to make sure you were safe."

"You should know me well enough by now to know I can take care of myself." She gave him a shaky smile. She couldn't take her eyes off of him. Never had she seen him look as good to her as he did now. There was a cut on his lip and a bruise on his cheek, but he looked incredible. She just wished she could hold him.

But Lorenzo didn't look happy. He looked frustrated. "Where were you during the battle?"

Angie was surprised. Of all things for him to talk about, she hadn't expected the topic to be about her activities during the battle. She hadn't even known he was aware of her escapades. But obviously, from the dark frown on his face, he was, and he wasn't happy about it. "It doesn't matter. You're here. You're alive. That's the only thing that is important."

His frown deepened and he leaned back into the shadows, concealing his face from her, effectively closing her out to everything that was going on in his mind. She didn't understand his behavior. When he had left her so many days ago, her heart had told her he felt something for her… that he needed her just as much as she needed him. Had she been so wrong? She didn't know what was wrong but, by God, she would treasure every last minute she had with him.

"Answer my question," he said softly.

"I was at the battle. But I think you already know that."

"Do you have any idea the risk you took?"

"Yes. The same risk you took."

Lorenzo leaned forward again and she saw a bandaged shoulder. "It's not the same. You can't do things like that! You can't just—"

"Why?"

Lorenzo raked a hand through his hair. "Don't ever put yourself in that kind of danger again, do you understand? I don't ever want to hear stories of your foolish bravery again."

Angie couldn't stand it any longer. She had to touch him. She had to feel that he was real. Setting down the lantern, she took three, quick steps across the room and kneeled in front of him. His face was a mask, though he didn't look happy with her move.

Tears filled her eyes as she saw the bandages covering him, from his shoulder all the way to his leg. The left side of his body was nearly covered in wraps.

"How bad is it?" she whispered.

He pulled back when her hands reached for him, his face anguished. "Don't."

Angie grabbed his face and forced him to look at her, her fingers lovingly caressing his cheeks, his lips, his eyes. "Do you know how much it tormented me when… when Olivia told me you were dead? Do you know what it did to me? It tore my heart out. It… it was as though I was dying, too. I couldn't bear the thought… I didn't want to…" Her throat closed up and she squeezed her eyes shut, trying not to let the tears fall, but she couldn't help it.

Lorenzo's hand came up slowly, hesitantly, and cupped her face. "Don't do this," he said harshly. "Don't make this harder than it already is."

Her eyes flew open and her eyes searched his face. "I know you have to leave. I don't understand, but I'm not going to force you to stay. I want you to stay because you need me as badly as I need you."

"I'm not the man you think I am. I'm not good enough for you."

Angie shook her head, though a smile tugged at her lips. "You're the only man I will ever want. Even though you are such a sorry excuse for one."

His thumb brushed at her tears. "You're the only reason I wanted to live."

Angie held her breath, not certain what he was telling her. But his skin on hers felt incredible, and she caught his hand, burying her face into his palm. He smelled fresh, clean. He must have bathed before coming to see her. The thought pleased her.

"I missed you so much," she whispered. "Every day— every day I worried if you were safe. And then when it was over... every day I watched the door to see if you would come back. When I thought... when...."

"How do you think I felt when I heard you were in the middle of all that mess?"

Her eyes searched his face. "I don't know. How did you feel?"

He closed his eyes and rested his forehead against hers. "Don't do this, Angie."

She slid her fingers down his neck and across his shoulders. "All I want is to enjoy what little time we have left."

"You're trying to force me to stay."

Angie pulled back. "How can I possibly force you to stay?" Her lips drew into an angry line. "You can't stop me from loving you, Lorenzo. Believe me, I've been trying. But you cannot accuse me of trapping you or forcing you into anything. I've told you I know you're leaving and I haven't tried to stop you. Delay you, yes. But I know it's inevitable."

"Why?"

"Because you said you have plans—your brother and all..."

"No, I mean, why do you love me?" He caught her hand when she began to turn away from him, forcing her to look at him. "Why, when everything pointed against me, did you believe in me? Why have you stood beside me through all of this?"

Angie drew a deep breath. She had thought she was finished with the tears, but her damp eyes proved otherwise. "I may not know your history, Lorenzo, and you may have committed crimes in the past that I don't want to know anything about. But I know you. I know the kind of man you are now. I know—I know that the money Armand pulled from your pocket was your own money. I know that you had been leaving some of that money at the homes we took weapons from."

He pulled away in surprise. "How do you know that?"

"I followed you into a home one night. I watched you put the coins on a table."

"Why? How?"

She gave him half a smile. "I've been watching you. I wanted to see if I could sneak up on an expert."

He shook his head. "I never had enough money to fully pay for what I took."

"But, still, you tried."

"I had stolen the money from the officer's quarters."

It was Angie's turn to be surprised and her eyes widened then she laughed, something she hadn't done in a very long time. Finally, she shook her head, catching her breath. "I love you, Lorenzo. I love the man that you are. And I always will."

Lorenzo watched her, drinking in the sight of her. He didn't know how to tell her what he wanted to tell her. Nor did he know whether he should even tell her what filled his mind. But he wanted her to know—he wasn't sure what he wanted her to know. "The whole time I fought in the battle... the entire time... all I could think of was you. You were the reason I wanted to get through everything... I wanted the battle to be over so I could see you again. Even though it would be just once more—I had to see you one last time. And that was all I could think about."

He shook his head, his hand weaving through her hair, loosening the knot and letting the waves flow down her back. "And then—then when I thought there was no chance I would live... I couldn't give up. I couldn't stop fighting, because I needed to see you. It was this fever burning in me, this need that consumed me. I had to see you one more time."

He paused, taking a deep breath. "I'll never be the same again, Angie. My leg is... I won't be able to take care of you the way a man should."

Angie shook her head at him. "Do you think that is something that is important to me?"

"It should be! How can I build you a home? How can I make you the life you deserve? You can't spend the rest of your life taking care of a cripple."

Angie refused to let herself hope. But the words he said made her think... made her believe...

She leaned in closer to him, her hands sliding around his neck. "I need you. No matter what condition you are in."

Lorenzo leaned forward and grabbed her for a fierce kiss, his hands cradling her face. "I don't want your love," he whispered, spreading kisses over her cheeks, her eyelids, her forehead. "I don't want it but, God help me, I need it."

Angie clung to his arms, afraid to hope. His hands ran through her hair. "From the moment I left you, all I could think about was you. I smelled you on my skin, I saw you in my dreams. You haunted me day and night until all I could think about was getting back to you."

Angie held her breath. Did he really care for her? Did he need her as badly as she needed him?

"I tried to leave," he confessed. "By midmorning today I was miles from town. I turned back, convincing myself that I had to make sure you were safe. It was a lie. I needed you."

Angie captured his mouth with her own, silencing him with her lips, her arms wrapping around his waist. "Does this mean…"

He smiled against her lips. "I can't leave you, *chula*. Someone has to make sure you stay out of trouble."

"Lorenzo…"

"I love you, Angie. I didn't want to. But I can't stop it. I love you. And I need your love."

Joyful tears filled her eyes. "I love you. And I always will."

Epilogue

T HE WEDDING WAS as small as they could manage. The entire town came. The church was packed so full there was standing room only.

As they repeated their vows and went through the rituals, Angie and Lorenzo exchanged longing glances at each other. The preparations had kept them apart for two days, and they both felt like they were going to lose their sanity.

As soon as the ceremony was complete, they were in each other's arms and a cheer rose from the guests. A grinning Lorenzo and a blushing Angie were escorted out to the *fandango* and the festivities rivaled the celebration that had followed the defeat of the Mexicans.

It seemed as though Angie and Lorenzo were never going to be alone. Though Lorenzo had to sit out for many dances due to the ache in his leg, his injury wasn't as bad as it had first appeared, and he was able to spend many dances in the arms of his wife.

As they danced together for the last song, Lorenzo's smile was positively wolfish. "I must remind you, Husband, that you should remain proper in front of our guests."

He raised an eyebrow. "I recall you lecturing me on propriety when we first met," he said as his hand slipped lower on her waist and she drew in a sharp breath.

Pulling his hand back to an acceptable position, she sighed. "And obviously you didn't learn a thing."

The town escorted them, with many suggestions for Lorenzo along the way, to the small boarding-room house they were residing in for their honeymoon. On the sidewalk, Lorenzo swept her into his arms and the crowd cheered.

She wrapped her arms around his neck and smiled at him as he carried her into the house and up the stairs. "I do wonder what is on that mind of yours."

He wiggled his eyebrows dramatically as he set her on the floor of their room. "I'm afraid it isn't very proper."

"Oh," she said, smiling, her fingers playing with the lace at the neckline of her dress. "In that case, Husband, I suggest you close the door and find out how very improper your wife can be."

The sound of their laughter ended with the slamming of the door.

The End

If you enjoyed Texas Conquest,
you'll love the next book in...

The Texas Legacy Series

Book 1: *Texas Conquest*

Book 2: *Texas Desire*

Book 3: *Texas Heat*

About the Author

Holly grew up spending many lazy summer days racing her horses bareback in the Texas sun. But whenever Holly wasn't riding her horses or competing in horse shows, she was found with pen and paper in hand, writing out romantic love stories of the wild west.

Later, in her professional life, Holly worked just blocks from the Alamo in a unique setting where the buildings were connected with basements and tunnels. The exciting history of Texas, the Alamo, and working in a historic building dating back to the 1800's inspired Holly to write about the Texas Revolution, and has evolved into a series all about Texas becoming the great State it is.

Today, Holly lives in a small community just south of San Antonio, with her husband and two children. On the family's 80 acre ranch, surrounded by cattle during the day and hearing the howl of coyotes by night, Holly has endless inspiration for her writing.

Thank you for reading

Texas Conquest

If you enjoyed this book, you can find more from all our great authors at TulePublishing.com, or from your favorite online retailer.

TULE
PUBLISHING

Made in the USA
San Bernardino, CA
22 November 2019

60196291R10273